One Saccharine Dream

Of Gods and Monsters

Dawn Darling

ONE SACCHARINE DREAM

OF GODS AND MONSTERS, BOOK 2

One Saccharine Dream (of Gods and Monsters, book 2)

Published by Dawn Darling, Author

Book cover by Ashley Boehme Art

Special edition reverse dust jacket by Killustrate

Edited by Jessica Jordan

Copyright © 2024 by Dawn Darling

All rights reserved. No part of this publication or its art may be reproduced, distributed, or transmitted in any form or by any means, including photocopying, recording, or other electronic mechanical methods, without the prior written permission from the publisher or author, except as permitted by U.S. copyright law.

The story, all names, characters, and incidents portrayed in this production are fictitious. No identification with actual persons (living or deceased), places, buildings, and products is intended or should be inferred.

CONTENT WARNINGS

PLEASE PROCEED WITH CAUTION, DARLING, FOR THE GODS ARE CRUEL

GRAPHIC VIOLENCE	MENTIONS OF SUICIDE
GRAPHIC LANGUAGE	RELIGIOUS SACRFICES
GRAHPIC SEX	STARVATION
MURDER	MANIPULATIVE SEX
TORTURE OF AN MC	TRAUMA
DROWNING	PTSD
NON-CON	GASLIGHTING
NARCISSISM	CAPTURE

IF YOU DISCOVER ANY SENSITIVE CONTENT NOT LISTED HERE, PLEASE EMAIL
DD@DAWNDARLINGAUTHOR.COM

Dawn Darling

Dedication

This is for all my darlings struggling to embrace the chaos living inside. Your darkness is not a monster, and your light does not define you.

"Embracing your chaos means finding peace in your heart and living with all parts of who you are. Even the ones you hide from."

Pronunciation Guide

ZEUS — ZOOS
PANDORA — PAN-DOOR-UH
BROOKS — BR-OO-CKS
XIA — ZEE-YUH
NYX — NIH-X
PHOBETOR — FOH-BEH-TOR
LYTTA — LIT-UH
GEIA — J-EE-YUH
MOLPE — MOLE-PAY
CLOTHO — KLAH-THOE
LACHESIS — LA-KUH-SIS
ATROPOS — UH-TRAA-POSE
MOIRAI — MOY-RYE
MELINOE — MEL-EEN-AW-EE
AVYSSOS — AH-VIS-OH-SS
EREBOS — AIR-EH-BUS

**some of the pronunciations do not align with the traditional Greek diction

A Playlist For Your Most Saccharine Dreams

One Little Nightmare

One Saccharine Dream

Want a vibe sneak peek for my Patreon serial?

Unleash your Chaos

Prologue

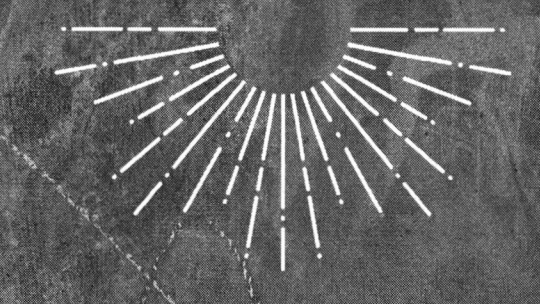

"Persephone?"

"Yes, mother?"

"Be sure to stay close while I tend the fields, darling. We will only be a moment."

"Yes, mother."

Demeter filled the gilded landscape with bushes and trees, the flora dripping with ripe fruit. Crops grew in rows on the rolling hillside far as the eye could see. Persephone swelled with pride watching Demeter work and admired her mother's elegant strokes as she painted the terrain with a wave of her hand.

With a hum and a smile, Persephone ran from the harvest and toward her secret haven of daffodils. While Demeter tended the crops, Persephone bloomed her favorite six petaled flowers in an alcove hidden by a copse of trees. Demeter often chastised her for frolicking, but the sweet flowers drew her every time nonetheless.

Birds flitted through the sky as they chased one another, their high-pitched songs the perfect tune to fill the silence. Once out of sight, Persephone walked without haste, running her fingers through the waist high grass that danced with the breeze and coaxing blooms where she touched.

Demeter was a goddess of the harvest, capable of growing grains and vegetables without a thought. But Persephone? Her gift was flowers. Delicate silk petals blossomed with whispered praises under her fingers. Everywhere she touched, beauty grew.

Persephone stopped on the peak of the highest hill, closed her eyes, and embraced the world around her. Water tinkled in the distance as the brook flowed steadily downstream. Light from the setting sun warmed her skin and the breeze ruffled the pink hair around her shoulders.

"Such a pretty flower," a hushed voice grazed her skin. Persephone didn't open her eyes or turn. She expected the whisper, and a shiver of anticipation pulled at the corner of her lips. The first time she heard it, Persephone ran back to Demeter without a backward glance, terror fueling her sprint. The second time she fled slower, throwing distraught looks over her shoulder and searching the meadow.

Each time, Persephone grew more hesitant to leave. The voice whispered her praises, doting on the braids in her hair or the chaos she wove through the ground. The low, masculine lilt in the voice intrigued Persephone and the closer she got to the water, the louder his whispers became.

This would be the seventh time the voice visited her.

Seven times she heard the voice.

Seven times she felt its presence.

Seven times, she'd been okay.

Persephone opened her eyes to the sun and descended the grassy knoll into the field of wildflowers. The world seemed to sigh as she connected her mind, body, and soul to the plants brushing her ankles.

The skin on her neck prickled as ghostly eyes roamed her body, but she brushed it aside. Her heart pounded as Demeter's warnings rang through her mind. "Don't go toward the streams, Persephone. Water from the Underworld trickles through these valleys and we are outside the protection of Mount Olympus. You don't know what may be lurking, and finding out could be your death."

And yet she still stood. Demeter had always sheltered her, but as Persephone grew older she found herself longing to make those choices for herself. So rather than run back into the safety of her mothers arms, Persephone stepped toward the brook and sat in a cluster of flowers at its side, dipping her feet into the cool water. As brilliant hues of the setting sun lit the sky, she twirled one finger around a strand of pastel hair lighting fuschia with the dawn. Persephone busied her other hand in the dirt to keep them from trembling as anticipation rolled through her belly.

Would the voice appear again? And who exactly did it belong–

A ripple of water lapped against her ankle and she startled, feet slipping in the softened ground as she scuttled backward. A man with tousled brown hair and a crimson silk robe rested his arms on the bank. "Easy, flower, everything is okay." *He lifted placating hands and offered a reassuring smile.*

"Who are you?" *The rise and fall of her chest was quick as adrenaline froze her limbs.*

"I've been watching you. You always leave my field looking so pretty." *He smiled, cheeks dimpling as he flashed teeth white as pearls.*

Watching her?

"Is that supposed to be comforting?" *Her tone held a clip of haughty defiance, one her mother snapped a vine across her knuckles for on more than one occasion. Defiance was not obedience, and good girls were obedient. Persephone swallowed and bowed her head, the epitome of submission.*

"Don't be shy. I was going for flattery. The blooms are most beautiful after you've touched them, and your radiance is blinding after they've touched you."

Persephone was taken aback as he smirked, the insinuation sitting heavy in the air between them. A familiar wave of suspicion deepened her brow as she watched the stranger, waiting for the moment he became just like the rest of them. No man wanted to know Persephone. They wanted to own her.

"Flattery will get you nothing. If you wish an alliance with my mother, you'll have to ask for my hand like everyone else," *she snapped.*

Suitors lined Demeter's estate to ask for Persephone's hand. Demeter was one of the twelve Olympian daemons worshiped as a god by the humans and served as an authority figure for their race, daemonkind. She had one of the more potent wells of chaos running through her bloodline. An alliance with Persephone, daughter of the goddess Demeter, was an alliance with The Twelve.

"Ask for your hand?" *The stranger tilted his head.* "Come now, little flower. Surely you don't mean to tell me that you have no choice in who you fuck?"

Her cheeks heated, retort dying on her tongue as he watched her strug-

gle. No one had ever spoken to Persephone so crudely. Demeter would have had him hanged on the peaks of Olympus. It was a scandal. Forbidden.

So... Why did it spur the butterflies in her belly?

"You're so beautiful when you blush," he huffed a laugh. "Your cheeks color like the softest of pink peonies. I wonder if they deepen when you come."

Persephone's breath caught, heart fluttering as she stared into his eyes. They were so deep and inviting, their points fixed on her. They weren't searching for Demeter. Just, her.

"I've never–" she stammered and cleared her throat. "I am untouched."

"Untouched? Even by your own hand?"

"Yes," she responded, her voice breathy. The admission shocked her, but she didn't have time to regret it.

"Can you show me?"

Her stomach dipped at the implication. He looked down to hide his wolfish grin and twirled a daffodil, plucking it from the dirt and tucking it into the brown curls behind his ear.

"Not that, silly flower. Show me your magic. I always watch it from afar. The way you push your fingers into the dirt and pull the most beautiful buds from its surface is mesmerizing. I'd like to see such enchanting chaos up close."

Persephone swallowed, the edge of suspicion still cutting through the smiles and innuendos like a sharpened blade. Though Persephone wasn't allowed to meet the suitors, she heard their reasons.

Power.

Beauty.

Alliance.

Bloodlines.

Never had they asked about the delicacy of her chaos nor the manner in which it was used. They never wanted details about her hobbies or the way she liked her herbal water in the morning. Not one saw the wonder in the world the way she did or cared to know her enough to ask. The man in the brook, though? He wondered how her face tinted if he gave her pleasure and how she connected with the soil as she encouraged it to hold life. He was curious about *her*, and not what Dememter could give him.

The small, defiant flame in Persephone's belly sparked. At that moment, the decision was hers. Not Demeter's.

Against her best senses and her mother's warnings, Persephone stepped toward the handsome man wading in the brook.

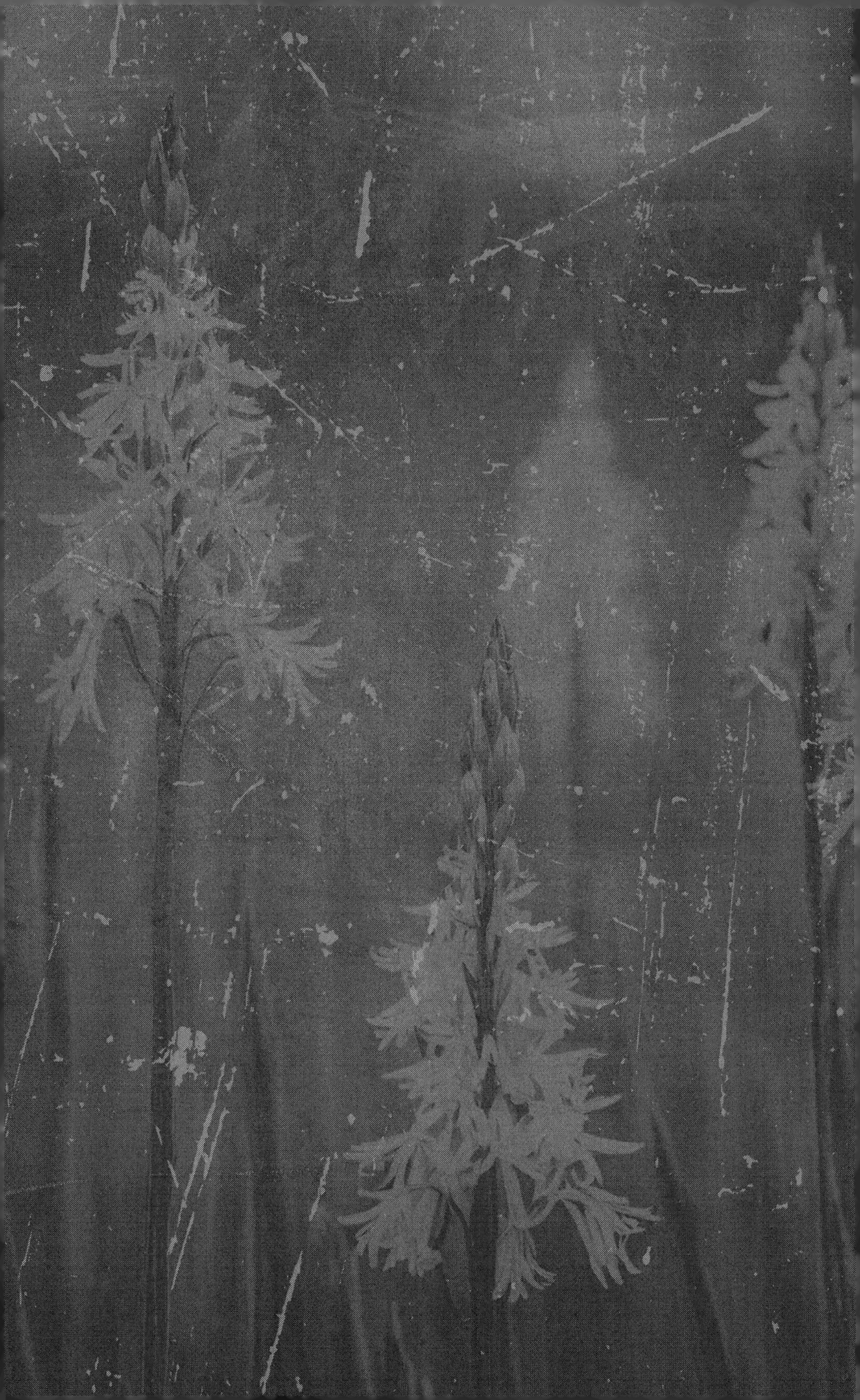

A MEADOW FULL OF ASPHODELS

Unleash your Chaos

Brooks

1

"I am the Father of Darkness, the Void Between the Stars, Creator of your Gods and the Eater of Souls. I am Chaos the Deathless God, and I will find you."

His promise to Xia rang through the night like the ticking of a timer, and Brooks was terrified it was at its last second. When he broke from the Asylum, Brooks scoured the universe through the intricate webbing of chaos powering the world. Everything had changed since his capture and it was obvious he had a lot of catching up to do.

Locating Club Hel took only moments and evaporating into the darkness took even less. With a thought, he was standing on the craggy black shore of Anthemoessa, the island that was both home and prison to his Siren.

A breeze rolled in icy waves off the ocean as Brooks studied the world he'd left behind. He thought Earth to be his greatest achievement, capable of creating and retaining even the most delicate of lifeforms. And what was there to show for his pride? Tainted land that was nothing but a sad remnant of its origin.

Silhouettes moved against the outside of Club Hel and Chaos rumbled in his chest. *We will make them all pay, starting with the sick son of a bitch who left our Siren weeping on a dirty floor.*

"Agreed." He stalked forward, eyes set on the catalyst of his rage.

Power caressed the island, shadows bending and writhing to

reach the vengeful god striding toward Hel. Bass thrummed over the crashing waves at his back, electricity sparking through the air as he searched for that endless well of chaos in his chest. He reached, and when his senses felt nothing, he reached further.

"What the fuck?" Brooks faltered. "Where is it?"

What used to be endless felt... drained.

We are not powerless. But we are not powerful.

"What does that mean?"

If I knew, we wouldn't be powerless, Chaos growled.

"It doesn't matter," Brooks said to his darker half. "Whether we have our power or not, Xia needs us."

Brooks kept to the shadows until the entrance of the building was visible. Strobing red lights filtered from the closed door as daemon of all variety stood in a line. He debated his tactics for only a moment before stepping from the shadows and into the line of club patrons. Without their full power, their chaos, he and his darker half would have to be strategic to avoid making a scene. He was unwilling to test its limits before he needed it most. Chaos paced in his confines inside his mind, but Brooks maintained focus. He had to get to Xia.

"Hey handsome," a shrill voice rang to his right as a vibrant pink claw traced his collarbone. "That's quite an outfit. Headed to Level Lust?"

A quick look down and the realization hit– he was naked.

Jeers and whistles followed her comment. *Kill her*, Chaos sneered.

When he'd created the world, nudity was the standard. The time spent sculpting their bodies until each inch was uniquely perfect filled his empty moments. The evolution of his creatures in front of him was remarkable, though, and the mixing of the bloodlines seemed to know no bounds. Their skin was a cacophony of colors from pastel blues to fiery oranges. Feathers and fur, wings and hooves. They were beautiful.

A glance around confirmed that it was now custom to clothe the skin in scanty shreds of fabric. His mind flicked back to the scratchy tan scrubs he'd worn in the asylum and he shivered. Brooks glanced around the standing crowd and caught the eye of a nymph dressed in ripped black pants and a white v-neck shirt.

That would do.

Brooks pulled on a small thread of chaos like a weaver holding yarn and knit the fabric of reality to his whims. He looked down to find his body clad in the same fitted ensemble.

"Aww, I wasn't complaining, honey. You can take it back off." The female was beautiful in the most exotic way. Her body was shaped like his original creation made in his image, but that's where the similarities ended. Her arms resembled wings– long feathers draped to her sides with a hand at the end of each. Smaller feathers covered her legs, groin, and breasts and a brilliant headdress sat atop her head. Her entire body, feathers and all, was one shade of magenta. All except for the piercing yellow eyes staring back at him.

"Either you like what you see, baby, or you've never played with a harpy before. I can make all your wildest dreams come true," she teased as the group of daemon surrounding her laughed. They were all harpies, each a different color with various arrays of feathers patching their skin.

He ignored her taunt and asked, "How do I get in?"

"Just buy me a drink, handsome." More laughter.

Kill. Her. Or I will drain her dry myself.

Ice spread from under his feet and crawled up the side of the club as Chaos fought for control of his body. The cold lingered with each breath puffing from the patrons standing closest in line. Stares turned their way as the group of harpies regarded him with cautious glares.

"Tell me how to get into this club, harpy." His fists clenched as he fought for control.

She will answer or she will die in this line.

A blue male with impressive muscular definition and a tall frame stepped in front of her and crossed his arms. "Or what, freak?"

Brooks imagined that most would be intimidated by the stance. If he were back in the asylum, he may have been frightened, too.

No longer.

The Deathless God feared nothing.

"Don't waste my time." Brooks' tone was menacing and dropped with the temperature.

"Don't make idle threats, asshole, and I won't waste my time shutting you down." His posse closed in and the pink harpy's smile turned venomous.

"They're not going to help us," he thought inward. "We cannot make a scene. Calm. Down."

Chaos' sigh was palpable. Brooks turned from the group and moved forward with the line surveying the area for an alternate entrance. When none appeared, he eavesdropped on the conversation between a few daemon and a hulking horned figure guarding the door, but their words were indiscernible under the bass pulsing through the walls. The bouncer pushed the couple back as a group of males escorted a pink-haired female in a scrap of silver through the front doors.

Maybe if you summon her dress next, they'll let us through.

Brooks rolled his eyes. He didn't have fucking time for this. His Siren was in there suffering and he was sorting through club politics with a sarcastic leech riding his ass. He moved to push his way through the line, but before he could take the first step a fist collided with the back of his head.

Unleash your Chaos

NYX

2

The smell of piss and opium filled the darkened alley as bodies stumbled along, hands grazing the brick wall to guide them toward the door into Hel. Moans lingered in every corner, just loud enough to be heard over the bass from inside.

Nyx checked her reflection in the pocket mirror and gave a weary sigh before tucking it back into her handbag. The long, pink wig she'd stolen from the woman passed out behind the club was less than ideal, but her self-cut shoulder-length black hair was too inconspicuous to gain entry into the infamous club. Black kohl lined her cat-shaped eyes to emphasize the violet of her irises. Pale skin stood out against the black lipstick painted on her lips and the beauty mark drawn just above them.

The stolen dress she'd donned was a barely-there silver piece that her curves couldn't quite fill, but it would have to do. If you wanted to be a patron of Club Hel you had to either know someone big or catch their attention. Wigs and flashy clothes were her best bet, since everything else about her was unremarkable.

Nyx wiped imaginary dust from her front as nerves set in, stomach rumbling just in time to remind her how important tonight was.

Helpless lives depended on it. On her. And she wouldn't let them down.

Unlike other daemon, Nyx hadn't been born with strong chaos.

She could muster a small illusion or trick of the light, but nothing flashy. In fact, such a small amount of chaos coursed through her veins that the more powerful of her kind didn't even recognize it as such– they taunted her with human words like, "magic."

Fuck them.

Nyx set her shoulders, released a shaky breath, and forced a swagger into her steps. The click of her heeled shoes rang through the night as she stepped around the corner to the main entrance. She'd already tried the side doors. Surprise, surprise, they were locked. Her mood turned to shit when she realized that it wasn't a lock she could pick either. No, the fucking Oneiroi magicked the locks. Only an employee and their essence could open one of those doors. She put plan B into motion because if you wanted to stay alive in Olympia, sometimes you had to get scrappy.

The line of daemon trying to whisk away into the levels of Club Hel was long and there was no way they were all getting in. A quick scan showed that most of them were female, as expected. When the high rollers of Olympia came to town, everyone ran to try their luck at snagging a god and Nyx knew that it would be harder to gain entrance because of it. Only the most beautiful and eccentric would make it past the black velvet ropes tonight.

A shout of laughter drew her attention to a group of four men walking past the waiting line. They stopped just short of the entrance to finish the cigarettes trapped between their fingers.

"Brilliant," Nyx whispered to herself.

This would be her ticket in. Cigarettes were not common in Olympia as they were from the human world. Anyone who had access to human garbage and flaunted it like these men had status.

Nyx inhaled, called upon the small spark of her power, and drew the shadows in around the group. It wasn't enough to catch their attention but rather drown out some of the neon light glaring from the Club Hel sign.

She approached the group with narrow hips swaying and a fake smile plastered on her painted black lips. Those facing Nyx looked up, attention caught by the clicking of her heels, and watched with predatory eyes as she sauntered to them.

When she was close enough to see the stubble on their cheeks, she reached out, dragged a finger around the nearest man's back and rested her hand on his shoulder. He tensed at the surprise intrusion but covered it with a suave maneuver.

"And what Level of Hel will you gentlemen be enjoying tonight?" Her tone was seductive, a trick she'd mastered by the time she was sixteen years old.

Rule number one of manipulating men? Touch. If you initiate, they will follow.

Nyx tossed him a wink. Her body burned as his eyes roamed from top to bottom, his suit jacket undone and the top buttons of his shirt open. Accompanied by mussed blonde hair and bedroom eyes, she could guess where they were going.

His name had to be Cupid.

"Depends on what level you're going to, sweetness," another said to her left. He had shoulder-length brown hair and was taller than the others with broad shoulders and a shirt one size too small.

He stood like a burly bear motherfucker.

She was going to name him Teddy.

"Well," she said, a sly edge to her voice. "I was going to start my night in Gluttony, but I'm beginning to think my plans are changing." She made a show of looking longingly at them while biting her lip.

Men were so fucking predictable.

Cupid wrapped his arm around Nyx's waist and pulled her in against his side. His cologne was dizzying and made her empty stomach turn, but she fought to keep the lazy look of lust in her eyes. He lowered his mouth to her ear and bit the lobe eliciting a sharp pinch. His stale breath blew across her cheek as he said, "What's your name, baby?"

Nyx turned her face to his, letting her lips whisper across his own as she spoke. "Ambrosia."

They all shared a knowing laugh before Teddy piped up. "I bet you taste divine."

"Only one way to find out." She winked.

Nyx strode toward the door without a backward glance. She was counting on them to follow. They were, after all, her one-way ticket to Hel.

She'd nearly made it to the door when a hand cupped her ass. "Slow down, baby. You trying to get rid of us?" Laughter rose from the group. Cupid was a fucking comedian.

Nyx kept walking until they reached the Club Hel bouncer standing guard at the entrance. One nod from Cupid and the velvet rope was unlocked, just like that.

Pompous, entitled sons-of-bitches.

Her anger burned like acid on her tongue, and it took every ounce of self-control to keep it from spewing past her lips. She wished her life had been that damn easy, but she didn't have a dick hanging between her legs.

A darkened hall funneled them into a small room where black velvet curtains hung from the ceiling. Two more club lackeys stood on either side and pulled the curtains open as they approached. Nyx covered her eyes as light poured into the small holding room. Smells of roasted meat and sweet ambrosia assaulted her nose as music blared from all sides. She struggled to overcome the attack on her senses. She'd come too far to fuck up now.

The inside of Club Hel was luxurious. Gilded metal adornments, plush carpet runways, and uniformed staff buzzing about to see to your every whim. The first Level of Hel was tame compared to the stories of the rest. Full length obsidian counters lined the outside of the room with bottles of liquor and assorted pills displayed behind it. At least twenty Club Hel employees were stationed behind the bar pouring amber liquid into glasses while others shook mixers in tin containers.

An enormous buffet stacked with savory dishes was placed toward the middle of the room, and in its center stood a fondue fountain flowing with ambrosia. It was one of the most potent intoxicants a daemon could consume. The chaos in their blood brought them immortality. In its battle to sustain life, any disease or drug was cleared hastily from their system. Ambrosia, however, was fermented by the Olympian, Dionysus, and he lived for creating substances that even chaos couldn't filter. The effects of ambrosia were immediate, lowering inhibitions and boosting confidence in euphoric bliss.

Nyx swept the room with an assessing stare. Daemon reclined on couches glutting themselves on food and drink– the perfect beginning to any night reveling in sin. With Cupid on her left, Teddy on her right, and the two others covering the rear, they walked into Club Hel like they held the fucking keys to the place.

Nyx made to move toward the bar but a hand caught hers and tugged. "No fucking way we're getting stuck in Gluttony," Cupid chided.

"Come on, sweetness," Teddy tsked as he wrapped a burly hand around her waist. "Bring your cute little ass along."

Nyx bit her lip to hold back her quip, inhaling a breath of patience and counting to three. The plan had been to ditch their loser asses just after they got her through security, but it seemed the boys weren't ready to throw away their plaything. She pulled the reins on her attitude and turned to face them.

"I wasn't aware 'fun' had a schedule." She smiled, trying to stop the quirk of her brow and annoyance in her tone. Teddy just winked as the others caged her in.

Great, now she was being herded by a bunch of animals.

"Okay," Nyx resigned. "To the elevators. After you, gentlemen." Nyx had been scoping this place out for weeks. There were eight levels in Club Hel and if she didn't ditch these losers quickly, she would never make it to the gold. A child's laugh chimed like tinkling bells through her mind, reminding her why she was doing this, and a ball of unease grew in her stomach.

Nyx had to make it to Level Pride.

The group started toward the elevators on the far wall of the room, making sure to keep her in the middle. Not for the first time tonight, she fought an eye roll.

Cupid grabbed a couple flutes of sweet champagne from a passing employee and handed one over. She didn't care for the bubbly liquid but sipped on it slowly for appearance. For all Nyx knew the fucker slipped datura into the fizzing amber liquid. The thought made her spine straighten. Datura was another substance brewed by Dionysus that affected daemonkind. It was often slipped into female's drinks by sleazeballs like Cupid when their dick wasn't big enough to fuck her with consent.

Once at the glass elevator, Teddy pushed the 'up' button and the doors opened with a *ding*. Nyx stole a glance at the control panel as she was ushered inside and took note. Gluttony, Wrath, Greed, and Lust were the only floors listed. Her brow furrowed as she recalled information gathered from the whispers surrounding Club Hel. She knew there were eight floors because you could see it clearly from the rows of windows on the outside. So why, then, were there only four Level's listed in the elevator?

She needed to learn what lay beyond Lust and figure out how to get there if it wasn't the elevator. Surely to Zeus you didn't have to walk up the fucking stairs. That had to be an activity below the rich.

They may break a sweat.

It would be unlawful, really.

Cupid pressed the button to Lust and Nyx had to fight the itch to run. Out of all her personality traits, nympho was not one of them. Sure, she was cunning and kind of an asshole, but she'd be damned if she exited the elevator on Level Lust with a group of Chads. She'd stolen enough human books to know how that would end, and the men who herded her were much more dangerous than the swine on those pages.

The elevator jerked to a start and the air became too heavy for comfort. The space darkened as they rose through the ceiling of Gluttony and arrived at the next floor. If the panel were to be believed, Level Wrath was next. The cable pulled them up slowly as if to showcase every floor they were passing.

"*Are you sure you want to miss this?*" It seemed to say.

A few seconds later the rumble of utter chaos breached the quiet glass box. Nyx stepped forward through the hulking group of men to peer out. What she saw shouldn't have surprised her, but the sheer brutality of Level Wrath made her swallow.

A fighting ring was in the center of the room surrounded by screaming daemon.

No, not screaming, she thought. *Cheering.*

They were in various states of undress, but all of them wore fighting garments. Some were in tights, others in leathers, but all held a dangerous gleam in their eyes. They were mad with wrath and chomping at the bit to get into the ring.

The two daemons fighting in the center were brutal. One was a tall, bulky man in white shorts with his torso bare. He looked mean as fuck and was scowling like he'd never seen the sunshine. His opponent was a small female who, if possible, looked even meaner than he did.

Nyx didn't need a rule sheet to know that in Club Hel, anything goes. Eye gouging, groin punching, biting... it would all be fair game here. Her kind were brutal and she expected no less from a club of sin hidden in the darkest and most ruthless of oceans, on the furthest island from Mount Olympus.

The ceiling to Level Wrath was much taller than Gluttony, and it wasn't long until the reason was obvious. As the elevator continued its journey up, a dimly lit balcony circled the perimeter far above the ring. There in the shadows, reclined in leather chairs with sophisticated glasses and computers, were the beginnings of the daemon elite. They were dressed in business casual, every pleated pair of pants and combed over strand of hair perfectly in place. Some sat alone while others stood, glasses in hand, pointing to the ring and whispering.

Level Greed.

A roar erupted from below and Nyx caught a quick glance of the female daemon on the back of the male. Blood trickled down his torso and stained his ruined pants. She held a victorious fist in the air, chin covered in the gore from his open neck. Nyx's heart leapt in her chest.

Evidently 'anything goes' includes murder.

Money exchanged hands on Level Greed and backs turned to the scene below. Some scowled while others smiled victoriously. The elite couldn't be bothered with the loss of life.

It was literally below them.

"It's not polite to stare, sweetness."

Nyx startled and cursed. She had let her guard down, too lost in the battle below to track the men behind her. *Fucking idiot*, she scolded.

"Blood lust is not impolite," she rebounded. "It's expected."

"Feisty little thing." Cupid smiled.

"I like it." Teddy licked his lips as if he could already taste her on his tongue.

She winked at them and turned back to the female celebrating her win. Nyx couldn't wrap her mind around what she'd witnessed, and it made her blood curdle. A pit arena full of rage and bloodlust, and a balcony full of spectators gallivanting their riches and betting on lives like they were livestock.

What had this world come to?

When the elevator went dark and Level Greed was hidden, Nyx took the moment of obscurity to collect her features and steel her spine as the elevator hummed. She was going to have to bolt when the doors opened, and quickly.

Seconds later the glass box illuminated with sensual pink light and the sight was a punch to the gut. She hoped the men behind her mistook her heavy exhale for longing rather than the shock and total dread making her heart race. Heat rose to her cheeks as the elevator *dinged* and opened its doors.

"Welcome to Lust, sweetness."

Unleash your Chaos

Xia

3

She'd been in the bath for what felt like hours waving her pruny fingers under the water and trying to find peace in the feeling. What feeling, she didn't know exactly. Maybe the tickle of flowing water between her fingers. Or, perhaps, it was the way the fragrant bath oils moved back and forth with every stroke of her palm. Regardless, she was happy to live in the moment, for the next could be her last. Xia recalled pieces of the conversation she'd heard through the vent a mere hour ago.

"Where is the song? Do you have it?"

"Of course I fucking have it," the Devil retorted.

Her tone was low and deadly when she responded, "Do. Better. This isn't enough. This doesn't work without her. I cannot hold him without her song and we are not finished."

Xia pondered those words over and over until she'd analyzed every letter.

What she knew– the Devil was holding her captive to collect her song. He and the mystery woman were using the drugging properties of her chaos to hold someone in an unconscious trance. What she didn't know, however, was the identity of the mystery woman and the victim of her song.

They had to be strong, whoever they were. To be dosed with her song and not given the anti-venom that only she contained, the daemon would be dead. Her song would bleed them dry to fill the well of her power. Of this much, she was certain.

So who was strong enough to receive large quantities of her chaos and, rather than die, maintain a sedative state?

Chaos, a voice whispered. *Brooks.*

Xia sat up with a sigh and hugged her knees to ease the anxiety squeezing her chest. The more she contemplated the situation, the tighter its grip became. The ominous feeling grew with every passing hour as the air thickened around her. She didn't know what the Devil was up to, but she did know him.

Xia knew that he was worse when he was angry. He took more than necessary from her and, when she thought she had nothing left to give, he took more greedily. She knew that he would be bitter after the meeting with his mistress. Resentful. His rage would know no bounds.

And who better to take it out on than the cause of his embarrassment?

When she overheard the conversation through the vent, his torture had been limitless. He constructed nightmares built atop her regrets, fears, weaknesses, but worst of all, he'd built them atop her shame. And still, it hadn't been enough to please whoever held his leash. It was only a matter of time before he made his way back to her to prove a point. If his mistress wanted more, the Devil would serve it on a bloody platter.

A crash disrupted the calm as a raging scream pierced the silence. "Where the fuck are you, Siren?"

Xia's pulse raced as she buried her head between shaking knees and fisted handfuls of hair. Panicked sobs wracked her frame, worsening with each footfall outside the door. She didn't look up when he broke through. Xia didn't have the courage to stare death in the face. She wasn't brave enough to help her sisters, and she was no longer desperate enough to help herself.

He stopped in the doorframe and the weight of his stare burned between her shoulder blades. "Get up," he growled. She couldn't move. Fear locked her limbs in place as her silent sobs turned to desperate wails. "I said get up, you fucking whore!" Her screams battled his malevolent roar.

In two quick steps, he reached her side, knotted his fist into her hair, and jerked her from the tub. Xia's scalp flamed as each follicle held on for dear life, the pain unbearable. The Devil pulled her face to his and she shriveled under the hate in his stare.

"This is all your fucking fault."

He yanked.

She screamed.

The acrid smell of sex was on his breath. She tried to turn away, but his hold was unforgiving. "Please, Tor," she cried. "I'll give you whatever you want, just please don't hurt me anymore." Tears mingled with the drippings from her nose and fell to her breasts.

The only warning she had was his snarl. In one fluid motion, he let go of her hair and swung his fist. The resounding crack against her jaw echoed against the porcelain bathing chamber. Xia fell to the floor with the copper tang of blood filling her mouth, heartbeat pounding in her ears as blurry black boots stepped in front of her.

"Get up," he snarled. "Do not force me to make you."

She could. If she just lay there and didn't move, maybe it would make him so angry that he'd finally end her. She wanted to. It would have been so easy. However, as she prepared her heart to concede, a darkness coiled around her soul. Xia cried, willing it to lay down and die with her, but it refused.

Fight, the demon inside her seethed. *We are more than this.*

She swallowed.

Do not give him the satisfaction of your death. It is a spurn of your worth to fall to such filth.

Her wet hands pushed against the tile.

You do not relent.

Her knees pulled beneath her middle.

You do not back down.

She placed her wobbling feet against the tile.

You do not accept defeat, it hissed.

Xia straightened and matched his stare with a scowl as blood trickled down her swollen lip. Flashes of blood lit skies and crashing waves danced across her vision as her song flooded her veins. The same serpent that called forth the storms rattled in her chest poised to strike. His smile was venomous as he watched her rally, and Xia squared her shoulders in challenge.

His fist was buried in her stomach before she could speak. Xia folded over and barely managed to keep its contents from spewing. She gagged as the pain lanced through her torso.

"Stand up."

It was a challenge as though he was saying, *"Let's see how much I can give before you break."*

"Stand the fuck up!"

Fury exploded behind her eyes, serpent hissing inside as she straightened and spit in his face. Her pink-tinged saliva coated his skin and he stood in silent rage before wiping it from his eyes.

"You're fucking dead."

His hand was back in her hair. Xia screamed and clawed at his death grip, her feet kicking in every direction as she fought to stop her fate. The Devil dragged her back to the porcelain tub and kicked the back of her knees until she was bowing before it.

Not a word passed between them as he used his iron grip to shove her head beneath the water. Her body grappled as it tried to save her, hands pushing, feet kicking and head thrashing, but he held steadfast. Tor thrust her forward until the lip of the tub had nowhere to go but through her, the crack of her ribs echoed like a bomb in the water.

Healing salts in the water burned her eyes and ran like a river of lava into her lungs. She spit and sputtered, hands clawing at her porcelain grave, but she wasn't strong enough to break the surface.

She was going to die. Gods, he was going to kill her in this fucking prison. The moonlight would never touch her skin again, and Brooks...

She'd never hear his voice again. Never laugh at his obscene jokes or pretend to be wrapped in his arms. The darkness inside her roared, fighting to be free as she gulped lungfuls of water. Xia sobbed, one last plea to the Fates as her vision blurred. Just as she started to fall, his grip lessened. A moment later, he lifted her from the water and tossed her aside.

Voices murmured off to the side, but her choked sobs overwhelmed the small space, quickly drowning out the Devil's angry whispers as she retched. The Devil pulled a towel from the rack to dry his hands before throwing it to the floor and stepping over her. He bent and grabbed her chin, forcing their gazes to clash.

"I'll be back. And when I am, you're done." He ran a hand through his tousled blonde hair slicking it back into place and straightened his button-up shirt.

In mere seconds, the battle ended and Xia was left to suffer in the wreckage.

Suffer, she scoffed. All she ever did was fucking suffer. She lay on the same spot on the bathroom floor as she did every time he left her to knit the pieces back together. Weak, her sisters had called her. Content to be a fly on the wall and cower at the first sign of conflict. Cold fury iced her veins unlike any she'd ever felt as her chaos slithered the surface. She was tired of being weak.

Helpless.

Useless.

Xia shattered the barrier between her heart and the monster she kept locked in its depths. She let rise the nature of her chaos as she stood from the floor. Frost settled over her heart and she lost herself to the fury and cruelty in which her monster basked.

Something took control of her then. Something she only faced when she screamed at the black sky and pulled blood from the sea. Her broken bones melded, corded muscle mended, and her waterlogged chest expelled every drop as Xia stepped from the body of the woman and into the skin of the monster.

Her kindhearted nature whispered protests. *See reason*, it begged. *This isn't you.*

But the darkness was all consuming. Xia's gentle soul tucked itself into the arms of the monster, and all she had left was rage.

To covet is to yearn
To yearn is to desire
To desire is to

Envy

NYX

4

Teddy placed a hand on her lower back and urged her forward. She was hesitant to go but put one foot in front of the other. She wouldn't let them see her tremble.

Nyx stepped into the large foyer and assessed her surroundings. Plush body-sized cushions were strewn about the floor, large couches and duvets sprinkled here and there, and a pleasure bar was situated in the corner. Sheer floor-to-ceiling curtains were placed strategically to allow privacy when desired.

Not that anyone here cared to use them. Nyx couldn't look anywhere without seeing a man stroking himself or a face buried in between someone's thighs. Gagged moans drew her attention to a pair of men, one reclined on a couch while the other was on his knees taking as much cock as he could handle to the back of his throat.

Nyx looked away, cheeks blazing. She prayed to whoever would listen that her blush would resemble heated desire rather than innocence. Women danced on raised platforms and in gilded cages hanging from the ceiling. Some were dressed in decorative fabrics that covered just enough to tease while others were naked and adorned with shiny jewels accentuating their assets.

Cupid took Nyx's hand and pulled her from the gala of flesh and toward the shadowed outskirts. Sleek black doors lined the outside walls with men in black suits interspersed between each of them.

"Where are you taking me?" She had to raise her voice to be heard over the groans and music. She'd be damned if she leaned in close enough to whisper. Encouraging these assholes more than necessary was not on the agenda.

"To get some privacy, baby," Cupid drawled with a wink. He approached the nearest Club Hel bouncer and leaned in close, gesturing to their group. With a quick nod, the man scanned his badge to the control panel on the wall. The door next to him lifted swiftly and disappeared through the ceiling. Only the best of technology for the patrons of Club Hel.

Panic settled in her limbs. Nyx needed to shake the assholes before she was forced into a private room with the four of them. She grabbed Teddy by the ear, pulled him to her level, and licked the outer rim slowly.

"I'm going to the ladies' room to freshen up. Grab me a drink, big boy, and find somewhere comfy. I'm riding you first." She bit the lobe and sucked the sting away. Teddy jeered and smacked her ass, and she was glad no one could see her eye roll. With a quick kiss on his cheek, Nyx sauntered away with the hopes of finding a bathroom to hide in. She needed a minute to think about her next moves.

The small hairs on the back of her neck stood on end, paranoia quickening her pulse. Someone was watching her.

Nyx grabbed a passing server by the arm and leaned in to ask, "Where are the bathrooms?"

The Club Hel employee pointed to the opposite corner and yelled over the music, "The first hall on the right. The ladies' room is the second door."

"Thanks." Nyx followed his direction and kept her pace nice and even. She didn't want whoever was watching to know that she'd caught on to their attention. A good thief was aware of her surroundings and played the underdog.

She shouldered through dancing bodies and avoided grabbing hands while trying to adjust her vision to the magenta light. Saccharine perfume permeated the air and she hoped to Zeus that it was body spray and not opium. She couldn't afford to lose her wits.

"Come back home, okay, Nini?" Evangeline's voice drifted through the mayhem in her mind and Nyx's stomach clenched. If she fumbled, Evie would starve.

Nyx caught sight of a clearer walkway and relief nearly forced her to her knees. It was short lived, however, when she saw the length of the line of women waiting for the bathroom.

"Just fucking great," Nyx murmured. So much for taking a minute to get her shit together.

Nyx reluctantly joined the line and threw a paranoid glance over her shoulder. She didn't know who was watching her, but seriously hoped it wasn't one of those pig-faced motherfuckers she walked in with. She hated standing still for too long. Like a rabbit ripe for slaughter.

She wiped her sweaty palms onto her sequined dress and decided she was tired of fucking waiting. Nyx pushed past the women in front of her with hushed apologies and ignored the dirty looks tossed in her direction.

"I'm just going to squeeze past you–" She nudged past a woman in a skimpy pink sequin dress with an awful brown wig and smeared eye makeup. Her breath screamed opium and ambrosia.

"Watch where you're fucking going." The woman shoved Nyx in the shoulder, her face contorted in a drugged rage.

Nyx stumbled across the hallway. Her heeled shoes caught on the carpet and her back hit the wall hard enough to force the breath from her lungs.

She had only a moment's notice before a familiar feeling of vertigo crept up her spine. A rush of magic burst through her veins crackling like electricity as Nyx threw her head back toward the sky. White glazed her eyes as she was thrown into a vision.

Men in black suits surrounded a body crumpled in the alley outside of Club Hel. Jewels glittered in the security light, reflecting off a dead woman's dress as her unseeing eyes bulged from the sockets. A small trickle of blood ran from every orifice. She was fragile and white as a corpse as if all of the blood and ichor flowing through her veins had been drained, the very essence sucked from her body.

The men parted as a menacing figure stepped through their line. He was not the biggest of the hulking entourage, but he carried an essence that would make any god cower. Time faltered, shadows reached, the whirring neon signs dimmed...

It was as if the world held its breath for him.

His dark blonde hair was slicked back with only a few strands out of place. Black business slacks hung low on his waist, tailored perfectly to the long length of his legs, and matched the color on his nails. Tattoos colored his forearms and slipped under the rolled sleeves of his black buttoned shirt.

But his face...

His high, proud cheekbones stood out prominently and added an elegant beauty to damper the cut of his jaw and menacing set of his brow. Eyes milky white as smoke trapped in glass stared down at the broken woman while his face flickered between life and death. Neither here nor there, but stuck somewhere in between.

A man made of both the sweetest dreams and the darkest nightmares.

Nyx stepped from the shadows to get a closer look at the scene. Her body shifted in between planes, the translucency of her skin like static as it projected into the alley. She swallowed as she thought of her physical body lying prone by the bathroom, but shook the nerves. If she couldn't see what her chaos wanted her to, Nyx wouldn't be able to go back to her body. Her sight was a curse.

Nyx dropped to her knees and crawled forward to peer through the security details' legs and a small gasp slipped from her lips at the close up state of the body. At the sound, the man made of nightmares looked up and those milky eyes pierced her soul. She froze, every cell in her body refusing to move. A slow, knowing smile fell across his lips.

Nyx was thrown back into her body, lungs gasping for air as she worked to tame the panic.

He *saw* her.

How was that even possible?

"Fucking weirdo." The woman who shoved her stared as if Nyx had the plague.

Nyx fumbled, the vision heavy within her mind.She placed her hand on the wall and used it as a guide from the bathroom hall and toward the cushioned alcove perpendicular to the bathroom. Couches lined either side of the small sitting area with an empty wall at its end. Her harsh breathing filled the space as blood pounded through her ears. The rising wave of panic crested, making it nearly impossible to grasp the calm she needed to work through the situation. Nyx sat in the chair closest to the back wall and cradled her forehead as she closed her eyes and breathed. Anxiety was a finicky bitch.

She was still being watched. She was still in danger. And she was no closer to securing money for her village, or the little girl waiting for her there.

A whisper of a breeze brushed against her clammy neck and drew goosebumps across the skin. Nyx turned her head and let it cool her brow as she worked to calm her racing heart. Nyx decided she would freshen up and go back to Cupid and his crowd of idiots. At the very least, she could slip some valuables off of them before going home to regroup.

She opened her eyes and prepared to stand, but froze when another rush of air bristled the strands of her wig. Now that she was collected, she realized the chill was rolling off the wall to her left.

"What the..." she murmured as she reached out a tentative hand. Nyx blinked hard and refocused her vision, turning her body to allow light to flood into the alcove from the bathroom. Nyx's fingers brushed the wall and shimmered like she'd dipped them into a crystal pool. Her breath caught, eyes bulging as she realized what she'd stumbled upon.

"A portal," she whispered. It explained why Level Lust was the last floor listed in the elevator. The higher up the floor, the more prestigious it became. You had to *know* how to get to Envy, it wasn't just offered.

Nyx stood and checked her surroundings before placing one foot into the hazy wall. She threw a final glance over her shoulder stepping through the portal.

The secret room was swallowed in shadows as the door closed behind her, nothing but a strand of LED lights on the floor. Nyx took a few tentative steps forward and perked her ears, listening for any sound that would indicate danger. When her senses picked up nothing, she followed the light strands down the hall.

It wasn't fifty paces before the lights made a sharp right and disappeared from view. Nyx approached the corner hesitantly, but as she peeked around it became clear where she had landed herself. Over a wide archway was a lit sign that read–

To covet is to yearn
To yearn is to desire
To desire is to Envy

THE LAST WORD FLOURISHED AND, unlike the other white letters, was lit in neon green. She found the secret door to Level Envy. Nyx crept around the corner and it became glaringly clear how Club Hel defined the sin of yearning.

Level Envy was a hidden layer on the outside of Level Lust.

Suited men stood before large two-way windows cast in the pink light of Lust, their gaze enraptured with the show before them. Some were still as predators, their eyes aflame with longing, while others braced against the wall on either side of the glass rubbing themselves through pristine pants. The bolder of the few stroked their cocks unabashedly in the open. Heat flamed her cheeks, but Nyx tried to adorn a front like she belonged in the room. While most of the patrons of Level Envy were male, there were a few females scattered about which was promising. Maybe she wouldn't get thrown out on her ass.

There were no lights on Level Envy other than the lazy haze of pink, its patrons left alone to envy in the dark. As Nyx stepped cautiously down the hall, she found her eyes lingering through the viewing windows. What she saw was carnal.

Every room held one or more daemon in various phases of pleasure. She stopped and watched four men bury their cocks wherever they could find an opening with their two female companions, their mouths open in silent moans.

It dawned on her that she recognized these men.

Cupid fucked his way to orgasm into a woman from behind while Teddy laced his fingers through her blonde hair and choked her with his dick. He pulled out after filling her mouth with cum, but only so he could stick his fingers in to feel her swallow it. She sucked greedily as she gulped it all down her throat.

Nyx couldn't turn away. Wetness slicked her thighs as the pressure in her lower stomach built. She felt guilty for watching, maybe even shame and a touch of fury, but couldn't force her feet forward. Nyx lived in a constant state of survival. She didn't have time for pleasure, and had never experienced a man between her legs. So why, then, did her mouth water? Why did her thoughts stray, envying the woman who was taking cock like it was her day job. Was that what she wanted?

Nyx shook the fog away and let herself become grounded in the anger that kept her going. She supposed that was the point of this whole sick fucking floor.

To be an envious voyeur.

"Do you see something you like, little thief?" A deep voice rumbled in the dark.

Nyx whirled, her fist already squeezed tight and aiming for whoever had the audacity to be so close.

Before her fist made contact, a tatted, muscled arm knocked it aside as a hand with painted black nails clasped around her throat. It pushed her up against the glass in a ruthless maneuver. Shock stilled her body as a man made of nightmares smiled down from the shadows, the bones of his skull flickering in and out along with a row of jagged teeth. He bent and pressed his face to her neck, squeezing just hard enough to make her vision dance. The man inhaled as he dragged his nose up the column of her throat leaving a trail of electricity behind, and it was like the oxygen was forced from the room.

"Do you know what I do to little thieves who sneak their way into this club?" he murmured against her ear, breath tickling the tiny hairs that stood on end.

Nyx fought for a moment of clarity to guide the situation, but his closeness muddled her mind. She was afraid, though not nearly enough. Instead, the pressure grew to a burning ache and Nyx hated herself for it. Shame stoked the rage as she choked out, "Let them go because you're a nice guy?"

His laugh rumbled through the space between them and the vibrations hummed where their bodies met. When did they get so close? She couldn't remember.

"I assume you were trying to make it to Level Pride to scrape the pockets of my finest patrons."

"Dude, can you back the fuck up? Your breath smells like ass." Nyx fought to hold back gasps as her lungs begged for the oxygen he deprived her of. The chokehold made her clit swell and it only fueled her anger.

He chuckled and it was a sinister sound that made goosebumps spring up along her skin. "Have your weeks of stalking my club taught you what lies beyond Level Pride?"

His club? *Fuck.*

"I'll take your silence as a no." He put his forehead against hers and stared deep into her soul with those milky irises. He was both stunning and terrifying. "Thieves go to the next Level. Desecration. It's where I enlist you in an auction of private, unnamed patrons and sell you to the highest bidder. Who knows what they would do to a little thief like you..." He trailed off, leaving her mind to wonder what sort of horrors would await her.

He placed his mouth back by her ear and touched the lobe with his tongue. If his hands weren't restricting the flow of oxygen, her body may have betrayed her with a moan.

"If you keep soaking your panties, however, I may have to take you to the highest floor. Do you know what's up there?"

Nyx had no response ready, no quips to wield like a blade as his words wreaked havoc on her body. Instead, she shook her head.

"That, my little thief, is my office. The Devil's Playground."

The fear she'd been missing struck tenfold as Nyx fought against him. Somewhere in the back of her mind she knew that when you were faced with a dangerous animal, you weren't supposed to fight or flee because they may give chase, but Nyx didn't have time to analyze it. She knew that if she let this man take her, she may not make it back home and that wasn't an option.

"There it is," he smiled. "Fear. I can taste it." He loosened his grip, yet caged her body against the wall with his muscled frame instead. She shuddered when something hard pressed into her abdomen.

Please Zeus let that be a gun, she thought.

"That's a good girl," he praised. "You should be afraid." He used his free hand to stroke her cheek.

Something else she'd learned about animals was that you're not supposed to underestimate one that's been caged. She tried to strengthen her spine, making her body as big as it could get compared to the lean frame of muscle standing before her.

"I'd agree with you," she spat. "But then we'd both be wrong, you hulking asshole. I'm not afraid of the likes of you, and I haven't violated any rules in your precious club."

"Feisty, like a little kitten," he smirked.

The living nightmare stepped back without warning and Nyx fell to her knees with a sharp inhale. She'd barely hit the ground before he caught her by the throat and pulled her up, motioning to others with his free hand. Something pinched around her wrists with a *zip* and Nyx lashed out with bucking legs, but it was useless.

He watched with a wolfish grin and she had a sick feeling that her fear was the finest of aphrodisiacs for him. She wondered how many times he sat behind the glass on Level Envy just to watch. A devil lording over his kingdom.

"Take her to The Playground."

It turned out that The Playground was a multilevel penthouse full of fucking torture. There were holding cells, BDSM rooms, and gods knew what else. They only made it halfway before one of the bastards shoved a ball gag in her mouth and locked it tight. Apparently, her screams were upsetting the patrons.

My fucking bad for being taken against my will.

They threw her onto a black velvet chaise in a cushy office and bounced like they couldn't stand to be in her presence a moment longer. She tried to yell 'untie me you fucking dirtbags,' but all that came out were muffled screams. After the door clicked shut, Nyx pressed her forehead against the chair and took a moment to gather herself. She was scrappy and never met a situation she couldn't slink out of, however the current predicament was probably the worst.

There was too much at stake to be killed or sold. Getting back to Avyssos was the priority. Nyx spent some time tinkering with her restraints while considering options of attack. The man was too good at pitting her body and emotions against her, and Nyx was too fast to fall victim.

She stood and walked to the sleek black desk situated in front of floor to ceiling bookshelves as she decided that fire and sarcasm was her best shot at leaving alive. If he moved her to auction, maybe she could slip free in transit. The man was a psycho. Nyx didn't want to give him any reason to get bored and kill her.

Nyx thought to rifle through the drawers, but no surprise, they were all locked. Probably for the best since her hands were bound. Besides, any place with an essence scanner on all of the doors had zero hope for a thief trying to escape the penthouse office.

She took a moment to study her surroundings as she calculated her next move. The office was modern chic and fifty shades of black. Not a single drop of color painted the space other than her hot pink wig.

It definitely belonged to a douchebag.

She would bet her last human chocolate bar that the bedroom belonging to the owner of this office had black satin sheets, gray marble flooring, and zero pictures on the wall.

Fucking. Boring.

She hopped up on the desk, which was no easy feat, and faced the bookshelves. If she were to be trapped, she was going to learn everything possible about the owner of the room. If she was lucky, there would be something to help her escape or, at the very least, outmaneuver him.

Her mind conjured the devilish face without permission and she used it to stoke the flames in her blood. Not only would she make it home, she decided, but Nyx would come back to Club Hel and rob him blind. What better way to form a plan than to understand the piece of shit in charge. In true douchebag fashion, however, none of the books on the shelves were real. They were all the same shapes and sizes with black spines and no lettering.

Fucking typical.

A door clicked shut and Nyx whirled. She wasn't surprised when the asshole with no respect for personal space sauntered through the door. He was even scarier in a well-lit room. The tattoos stood stark against his pale skin and the flickering of his face was even more prevalent. He watched her, and she eyed him right back.

Let the game begin.

Nyx was used to being underestimated and smart enough to use it to her advantage. He circled the room, each step bringing him closer to the desk she still perched on. The air was taut as if the steps he took reduced the size of the space. Men made her alarm bells sound in general, but there was something about this one that paralyzed her. It was almost as if her body knew that running would only make him chase her.

He was a man who liked the hunt, and she was determined to never be his prey.

The man made of nightmares stopped just short of the desk and they stared intently at each other. She was afraid to breathe. Terrified to blink. But she never backed down. She was a survivor, and survivors couldn't afford to flinch. She didn't let self-righteous bullies push her around and damn sure wouldn't start with this one

In a move so swift she couldn't track it, he closed the distance and put himself in between her thighs. He towered over her, pulling the air from her lungs as he dominated the space between them. She knew it was purposeful. It was a power move. He wanted to get in her head. Make her cower.

"You look like a sweet dream, sitting pretty on my desk." His voice was low and seductive as he lowered his mouth to her ear and whispered, "But I bet you'd be a beautiful nightmare bent over it."

Her labored breathing through the gag was harsh in the silence and when he lifted a hand to trace a pink strand of her wig, she almost quit breathing entirely.

She froze and flamed all at once, the fire and ice fighting for dominance. Was she scared or turned on? The momentary lapse in attention cost Nyx more space as he reached around her. She expected him to pull the wig off, but instead his hand settled on the clasp at the back of her head. He released the gag and tossed it aside. The gesture caught her off guard, and the smirk dimpling his cheek said he knew it.

"Do you always look like that?" she blurted, surprising even herself. Her jaw ached from the gag but it wasn't going to deter her questions. Questions, much to her chagrin, that popped up out of nowhere. Like he wasn't a dangerous daemon ready to feed her to his hellhounds or sell her off to the highest bidder.

"What do I look like to you?"

Nyx's tongue snaked out to wet her lips, her mouth suddenly too dry to speak. Her cheeks heated as she watched him follow each swipe of her tongue.

"A nightmare," she whispered.

His smile was wicked as it stretched slowly across his face.

He reached to unbutton his black shirt and Nyx's greedy eyes followed every motion. Fine muscles flexed with each maneuver as the tattoos stretched over his skin. His hands were deft and handled each button with ease. "What am I going to do with you, kitten?" His tone was more of a reprimand than a question.

"Maybe let me go?" she quipped, but it lacked fire. No, the fire in her spirit was burning somewhere much lower as one... two buttons were freed.

"If only it were that easy. If I let you go, you'll just turn around and try to steal from my customers again, and I can't have that." Another button loosened, but this time his thumb gave it a gentle swirl before stroking down to the next one.

"What if I pinky swear that I won't?" Nyx swallowed, eyes glued to those godsdamn buttons.

"Now what kind of businessman would I be if I believed the lies of little thieves?" The fourth popped free and those clever fingers teased the slit.

Nyx shifted and bit down on a moan as the desk pressed against her aching pussy. "I already told you," she ground out. "I didn't break any rules in your stupid fucking club."

He leaned forward, lips brushing her ear as he whispered, "I know." He stepped back, dropped his hands to the desk, and swiped his tongue across perfect teeth as he smirked. Shame and anger clashed in her chest, outrage warring with humility as she realized the trap he'd set and gods fucking dammit if she hadn't fallen straight into it.

"You know?" Nyx said incredulously. "What the hell do you mean you know?"

"I know because I've been watching you." He held his ground, fists planted on either side of her hips daring her to shrink, to flinch back or yield.

"Well, that's the creepiest godsdamned thing you've said all night," Nyx spat, spine straightening with every word.

"Did you think you could steal clothes and a wig from someone off the street and come into my club unnoticed? I see everyone who walks through those doors. I know when they do and do not belong in Club Hel and you, kitten, do not belong. I can smell your innocence."

"First the fuck of all," she snapped as she sat up tall and stretched her neck out until they were nose to nose. "You know nothing about me. Don't pretend to understand my intentions when you don't know what I need or what I've been through. I just wanted to have a good time, and I was doing a damn good job of it until I was interrupted by some asshole and his brooding group of bullies."

"Such pretty lies," he whispered, his hand reaching to trace her jaw. Her heart pounded at the promise of his touch and she wanted fuck him almost as bad as she wanted to rip him apart.

"Stop playing games. Let's lay it all out on the table. What are you going to do with me, since you're obviously not going to let me go."

That milky stare pierced hers as he dropped his hand and stood in silence for a few heartbeats. Those seconds felt like hours.

"What's your name?" he asked.

She was quick to answer, "Ambrosia."

The twitch of his eye was all the warning she got before he pulled a blade free from his side, twisted it on the upstroke, and stabbed it into the desk between her thighs on the down. Nyx's heart thundered in her ears as a bead of blood welled and trickled down her inner thigh. He wiped the trail with one black tipped thumb and Nyx watched with bated breath as his tongue snaked out and licked it clean. "I thought we weren't playing any more games, Nyx."

Her blood ran cold.

Fucking balls.

He smiled and went on before she could answer. "I told you, I've been watching you."

"Who are you?" She whispered, voice cracking on the last word.

"It doesn't matter who I am. It only matters who you are."

"I'm nobody."

"A nobody who is going to fetch a high price in level Desecration if you keep lying to me."

"Fine!" she snapped as every fraying emotion imploded inside. "I'm just," she stumbled, searching for honest words to sprinkle in with the lies. "I'm just a girl. A nobody. I've been orphaned and I thought I could find someone... someone to be with in your club. Someone who could take care of me."

Lie: finding someone to take care of her.

Truth: finding someone rich to steal money or secrets from so she could take care of those counting on her back home. Nyx needed to find even footing. Needed to figure out where his strings were and how to pull them.

"First you're an adult, and now you're a little orphaned girl with no one to take care of you?"

"I am an adult. I'm twenty years and I *was* orphaned."

"How does an orphan girl make it onto this desolate island of Anthemoessa?"

"I tricked someone into bringing me. I've heard rumors about the types of people who patron your club. There are hundreds of daemon here right now who wouldn't mind my company in exchange for housing and food."

"So your plan is to whore yourself for a roof?" Anger lit those milky eyes, and Nyx paused. Had she struck a chord?

"No," she sneered, rallying every ember of fury she could muster.

"What then? Do you think someone is going to allow you living space while you rob them blind and curse them into oblivion?" His voice rose an octave with each word as strands of hair fell free from their neatly styled hold.

That's it, she thought. S*how me what you're hiding.*

"It's none of your fucking business!" she yelled.

"I am making it my business," he roared, closing the small space between them and putting his face to hers. He withdrew the blade from the table and slipped it under the hem of her dress, pressing the tip against the junction of her thigh.

She tried to ignore where their bodies touched, how his breath heated her skin, or the racing of her heart. But more than that, she tried to ignore how much she fucking liked it. How she seemed to hold this man in the palm of her hand as he held her by the throat.

"What use will you be to a man when you don't know what to do with his cock?" His words were menacing and they stoked the fire in her belly.

"I know exactly what to do with a cock–"

His bellowing laugh cut her off, and godsdamn if she didn't want to knock his fucking lights out. He was lucky her hands were tied.

"You wouldn't know what to do with a cock if I gave you an instruction manual and a godsdamned tour guide."

"You slimy motherfuck–"

A hand covered her mouth as the other grabbed the back of her neck, the forgotten blade digging into her spine as his hold forced her lips shut. "If you're so confident about your skills, we will put them to the test, eh?" A sinful smile spread across his lips and she didn't like the gleam in his eye. She'd intended to push him, force him to show his cards, but gods... Had she just pushed him over the edge instead?

"Level Desecration or a night in my Playground. You choose."

Nyx's stomach lurched. What kind of fucking options were those? Be put up for auction to a bunch of strangers or spend a full night doing gods knew what with a maniac? Her brain went straight to the BDSM rooms she'd seen on her way to his office and that was not something she wanted to be a part of now or ever.

Lies.

She looked pointedly at the hand covering her mouth as rebellious rage burned her chest. He smiled that wicked grin and removed his hand but kept his face pressed to hers. Their breaths mingled, the force of their crash reverberating in dizzying waves.

"I'm jealous of all of the people who have never met you," she spat.

"Come now, kitten. That hurts me." Anticipation sparked in his eyes, his muscles tense and waiting for those words of confirmation to fall from her lips.

Nyx leaned forward, their cheeks grazing as she placed her lips against his ear. "I would rather sell my soul than spend even one night with you."

Chaos rippled through the air as a great pair of shadowed wings flexed on the wall behind him. Nyx held her breath, preparing for the onslaught that never came.

"Fine." His cool mask slipped back into place as he took two steps back. "This arrangement could have been fun but now I suppose it's just business."

"What fucking arrangement?"

"Watch your mouth kitten, or I'll fill it with something big enough to tame it."

"Don't you dare talk to me like–"

"She's a cute one, you know. Evangeline." His words were too matter-of-fact to cause the amount of destruction she felt in her heart. Bile burned the back of her throat, the heat from their argument dying like a flame under water. His smile was asinine. "You see, sweet Evangeline is having quite a nice dinner with my friend Epiales. Do you know who that is?"

"The black dream," she breathed. Fear incarnate.

Oh gods...

"So smart for a little street cat," he drawled. "I've made sure he fills her little belly to the brim with anything she's asked. Meats, breads, cheeses, sweets... you name it. Little Evangeline has it."

"Please don't hurt her." Tears splashed in her lap. "She's just a girl. She's never done anything to hurt anyone, please, you have to–"

"One word from me and Epilaes snaps her pretty neck."

"What do you want? I'll give you anything." Her voice was a raspy whisper laced with fear and regret. What had she done?

"What I want, kitten, is your undying loyalty."

Words. She couldn't find them.

"Our fates are twined, and the last thing I need is you out in the world fucking everything up."

"Fucking what up? I don't even know–"

Her words were cut short as he sliced the ties holding her hands. Her fingers throbbed as blood rushed back into the tips. Nyx didn't even have time to whimper before her right hand was between their bodies and he drew the blade down her palm.

She gasped and recoiled, but his grip was firm.

He met her stare as he pulled the wounded hand to his mouth and lapped the cut. His tongue was tinged in red and he watched her with every sinful lick. His blood stained lips pulled into a devilish grin, pointed teeth on full display. "Your turn."

That was all the warning she got before he pulled the blade across his neck and forced her mouth to it. She resisted at first, closing her mouth and shoving at his chest. But he grabbed her neck in a bruising hold and growled, "Take my fucking blood or I'll slice sweet Evangeline from neck to navel and drown you in hers."

Nyx sobbed as she closed her mouth around his skin.

If he thought subservience was in her nature though, he was mistaken. She wanted to hurt. Wanted to hurt *him*.

Nyx pulled back just a fraction before sinking her teeth in hard enough to make her jaw ache. She hoped it would make him hurt. Make him regret ever crossing her path. She should have known better.

A mix of laughter and moans burst from his lips and the harder she bit, the louder he got. He held her neck tighter with one hand and placed the other on her lower back and pulled. His hips ground against her with every brush of her tongue, his erection nearly bursting through his tailored pants.

She intended to rip his jugular out with her teeth, to tear the skin from his neck and watch him bleed out on the floor. But when Nyx tensed to act on it, he grabbed her cheeks in a menacing grip, and forced her teeth to release him.

"I'm going to have fun taming you, kitten."

Evil was written all over his face, the spear of insanity glinting in his eye along with the promise of pain. He would hurt her, and he would enjoy it.

Nyx summoned the rage that fueled her hatred and spat the blood coating her mouth back into his face. He closed his eyes on impact but didn't make a move.

When he opened them again, the milky whites bled black. His skeleton form flickered in and out, jagged teeth yawning, and the blood spatter emphasized the nightmare of a man. "I like you, Nyx."

"I don't fucking care if you like me."

"You should. I kill people I like."

Nyx was in over her head, and the water was too turbulent to break back through the surface. Her words dripped with venom but he liked the taste. The lower she fell, the higher he rose.

"There's nowhere you can hide from me, kitten. Our bond is

sealed in blood. If I die, you die. We are bound. This can be as easy or as difficult as you make it."

"And what if I just kill you right now? What if I decide that losing my life is worth wiping this world free of you?"

That hungry gleam returned to his eyes as something heavy pressed against her palm. He wrapped his hand around hers and brought them both to his chest. Nyx's heart fluttered when she realized she was holding the dagger, and he'd placed it to his throat.

"Do it."

"Why? Why are you doing this?"

"Because I have a little problem I need solved, and I like you Nyx." His throat bobbed against the blade as he swallowed and nicked the skin. "I think you and I have an understanding. You help me, I don't drain little Evangeline dry for my next bath."

Her hands trembled and she fought to keep the shake from her voice. "What do you need?"

He smiled, canines glinted against the lights. "Someone let the Soul Eater out of his cage, and I need insurance to barter my safety." Nyx didn't have time to process his information or the absolute terror it filled her veins with.

The Soul Eater.

Words felt heavy on her tongue as she spoke. "Why would the Soul Eater, the Father of Chaos himself, spare your life because of me?"

"Because, little thief, our souls are now bound. A blood bond is a soul bond. If you die, I die." Nyx was frozen on the desk with her face still gripped between one of his large, tattooed hands.

"What does Chaos have to do with me?"

"Everything, Nyx. You will escort him to that tragic little town of yours and feed him some bullshit sob story about your crumbling slice of Olympia. Tell him how he failed you all and let him watch as you starve, and then tell him his little problem can be solved on Erebos. Tell him an old friend is waiting for him there, and she's *very* excited to see him again."

It didn't make sense. Any of it.

"You think he won't kill me? I'm nothing to him! He's primordial. He is Chaos."

"I guess you're going to have to get scrappy. Make him like you. Make him love you. Use that charming personality of yours and get scrappy, Nyx."

"And If I fail? If I can't get Chaos to Erebos?"

"If he doesn't make it to Erebos, she will kill me. Do you understand Nyx? If I die, Epiales will kill Evangeline and burn your little run-down village to the ground "

Her only response was a sob.

"Good girl. I knew you'd see the full picture."

The Devil released her and stepped back.

"He's here in Club Hel. You best run along and find him."

"And what about you?" she retorted with every ounce of venom she could muster.

"I'll be enjoying the Freakshow." He winked and the action made her blood boil. "If you ever want to join me on Erebos, virgins go for a pretty penny."

Her cheeks flamed and, though it was the last thing she wanted to argue about, she couldn't help but bite back. "I'm not a virgin."

They both knew better. His mischievous grin said as much.

"If you weren't a virgin, I would already have you bent over my desk with my cock buried inside your wet cunt and spanking your ass for your insolence. Consider yourself lucky that I've some restraint." He walked toward the door and opened it in three quick strides before he turned to say, "And the next time you *see* me, I prefer to be naked and not standing over a dead woman."

Unleash your Chaos

Brooks

5

Brooks blinked away spots coloring his vision, ears ringing from the force of the hit to head, but he was primordial. It would take more than a punch to subdue him.

Chaos' laugh rumbled through his chest.

Brooks turned to the harpy who'd been brave enough to hit him. The harpy held a cocky stance, but the fear bleeding into his expression told Brooks all he needed to know. Harpies, evidently, were prideful creatures. It seemed that the blue male would rather die where he stood than look weak in front of his pink mate. It was a trait Brooks could admire.

Not that it would matter. He had a millennia of rage begging to be unleashed and a bird willing to take it. "Do it again." His menacing tone cooled the air around them, ice creeping along the dead soil.

The harpy huffed a laugh and looked around to his friends. Their postures remained relaxed as if they couldn't sense death breathing down their necks.

"Or what, freak?"

"Do it," Brooks growled. "Hit me again."

Indecision mixed with fear flashed across the harpie's features, but still he did not back down.

Good.

The harpy tensed as he swung and cracked his fist against Brooks' jaw. The thrill of pain made him feel grounded. Alive.

"What's with this fucking joker?" A green harpy with spiked hair and black feathers laughed.

"You want some more, asshole?" Another asked from the back of the group.

Several tall, muscular forms stepped forward, their chests puffed and shoulders pulled tight. Blood lust flooded his veins as Chaos grappled for control.

Brooks knew he should shove the assholes aside and find Xia, that the fight was precious time wasted on beings that mattered less than shit. But as the group of harpies puffed their chests, Brooks found himself sharing space with Chaos. All of that rage boiling between the two of them was desperate for an outlet, no matter how small.

The group of harpies surrounded him as the other patrons in line backed away. None of them paid any heed to the god standing before them. How far his world must have fallen.

"If you want a fight, freak, you've got one."

"Yeah, Tobias! Kick his ass!" The pink harpy cried out from behind the approaching males.

"Yeah, Tobias," Brooks taunted, his voice deep and ethereal. "Kick my ass." He grabbed that string of chaos and pulled, calling to the shadows and smiling as they danced along the ground and curled through his fingertips. The black bleeding through his veins pulsed and he knew from the wide stares that his eyes glowed. And yet none of them backed down.

"You stupid motherfucker," Tobias yelled before launching himself forward.

Pride. A disgusting amount of pride. Tobias didn't make it a full step before Brooks released the poised darkness. Using them was as simple as breathing.

They were an extension of his chaos.

Of his soul.

Tendrils of inky black lashed out and restrained Tobias while another wave barred the crowd. Brooks held the invisible cord of chaos and pulled taught, but when it fizzled and slipped his breath caught. His power waned and surged, one minute as easy to wield as a thought and the next impossible to capture.

Chaos bared down on the flow and pushed it into the wavering shadows until they were solid as stone and growled. *I don't know what is happening, but we cannot call on the well of chaos many more times before we're dry. Take it from the bird so we can save her.*

There was no indication that the daemon noticed his lapse in power. The crowd continued to roar and the harpy's face was stuck in a fit of rage, but fear glinted like a blazing sun in his eyes. Brooks stepped toward him and once they were toe to toe, he inhaled deeply and listened to the shadows around him. Through them, he could taste the sour tang of fear and the spice of hate. Brooks sent tendrils of shadows forward and caressed Tobias' face. The bitterness on his tongue thickened and a shiver of pleasure tingled his spine.

Brooks wrapped the harpy in darkness. Tobias' eyes disappeared up into his head, a silent scream on his lips as the shadows seeped into his body and soul. Brooks knew it hurt, tearing the mind apart from the inside out in search of memories, but he didn't give a fuck.

The Deathless God only gives one chance at mercy.

Brooks closed his eyes and sniffed the air, pulling in the harpy's mind through all of his senses. His shadows filtered through sounds, smells, and sights, pillaging memories and tearing through thoughts. Within seconds Brooks had a clear map of Club Hel. Each Level represented a sin the daemon glutted themselves in. Tobias, it seemed, liked to feed off of the fear of those weaker than him and force himself on females while his brothers watched. Brooks rummaged through the memories, each more disgusting than the last.

"What a man, Tobias, to take advantage of others to make yourself feel big. To force your cock somewhere it doesn't belong just to stroke your pride. You're nothing," Brooks spat. Something dripped to the pavement, and Brooks looked down to see piss running from the navy feathers. "Now everyone knows how small you are."

Brooks smiled and sent his shadows plunging through Tobias' every orifice above the shoulders. They forced their way down his throat and into his ears as they tore him apart from the inside out. Brooks gripped Tobias' neck in a crushing hold and forced his chin up. He closed his eyes and urged his shadows toward the pulsing life in Tobias' chest as the harpy screamed. Chaos swirled there and Brooks urged it forward, calling it back home.

It came eagerly and left Tobias' body in a rush, mingling with Brooks' own darkness. He sighed as it swelled within. The daemon used to fear him. *The Soul Eater,* they would whisper.

They weren't wrong.

When any living being was born, a small bit of chaos intertwined with their soul and gave them life. When they died, their essence was ushered into the Underworld and eventually pulled back into the well of chaos. From the well, others were born.

It was a great cycle and keeping balance was imperative. If the chaos wasn't recycled, then the new souls would get less than those before them.

The world he'd created so long ago could not function without the chaos he fed it. Since he was the power that all beings were born from, taking a soul did not affect the balance and he could choose whether or not they were reborn.

Without his chaos, the harpy was just a shell. Brooks decided that Tobias would end there. Sins as great as his didn't deserve to be reborn. Red trails of blood wept from Tobias' eyes, nose, and ears. It was a mercy really, that Brooks had ended him quickly.

Take the others, Chaos growled.

Screams rent the air as his shadows swelled over the crowd and plundered their captive souls. Bodies fell to the ground around him, the darkness swarming back to curl around his ankles once more. The shadows were darker than they'd been before the harpies, but nothing like the endless void he was used to wielding.

"For now, it will be enough. We just need enough to find her and run." Brooks spoke inward.

Agreed. We will figure out the cycle once she is in our arms.

Brooks turned to stalk toward the entrance. The original plan was to find a quiet way in, get to Xia, and leave before her captor knew she was missing. But now, eyes tracked his every movement as the patrons of Club Hel moved out of his path.

Their whispers filtered through his ears.

"...Soul Eater..."

"...Is he real..."

"...it can't be..."

Brooks ignored them as he approached the wall of muscle standing guard at the door. He was going to walk right through the front fucking door to Club Hel and hoped someone dared to step in his path. He was in the mood to make blood pour from the sky.

Brooks didn't deign to look at the man before sending his shadows forward and ripping the guard's mind apart piece by piece. From it, he learned that the lower levels were for the lowest of patrons.

He needed to be at the top where the real darkness played.

We do not have time to walk through this disgusting club. We are God.

Chaos gathered a burst of power from within and Brooks bled into the shadows, following its whispers as they guided him toward traces of sunshine and sea salt. The smell of her hair still coated his senses and it was maddening. Bouts of vertigo sent him spinning as his chaos drained, but the closer he got to Xia the more blinded by desperation he became.

I can feel her.

He followed the shadows through rooms of sin and sex, blasphemy filling every inch of the club. He was both intrigued and disgusted by the behavior of the race he'd created so long ago.

The discrepancy of the club played to his advantage. There wasn't a single space he didn't have access to. The dark was where daemon came out to play, after all.

He'd made it nearly to the top of the club when angry, hushed voices caught his attention. It was the first time a sound other than breathy moans sounded in the club. Maybe they would know something about where his Siren was.

Brooks slinked through the shadows under the door and settled in a corner as two figures engaged in a battle of wills. A small, pink haired daemon was bound on a desk with a fire in her eyes like none he'd ever seen. Her valor was awe inspiring and Brooks found himself impressed by the fight she possessed. Especially as a menacing figure pressed himself in between her legs and held her captive.

His sense of urgency grew as electricity thickened the air. Pressure weighed his chest, his blood pounding through his ears as his body begged him to keep searching.

His heart was out there somewhere and he ached to reach her.

Fuck this, Chaos growled. *Leave them.*

Brooks couldn't agree more.

He left the feuding couple in a drift of shadows. There was one more floor to search before he'd have to get crafty.

Where the fuck is she?

As the thought wound its way around his nerves, a rattle of power caressed his chaos and set his blood roaring. It tasted of sunshine and sea salt and felt as much a part of him as his own soul.

Xia.

Her power sang to him, reverberating straight down to his godsdamned marrow.

Brooks moved to go to her, to find the other piece of his soul, but a single breath was all he got before an earth-shattering scream cracked the world to its core.

Unleash your Chaos

Nyx

6

"He's here in Club Hel."

Nyx tried to process the information dumped in her lap. She wasn't sure where to begin, but she did know three things for certain.

The Soul Eater was real.

Evangeline was in trouble.

And she'd made a blood bond with the Devil.

Panic seized her muscles as her mind raced to find a solution to her current mess. A mission to secure food and trade items for her home had become a complex nightmare.

"Fuck!" she yelled as she slid from the desk, hands fisting into her eyes as if she could rub hard enough to wake from the dread. Pressure built in her chest, and it was not something she could afford to deal with. Nyx focused on her breathing to calm her restless mind. She was scrappy. Driven. Stubborn. The cards had been stacked against her since birth, but nothing had ever brought her down. She'd be damned if that disgusting dirt bag would be the first.

Determination steeled her frame as she turned to the cracked door. He wanted to dabble in nightmares? Fine. By the end of the road, she'd make sure he was the one begging to break the bond.

Her footsteps were quick and sure as she raced toward the door. She would find that fucking God of Chaos and force the bastard to Erebos even if it meant dragging him by the flaccid dick. Imagining stepping foot into Erebos made her skin crawl, but it wasn't a thought she could afford to dwell on. Evangeline needed her. The land of eternal darkness behind the rising sun was where the monsters roamed, and even the worst of her kind were afraid to show their faces there.

Nyx burst through the door frame and stopped mere inches across the threshold. The air grew heavier and the dim candelabra lining the walls flickered. Static clung to her skin as the fine hairs stood on end. Even the plastic strands of the wig rose. Something was coming. Her instincts begged her to run, but her heart kept her studded silver heels firmly planted. She had to find Chaos. Her promise to keep Evangeline and the others safe would not be broken tonight.

Without a second thought, Nyx turned and ran toward where the power felt heavier. She would bet her last good bra that it was coming from the Father of Chaos himself. Nyx made it halfway down the hall before a thundering crack resounded through the island. The quake took her to her knees, her body crumpling into an ungraceful heap as her face slammed into the unforgiving marble. The first impact stole her breath, but the second?

It left her nearly unconscious.

A black figure fell directly out of the shadows housed beneath the lights and crashed on top of her prone form. If her nose hadn't been broken before, it definitely was then. Nyx was stuck face down, arms pinned to the side as nausea rolled her stomach. Whoever was on top of her was heavy as fuck and if she weren't so dizzy she may have been pissed.

A masculine groan rumbled across her back as two hands with pale skin and long fingers pressed into the floor on either side of her head. It was a small mercy when he lifted himself. Nyx took that moment to peel her broken nose off the rattling floor and suck down air.

It only took Nyx a few moments to gather her wits. She rolled into the pair of leather clad knees straddling her body, nearly toppling the stranger. Dancing black shoulders lunged to catch him, and Nyx swallowed back her surprise as she spat blood off to the side and blinked to clear her vision. Dust fell from the ceiling as the foundation of the building continued to rumble and quake. Nyx wasn't sure what was happening, but she damn sure wasn't going to stick around and find out. The stranger held his head and rubbed at his eyes as he tried to force his legs to stand. Was he experiencing vertigo too?

"Hey," she said. "Can you get the hell off of me?" Would it matter? It wasn't as if she could stand.

He stiffened as those pale hands lowered and her breath caught. Staring back was the most beautiful man she'd ever seen. His symmetric features were amplified by a strong jawline and piercing blue eyes that held an ethereal glow. His jet-black hair was messy, but seemed as if each strand was placed by Chaos himself.

At that thought, her stomach sank.

Nyx tested the air with what small amount of chaos she had and fought the urge to cower when it brushed up against his pulsing shadows. The power rolling off of that man was endless. It spoke of imploding stars, the creation of galaxies and all of the darkness in between. The blood drained from her face and Nyx could have sworn that even her heartbeat slowed so as to not catch his attention.

Holy fucking Zeus.

Chaos.

"I– uh, I'm so–" she stuttered, words failing at every turn.

"I'm looking for a siren. She's been held captive here. Have you seen her?" His voice was smooth like dark chocolate after a shot of ambrosia.

Time slammed to a halt along with her brain. She couldn't speak. Couldn't breathe as the world shook around them. That annoyingly handsome face searched the hall as what she could have sworn was concern etched his brow. Surely to Hades a being like Chaos didn't feel concern for anything. While she was thinking about it, why was he at Club Hel in the first place?

"You will escort him to that tragic little town of yours and feed him some bullshit sob story about your crumbling slice of Olympia." The Devil's deep, cloying voice filtered through her mind.

Chaos grunted and didn't spare her a second glance as he shoved off from the floor and started down the hall.

"And If I fail? If I can't get Chaos to Erebos?"

"If he doesn't make it to Erebos, she will kill me. Do you understand Nyx? If I die, Epiales will kill Evangeline and burn your little run-down village to the ground "

Time started back at breakneck speed and Nyx forced her body to stand as the one person who could save Evangeline walked away.

"Wait!" she yelled after him.

He stopped but didn't turn.

"I, uh–" Her voice faltered as a broken plan formed on her tongue. "I know where she is. The Siren? I know where he keeps her." Nyx made a leap of faith assuming that it was the Devil keeping the siren.

If he wasn't? She was completely and irrevocably fucked.

His head swiveled just enough that the dim lighting cast his profile in shadows, making his illuminated blue eyes even more neon.

"Do not lie to me." His monotone voice was quiet, but the undercurrent of menace laced beneath those words made her lip tremble.

"I'm not lying." Her reply was breathy and broke at the end. *Way to go, dumbass. That was really convincing.*

He faced her fully and his expression was anything but kind or patient.

Gods, she was screwed.

Her tongue snaked out to moisten her dry lips. Bravado had never been so hard to force. The distrust on his face grew and the shadows he kept tucked tight around his shoulders unfurled to the width of the hallway.

She was *royally* screwed.

Nyx was scrambling to form her next lie when screams filtered in from the levels below. They were guttural and desperate. Some rang of pain while the others tainted the air with desperation. Daemon were dying in Club Hel and if she didn't find a way to convince their creator that she was useful, she would be the next swimming in the river Styx.

Chaos was a flash of shadows and fury as he stormed down the hall toward the screams.

"Wait!" Nyx called after him. Which was stupid. Of course, he wouldn't fucking wait. Nyx forced her body to move and pounded down the hallway on his trail. She wasn't sure what her next move was, only that she couldn't lose him. She was no stranger to life threatening situations, but running after the deathless god was a new one even for her.

Unleash your Chaos

Xia

7

Xia stood on the cold bathroom tile and stared at her gilded prison. Hate was but a burning ember in the pit of rage fueling the monster within.

Take it all, she told it. *We are done being its slave.*

A dam broke inside her heart and there was no holding back the power trapped behind it. Xia had feared that power her whole life, locking it down to protect the world from its cruelty as she took the brunt of its punishment. It ate at her as she forced it to wither, sentencing her mind and soul to the most painful kind of death an immortal could face. Never again would she subject herself to torture for the sake of others. She was done punishing herself.

And the Lord of Nightmares? Returning the favor of his treatment would seem like a mercy after she was finished with him.

She recalled the way he'd held her head under the water. The times he made her rewatch her sisters die and then twisted their mutilated corpses until they spat venom at her feet. All of the times he pressed his skin to hers to deepen his hold. The chaos he'd ripped to fuel his disdain for the world around him. The way his cock pressed into her hip as he laid beside her and reveled in the misery he caused.

Those memories curled like a grove of razor vines through her body, nicking and slicing until she was left in bloody tatters. But this time was different. Xia didn't run from the pain. She welcomed it. The agony she'd felt when her sisters were slain, the despair she'd nearly drown in when he laughed at her tears. Every shiver of disgust, the longing she felt for a man she could never have. The collision was soul-shattering and Xia embraced every shard.

She would never allow herself to be numb again.

Never. Fucking. Again.

She used every miserable moment of her life to encourage the monster to rise. Her jaw ached as she seethed, her face twisted into indescribable fury as tears streamed down her face. All of the agony... all of the suffering, and all of the rage ripped from her throat in one guttural scream. Everything she'd ever felt poured into one moment.

The sea thrashed and roiled as her chaos called it forward. It lunged in crashing waves against the glass, the surface fracturing and spewing foamy water as it fought to get to her. She screamed until her lungs had no air to give, her nails digging into fisted palms and face flushing from the force of her anger. Xia stared with intent, urging the water to fight for her until the final chime of redemption rang through the air.

It reminded her of clinking ambrosia flutes as the cracks in the wall ruptured.

The monster within smiled, canines fully extended and dripping venom as the confines of her prison shattered.

Unleash your Chaos

Brooks

8

Only one thought ran through his mind as he raced toward the screaming patrons of Club Hel.
Find her.
Help her.
Save her.

Brooks jumped through shadows and shoved past the panicked mobs of people. He had no idea where the shadows had taken him. Only that when he heard that scream, heard *her*, chaos exploded in shock waves that rattled the Earth. Her unique essence left a tinge of sunshine in the air, a hint of sea salt on his tongue.

He didn't know how to navigate Club Hel, but it didn't matter. If he couldn't find Xia through his shadows, he would become the storm to clear a path to her no matter the consequences. He followed the lingering smell of her hair and the sound of her heart through the darkness. He wasn't sure if he had a soul, but she called to something deep within.

Brooks' feet pounded against the hallways of Club Hel. Lights flickered all around as the foundation shuddered. Jagged cracks splintered up the walls as the building groaned under pressure. He stopped to gather his bearings and listen for where her chaos called. It brushed against his skin like a warning, the sweetness of her light sparking to an ember before lashing out like a solar flare. Her rage was palpable, a craving for death that spoke to blood rushing through his veins. His Siren was a goddamn force to be reckoned with.

Gilded cages hung from the ceiling with panicked females begging for someone to let them out. Some were scantily clothed while others wore nothing but a shimmering oil on their naked skin. They gripped their chests and wiped at their eyes as they screamed, but he didn't have the luxury of time or concern for them.

The walls were lined with doors, some blocked with large pieces of the fallen ceiling while others appeared unharmed. Some of them were covered in black spatters that seemed to darken as the drone of red lights flashed across. Strings of flashing black and ruby crystals hung low from the ceiling catching the light at all angles.

A loud, rupturing boom rumbled through the floor as fissures webbed down the walls and spread toward the floor.

Brooks made to run but was so focused on finding the source of her power that he didn't notice the clutter on the floor. When he stepped forward, his foot caught and he stumbled to the ground, his knees hitting the unforgiving marble as his hands landed in a pool of black oil.

No. Not oil.

The smallest of molecules lifted from his hand and floated lazily toward the ceiling. Brooks turned his chin up to follow and realized that it wasn't crystals or rubies dangling luxuriously from the ceiling.

It was blood. Hundreds of thousands of droplets catching the droning red light and reflecting it back to him. He turned his gaze back to the ground, toward whatever it was that had tripped him.

Bodies.

Hundreds of them lying on the ground bleeding from every orifice, their faces gaunt and eyes bulging as the final proof of their fear was forever engraved in their expressions.

He looked back to the gaudy cages to find the women in much the same condition. Their screams no longer pierced the air. Arms protruded from in between the bars as their soulless eyes stared down at him. They'd spent their last moments begging.

It's her Song, Chaos murmured, a crisp breath of awe flowing between them. *Her Siren. She's bleeding them all dry.*

Brooks stood and grasped his chest as the pressure in the air squeezed him tighter. He felt helpless as he reached for his well of power, grasping for something that simply wasn't there.

"Goddammit!" he raged, voice carrying across the universe as he kicked at the bodies on the floor. He needed more chaos to fuel him, but once a life was extinguished their chaos filtered back through the cosmic well and not even he could pull from it.

If he could just pull a little more chaos, it was possible he could latch onto her essence and travel straight to her. He should have done it from the beginning, but he was an immortal god. He'd never felt emotions like panic or worry. Only a deep loneliness that resounded straight to his very marrow. Brooks struggled to keep his fucking head on straight and put a goddamn plan together.

More screams erupted through what sounded like the doors lining the wall. The walls continued to crumble around him, dust and rubble falling like the sand through an hourglass.

"Help us!"

"Somebody help us!"

"Please, Zeus save us!"

His ears perked.

If there are still living daemon in the building, there is still chaos to be consumed.

Brooks moved with purpose to the echoing screams. They came from a corner swathed in shadows and his anger rose as he neared. There was no door, only a hallway leading to the restrooms and a small open seating area with couches lining two of the walls. Couples lay naked on the velvet furniture– one gripping each other chest to chest with their faces touching as if they knew they were spending their last moments together. The other couple? He was giving her all he had from behind. Brooks could imagine they all died exactly how they would have wanted to go.

He reached out his arm and touched the wall with cautious fingers. As the tips touched the surface, it broke in waves like a drop falling into water. The wall was an illusion and gods knew he was no stranger to that.

He stepped through with zero reservations and surveyed the area. A neon green sign lit the entrance to a hallway where the walls were lined with transparent material. It had to be stronger than glass, whatever it was, because the large chunks of debris laying around surely hit it while falling. Not a single pane was fractured.

Brooks followed the echo of fists banging against the mirrored walls. In one of the middle rooms was a group of screaming daemon, their eyes weeping red as color drained from their panicked faces. Four males sat on the assortment of furniture with their heads in their hands, fists gripping locks of hair while two females beat on the glass. He recognized the men as the group who entered the club with the pink haired girl.

When Brooks approached the glass, the females' expressions turned gratuitous as rays of hope shone in their tear stained eyes. They thought they were looking upon their savior. They never imagined that the greatest darkness of all had come to seal their fates. There would be no afterlife for them.

The Soul Eater left nothing behind.

One of the sobbing females pressed her hand against the clear wall, words of thanks falling from her lips. Brooks lifted a hand and placed it against hers, a pang of emotion he didn't quite understand sticking to the back of his throat.

We do not have time for your growing sense of empathy. It is weak and not fit for a god. Kill their souls, drain their chaos, and get us to our Siren. I will not be so kind if you force my hand.

He urged his remaining chaos forward, hands staining black as the darkness webbed its way up his arms. The reflection in the window emphasized his glowing blue eyes and he quickly averted his gaze. Shadows unfurled from the darkness in his palm.

The women grimaced and shared a look, brows furrowing as a frown creased the corners of their lips. He could imagine that they had no idea who he was. This world had changed so much since he left it. Chaos, the Deathless God, was nothing but a memory.

The one closest pulled her hand from the surface and backed away, the other female hiding behind her with the same bewildered expression.The men stood and cowered to the other side of the wall, leaving the woman to hold the front line.

Cowards. They die first.

His shadows slipped through the smallest of openings and fell to the floor curling like smoke across the room. The females sobbed as the males shoved them forward. A burlier brown haired man begged Brooks to spare him and his friends in place for the women.

Brooks' blood boiled by the weakness bred into this new society. When he'd placed drops of chaos into the first living immortals, it was to encourage strength and honor. Morality and protection. They were to be the pillars of strength holding the foundation for generations to come. Somewhere along the line, they failed.

We failed.

His shadows were swift as they curled around the screaming daemon and latched onto their skin. Hands smacked and rubbed frantically to dispel the darkness calling for their death.The group fell silent as the living extensions of his soul twined around their necks and pressed them to the wall. It would go faster if they didn't fight.

Brooks closed his eyes and exhaled a breath with intention. He would do the females a mercy and make sure their conscious mind was unaware of the pain and fear of death. An emptiness echoed in his chest as the well of chaos in his veins emptied save a few drops. Their eyes closed as their bodies fell limp. No wrinkles gathered on their foreheads and the tracks of glistening tears dried.

The males, however, continued to scream and beg for their lives. They stared in horror at the limp women and fought uselessly against his shadowy restraints.

It would do them no good.

"You're disgusting, craven gods who don't deserve the gift I've given. You spineless pieces of shit will die as cowards, and my sentence is the wrath your kind will learn to fear." Chaos' voice entwined with his own, their tone low and ethereal.

Upon his last words, the shadows burst forward and funneled down the throats of the men in a violent, punishing wave. Their frantic screams were muffled as his darkness forced its way down into their chests and up into the brain. Curls of inky black left their noses as he shredded them apart from the inside out. He was going to pull every last drop of chaos from their tainted souls.

Brooks' shadow grew darker as it pulled the chaos out of the writhing group. It was a slow drain at first, but once he had his claws in, the power flowed back in a rush.

Fuck, he thought, hair raising along his arms as the tingling high flowed through his veins. Brooks closed his eyes once more and inhaled, welcoming the rush. It was nowhere near enough to bring him back to full strength, but it would be enough to take him to her.

It had to be.

When there was nothing left but marrow and sinew, he recalled the shadows and ignored the thud as the bodies dropped to the ground. Milky eyes stared at the ceiling, their hollow cheeks frozen in a scream.

Something cool and wet soaked his shoes, pulling him back to the task at hand. The hallway was completely flooded and the water level was rising fast. He bent down to wet his fingers and touched them to his tongue.

Salt water.

She is calling forth the sea. We must hurry.

Another ripple of power echoed through the world and he tasted her in every wave. Chaos stirred in his veins and reached for the sunshine that sang to his very soul. Xia awoke a beast that had been sleeping since the dawn of time, and it was ravenous.

He was desperate to have her.

Hungry to taste her.

To *devour* her.

Brooks closed his eyes and urged his mind, body and soul to follow that ripple back to the source. His scattered pieces clung to hers and reached desperate hands toward the light calling him home.

She is our beacon.

Molecules spread and rode the trail of power back to the one thing that promised to make him whole. He traveled through darkness until the bitter brine of sea water hit his scattered senses and static electricity thickened the air. Light pierced the darkness in jagged bolts and illuminated the black sandy beach in bursts of brilliance.

Brooks threw himself from the shadows and bid the chaos to piece his daemon form back together. His feet crunched on the sand as the clouds ripped open and poured their rage upon the surface.

Two silhouettes stood stark against the flashes of lightning– one cowered on the ground while the other... His pulse jumped as his heart lodged itself in his throat.

Xia.

She stood over the slumped form on the ground in a menacing stance as the tumultuous waves reached and crashed against the cliff face. He didn't know where exactly they were. Club Hel was somewhere above them but they weren't on the strip of sand he'd seen in his dreams all those weeks ago.

It didn't fucking matter.

He ran to them, his feet kicking up sand as his arms pumped at his sides. Rain stung his face and battered his eyes, but he wouldn't stop.

"Xia!" he shouted, his voice booming as deep as the thunder rumbling around them. Her spine stiffened and she looked up, those glowing green eyes like a beacon to his soul.

Their stare never faltered as he ran. When he was a few paces away, he slowed to a jog. The last thing he wanted to do was crash into her and send them both flying from the cliff. If he were a good man, he would stop. If he were a patient man, he would let her come to him. Brooks stood before the raging tempest his Siren had become and reveled in her twisted beauty. He yearned for her more than the moon longed for the rising tide.

We are not men. We are neither good nor patient. We are God. Now go.

Red dotted his vision and splashed against his jacket as he realized it was not rain that fell from the sky. No, she'd called forth the storm that raged in her veins and drenched the sands in the blood of every patron from Club Hel. The red droplets mixed with the spray of sea water and soaked her moonlit locks, staining them pink against the blazing storm on the horizon. It ran in rivulets down her face, dripping from her chin and streaming down the curve of her breasts.

Their ragged breaths mingled, each afraid to touch the other. Her skin pimpled as she stared into his eyes and that piercing neon glow dulled to a turbulent sea green, lashes fluttering against the bloody beads still dripping from her hair. "Brooks?" she whispered, her voice hoarse and broken.

His name upon her lips brought him to his knees.The Deathless God of Chaos knelt before his queen and, as the sky bled and the world burned around them, he knew he was where he belonged.

Xia reached a hand toward him just as her eyelids fluttered closed and her knees buckled. Brooks jumped forward to cushion her fall and cradled her limp body in his arms. When the winds died down and the sea calmed, her panicked words reached his ears. Her lips moved as she whispered unintelligibly, the storm around them fading with her consciousness.

"I can't make it stop, Brooks. The demon inside... I can't make her let go..."

He placed his cheek against hers and ran a soothing thumb across her jawline as Chaos bled from the shadows and held her from behind. His darkness whispered to hers and the storms calmed on the horizon. Brooks brought his lips to her ear and said, "It's okay, Xia. Let go. You can fall... I will catch you."

Unleash your Chaos

Nyx

9

Nyx stood at the open cave mouth and watched the scene play out before her. Chaos bolted toward the monstrous female wreaking havoc on the island. Puddles of blood soaked through the black sand and illuminated in the bolts of electricity ripping through the sky.

But all she could see was *him*.

She wasn't sure how she knew, and she would figure it out later, but the figure slumped on the ground by the electric couple was the Devil.

The cut on her hand burned. Nyx didn't know the rules of being bound to someone by blood, but the weightless, nauseating feeling roiling in her gut bet he was dying. She could feel it down to her marrow as her vision dotted, instinct urging her to save him. The pieces of his soul entwined with hers were losing the battle and they weren't going without shredding hers along the way.

"Shit," she whispered, sweat dotting her brow as her hands shook. She had to make a decision.

Save the Devil. Befriend the Soul Eater. Don't die trying.

"Simple," she breathed as her head spun. Talking to herself made it better. Sometimes.

Bolts of lightning illuminated the beach in an ominous haze. Nyx was counting on the white-haired beauty to keep the God of Chaos occupied while she dealt with the Devil. She didn't have time to be too calculated. He'd managed to crawl away, but Nyx was afraid the distance wouldn't be enough to hide them.

Nyx's feet stumbled as she ran, her life draining out on that sand right alongside his. As she reached the Devil's side her heart pounded louder than the thunder reverberating through the fire-lit sky. Nyx dropped to the sand and shook the man vigorously. He was lying on his stomach, head turned just enough to not suffocate. Bloody droplets stood stark against the pallor of his skin. Death had its boney fingers wrapped around his throat.

"Wake up asshole!" Her voice came out as a shaky whisper-scream as anxiety dug its claws in.

She tucked the pink wig back and leaned forward to place her ear by his mouth. He wasn't breathing. "Shit!" she cried as her vision swam. Air squeezed from her lungs as the pressure of their bond clamped around her heart. He was slipping away and she didn't know how to hold on.

Nyx looked over her shoulder to make sure she hadn't been spotted with the monster dying beside her. She didn't know their story, but it was clear that she wouldn't make it out with her life if she was caught with the Devil. He was dying for a reason.

"Okay, get a hold of yourself, Nyx." She wiped her eyes and sniffed, pulling composure back into her spine.

She tucked her hands under his arm and settled a hand under his left pectoral. Her hand met meaty flesh, and not the muscled kind covered in soft skin. Jagged tears and stringy muscle corded between her fingers and it took all of her resolve to keep her hand where it was as she gagged.

"One, two, three–" She heaved, toes slipping in the sand as she grunted and shoved. Nyx placed a hand on his black denim clad hip and pulled, her strength waning with his life. Just as his back met the shifty ground, a flash of light put the severity of his injury into focus. Horror froze her rigid body. His chest had been torn wide, white bone protruding through shredded muscle as splatters of clotted blood and ropey vessels dotted his clothes.

"Zeus almighty," she breathed. Her body was begging to flee, but her mind urged her to stay. If he died, she died, but if her heart was still beating, she still had a chance.

Nyx patted the rest of his body searching for other injuries.

"What will you do if you find one? Who knows. Surely it can't be worse than the godsdamned hole in his chest," she muttered under her breath.

Her hands pressed against his ribs and she shuddered as the left one gave way. Down she went, roving over his lean, athletic frame. She lifted his bloody shirt to examine the skin. Black tattoos wrapped around his sides and disappeared under the low waistband of his pants, but the skin seemed untouched.Her fingers traced the fine lines and she caught her mind wondering how low they went. Luckily, reality bitch-slapped her before she had the chance to do it to herself.

Dying man at her front, angry god at her back.

"Get a hold of yourself, Nyx. Now is not the time to act like some drooling virgin idiot. They always die first," she scolded. Nyx was careful to stick to the outside of his thigh. If his dick was mangled or missing, it was his problem.

As she patted his left thigh, her knuckle met something lying in his lax palm. Nyx closed her eyes and swallowed against the shiver. "Fuck." Slowly, Nyx turned her head back to the Devil and peered at the mutilated mess nestled into his hand.

Laying there was the Devil's heart torn from his chest. What was more disturbing was the way it beat erratically, clinging to the living plane as stubborn as the man it belonged to. That son of a bitch probably should have died a hundred times over, but people like him always made it in the end. It was almost as if the taint on their soul was so heavy that even the underworld couldn't contain its darkness.

A true villain.

"Come home, Nini." Evangeline. She was there for Evangeline. Morals were a luxury, and she couldn't afford them.

Nyx closed her eyes and silenced the lingering guilt as she went inward and searched for the mark of the blood bond on her soul. It had guided her this far. She imagined it would see her to the end. Or at least she hoped. She sure as shit didn't know how to put a beating heart back into a butchered chest cavity.

As the thought crossed her mind, a feeling of rightness caressed her senses.

No. Did it want her to–

"Seriously?" she asked it aloud. Nyx opened her eyes and gulped. She reached out, her fist closing around the Devil's heart as she raised her hand and turned it left to right. Was she supposed to wipe the sand off of it?

Nyx held his heart to the sky for inspection and as the moonlight fell over the heart in her hand, a low drumming filled her ears. The sound resonated in her chest, and as she watched the fading rhythm in her hand, Nyx realized it matched her own.

"Double fuck," she breathed. "Here goes nothing."

Nyx hovered over the Devil, cradling his heart in both hands as she took a moment to look over his face. The man made of nightmares didn't look so scary then. She almost pitied him.

She descended into his chest, keeping her hands cupped around the organ to protect it from protruding bones. The jagged edges of his broken ribs sliced at her hands and stabbed at her forearms as she pushed. Nyx swayed on her knees, her muscles cramping and vision blurring as her pulse weakened. Pressure built in her chest and worsened with each push like she was returning the heart to her own chest.

Nyx stopped when her fingers met the backside of his ribs and released the heart. Was she supposed to put it in a certain way? Or make sure that all of the arteries matched up?

She whined as she retracted her arms and stared down at the puncture wounds from his ribs. She couldn't stop the blood from running down her arms and into the Devil's chest. Not that it mattered. He'd taken more than his fair share earlier. He obviously hadn't been too worried about her lowly peasant blood mingling with the pureness of his own.

Nyx sat back on her heels and waited for something to happen. Anything. The sea calmed and the blood stopped falling from the sky, and Nyx fought the urge to fidget. He didn't dare look over her shoulder again. It was only a matter of time before she was caught. And what would she say?

Hi, I'm Nyx. I saved this piece of shit for the hell of it and have been spying on you. Want to be besties?

"Ow! What the–" she exclaimed as a cold hand flew to her wrist and enclosed it in an iron grip. The Devil stared back at her with those milky white eyes and she shuddered as she watched the hole in his chest weave itself back together.

A flash of movement from the side drew her attention. The Soul Eater caught his fallen beauty as her knees buckled. He moved strands of hair from her face and rubbed her jawline so gently that it sent a pang of guilt rocketing straight through Nyx's bones. If the moonlit goddess had been the one to kill the Devil, what must he have done to her to earn it?

"We have to go," he croaked.

She pulled her gaze from the lovers' caress. "How do you suppose we do that? I can't carry your heavy ass anywhere, and this may be my only chance to get to him. I will not risk my family to get you off this beach. I did my job and saved your worthless life," she spat.

Anger deepened the lines across his brow. "Give me a nightmare and I can take us back to the cave. If I die, little thief, then so do you."

"What? I'm not giving you shit–" Her temper flared, and the regret was immediate. The Devil used her distraction to weasel his way into her mind. Her vision clouded as she was thrown back in time to a place she had sworn she'd never revisit.

Putrid breath assaulted her nose as he pinned her wrists against the wall.

"You owe me, you piece of shit." Spittle dotted her cheek and if his unwashed hand wasn't covering her mouth she may have vomited.

Unnamed brutes scoured her rundown village and bullied the starving citizens into paying protection costs that they simply didn't have the funds to cover. Nyx couldn't live with herself if a family was torn apart. She was an orphan with no one to miss her. If it meant saving even one family, she would deal with soldiers of Ares. It had always been her burden, and it would be so until the day they took her life.

The brute lifted her arms until her feet dangled. She winced at the coarse brick shredding the top layers of skin as he dragged her up, but Nyx wouldn't give him the satisfaction of crying out.

"Where are the dues for our services?" he spat, voice raised an octave.

Nyx looked down at the hand covering her mouth and back up. Strong he may be, but smart he was not. He pulled his hand away with an annoyed grunt and she spat in his face.

"There's your payment you ugly piece of—"

His fist connected with her face and the darkness damn near took her. She'd taken punches, but it was always worse when your head was pressed to a brick wall. Tears mixed with blood and ran in streams down her face, the tang of copper coating her tongue as it flowed over her swollen lips.

"You're gonna regret that, you half-blood filth. If you don't have the coin, you'll pay another way."

Fear fueled her outrage as she kicked and bucked against him. He delighted in her struggle. Nyx fought as he ripped her shirt. Screamed her fury into the sky when he palmed her breasts in a bruising grip and rubbed his dirty, stubbled cheek against them.

Nyx was thrown from the nightmare and curled to her knees as she spilled the contents of her stomach into the stand. The Devil wore a stormy expression she couldn't identify, jaw flexing and those eerie eyes swirling. "Did he touch you?" he said, his voice nearly a whisper.

"How fucking dare you!" she screamed, pain squeezing her heart as her body shook with the memory of those hands on her body.

In the next breath her wig was thrown to the side, short black hair falling around her neck as he gripped it tight. She cried out as he pulled them nose to nose, fury written across his features as dark as a storm about to break. Their ragged breaths mingled in the small space between them as each refused to back down. His nose scrunched right before he let out a growl and released her. They stood, frames rigid as they watched each other.

The Devil took a few more tense breaths before closing his eyes and wiping the sand from his shirt. She gaped as the tension melted from his body and in its place stood the suave business man she'd had in between her thighs earlier that evening.

"Don't forget our deal, kitten." He turned to walk back into Club Hel, but stopped short to say, "Oh, and don't tell our friend about me. I'll be checking up on you and don't want any more kinks in the plan. Unless they're yours, of course." His wink was sin, but she couldn't tell if it was butterflies or centipedes in her stomach. Disappearing into the shadows, he left her in a pile of her own misery.

Nyx swallowed and looked to the man hunched over the goddess on the sand. The nightmare pulled from the depths rattled her to the core, but she didn't have time to dwell. The people she protected were counting on her.

Evangeline was counting on her.

Nyx took a deep breath and let it out slowly before donning the mask of her new role. She scrunched her face until she knew fear was painted across it and took off toward Chaos.

"Hey!" she yelled, but it didn't carry past the sound of waves beating against the sinking cliff face. She tried once more, bellowing as loud as her scratchy throat would allow. *"Hey!"*

Nyx waved her arms to get their attention as she ran. Chaos glanced her way and froze, distrust was written all across his features. Nyx slowed down and held up her hands as she approached. "Look, I know you don't know me and you're smart not to trust me." He would never know how true those words were, but she shoved down the guilt and forged ahead. "But there's a man inside and he's looking for her. I think he wants to kill her."

He said nothing and her rising impatience fed the irritation bubbling to the surface.

"I can take you somewhere safe, where she can recover and no one will find you. You just have to trust me."

He looked down to the beauty in his arms and the way his eyes softened made her stomach roil. This betrayal would be the one to end her life. But she had to do it for Evangeline.

Nyx held out her hand to the most powerful being in the universe and said, "Just take my hand. Use your chaos to move us and I'll use mine to guide us."

He gave her one last thoughtful glance before stepping forward to take her hand. What she thought would be a companionable hold turned menacing as the fine bones in her hands crunched and popped beneath the force of his grasp.

She couldn't catch a fucking break.

"I don't want to end your life, but it is but a mere ember of light in my world compared to the rays of her sun that I orbit. If you betray me, I will kill you. If you get her hurt, I will kill everyone you love. Do you understand?"

His eyes glowed a piercing blue as she nodded, nervousness dotting her upper lip with sweat. "I understand," she gulped.

Understanding was not agreeing. He had a lot to learn in this new world.

He nodded and sent a burst of chaos so pure through her soul she nearly wept. Hers was a murky puddle of piss and rain water compared to his. Traveling with the God of Chaos was an ethereal experience that urged her to fall to his feet and worship in his wake.

"Take us," his voice echoed in her mind.

Right.

She thought of Avyssos– it was full of ramshackle homes pieced together by whatever material was available. The sky was always dreary and the sterile soil made it impossible for crops to grow. But it was home.

She let the love for her village mingle with his chaos and before she could close her eyes, their feet thudded on the mossy grass surrounding the place she held most dear. Nyx didn't give him a backward glance before walking toward the shabby line of homes. She didn't know how she was going to explain the pair to everyone, but it was definitely a future Nyx problem.

Unleash your Chaos

Persephone

10

The brown haired stranger grinned ear to ear at Persephone and the most handsome dimples dotted both cheeks. The sight of them did impossible things to her brain. Adoration sent butterflies fluttering in her stomach and she giggled like she used to when she was child, before the politics of gods consumed her soul.

Persephone and her perfect stranger laid together next to the tinkering brook. She looked forward to their secret visits as Demeter tended the famine, counting down the minutes from the moment she left his side.

"Surely of all the flowers itching to bloom from those delicate fingers, the daffodil isn't your favorite."

"Why can't it be my favorite?" she asked. A smile she couldn't shake stuck to her face. If he made her smile any harder, she would have to frown for a week just to relax the muscles.

"Because it's too simple. Six petals and a cone, and most are only yellow. They're the most ordinary flower in the fields. A beauty such as you can bloom dimensional roses, or bold blues and purples that unfurl and wake with the rising sun."

Their bodies were angled apart, but their heads were mere inches from touching. His touch was one that she found herself longing for all hours of the day. Persephone twirled one of the beautiful, six-petaled flowers in her hands as he reached back and fingered a string of her pink hair. The first time he'd done it she nearly fainted. No one dared touch the daughter of a ruling Olympian without their permission.

What she loved about him though? He didn't ask anyone for permission.

Except Persephone.

"I spend my life surrounded by intricacy. The politics are nauseating and the pompous contests are exhausting. All of the kind gestures are but a test of your cunning. They're all waiting for you to turn your back so that they can sink in their hands and rip the heart from your chest." She paused as she considered her next words, feelings that had always been there but she'd never voiced. "There are plants with hundreds of blooms on a vine, or single stalks with layers of petals filing atop each other. They look beautiful because all of their flaws are hidden beneath grandeur. The daffodil, though? Six petals with nothing to hide behind. What you see is what they are— nothing more and nothing less. There is beauty in simplicity."

He was silent as she pondered her own words. Persephone had never spoken such slander aloud, and a creeping fear made her shiver. "Never be loose with your words, Persephone. There is always someone listening." Demeter's warning rang through her mind and it was hard not to dwell on it.

"Sounds to me like they're all measuring their cocks to see whose is the largest," he spoke, his light tone pulling her from the darkness constricting her thoughts. "They wouldn't have an inch on me, though." He winked.

It took a moment for her to catch his intention, but as it clicked laughter burst from her chest and rang through the meadow. He joined in the raucous and they laughed together until her chest ached. Even after they stopped, her smile refused to falter. She'd never know such joy in the company of another.

A heavy awareness fell between them. She turned to look at her mystery prince and found a pair of soulful brown eyes staring back. Hesitantly, he brought a hand up and traced the line of her jaw as he whispered, "You're so beautiful, Persephone."

Her cheeks flamed and she shied away, but the hand on her jaw held firm.

"Don't hide from me, flower. I see you and all six of your petals."

Her breath caught as tears sprang to her eyes. No one had truly seen

Persephone before, only the layers Demeter laid so heavily upon her shoulders.

"Why are you so kind to me?" Her voice was shaky as the dam holding her tears shuddered under the pressure.

The man didn't respond, only rolled to his stomach and braced his weight on his elbows. Their gazes locked together for what could have been moments or years before his flicked down to her lips. Her tongue swept out to dampen them, suddenly dry from the heat of his stare. He lowered his head tentatively, his eyes looking back to her as if saying she could stop him any time she needed to.

She did no such thing.

Her pulse quickened as his gaze dipped once more. Persephone closed her eyes as their lips met. His kiss was gentle and made bliss rocket through her senses. She melted under him, her body so warm and fuzzy that she couldn't do anything but kiss him back.

She knew he would be a good lover because his energy always seemed to match hers. When she was hesitant or contemplative, so was he. Now, however? Persephone was ravenous and he was eager to feed her hunger.

She had never kissed anyone before but it didn't matter. Where she faltered, he took control and corrected. Their kiss was a dance and he taught her every step until she was a master at leading.

They sat up as their kiss became more passionate and their hands desperate. She nipped at his swollen lips as his tongue teased, their ragged breaths mingling between. Soon, kissing wasn't enough. She was desperate to explore his body, her hands clenching and releasing in his shirt as she tried to tell him what she wanted.

She broke the kiss and threw her head back. His mouth touched every inch of her exposed neck and each press of his lips sent tremors racing through her. Persephone whined a breathy, frustrated moan.

Laughter vibrated from his chest as he bit her earlobe and sucked away the sting. "Do you want to touch me, flower?"

"Please," she cried.

"Do you know how?"

She shuddered, more than a little self-conscious of her virginity. But what was scarier than her ignorance was the complete trust she felt in him to be her first. Persephone turned to meet his stare and whispered, "Show me."

His smile was devilish as he pulled the shirt from his back. Her eyes roamed his taught torso and heat flared in her belly. She thought there was already a fire, but it was embers compared to the flames his naked skin stoked.

"You look..." She hadn't the words to continue. Beautiful didn't do him justice.

"I know." He smiled.

She reached out a hand and ran her fingers through the patch of brown curls on his chest. They were coarse against her skin, but she found pleasure in the contrast. Where she really wanted to go, however, was down the small trail of hair dipping below the cotton pants at his waist. Persephone's hand traveled slowly, reveling in every inch of his tanned skin.

"Put your lips to my chest and kiss your way down." His voice startled her, her mind too lost in awe over the god before her.

Confusion must have been painted across her expression judging by his answering smirk. He laid back on his elbows and flexed the muscles in his abdomen. Her mouth flooded and she wanted nothing more than to do as he asked.

"It's okay, flower. I know how tempting I am. Bask in me as I do you."

Her mouth watered as she lost herself in the looks of him, but as she moved forward to touch him again, she hesitated. She was supposed to save her body. It was her duty, after all. To be untouched and presentable. Demeter said that's the only way a man could ever want her.

She scoffed, a sneer sneaking into her expression.

Persephone would be bonded to a man of her mother's choosing and forced to bear him children all for the sake of powerful bloodlines. She had no control over her life, and all that awaited was misery

The one thing she did control... Her body. Defiance raged in her heart. She didn't want to be taken demurely out of duty. Persephone wanted to be fucked and by a man of her choosing.

"Surely you're not thinking of leaving, flower? Are you seeing something you don't like?" His tone was sharp, but she would have been flustered if the role were reversed.

"No. You're perfect."

With that, she dipped her mouth to his chest and laid a kiss to the center. The coarse hair tickled her lip and she rather enjoyed the scratchy feel of it. Persephone explored his torso, kissing and licking until she was sure she'd taste every inch. He whispered soft praises as she bit his nipple and sucked it teasingly, just as he had shown her when he'd bitten her ear.

"You're a quick learner, flower."

She grinned as the compliment bloomed in her chest. "I've got the best teacher."

"Yes, you do. The very best." She questioned his haughty response for a moment, but it slipped away when he ran his fingers through her hair and pushed her mouth lower. Persephone hesitated. She knew what he wanted, but she wasn't sure how to begin.

"Don't worry, flower. You'll like it."

Would she?

Persephone heard whispers through the servants' quarters at her mother's estate often from the maid staff. They spoke giddily about nights of sin and how they chose to pleasure the men in their beds. Some used their mouths while others preferred suggestive clothing or dance. They all seemed to enjoy cock in one way or another.

Surely she would enjoy it, too.

Her lover was arrogant, but also sure. He knew what he was doing and had brought nothing but pleasure to her body so far. She could trust him on this.

Persephone kissed his waist line as one hand worked to lower the brown cotton pants. Her hands were shaky and she struggled to move both sides of the garment at the same time. She was fumbling and it made her nervous.

She breathed a sigh of relief when he chuckled and pushed the band of his pants down. He kicked his legs until the fabric flew free and placed both hands behind his head. His smile radiated confidence as his erection jutted proudly from his hips.

"What—" she stammered, unable to turn her stare from his prized possession. "What do I do?"

"Whatever feels right, beautiful. Play around. Touch it with your fingers, your tongue... You'll get the hang of it."

Persephone swallowed and attempted to force some bravado in her posture. How hard could it be? The maids said that the men always finished first, some even before they got to the actual sex part. Maybe she would get lucky and find the right combination of movements.

She reached out a hand and capped the tip with her palm. Unsure what to do next, she rubbed small circles and cringed inwardly. It didn't feel right. He sat up and grasped her hand. Before she could question, he opened the fingers and spit in her palm.

"If you're going to play with my head, it has to be wet. Otherwise it's irritating. Try again, but this time start at the base. Grip it tight and move it slowly up and down. Got it?"

Persephone nodded as she stared at her hand. She was taken aback by the filthy move, but... she didn't hate it. She did as she was told and worked him from the base up. The act made her flush. It was more embarrassing than it was arousing. Maybe it was because she was nervous. She didn't know what she was doing and the inadequacy was grating on her nerves.

There was that temper her mother chided her about. Always quick to rage but never to stop and learn.

He sat up and removed her hand once more. "Okay, I can tell you're not into it. Maybe we should do something different. How about if I work my magic on you?"

Persephone still struggled with her warring feelings, but nodded. He laid her back on the grass and rubbed a thumb across her lower lip.

"Do you remember when we first met, and I told you I wanted to see what color your cheeks turn when you come?"

Words failed her, so she nodded again.

"I'm going to put my mouth on that pretty pussy of yours and find out."

She was absolutely breathless.

He didn't trail small kisses down her abdomen like she'd done, but maybe that was her inexperience talking. Persephone inhaled deeply and released the breath slowly. She needed to calm down if she were to enjoy their time together.

He raised her skirts to lay against her stomach and placed his hands on her shaking thighs. She knew she was exposed because the breeze rolling off the hills chilled her flesh.

"You're just as pink and delicate as the flowers you bloom."

Persephone closed her eyes and in the next breath his mouth was upon her. His wet tongue glided sinfully and her hips arched without her permission. He drove her wild with teasing licks, and when she was aching for more he answered with the full force of his mouth.

She didn't know what he was doing down there, she only wished it would never stop. A burning ache built in her belly and worsened with each wet swirl of his tongue. Persephone cried out, desperate for him to relieve the pressure.

"Let go, flower. Falling is the best part."

She whimpered as he continued and, just when she thought she would die from the throbbing in between her legs, a dam broke. Pleasure burst from her center and tingled down every limb as her back arched from the velvet grass. Her hands flew to his head and held it in place as he licked and sucked at her furiously, wringing every wave of pleasure she was capable of giving.

When her body stopped convulsing, she lay breathless wondering what in the hell just happened. It was the most intense and pleasurable thing she'd ever experienced. And she wanted more. Stars danced behind her eyes as she urged the lids to open, but found them too heavy to move.

"Do you want more, flower? Do you want me inside you?"

"Yes," she moaned and nodded vigorously.

"I knew you would." She could hear the smile in his voice, but still couldn't open her eyes to see it. The atmosphere shifted and as he positioned himself over top of her. "It's going to hurt when I'm in deep, but you have to trust me. Okay, flower?"

"Yes," she breathed. Persephone wasn't sure what to expect. All of the maids were long since untouched and never spoke of their first times. Just as she felt the soft tip swipe up her center, she cried out, "Wait!"

He stopped, but didn't take himself from her.

"Your name," she said.

"My name?"

"I don't even know your name." Silence fell, and she flinched from the air of annoyance coming off from his stiff posture.

"Do you need to know my name?"

"Yes." *Her response was a whispered plea.*

He huffed an agitated breath, but still didn't pull himself from her.

"Narcissus," *he ground out.*

She chewed that over, trying to recall if ever she'd heard that name spoken between the Olympians, but nothing came of it.

"Narcissus," *she repeated.*

"At your service." *His smile was forced, but she was relieved he was trying.*

"I just wanted to know so I could remember," *she blurted.*

"Remember what?"

"I want to remember the name of the man I chose so I can think of you while I'm lying under a man forced upon me."

His smile was genuine when he said, "Oh, my sweet flower. You'll never forget me, and I'll never let you go." *There was an edge to his voice, but as he slid inside her it became a fleeting memory.*

Persephone lay *in a breathless heap upon the ground, grass tickling her bare flesh as the breeze dried the damp sheen covering her brow. Her thighs were slick with their love making and the rumble of approval beside her made her smile. They lay like that for gods knew how long with his fingers entwined in her tousled pink hair.*

"Is it always like that?" *The question had been swimming in her mind since the hazy fog of orgasm lifted.*

"With me? Always."

She huffed a laugh at the haughty remark but couldn't stop the corners of her mouth from creeping back up. That was until she caught the fall of the sun. Demeter would be finished battling the famine soon and Persephone would have to be back before then. Demeter did not like to be kept waiting.

"I have to go." *The sadness in her words was noticeable even to her own ears. She didn't want to leave the spot where their bodies had flattened the grass. Didn't want to leave her little slice of Elysium in the furthest corner of Olympia.*

Narcissus sat up and looked down on her. His brow softened as he spoke, "Come. At least let me nourish and wash you before you present yourself. Can't have you dripping with cum when you meet your mother."

Gods, that man's filthy mouth. Color rushed to her cheeks as her shy gaze looked anywhere but at him.

"You're so delicate sometimes, flower." *He smirked.*

"You're quite different from the men I meet. I'm not used to such language in the presence of a daughter of The Twelve."

"You're no daughter of The Twelve here, Persephone."

Her eyes watered at the sincerity lacing his voice, but she couldn't find the words to express how they made her feel.

"Come on, flower. Let's get you fed and cleaned up."

She took his proffered hand and hoped the gratitude swelling in her chest showed in her expression. His kindness never ceased to surprise her.

They walked hand in hand down the bank with the flow of water. What started as a small stream widened into a thicker stream with a heavier current. It was nothing dangerous, but the water ran more freely than the others.

"Where are we going?"

"There's a pool of crystal water where the brook flows downhill. It's hidden by a grove of fruit trees and is the most peaceful of places. I spend a lot of time there and I think you would enjoy it. It's nearly as beautiful as the two of us."

"You're pretty full of yourself aren't you, Narcissus?" *She laughed as she spoke, but she had been thinking about it a lot. Were all men like this? She wouldn't doubt it if they were. She was surrounded by The Twelve and their offspring, and their pompous natures truly knew no bounds.*

"Why should we be bound by modesty when it only hinders the truth? You live your life so humbly Persephone, but how powerful could you be if you embraced your beauty and used it to your advantage rather than cover it like a weakness? It's rather hypocritical."

That threw her off guard.

"How so?" *She couldn't keep the offense from her tone.*

"You prefer the daffodil because it's simple. Honest and open. Yet you hide yourself away in the same layers you despise. You hate the gods on Olympus because they lie and manipulate behind their layers, but how is that any different from what you do? So which is it, Persephone?"

She couldn't speak. With one speech, Narcissus had turned her world upside down. He was right. She had become the very thing she hated. She thought that by keeping her intentions pure it kept her honest. But instead she hid everything about herself inside where no one else could find it. Underneath layers.

Persephone's thoughts drifted so far that she didn't realize they'd stopped.

"We're here, flower. Take off your dress and I'll help you in."

She hesitated. No one had ever seen her completely naked except for her mother. Even her time with Narcissus was spent covered from the waist up, and she didn't dare look at her exposed flesh as he had devoured it.

Yet another instance she hid behind her imperfect layers.

"I've fucked you, flower. I've peeled one flawed petal from your core. It's in your hands to peel the next."

His words struck her yet again, and she wasn't sure if she was upset with herself or feeling discomfort in his presence. She needed time to swallow everything, but the pressure of indulging in these last moments forced her hand.

With shaking hands, Persphone pulled the thin silk straps of her ivory gossamer gown from her shoulders and shuddered as it pooled around her feet. It took every ounce of control not to curl within herself.

How powerful could you be if you embraced your beauty? *Narcissus' words echoed in her mind.* He was right. She should find power in her beauty and watch gods fall to their knees before her.

Narcissus stood proudly in his nakedness, waiting for her to make the next move. Persephone forced her gaze to hold steady as she said, "Would you offer a hand, please? I'm afraid blooming flowers all day doesn't require much agility."

"Of course."

Persephone grasped his hand and stepped into the most beautiful, crystalline water she'd ever seen. She kept her movements elegant with a force of bravado. If she was going to try to be this new goddess Narcissus was molding her to be, she had to start believing it herself.

The cool water was the perfect contrast to the beating sun. She basked in its perfection as she waded to the middle. Persephone could reach the bottom with her toes, but the water was up to her shoulders.

Narcissus walked in after her and wrapped his arms around her waist. They took a moment to enjoy their quiet haven before he moved to wash away the evidence of their secret meeting.

She closed her eyes and enjoyed the way his large hands rubbed gently across her body. The way that something so masculine could move so delicately was wondrous.

"I used to come to this pool and lose myself within it. I imagine I lost hours, if not days, to the beauty I found reflected in it."

Persephone looked up at the trees surrounding the haven. They were mature with stout trunks that grew to support a network of branches holding the most lusciously ripened red fruits. They looked even more beautiful reflected on the surface of the water.

"I can imagine it would be easy to lose oneself here. What are those?" She pointed to the lower hanging fruits.

"You're telling me that your mother is the Goddess of Harvest and you've never seen a tree like this?"

"Never," she said, in awe.

"I suppose that makes sense. This is the only place these trees grow in Olympia." Narcissus waded toward the lowest hanging limb and plucked a plump fruit. He shifted to the left where a sharp, red stained rock protruded from the bank. The tip was saturated while the rest was dotted in drips and splatters. Narcissus raised the fruit and beat it against the point, and when it cracked fully she understood the staining. Handfuls of ruby seeds were nestled in rows within the shell of the fruit. Juices ran down Narcissus' wrist and Persephone's mouth watered.

As he walked toward her, he spoke, "This is a pomegranate. All of these red sacks are filled with tiny seeds and juices. They're truly delightful. Here." He offered half of the fruit. "Give it a try."

Persephone took what he offered with greedy hands and plucked a single seed from the top. Slowly, she placed it on her tongue. When she bit down, a beautiful blend of tart and sweet burst on her tongue in the most delightful explosion of flavor. Had she not been lost in the taste, she may have been embarrassed by the delighted moan that slipped from her lips. Persephone gathered more seeds from the shell and ate them by the handful as Narcissus watched.

"Did you know that Aphrodite used to frequent this hidden treasure grove?"

She looked at him but couldn't stop shoveling the juicy buds into her mouth. Instead, she shook her head.

"She would come every day and look upon her reflection, and every day crystalline perfection of the water would transfer some of its beauty to her."

Persephone recalled her lessons with Demeter when she was a child. Aphrodite was one of The Twelve gods of Mount Olympus. Her beauty was that of none other and was said to make men and women alike weep at her feet.

"As her beauty grew," he continued, "so too did her power. Aphrodite radiated chaos and the effects of its potency were immediate. She spread love like a wildfire and it's rumored that she is the cause of monogamy, the bonds her powers forged too strong to break. But love wasn't the only thing she spread."

"Can I have another?" Persephone interrupted and a flicker of agitation crossed his face. Narcissus plucked another fruit, opened it with the rock and placed both pieces in her waiting hands.

"Thank you," she muttered, feeling a bit like a punished child.

"You're most welcome, flower. May I continue?"

"Yes please," she said around a mouthful of fruit.

He nodded and continued his story. "You see, Persephone. There are two sides to the pond. Come with a true heart and gaze upon your reflection, and you'll be blessed. But if you stare upon the surface with any taint in your heart, you'll be cursed."

Unease crept in her gut, for only moments ago she'd looked at herself in its mirrored surface. "How do you know whether it's cursed or blessed you?"

"You don't. Not for a while at least. You see, by the time Aphrodite realized what was happening it was already too late. The pond had blessed her with unimaginable beauty, yes, but her curse was not worth the price."

Fruit soured in her mouth.

"By day she spread love and beauty and held the most sinful orgies in rooms of luxury and grandeur. But at night? The pool cursed her into the most hideous being in Olympia. Boils and pustules riddle her skin as it sloughs from her bones. Tainted chaos spreads just as powerful as it does during the day, but it isn't lust she radiates."

"What is it?"

"Famine." His eyes darkened and the smile that spread across his dimpled cheeks was eery.

"But my mother..." she trailed off. Demeter spent her days whispering to soil, urging it to fertilize and grow the crops the world so desperately needed to thrive. Was Aphrodite the reason for their famine? What her mother worked so hard to fight against?

He only nodded.

But then another thought occurred to her. "Narcissus, you said that you've looked within the depths of the water too."

"Indeed I have, flower."

Her heart stuttered before it picked up a pulsing, irregular beat. "And what did it gift to you?"

"Ah, that is the question indeed. You see, if you look into the water with a tainted heart, it senses that darkness and gives it back tenfold. Part of the curse is that you're too blinded by the blessing to see the curse."

Persephone gazed upon her reflection as an ambush of worry flooded her thoughts. Demeter instructed her not to wander too far. She'd warned Persephone of the dangers in the world and Persephone hadn't listened. She had lied, broken the bond of trust between them, and tainted her body with the hands of a stranger. Persephone disobeyed her mother with defiance in her heart.

"What will it do to me?" Tears ran in rivulets down her cheeks and rippled the water like raindrops. Her reflection wavered as she cried.

"You? Oh, my sweet flower. There is no room in your heart for taint. You are as pure as you were when you were pushed from the womb."

A sharp sob of relief burst from her chest and she made to move, to run as far away from the pool as possible lest it find her unworthy. She didn't make it a step before Narcissus grasped her wrist in a bruising hold and jerked her back to him.

"Look again, Persephone."

"Please, Narcissus, I want to go. I don't want to—"

"Look at it!" He snapped. Madness rolled off of his confrontational form and permeated the air around him. It was suffocating.

Screams tore through her chest as she resisted his hold, but Narcissus wouldn't take no for an answer. What was happening? How could the man she'd put so much trust into turn on her so fiercely?

A dominating hand grabbed the back of ner neck and forced her face to the water. "What do you see Persephone?" Her sweet talking lover just moments ago had morphed into a thing of nightmares.

"Please, you're hurting me, Narcissus. Just let me go, please! I'll do anything—"

"Do not make me ask you again, you perfect little cunt," he spat. His rage was palpable and Persephone thought she may be sick.

"I– I don't know," she stammered.

"Of course you don't. To be so pretty, Persephone, you have to be the dumbest fucking daemon I've ever met."

She couldn't speak over the sobs.

"When I look at you I see a pretty little halo of shimmering gold around you. Don't you see?"

She nodded desperately.

"Now look at me. What do you see?'

"Nothing," she sniffled as glanced down into the pool. "I see nothing." No halo glimmered around his head, and his reflection was murky. "Please, Narcissus," she whined.

"Oh shut up. All of your pathetic cries and whimpers won't help you here. Do you know why you see nothing around me?" He didn't give her time to answer. "Because I'm tainted. Cursed. Those looking upon their reflection would never know their dark fate because to them, they see a normal reflection. People like you though, Persephone. They would know they've been blessed because of that shimmering goddamned ring marking you as innocent."

"What does this have to do with me? I've never hurt you. I've never hurt anyone!"

"Oh, but I have. You see, when I looked upon the pool for the first time it was because I followed Aphrodite. I watched her gaze upon her reflection and shine with the gift of beauty it transferred to her. When she left, I walked to the water's edge and stared at myself."

Narcissus looked at his own reflection as his eyes drifted to a time in the past, his hand still gripped tightly around her neck.

"What I found Persephone... Gods, what I found was the most beautiful man I'd ever seen. I spent days by the pool basking in the lust Aphrodite left behind as I gazed upon my reflection with my cock in my hand. I would come over and over and over again. I loved every fucking minute of it."

He pulled his eyes from the water and stared so deeply into hers she feared he may take her soul.

"But, soon, the touch of another couldn't satisfy me. I stuck myself into so many men and women, but nothing provided blissful surrender the way I could. But it wasn't my hand, Persephone. It was my beautiful face. Every time I looked at myself in the pool I wept. I am truly the epitome of beauty and carnal release."

"Gods what are you talking about, Narcissus? Do you hear yourself?" He had gone absolutely mad, and she was terrified of what that may mean for her safety. Mad men were the most dangerous of men.

"Oh, I do, dear Persephone. Just the sound of my voice makes my cock stiffen. I couldn't stay away from the reflection, and each time you look at it the curse deepens. It has been harder throughout the years to find release, but I think that with your sacrifice, Persephone, I can find it again."

"You don't have to do this," she cried.

"No," he smiled, and it was truly the most evil thing she'd ever seen. "I don't have to, Persephone. I want to."

"Please."

One last try.

One last beg for mercy.

"The pool has shown me the greatest beauty in the world, but with it came the curse of simplicity. Nothing will ever be enough to feed the need to have *myself, and I can't let you look upon the pool to be graced with a beauty greater than mine. So when I look into your eyes, dear flower, and see my reflection within them... Just know that I will feel bliss in knowing you'll never compare."*

Before she could scream, Narcissus used his brute strength to shove her head beneath the water. She kicked and clawed desperately, reaching for anything to help pull herself up. Panic seized her lungs and she inhaled gulps of water, unable to stop the instinct to breathe.

Narcissus grasped his cock and stroked himself to the pounding of her heart. Her fight was nothing compared to his strength. Her lungs burned as her body rejected the water but only in vain, for as she coughed and gagged, she only inhaled deeper.

He gazed through the crystal clear water and watched himself greedily in the reflection of her eyes. The more her life waned, the harder he fucked himself. The last thing Persephone saw as her body slowly died was the absolute carnal bliss on his face as he came.

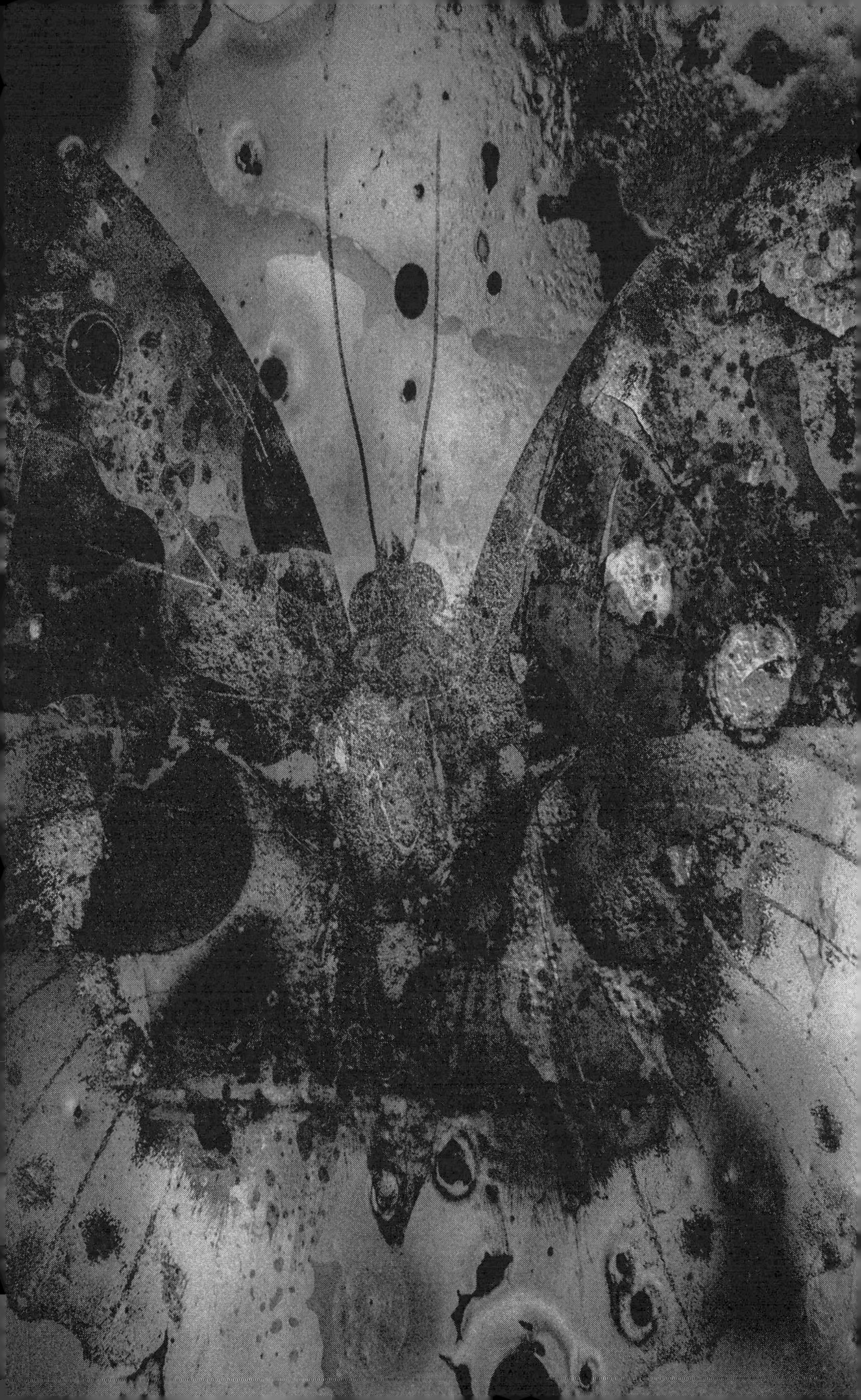

Xia

11

Xia washed up on the shores of consciousness, each wave bringing her closer to awareness. There was a pounding in her head that worsened with every waking beat of her heart and she was sure it would split her in two. Her muscles ached like she'd fallen from the cliffs of Anthemoessa.

She was laying on something soft and a warmth surrounded her like none she'd ever felt. It was cozy, and Xia wanted to melt into it and never leave. A rumble vibrated at her back as a low murmur filled her ear. She froze, breath catching as she fought past the fog.

Where was she?

Oh gods...

Was she still in her glass prison? Was the Devil waiting for her to–

"I've dreamt of you for a hundred lifetimes, Xia," a man whispered. Something tightened around her waist as the voice nestled more closely. His breath blew tendrils of hair across her ear and she shivered. His voice was full of longing and sadness, and her heart ached for him. "I've painted thousands of sunsets with the most brilliant of colors."

She... she knew that voice.

"I've filled millions of skies with the brightest of stars." The pressure lifted from her waist and she found herself wishing it would come back until a gentle hand stroked the hair falling across her face. "But none of it has captivated me the way that you have."

Brooks.

"I–" His voice broke. "I've been so lost without you."

A flood of emotion burst through the dam with only six whispered words. She urged her body to wake so that she might turn and look at him. Hold him. To tell him that she had longed for him too.

"I don't know if you can hear me, sunshine…"

Something splashed on her temple and rolled to the bridge of her nose, leaving a damp trail down her face. He swallowed hard and pressed himself closer. She fit snugly into the curve of his body and the most divine feeling of rightness filled her chest.

She wanted to stay there with him. She wanted to touch his arm and nuzzle her face into his neck. She would tell him everything was okay and that he didn't have to live in the darkness anymore. Xia ached for all of those things, but her mind, body, and soul had been beaten until there was nothing left to take. For now, as her body shut down and dragged her mind with it, Xia found peace within his arms.

For now, she was safe.

She was home.

"You saved me."

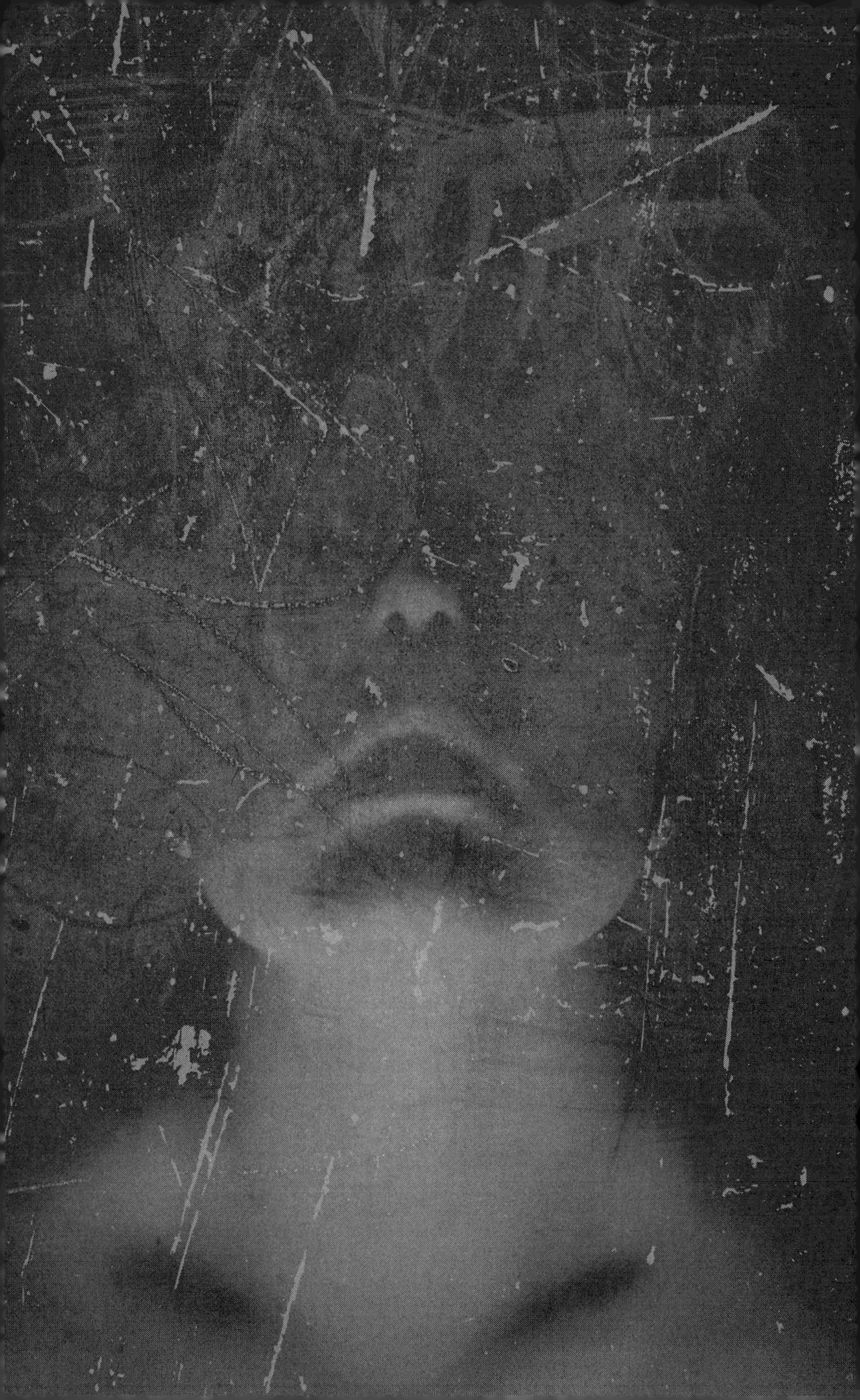

A SECRET SHE WILL
NEVER TELL

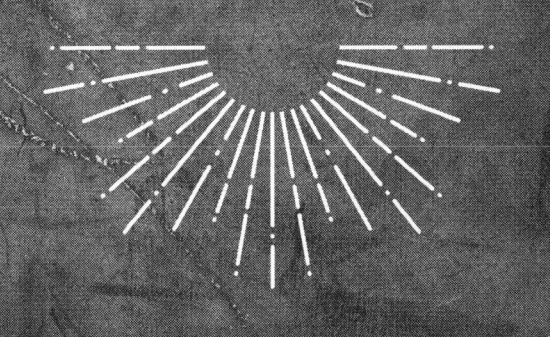

Unleash your Chaos

Brooks

12

The last few hours had been surreal.

Brooks lay on a bed made of thin cloth and hay that poked him at uncomfortable angles. He thought he'd known discomfort in the asylum. The scratchy tan scrubs and harsh springy mattress were daily pains in his ass, but compared to the clothes and bed he occupied now? The feelings from the asylum were dull. They were never real.

He basked in the relief of the discomforts of true life. Because he was laying in a bed with *her*.

Chirps filtered through the single window and mumbles came from the room just outside the door. But there, the girl of his dreams was tucked safely away in his arms on a bed of his shadows. They wanted to be near her just as much as Brooks, and he refused to let her healing body rest on such an awful bed.

He, however, needed to feel it. All of it.

The fear that it could all be an illusion gripped his heart. That fear urged him to recede back inside where it was safe, just as he'd done all of those millennia ago. But as he stroked the white strands of hair falling around Xia's shoulders, he knew that it was a worry for tomorrow.

Brooks tucked his nose into her hair and inhaled deeply. She smelled just as she had the night they spent together in their dreams–sunshine and sea water.

A loud gurgle broke the silence and his middle cramped.

"The fuck?" he whispered into the darkness.

He'd ignored the growing feeling of emptiness in his stomach since falling into the daemon plane and it seemed it wouldn't wait much longer.

As if she'd heard his bodily grumbles from the common room, the short haired pixie turned the doorknob and poked her head in. "Hey," she whispered. "Are you awake?"

He debated not answering. She was shrouded in mystery and Brooks didn't like the unknown, especially where Xia was concerned. He was still trying to determine what her motivations were. Soft footsteps crept toward the bed and a possessive instinct forced him to lash out. Brooks sent his shadows flying like daggers through the air and stopped them just short of piercing every major organ.

"One more step and you'll be a permanent bloody fixture to the wall." Chaos' menacing voice echoed in her mind, but never left his lips. He could tell her bravado was fake as she forced her breathing to ease, but the pounding of her heart filled the silence.

"You've been in here for nearly twelve hours. You need to eat, and we need to talk."

Leaving Xia was the last thing either of them wanted, but if he didn't take care of this newly manifested body, it may wake her. Xia needed to rest, and heal.

He nuzzled her hair once more and placed a soft kiss on her temple. "I'll be back, sunshine." He slipped from the bed, careful to not jostle her head as he pulled his arm out from under her. Brooks wrapped Xia's prone form in shadows and didn't step from the room until he was satisfied the inky shield was enough to keep her warm and safe. If anything or anyone so much as stepped in her direction, he would know. And he would kill it with no questions asked.

When the strange girl moved to shut the door, he stopped her with a silent warning. Her hand shook as she said, "I just didn't want to wake her while we talked. It would be more quiet with the door closed."

"The door stays open." Her eyes widened further at Chaos' intru-

sion to her mind, but he didn't seem to give a fuck. *This is my world now.*

They walked down the hall to the larger room that acted as both a central gathering space and the eating area. To the left was a hearth and fire, wood crackling in the dingy space. Tattered cushions were laid about with daemon, young and old in a range of disarray, doing their best to rest. None of them were clean, and their clothing was just as torn as the ragged furniture. What had his world become?

In front of the fire sat a mother and her child. Her golden curls were untamed and frizzed as if they hadn't been washed in a while. Unlike the others, though, her skin was mostly clean. In that moment, the small daemon looked to him, her bright blue eyes glistening in the fire, and he lost himself in her innocent stare. Her smile radiated outward, filling his icy heart with a spark of joy. Even Chaos seemed to sigh.

The girl tugged on her mothers sleeve and pointed to Brooks. The woman glanced his way and tensed, weariness plastered on her face as her grip tightened.

"Are you coming? Or are you going to stand there like a dumbass all night?" His host stood in the door frame, the outside a darkened blur behind her.

Brooks grit his teeth, but didn't say anything as he followed her out into the chilly night. He'd barely noticed the state of the village as he'd carried Xia through it. His only thought had been getting her somewhere warm and safe where he could assess any injury. With Xia safely tucked away under the protection of his chaos, he focused on his surroundings. What he found was dreadful. Ramshackle buildings, dead soil, ragged clothes hung to dry over string woven from foliage, and a musty smell hanging over everything like a plague.

"I'm sure you have a lot of questions." Her voice was a soft whisper as she stood beside him. She, too, looked over the village, but the look in her eyes didn't mirror his own. He found a fondness in her soft purple stare with a tinge of sadness creeping in around the edges.

"A millennia worth," he sighed.

She nodded, but didn't say anything as she waved him forward. Behind her home was a winding river that rushed steadily along the village edge. She sat on the bank and curled her knees to her chest.

Brooks reached for his chaos to ensure Xia was still resting securely. When the heartbeat thrummed soft and steady down their shadowed bond, he sat. Muffled clicks sounded from her direction, and he glanced to see her picking at her fingers. The nails were chewed down to stubs and the scarred skin ringing them bled in several places. She caught him staring and stopped, a flare of embarrassment shading her cheeks in the moonlight.

She passed a shallow wooden bowl with an assortment of food. Brooks remembered eating in the asylum, but never felt the pangs of hunger. He ate because that was what he was forced to do three times a day. Before he'd lost himself, he didn't have to eat. He just... was. But something had changed. His well of chaos was drained, and he was in a body that breathed and withered. His muscles ached from the action of the night and he was overwhelmingly exhausted.

"What is this?" He poked at the food and rolled it around.

She pointed at every item as she listed them off. "This is bread. This is cheese. And this is cured meat." Everything was hard and smelled unappetizing. "It's not much," she said. "But it's all we've got."

Brooks raised the bread to his lips. Green spots dotted the middle and he tried not to taste it as he bit into it. The cheese and meat weren't any better, but as he continued to fill his stomach the grumbling and aches stopped.

"What's your name?" He asked around a mouthful of cheese and glanced toward her. She hesitated, catching her bottom lip between her teeth as she picked at her fingers again.

"Don't lie," Chaos whispered into her mind. *"I'll know if you do."*

Her eyes bulged as her head whipped toward him. "How would you know?"

He huffed a laugh. "Don't you know who I am? What I am?"

She looked away and picked at her torn skin again. "No."

Anger rushed to the surface as ice coated the ground beneath them.Brooks lashed out, grabbing her cheeks with one hand as he jerked her face around. "Do. Not. Lie." The glow of his blue eyes was reflected in her terrified stare.

Good. Let her be afraid, Chaos seethed.

"Nyx," she breathed. "My name is Nyx."

She didn't break eye contact as he assessed her words. Good enough. For now. Brooks released his grip and turned back to the water. His protectiveness of Xia put him on edge and he struggled to rein the chaos back into his chest.

"I know you're lying because I can taste your soul, Nyx. Your entire race contains a piece of my chaos in your core and you cannot hide it from me. You cover it in layers of life, deception, emotions, and power. But once I call to it, it unravels every single one of those layers and shows me your true self."

"Soul Eater," she breathed. Her breath hitched and the pounding of her heart grew louder than the flow of running water..

He stared into her violet eyes to drive his point home as he said, "Remember that when you lie to me."

Brooks gave Nyx time to sit with her thoughts and emotions. She needed to understand the weight of their situation. Nyx offered her plate to him after he finished his food, her meat and cheese untouched. He didn't argue. If this body needed food to stay strong, he would give it everything he could.

"So, Nyx. Tell me about this world."

"Where should I start?" she scoffed.

He pondered that. "When I was..." Words failed. Where had he been? "When I was away, Atropos came to me often. She spoke of a darkness spreading in the world. I swore to never involve myself in what I've created, but it seems I will lose it if I don't."

"A darkness, huh? Did she elaborate? Because this whole world is a shithole."

"What do you mean?"

"Of course you wouldn't see it." Her mocking tone should have pissed him off, but it only made him more curious. What did these daemon know of him other than his part in their creation?

"Well," she started. "While you were off gallivanting through the stars, the rest of us were down here being starved and slaughtered."

Nyx looked away into the distance, but he caught the sheen of tears coating her eyes. She was silent for a long time before her shoulder squared. When she looked back to him, a fiery determination had slipped over her features.

"They believed in you." Her voice was strong, but he could still hear the small shake within it.

"Who did?"

"Everyone left to rot in this village. In all of the fucking villages just like this. The Olympians wipe us off their feet like dog shit and you could have been helping this whole time. With one blink you could have knocked them from their ridiculous fucking mountain."

He nodded but didn't object. One young girl would not understand the consequences of those actions.

"If I intervened in everything, Nyx, it would be a lot more scary than those you call Olympians."

"Oh yeah? Because you're so fucking tough? Some big, scary asshole who uses intimidation to frighten those with nothing?"

"Yes," he said simply as he met her gaze. Her deep, violet irises changed to shining amethyst and he was almost endeared by her strength.

Almost.

"If I were to decide to rule here, Nyx, no one could stop me. You could raise every army of the gifted against me and you would never even breach my doorstep." Brooks held her stare. He wanted her to see the truth in his words. He was not one of her cruel leaders inducing fear.

He was Chaos.

"It would be a gamble to ask me to," he said. "How do you know I wouldn't be worse?"

He let her ponder his words as he watched the current of the river. He'd spoken true. At his full power, he could wipe this galaxy from existence and start fresh on a virgin canvas. Nyx didn't need to know that he wouldn't, though.

Couldn't, really.

Though his chaos was still a well of power in his chest, something was wrong. Where the well was once an endless flow at his fingertips, it waned. Rather than having the entirety accessible at once, he had to wait for it to regenerate and it was too fucking slow.

"Have you ever heard the 'devil you know' saying, or was your head so far up your ethereal ass that you couldn't hear it?" Her sharp voice broke the silence and if it hadn't surprised him, he probably would have laughed.

He liked her fire despite himself. It reminded him of Lytta. Pain seized his chest as her name crossed his mind. He turned his eyes to the stars and found the cluster of five that was his best friend. She deserved more than she'd been given, but it was her wish to be laid to rest within the stars. It was selfish of him to put her to the forefront. She would have wished to spend her afterlife in peace where the darkness could bear the weight of her heavy soul, but instead he placed her amongst the brightest of them all. Her fiery soul had burned brilliantly, and he couldn't stand to see it dimmed.

Lytta, his best friend.

Gods how he fucking missed her.

"Hello!"

Brooks snapped his attention back to the ball of fury to his right. The outline of Nyx's body seemed to buzz with rage and it put him on edge, his chaos rushing to the surface to meet her onslaught.

"Do you even care?" Her breathing quickened as a small vein throbbed in her forehead.

"Care about what?"

"Unbelievable," she scoffed.

"We are getting nowhere," he sighed, more so to himself than anything. "Perhaps I'll find someone else to update me on matters."

"Perhaps," she mocked. "You should just take a fucking look around, Chaos. Can I call you that? Or should I call you Father?"

"Why would you call me that?"

"I'm not calling you daddy. Fucking forget about that."

He was done. He and Xia would find somewhere else to collect themselves and gather information. He needed solid grounding in this new world before he could determine what to do. Brooks stood intent on doing just that

"Wait!" she called as he walked away. "I'm sorry, okay? I'm just–"

"A pain in the ass?"

Soft thuds rushed his way before a hand grabbed his shoulder.

"I–" she stopped, her voice cracking at the end. "When I woke up this morning I had no idea how I was going to feed those people in the house. They depend on me. I'm the only one," she swallowed before trying again. "I'm the only one with nothing to lose."

Brooks did look over his shoulder at the shame in those violet eyes. She was just a girl with the weight of the world on her shoulders.

Don't you dare turn your softness toward this pain in the ass, Chaos huffed.

"I served you our last ration of food hoping that my gamble would pay off and you could help us."

Here we fucking go.

He recalled the beautiful little girl in front of the hearth holding her mother close, her blue eyes glittering in the burning embers of the fire. He thought the gauntness of her eyes was just a trick of the light. It made him sick to think it could be because of starvation.

"We will sit, and you will tell me what has become of this world. I cannot right the wrongs that I do not understand."

"Fine." Her tone was clipped as if she had more to say but held back. There was something simmering beneath all of that bravado and Brooks found himself wanting to explore it.

We do not have time for her. We do not care for her. We do not need her.

"Making connections with other daemon wouldn't be so bad. You never know, you may find one willing to pull the giant stick out of your ass."

"Do you mean it?" She whispered.

"Mean what?"

"That you intend to fix it. The world, I mean."

Brooks sat and faced the water. "I intend to end those who have hurt the only two beings I've ever cared about. And then I will find the one who wronged me and watch her bleed."

"And what about the rest of us? Have you never cared about the rest of us?" Nyx asked incredulously. "You have people here who still worship you. Who hold out belief that if they pray hard enough, you will come and save them from their shitty lives and their even shittier deaths."

He swallowed as he pondered her words. What about the rest of them? The truth was he'd never been close enough to care. They were so small and busy, lives beginning and ending faster than he could blink. He could imagine that his view looking down on them was much like their view looking up. You could see beauty, wondrous mystery, and a longing to be a part of it. But in the end, it was impossible to be a part of.

But now that he walked among them... Xia was one of those lives, and she was not small. She wasn't nothing.

She was everything.

And she was only one daemon out of thousands. More than the daemon were the beings they'd created– humans. What were mortals like?

Brooks, there is nothing for us here. We have made hundreds of planes just like this one. We give them life and they live it. We owe them nothing.

"I... I'm just not sure that's true."

"Avyssos was built on sacred ground," Nyx said, breaking the silence as she waved her hand. "It's one of the two places where our connection to the well of chaos is the strongest. The daemon you created, our gods, blessed the ground so that no harm could ever come of it."

"What kind of harm?" Brooks fought the urge to look at the homes falling to ruin downriver.

"Well, it used to be from anything. Those with ill intentions, or tainted chaos. I was taught that before The Twelve ruled Olympus you couldn't even wield chaos on sacred ground. Only those ordained by Gaia could, and they had to be dedicated to priests of the temple."

Sarcasm crept into her voice and by the end that sharp temper surfaced.

"And after The Twelve?"

"I don't know. It's... fading. Gaia stopped answering our calls. No more priests were ordained. Those we had either lost their faith and left or wither away in the old temples. Our link to the well is dying." Nyx's brows knit as she chewed the inside of her lip, her eyes gleaming in the moonlight as if this wasn't the first time she'd questioned the slow decline of her home. "Anyone can cross the grounds now. The Olympians come to claim taxes on food or coin that we don't have, but it's just an excuse to look for the temple," she scoffed as her inquisitive expression fell. Her eyes narrowed, lips thinning and she shook her head.

"Why do they need the temple?"

"Why do you think?" She threw her hands up, that sarcastic demeanor she wore like a shield flaring. "I just told you. The connection to the well of chaos is stronger here than any other place in the world, and they're the most conniving, power hungry assholes alive."

They mean to control it.

"What happens if they do?"

Pieces of us live in each of them, and those pieces long to join the whole. It is why the cycle works. Once the soul loses its piece, it rejoins the flow. It is possible that if a daemon had access to the well, they could siphon more for themselves. But they were not made to contain more than what we've given. It would overpower the soul and eat them alive. Rotting away, from the inside out.

Brooks' stomach dropped as a memory resurfaced. A raspy alto voice filled his mind, her eyes desperate and enraged as she straddled him on a surgical table. *"I have spent my life in a miserable endless cycle– Receive the taint, purge the taint, regret the purge, and try to die. I am Lytta, Goddess of Madness, bred by the taint within Zeus himself."*

Ice crackled on the ground around them as Chaos' wrath rose to the surface. *They steal from the well. They steal from us. This world will fucking burn.*

"Hey!" Nyx shouted! "I'm godsdamned talking to you!" A smack landed against his cheek and he lunged. Brooks gripped her throat, Chaos bleeding into the forefront as he squeezed tight enough to make the veins pop in her forehead.

"Do not ever touch us like that again, girl, or you will be nothing more than a stain on the ground."

"I'm not afraid of you," she choked out, her words sputtering as she fought for the oxygen to fuel them. "And I am not afraid to die. Do your worst, asshole."

Chaos growled, and Brooks had to fight to pull him back.

"Get a hold of yourself!" He scolded.

Nyx wheezed and coughed beside him. He tried to apologize, to reach out and touch her shoulder but she swatted him away. Nyx glared with every ounce of hate she could muster.

"I'm so sorry, Nyx. I didn't– he just, *we* are still learning how to cope with this new reality."

Hatred mixed with confusion as she frowned and asked around labored breaths, "We?"

"It's complicated." Brooks rubbed his eyes. "When I went to sleep, I was Chaos. Father of Darkness. Deathless God. When I woke up, I was someone else. I was eternal, but I felt... longing. Loneliness. That part split from the eternal god, and now," he gestured to himself. "*We are this.*"

Nyx huffed an incredulous laugh. "This world is so fucked." Her voice was scratchy, and a pang of guilt hit his chest like a stone. At least she wasn't coughing any more. "So when you go all blue and icy, it's him. But when you're this," she waved. "You're just–"

"Brooks. Just Brooks."

For better or for worse, the asylum changed him. He was no longer a nameless god roaming the darkness. He had become Brooks, and Brooks had a range of emotions he didn't quite understand. Brooks was the part that felt lonely while watching his creation laugh and love, indulging in a companionship that'd never been on the table for something like him. That was the part that longed to find companionship among the broken, just as he had with Lytta. Perhaps, even, with Nyx.

Chaos grumbled his disapproval, but Brooks pushed him to the side. *"Go take a nap you fucking grouch."*

"The world will be so happy to hear that that empty chest of yours finally holds a bleeding heart," she sneered. "Make sure to let them down easy when you announce you're only here to avenge two people."

Nyx plucked a weed from the ground and busied her fingers pulling it apart. Her body vibrated with tension. He watched, but didn't say anything as the storm brewed.

"I knew you wouldn't be worth it." Her lip culled as she plucked another weed from the ground. "Even when I prayed at your altar I knew it was for nothing."

Brooks simply nodded and looked out over the river where the stars reflected on its surface. "For what it's worth, Nyx, I'm sorry."

"Save it for someone who gives a shit." She was silent for a moment before she turned, disdain dripping from her pursed lips. "I was raised in that fucking temple. My entire life was spent in service to a creator who was so bored with us he went to sleep." Nyx threw her hands up in the air with a sardonic laugh, tears glistening silver against her violet eyes. Her voice raised with each sentence along with her fury. "I was taught that the single most powerful being in the universe gifted Gaia and Uranus the power of chaos and let them pass it down to their children. They charged priests with keeping a fellowship to pass their knowledge down through centuries, hoping that if there were still people left to make sacrifices to the great God of Chaos, he would grant us mercy when he returned to raze the Earth and rid it of evil."

She stood then and paced, fists clenching like they were begging to strike.

So much wrath, Chaos whispered.

"They built two temples in *your* honor. Sacrificed innocents in *your* name. Daemon starve and die on sacred ground all while pleading at your altar to grant them mercy!"

"I never asked for sacrifices, Nyx. I never required it. I gave this world my power and expected nothing in return."

"Oh." Another wry laugh. "Is that supposed to make me feel better? It didn't matter that you didn't ask for it because it happened anyway and you did *nothing* to stop it."

Brooks opened his mouth to argue, to tell her that it wasn't his place to see to every whim and plight, but she didn't stop.

"My entire life was planned around my death. I was raised like an animal for slaughter, and it means *nothing to you!* Those fanatic priests were going to slit my throat and pray as my blood soaked your feet. But I wasn't going to die in the name of a stupid, worthless god who wouldn't help." Nyx stopped pacing and pointed her finger at him, jabbing it forward with each blow. "Instead I decided to say fuck the priests, fuck this stupid religion, and fuck you."

Brooks bowed his head. Even Chaos had nothing to say.

"My death at your altar was not going to feed them, or keep them clothed. It wasn't going to make sure they had money to pay Ares or prepare their homes for the winter. If they resent me for it, that's fine. At least I know they're alive." She swallowed past the lump in her throat, voice shaking as she pinned him with her glare. "I love this village, and I love these people. I would *die* for them. But I will not die for you."

Unleash your Chaos

Xia
13

"*Y*ou saved me."

Those words echoed through her blood and wove themselves into the very fabric of her being. Xia didn't know how long she slept. It could have been minutes or dragging days, but her body ached like years had passed. She wasn't ready to wake and face the Devil. She wanted to hold onto the dream of Brooks for just a while longer.

A quiet, steady pattering filled the space and she reached to pull her fluffy duvet to her chin. When her hand grasped only air, she froze and awareness flooded her system. Her breath caught as she opened her eyes to the thinnest of slits, but she was met only with darkness.

The air smelled dank and musty, assaulting her nose and sticking to the back of her tongue. The atmosphere felt completely at odds with the bed she rested on. The bed felt as if it were made of clouds—soft and yielding to every curve, its hold as gentle and warm as a caress.

Xia strained her ears hoping to hear anything that may tell her where she was. There were no voices. No thumping bass lines from Club Hel or rushing currents whooshing along her glass wall. Nothing but the soft patter of water in the distance.

It was... peaceful.

She opened her eyes wide and was immediately taken aback by

the unnatural darkness. There was no filtered starlight or stray beams of sunlight through water. For a moment, Xia feared she'd been swallowed by a void and was forever doomed to live in its infinite darkness. Until, however, she caught swirling tendrils moving within the blackness.

Xia reached out a tentative hand. What she intended to do, she didn't know. Wave the darkness away as if it were smoke? Or perhaps determine whether the wall was solid or more fluid? What she met was neither.

Her hand brushed against swirls of shadow that flowed against her skin like watercolor paint. She watched in awe as it floated through her fingers and wrapped around her arm. The surrounding darkness hummed as it continued to caress her pale skin, and something in her chest squeezed. The shadows felt like... home. As if they'd been missing from her heart and finally found their way back to wind around her soul.

Xia reached her other hand out and more inky tendrils slinked from the mass. Her skin prickled as the shadows moved lazily along her body, teasing and exploring her like a lover. She'd never known shadows to feel like anything, but these?

They felt like *everything*, moving against her skin lightly like the softest of fingertips. Others were more firm like the brush of lips. The feeling made her heady and she lost herself in the touch of those shadows.

Xia was so caught up that she failed to recognize the cold seeping in or the uncomfortable sharp points of the hay sticking through the makeshift cot. She didn't feel the drops of rainwater atop her head from the faulty thatched roof, nor did she see the figure standing in the doorframe.

"Good morning, sunshine," a smooth, deep voice sounded.

Xia startled, her hands falling from the shadows as she pushed herself back toward the wall. Her mind was still fuzzy from sleep and made it hard to focus her eyes. The wisps of shadows thinned and light poured in from an open door. It was damn near blinding after being wrapped in complete darkness.

When the man made no move toward her, she risked wiping her eyes to clear the haze. He was still painted in darkness as the light cast him in shadow, but her body caught up before her mind did. Xia's palms sweat and some invisible string in her chest pulled taut, urging her to go to him like he held the other side of it.

He moved toward her, each step cautious and silent. Her anxiety didn't ease, but she didn't run. Not that she had anywhere to run to.

Xia reached for her Song, but didn't hold it. She had enough blood in her ledger, but she was a survivor and she would not die here.

"It's okay," he whispered.

When she backed away further, he stopped and raised his hands placatingly. His face was still cloaked in shadows, but enough light filtered in that she could see a mess of black hair curling in a rather unkempt fashion around his ear.

"Come on now, Siren. You know I'll only bite if you ask me to."

Her breath caught and she was sure her heart would stop beating. Tears blurred her already hazy vision and a hiccup of relief escaped her lips. "If you bite me, it'll be your dick stuffed and hung above my mantle."

"It'll be your biggest trophy, too."

She could practically hear the smirk in his tone and the skin along her arms prickled in anticipation. He stepped toward her again, but this time she didn't back away. Xia pushed herself up to standing and lunged toward Brooks. Her last steps faltered, legs shaky beneath her as she stumbled into his arms. He caught her in a strong hold, his arms warm and firm around her body as she tucked her head against his chest.

Xia had never experienced an embrace that didn't feel like a prison, but that didn't hold true to Brooks. He covered her from every angle, his arms a massive shield hiding her from the sorrows of the world. Her heart raced in her chest and she could have sworn that his pounded to the same beat as her own.

She inhaled deeply, wanting to know and feel everything about the man in her arms. Remnants of smoke clung to his rain-dampened shirt mingling with the fresh scent of birch and ozone. He smelled like the perfect storm. Her breath faltered when he nuzzled into her hair and inhaled just as deeply as she had, like he was memorizing every piece of her, too.

"Is this real?" she asked, her words muffled by the thick leather jacket he wore. Memory flooded in from their night together what felt like so long ago. Brooks, bruised and tattered from that gods-damned asylum, and her... just as shattered as he. He'd nearly broken her when those three words rolled off of his lips, desperation weighing them like an anchor. *"Let's just pretend."*

He squeezed her tight, lips whispering against her hair as he said, "Yeah, sunshine. It's real. You're safe, and I'm never letting you go." Xia flinched as her mind morphed those words into a deeper voice. The voice of a nightmare. She was quick to shake it, but her body betrayed her with a shiver. Her skin prickled as the cold seeped into her bones. Brooks pulled back and gently urged her to release her hold. It was the last thing she wanted, but Xia obliged.

"We need to talk. I don't even know where to fucking begin, honestly. But this... this embrace felt like a good start." His voice was soft as not to disturb their small slice of calm. Perhaps they were both afraid that if they made too sudden of a move, reality would shatter and send them both careening back into hell.

"Okay," she whispered. "Then let's talk."

"There's a fireplace in the other room. We'll soak up some heat and light. I want to see your face somewhere other than my dreams."

Maybe it was the absurdity of the last day. Or, better yet, maybe it was the euphoria flooding her system. With his words, a bubble of laughter rose from her belly. "Who are you?" she asked around the deep belly laugh shaking her shoulders. A lightness filled the space between them and she felt the soft rumbles of his laughter vibrate against her chest.

"Here I was trying to adore you and shit. Remind me to never be nice to you again," he teased.

"I'm sorry!" she said in between giggles. "I don't know what's happening." Her knees went weak and his arms closed tighter around her, lending her strength when her own failed.

"I always knew you were crazy. This just kind of confirms it."

She felt the lift of his smile in her soul and happiness spread like wildfire. "Says the man who's been living in an asylum for the insane."

"You were obviously just better at hiding your crazy. You can't fool me though, Siren. I know that deep down you're godsdamn batshit crazy."

They laughed together for a few more moments before settling. Xia stepped back from the embrace and sighed, donning the armor that would help protect her spirit from what was to come. "Alright," she said. "I'm ready."

He stared at her for a moment before his silhouette nodded in the dark. His fingers laced with hers and he guided her out into the dimly lit hall.

Xia looked at him then. Really looked at him. Gods, he was the most beautiful thing she'd ever seen. He wasn't bulging with muscle. His hair wasn't combed to perfection, and he didn't wear a persona dripping with sexual desire like other daemon. He just... *was*. And the beauty in that left her breathless.

They entered an open room that served as both a sitting and eating area and walked quietly to the fireplace so as not to disturb those snoring softly on the floor. Her brows furrowed, concern squeezing her heart to see people wrapped in tattered blankets and huddled against the cold.

Where were they?

Brooks guided her to two torn cushions settled close to the fire, gesturing to the one closest to the hearth. They sat and Xia shifted toward Brooks. He stared into the fire, and she admired the features illuminated by firelight. Dark stubble shadowed his jaw, the muscle jumping back and forth as he clenched. His skin held some color and she could imagine it tanned effortlessly in the sun.

Unlike her own pale complexion. Xia was born of the sea and moonlight. Her features were leached of color. She'd often felt like a wraith in the halls of Club Hel in more ways than one as Tor would usher her to and from his Playground.

Fire danced in his navy eyes, and he looked as fierce as a warrior bathed in its light. His eyes narrowed as the words churned in his mind, the battle he fought to choose them evident.

Where to begin? She wasn't sure either, but wanted to ease the waging war he fought. "I'm sorry you had to see me like that. On the beach."

Monster.

Xia feared his disappointment, so afraid that he'd seen the monster and could no longer see *her*. Xia turned her face to the crackling fire. She didn't want to hear the disparaging words sure to follow, so she continued. "He'd changed. I could see it in his eyes, Brooks. He–" she stopped, tears gathering as she recalled the crazed look in the Devil's eyes in that cold bathroom. "He was going to kill me this time."

The fire banked as ice swept through the room. Xia glanced around for an open window or a hole in the makeshift lodging, but when she found neither, she pulled her knees in and wrapped her arms around them. Brooks shifted, and warmth hugged her skin as he placed his jacket around her shoulders. He didn't offer words of defiance or comfort, just an act of kindness. And it meant more than declarations ever could.

Encouraged by his presence, she continued. "He held my head underwater. I should have just pushed the water from the tub or away from my face, but I was so scared, Brooks. I couldn't think straight. I just... panicked."

She took a steadying breath, pushing away the memory. You could tell a story without dredging up feelings, and she was intent on doing just that. Xia vowed that night to *never* feel so powerless again.

"He got called away, but swore he would be back to finish me. I considered staying. Lying there in wait for what was to come. Or even taking fate into my own hands, to die with a sort of dignity only I could give. But instead something happened. A darkness rose in me – so cruel and vile."

Monster.

It was then she looked at him, to face whatever judgment he would cast upon her as she released her truth. "There's a darkness inside me, Brooks. A monster that I've never let out of its cage because I'm so scared it will destroy me."

Xia stopped to swallow, to breathe, anything to calm the tidal wave of anxiety driven by a lifetime of trauma. She turned her gaze back to the fire but found it disappearing behind a wall of shadows black as the void. Her skin was too tight. Her chest caved in and refused to let her lungs fill. What had she done to deserve any of it? The curse of her darkness. The wrath of the Devil. The sea of nightmares. It was too much.

It was all too much.

Just as she approached the edge of that depthless hole of despair, a warm hand brushed against her own. Fingers slid between her clenched hands and gently urged them away from where they clawed at her legs. His grasp was firm and reassuring as he laced their fingers together and laid them in his lap. Brooks didn't say anything. He didn't use words of placation or try to convince her that there was no monster inside. He didn't persecute or judge. He simply watched and waited, offering a wall of strength for her to lean on as she crumbled.

Xia let the trauma roll through like a hurricane. Sobs wracked her fragile frame as she allowed herself to finally just... *feel.*

She buried her head in her knees and fell apart until she hit the bottom. The anxiety of being without purpose. The sickening dread when Phobetor and his brothers landed on Anthemoessa. She mourned her sisters and let the pain of their loss break the dam holding back her sorrow and despair. As memories washed over her, she relived Phobetor chaining her to the floor, Molpe spiked to the wall of Level Desecration, and Geia thrown from the sky when Morpheous decided he had no use for her anymore. The splintering of bones and sinew rang through Xia's mind as she replayed the cracking of her ribs over the bathtub.

Xia let the memories rise like the tide before washing them away. When she was silent but for a few hiccupping breaths, Brooks released her hand to brush a few stray strands of hair behind her ear. Running a thumb down her cheek, he hooked his fingers beneath her chin and pulled to lift her head.

"Don't look at me," she whispered. "I'm a mess." Her eyes and lips were swollen, tears and nose drippings covering her cheeks and chin.

"Yeah," he whispered, his voice gruff. "But you're my mess. And I'll take you however you come. Whether it's whole or in pieces, you're mine."

Unleash your Chaos

Brooks

14

He watched his Siren until something like awe fell over her features. Her red rimmed eyes were swollen, flames from the fireplace reflecting and dancing in unshed tears as her head shook almost imperceptibly. She huffed a small laugh as the corners of her lips rose. "Where have you been all my life?"

Just like that, Brooks was thrown back into the asylum where he and Xia bonded through their trauma. She appeared in his mind when he desperately needed a ray of light in the dark. So he smirked and did his best to give her that same feeling. "In your wet dreams, baby." He followed it with a wink for good measure.

A snort of laughter burst from her swollen lips, and she slapped a hasty hand over her mouth to cover the sound. Xia tried to peer through the shadows to see if she'd woken anyone, but they were impossible to see through.

"They help with the sound." Brooks gestured around before Xia landed a punch to his shoulder.

Brooks mocked disbelief and covered his arm. "My lady," he said aghast. "You wound me!"

"Shhh!" Xia exclaimed, struggling to hold back her laughter as she pushed at him. "You're going to wake someone, and I will not help if they want to fight you over it."

"I told you, near sound proof."

"I don't believe you."

Her lighthearted banter pulled his heart strings. He'd decided a long time ago in that dreadful fucking asylum that he'd do anything to hear her laugh for eternity. It was about godsdamned time he started making good on it, repaying her for every time she'd saved him.

Stray tendrils of darkness curled around her arms and drifted upward until they caressed her face. She leaned into their touch, closing her eyes as she nestled against them. Brooks felt the touch of her skin through them as surely as if it were his own hand.

"How are you doing this?" she whispered.

"I don't know."

Xia opened her eyes, brow crinkling as she asked, "What do you mean?"

"I mean, I can call the shadows, but this isn't me. It's all… him."

"Him?"

"You're not the only one living with darkness inside. When I went to sleep, I was Chaos, the Deathless God. When I woke up, I was Brooks. Now… We don't really understand it, but we're on the path to figuring it out."

Xia nodded, her brows still the picture of concentration as she nestled back into the shadows. "I think he likes me."

If I could live inside of her, I would.

Brooks scoffed. "He definitely likes you, Sunshine. We both do. He's smitten, actually. Gushes about you like a child with a crush."

Xia laughed, fingers twirling in the shadows as they brushed against her.

I will make your life miserable.

"You already do, bud," Brooks mumbled under his breath.

"What did you say?"

He looked up at Xia and smiled. "Nothing."

The shadows receded as Chaos tucked himself away and slinked back into the corners of Brooks' mind. "Do you want to take a walk? There's a river just behind this house and the sound is pretty soothing."

"I would love that, actually. The water always helps me calm down."

Brooks stood and offered his palm. The pair walked from the house hand-in-hand in comfortable silence. The closer they got to the steady flow of the river, the quicker her stride became.

The night was full of shadows cast by moonlight and a light breeze shook the tall grass by the water's edge. The air was dry and smelled of musty decay from the changing season. The chill in the air was cutting, but he didn't mind the cold. Discomfort was just a reminder that he was alive.

Brooks threw subtle glances toward his Siren to admire how the light fell upon her face. Half was illuminated so perfectly in the light, he could make out the pouty set of her lips and the flutter of her lashes as she watched the water rushing by. He imagined the other side would be swathed in shadow, just like the dark side of the moon.

Brooks recalled the time in the asylum when Xia told the story of the moon and sea. *"The moon and the sea were once lovers. The way the waves danced with the pull of the moon was so beautiful that even the stars were jealous. But now they spend their lives mourning the loss of a lover's touch. The tides rise as the sea reaches for the moon but, as she falls to the sun, so too does the tide."*

A pair of star-crossed lovers who found something beautiful among their chaos and were cursed because of it. He remembered the somber tone with which she'd spoken, and by the end he'd known why. Xia was born of the moon and tide. She was a reminder of how painful love and the sacrifices surrounding it could be.

When they stood on the bank, his heart warmed at the brilliant smile gracing her face. Even the stars could have fallen in shame compared to her beauty.

Xia sat and Brooks followed her lead. She nudged his shoulder with a grin and looked down toward the water. Her hands flickered and he watched in awe as Xia pulled small streams of water from the river and wove them in between her fingers like a shimmering necklace.

Xia lifted her other hand and swirled her finger through the water. Beads of water lifted from the surface, the edges rippling as they formed tiny fluttering shapes. Xia guided one forward into her upturned palm and it pooled to form the beginnings of a butterfly. She manipulated the water almost as if there were strings attached to it. Wings fluttered as the delicate shape flew around her hand and through her fingers. Dozens of tiny iridescent butterflies dotted the water at their feet.

"When it was just my sisters and I on Anthemoessa, we tended a small patch of lilac bushes. The blooms were–" she stopped, her smile widening and head shaking as she tried to find the words. Her eyes were on the crystalline figure fluttering around her fingers, but her gaze was far away as she recalled the memories. "Magnificent. The bursts of purple with subtle pinks and blues hidden in the tiny buds was such a wonder. We would sit in the grass, sometimes for hours, and watch butterflies of all sizes and colors flit around the bushes. I was always so amazed at how something so delicate could carry such beauty and grace. I..." Her voice drifted as her face fell, and the pain radiating from it hit him like a strike to the heart. "I miss them," Xia whispered. "After the Oneiroi came, the island just died. And so did the butterflies."

Brooks could do damn near anything. He could create life just as easily as he could take it. He could build a world and paint its night sky with stars. The one thing he couldn't do was rewind time. Time was a concept that he couldn't grasp– the one and only power that made him bow.

He couldn't bring Xia's sisters back from the past, but he could make sure that her future was full of family and love. He would be her family.

Brooks swallowed and placed his hand beneath hers so that the back of it rested in his palm. He called forth his shadows and bid them to mingle with the butterfly. The darkness bled like ink into the water and formed unique patterns throughout the wings. The contrast of his shadows to the moonlight streaming through the water created an effect that made the insect look more alive than any that could be found among the flowers.

Brooks leaned forward and exhaled the breath of life over the crystalline shape in Xia's hand. He smiled as the water changed from liquid to solid, its wings still decorated with the watercolor streams of his darkness within. It was a butterfly unlike any other, composed of the purest, shimmering light and deepest, gaping darkness.

"No creature can be made only of light," he said, his voice low and scratchy. "There is always a flaw, or a taint. Everything is capable of being corrupt. Only those who learn to let their darkness find solace within the light can control their outcome. It's part of us all, Xia."

As he spoke, the butterfly lifted from Xia's palm and flittered to his arm. They both watched as the wings moved steadily up and down.

"Embracing your chaos means finding peace in your heart and living with all parts of who you are. Even the ones you hide from."

He turned from the butterfly to find tears glistening on her cheeks.

The warmth of the fire had hidden the pallor of her skin and deep shadows beneath her tired eyes. Her cheeks were gaunt and the white light from the moon deepend the bruises he was beginning to see around her neck.

Chaos roared to life inside him, ice flooding their veins as he growled. *We will rip the soul from the daemon who laid hands on her. I may have been suppressed in the asylum, but we are no longer held by the chains of illusion. We are the Father of Chaos, and with our awakening will come a tide of vengeance this world has yet to see. We will glutton ourselves as we watch them burn for her.*

Chaos' anger boiled with his own, the man and the monster uniting as one in their rage.

"Your eyes are glowing."

Xia's voice filtered through his thoughts of rage and ruin as she covered the blemishes with a curtain of hair.

"Don't," he said. "Don't ever hide from me, Xia."

"Brooks, I don't–"

"I want to see it all," he interrupted. "The pain you've felt. The trauma you hold. I want it all. Do you understand?" His voice was guttural. "Your burdens are no longer yours to carry alone."

Xia flinched as she answered with a small, shrinking nod, the raging fire in his heart banked. How often had she taken the brunt of another man's anger? How many times was she forced to be submissive for the sake of pride and dominance?

"I'm sorry," he said in earnest, Chaos' voice melting away. "I lashed out. It wasn't your fault, and it wasn't meant for you."

"I know."

The silence stretched like a yawning chasm between them. Their arms touched, but Brooks felt miles away from her. Xia's lips pursed as she stared out over the water, butterflies still fluttering around them.

"I learned a lot on that beach, Brooks," Xia whispered. "About myself, and about this anger inside of me. She feels the way you described Chaos, just this ever present being stirring within. I've starved her, shoved her down into the deepest pits of my soul, all because I was afraid she would make me a monster. But..." she drifted, eyes falling to a butterfly that landed on her knee. "I think that was a mistake. She needs me to nurture her, and I need her to find the girl I could have been all along. You were right about embracing the chaos inside, and I'm ready to build that with her."

Xia placed a palm on her chest and rubbed slowly, pressing protectively against her heart. Brooks knew that feeling all too well. That was where he felt Chaos.

"I appreciate your willingness to protect and avenge the wrongs committed against me. But I don't need you to do that for me. Okay?"

Tears glistened in her pleading eyes as she asked him to understand. The problem was, he didn't. She was so fragile, her pieces so broken that there was no possible way to put them together alone.

But she is not alone. Her Siren is with her.

"I can try, Xia."

She nodded and swallowed. "I think trying is a good start. I don't want to be some burden you carry along. I want to walk by your side."

"I can be anything you need."

She scoffed, but a small laugh followed. "That's pretty open ended you know."

"Well, I meant it."

"You're lucky I kind of like you, or I'd have a mind to exploit your lack of details in this contract."

"Oh, it's a contract now, is it?" Brooks laughed and some of the tension melted from his body just her shoulders relaxed. The easy flowing banter between them was a safe spot, and he was relieved they found their way back to it. "How about this? If I ever act like an asshole again, you have the right to judge the severity of my crime and punish me accordingly."

"Well, in that case, I think I've earned the right to punish you right now. How about a swim?" A mischievous gleam crept into her eyes.

His head whipped toward hers, mouth agape. "What?"

"A swim. You know, that thing you do when you submerge yourself into a body of water and flail around to keep your head above water?"

"I know what swimming is, Xia. In case you haven't realized it yet, though, it's freezing out here."

"I don't know. This jacket is keeping me pretty warm." She smirked. "You said I have the right to judge the severity and punish accordingly. I think your outburst was pretty severe."

"No, I said if I ever do it again. Keyword, Siren. *Again.* That means the agreement is valid *after* the initial crime is committed."

"I see your lips moving, but all I hear is that I'm the one holding Themis's scales of justice and you, my friend, have tipped out of balance."

"Fucking hell," he sighed. "You're going to make me regret the day I ever talked back to you in my head."

"I'm going to make you regret a lot more than that, buttercup." Xia threw him another smile and stood with the grace of a goddess. Her movement disturbed the air and filled it with his favorite scent in the world— sea salt and sunshine.

Xia shook the jacket from her shoulders and took off toward the water, silver light gleaming against her skin with an ethereal shine.

"We're in so much trouble," he thought to Chaos as he swallowed.

I've been craving a challenge for our entire existence. If I had a dick right now, it would be hard.

"Seriously?"

"Brooks!" Xia called. "What are you waiting for? Come on!"

"Keep it in your pants. This is not the time."

It is always the time.

Brooks stood and took a deep breath before walking toward the water. Xia disappeared beneath water, bubbles surfacing from her exhale before she reappeared. Her white hair turned silver as the hazy light of the moon reflected off the water soaking her hair.

When he got to the water's edge, he hesitated while debating whether or not to take his clothes off. His well of chaos was near empty, so summoning the dry clothes wouldn't be an option. The bigger problem, however, was that Brooks was naked under his pants.

It was an all or nothing scenario that he wasn't sure how to navigate.

Don't be such a bitch. Get in the water.

"I will make your life miserable if you don't shut up and go the hell away."

"You're not scared of water, are you?" Xia asked. She was chest deep in the river now and staring at him with a half smile.

"Uh, no. I–" he stopped and blew out a heavy breath. "I would like to come back to dry clothes after our incredibly questionable night swim."

"So leave your underwear on."

"I didn't think about those when I dressed myself."

His Siren threw her head back and cackled up to the night sky and, though he loved the sound of her laugh, it didn't help his predicament.

"You know, I haven't been in this world very long but I'm pretty sure it's a universal rule that you don't laugh at a man when he talks about getting undressed."

"I'm so sorry," she said around laughs and pressed her hand to her mouth. "You just caught me off guard."

Just so we're clear, I'm laughing, too.

"How about this," Xia interrupted before he could let the insults fly. "You get undressed so your clothes stay dry, and I'll turn around while you get in. I promise I won't peek."

Tell her she should definitely peek. We have a lot to be proud of.

"You're dead," Brooks seethed.

You wish.

Xia's eyes flicked down, a faint blush tinting her cheeks, before she turned around. Brooks exhaled, already regretting his poor decision making. He pulled the gray shirt over his head and popped the button of his pants free, sliding them down to his ankles. He tossed both toward the grass and stepped into the water.

Brooks dipped his head under the water as he approached and resurfaced in front of her. He shook the water from his black curls and Xia laughed as it splashed across her face.

"Don't start a war you can't win, Deathless God," she teased. "You may control the shadows, but the water is my domain, and you're surrounded."

"Alright." Brooks held up his hands in defeat with a smile. "Is the cold water my punishment or did you have something worse in mind?"

"I'm still deciding, so you have time to plead your case."

"Shall I sing your praises? Would that convince you to take it easy on me?"

"I don't know," she shrugged. "Wouldn't hurt to try."

"Hmm, where do I begin? Your laugh sounds like tinkling bells and it's cute as hell."

Her lips are soft and stir a hunger inside me when she bites the bottom one.

His eyes dropped to her lips and he cleared his throat as he looked away.

"Go on." That mischievous gleam returned and was all the encouragement he needed.

"Your hair dries into soft waves and makes you look like a wild kind of beauty, especially when the green in your eyes turns into a turbulent storm of different shades. How am I doing so far?"

Not well enough.

"It's a start, but I'm not inclined toward leniency yet."

"Okay, okay. Let's see. Your nose crinkles when you laugh. It's pretty adorable."

Her Siren is fiery and sparks a passion inside us like no other being in creation.

"You're shy, but not in a timid way. You're so kind, it hurts. It honestly makes me feel like an asshole, because I'm pretty sure you've never had an indecent thought."

I've had enough for the both of us since she stepped into the water.

"That is not true, and you are not an asshole. You're colorful, but far from impure."

"You don't know the half of it, Sunshine," he mumbled.

"Oh yeah, what am I missing?" Xia drifted closer and into a beam of light. It caught the shear wave of her gown and, despite the cold, his dick hardened.

I want her.

"I am an asshole, though," he swallowed. "You just poured your heart out, and all I can think about is the way your lips move when you talk along with about ten different ways they could be the cause of my ruin."

Her breathy exhale was near silent, but it sounded like an explosion in his ears. Chaos paced the corners of Brooks' mind, the anticipation rolling in waves through their shared body.

"You're still not off the hook," she whispered, heat blazing in the storm of her eyes. "What else?" Xia took another step toward him. Any closer and she would know what was happening under the surface.

Touch her. Taste her.

"I can see everything through your gown and I'm having a really hard time respecting the space you asked for. Especially when you stand in the moonlight." His gaze dipped without permission and a slam of longing sent a shiver down his spine. Her nipples were peaked, creamy skin illuminated under the water and he could see every detail.

Xia's eyes darkened before she looked at herself. She didn't move away or hide behind crossed arms, and she never faltered as her chaos slowly moved the water away from her chest to her navel. Every brilliant inch from the waist up was exposed to the night air.

Brooks opened his mouth, but no words left his tongue. He tried not to stare, to look anywhere but at the perfect curve of her breasts, but it was a war he wasn't sure how to fight.

Go to her, Chaos growled. *Fuck her.* Claim *her. Or I will.*

Chaos was a force inside, and Brooks had a feeling down to his very soul that when he and his Siren clashed, the world would feel the aftershock. Blood pounded in his ears as he took her in.

He'd denied himself the pleasure of a lover longer than the first particles of space combusted. He was a god above all else, never dipping his toes into the worlds he molded. Pandemonium was the only outcome for his intervention and he swore to never put himself before creation again, but as the daughter of the moon and sea stood swathed in the pearlescent light of the night sky, Brooks knew without a doubt that it was a damning lie. He would shatter the universe and build a throne crafted from its bones to kneel at her feet for eternity. If she was starving, he was *ravenous*.

He cleared his throat in an attempt to keep the desperation from his tone, one last attempt to offer her a way out. "This hardly seems like a punishment, Sunshine. If you reward my dickish behavior with a peep show, I may be inclined to do it again."

The water parted more under her expert fingers and lapped against their knees. His hungry gaze followed her dips and curves, memorizing every inch of porcelain skin peeking through the gown. Brooks closed his eyes and swallowed. If he looked between her legs, there would be no turning back.

Memories of their night in the asylum flashed behind his eyelids, his mouth watering as he remembered the smell of her on his scrubs after she came. Chaos rumbled in his chest as he savored the memory alongside Brooks.

"Your eyes are so blue when you're desperate." Her voice had been so fucking sultry and images of her lust-glazed eyes would be burned into his mind forever.

I can still feel her squeezing around our fingers, tight and wet just for us.

"Xia," he pleaded. "I don't want to push this on you."

"Good thing I'm in control of my decisions."

"I'm not sure if you know this, Siren," he started, his tone a mix of trepidation and anticipation. "But you're playing a very dangerous game with my self-control."

"And you're testing the limits of my restraint. I want to see if you feel the way I remember you in my dreams."

Gods, he couldn't deny her.

I have no self-control left to give. Take her or so fucking help me–

"She sets the tempo. She is in control. We only take what she gives."

The only answer he got was a thick stream of shadows unfurling through the ripples of water. Black ink webbed through his veins as Chaos stepped from the confines of their shared body. Brooks stood beside Chaos' shadowy form, and they held their breath as they stepped from the curtain of water and into the open beside her. Xia's eyes widened as she took them in before pressing herself against Brooks. Her soft, feminine form felt like a godsdamned sin and he couldn't stop his hands from roving over every inch.

Chaos stepped behind Xia and ran his hands down her side, the darkness dipping with every curve. Xia tilted her back, resting it against his shoulder as Brooks grabbed her waist and pulled. His cock was pressed against her belly and the softness made him shudder.

Chaos kissed a trail down the side of her throat as Brooks leaned in and teased her collar bone with his tongue. He was hungry for more, desperate to taste her as he pressed his lips against hers. The kiss was tentative, but Xia grasped the back of his neck and laced her fingers through his hair, pulling him in closer. Their ragged breaths mingled as the embrace became desperate.

These fucking shadows, Chaos growled. *They are not enough. I want to feel* more. He pushed a knee between her thighs and dipped his fingers inside her tight pussy. Xia's head fell to Brooks' shoulder, her knees trembling as she shivered, crying out as Chaos teased her with his fingers.

"I want to taste you," she panted.

Not tonight, Siren, he growled and withdrew. *Tonight, you are ours to taste.*

Chaos stepped back and Xia whimpered at the loss. The shadow dissipated and flowed back into Brooks, the man and monster becoming one once more.

"Where did he go?"

Brooks pressed his lips against her ear, Chaos' voice mingling with his own as he said, "I'm still here, but this way I can feel you as you do me."

He gripped her ass and wrapped her legs around his waist as he kissed her, fingers tangling in the wet strands of her hair. He broke their kiss just long enough to say, "Hide us with the water."

He could feel the question bubbling on her lips as she pulled back, but he didn't have the patience.

"Please don't make me ask you again. Hide us. With. The fucking. Water. Siren." Each word was accentuated with a bite of her lip or tease of the tongue. "I don't enjoy being on the brink of madness, Sunshine, and I am not a patient man. I'm either drowning in this river or your pussy tonight. Your choice. But I suggest you make it quickly."

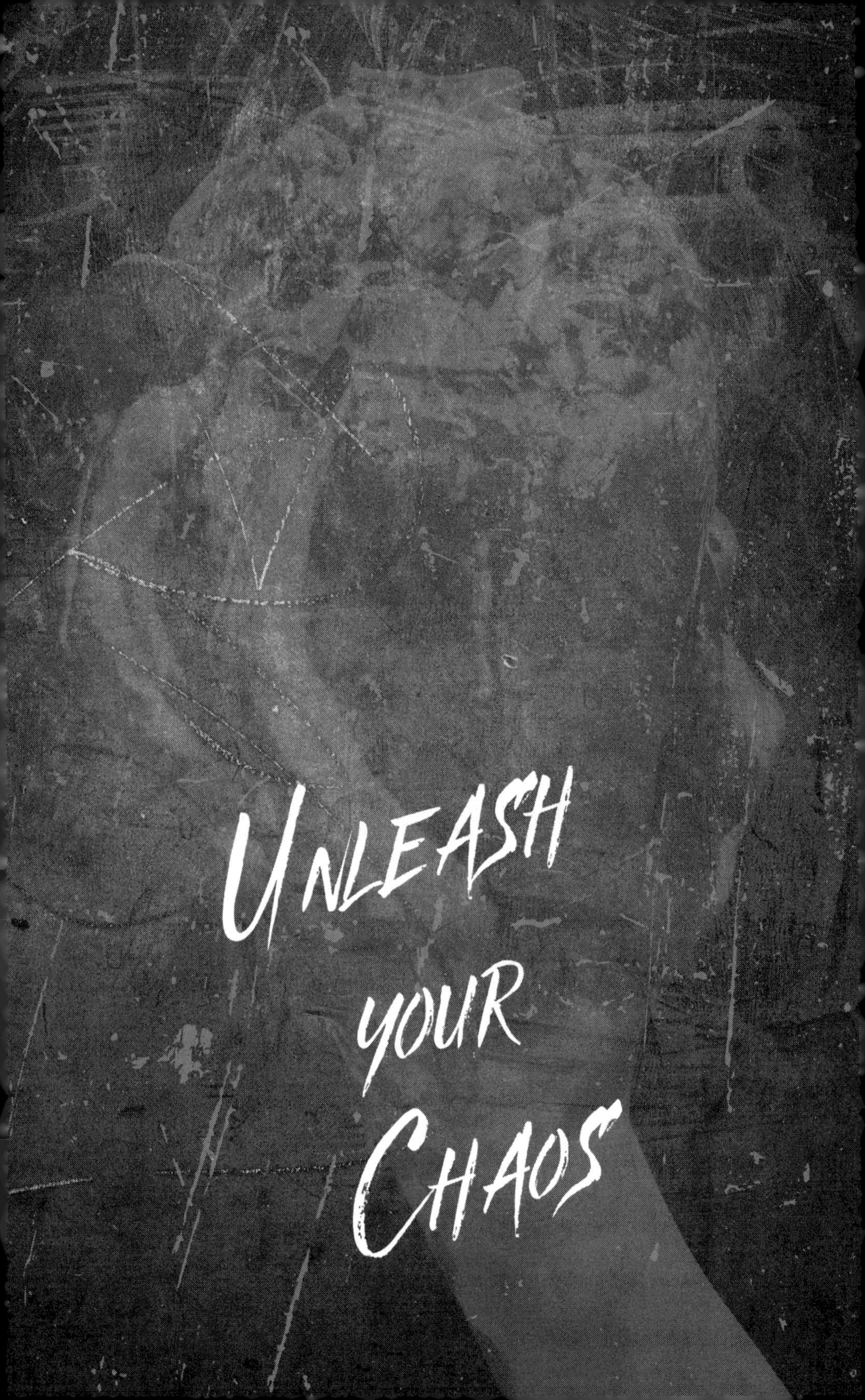
Unleash
your
Chaos

Xia

15

"Gods," she moaned as she summoned the chaos pumping through her body and pushed it away. Thunder rumbled overhead as flashes of lightning illuminated the sky, a storm building alongside her anticipation as the Siren inside awoke. Brooks didn't waste time getting them to the ground, but his maneuver took her by surprise.

With Xia's legs still wrapped around his waist, Brooks dropped to a sitting position and laid back against the muddy river bed. Her control slipped on the water as he grasped her hips with strong hands and pulled until she was situated over top of him. The hunger in his eyes made it near impossible to focus and tendrils of river water ran toward them.

"Raise the water around us and sit," he said.

Her Siren hissed, temper flaring at the sound of command. "Are you going to ask nicely?"

His eyes flared as she saw a bit of the monster slip through and her Siren writhed under the intensity of his stare. Without warning, Brooks pulled her hips up his body to meet his mouth and stroked once with his tongue. Xia threw her head back and cried out, shock mingling with the intensity of his touch.

"Raise the water to cover us Xia, or whoever has the misfortune to walk by and see you riding my face will pay in blood. You are mine, and I do not share." Xia's thighs tightened around him as his declaration rang through her mind.

We will not be owned, her Siren seethed. *We will reap the rewards of his mouth, and then we will show the great God of Chaos what it's like to be dominated.*

Xia did as she was told, using a burst of chaos to fling a torrent of crystalline water toward the sky. Her skin prickled against the fine mist rolling off the tide as his lips brushed against her inner thigh. A phantom hand slid up her belly and Xia looked down to find shadows roving over her body. The darkness came to life against her skin and worked her nipples as if they were his hands. The sensation of his lips against her pussy and the brush of his chaos nearly made her come undone. Even the Siren was writhing as she anticipated the onslaught of pleasure.

"Three rules, Siren." He teased her with his tongue. "I don't ask, I take. But I will stop if that's what you need. Understood?"

He sucked at the skin above her clit, and she moaned as she nodded.

"Say it, Xia. Say you understand."

The Siren sneered, but Xia answered, "I understand."

"When you come on my face, I want your thighs locked around my neck until you're finished. If I pass out, you're doing it right." He reached around and used his fingers to lay bear every inch of her to his greedy stare.

"Gods, Brooks!"

"Rule number three is the most important." He covered the entirety of her with his mouth and swirled his tongue greedily, his moan vibrating against her swollen clit. "Are you listening?" he asked, his lips keeping her on the edge.

Xia nodded hastily, determined to do anything to make him shut up and fuck her the way she'd always dreamed he would. Shadows gripped her chin and pulled until she was staring into his glowing blue eyes.

"Eyes on me, Sunshine."

Brooks placed a hand on her belly and pushed until her ass rested against his chest, exposing the entirety of her to his mouth. Shadows supported her back and teased her nipples, swirling in time with his tongue. He ate her pussy greedily, his moans vibrating against her swollen flesh.

The shadows pushed her forward and Xia groaned for more as he found a new angle. Brooks squeezed her ass, his tongue dipping inside before swiping back up to her clit over and over again until the ache between her thighs had her legs shaking.

"Come, Xia," he panted in between licks. "Come on my face and choke me with your thighs." The desperation in his voice was his downfall. The Siren grabbed a handful of his messy curls and pinned his head to the riverbed.

"Fuck," he moaned, hips lifting as he squirmed.

"I'll come when I'm ready, God of Chaos." She summoned water and wrapped it around his hands like manacles, pulling both above his head.

His frustrated growl sent a shiver of power down her spine and the euphoria made her ravenous for more.

Xia repositioned so that she sat overtop of him in the opposite direction and crossed one leg over his throat to hold him down as she bent forward to press a kiss to his navel.

"Follow my instructions like a good boy and you can make me come. Got it?" When he didn't answer, Xia leaned back to hover over his face. Brooks fought the restraints, naked hips arching as he pushed against the leg over his throat. She got close enough for him to touch, not to taste.

"Godsdammit!" he snarled, voice echoing into the night as droplets of water fell from the sky. "Fine! Yes, I understand!"

Xia hummed her approval as she lowered back down and placed her hands on his heaving chest. Brooks covered her pussy with his mouth again, but didn't waste time with teasing licks. Xia rode his face as he ravaged her, the feel of his stubble against her skin with the press of his tongue driving her mad.

Her hold slipped on the chaos keeping him restrained, the manacles weakening against his pull before he slipped free. Brooks' hands flew to her hips, torso trembling as he lifted himself to meet her. "Your fingers," she moaned. "Use your fingers."

Shadows unfurled at her command and writhed around them as he lost control. Brooks slipped two fingers in and pressed against her wall, pulling a desperate scream from her lips. Xia wrapped a hand around his cock and synchronized her strokes with the pulse of his fingers as he fucked her.

"You're going to finish," she rasped. "And then you're going to make me come, Brooks." His muffled curses vibrated through her core and she moaned as he arched into her hand.

Xia strained as she held back her orgasm, the ache in her clit throbbing. She needed him to come and could tell he was close as his fingers lost their tempo. Xia bent forward and spit on the head of his cock, swirling her thumb over the tip while he pumped into her hand.

"Fuck, Xia. Shit, I'm going to–" Brooks arched as he yelled, cum shooting onto his stomach as Xia's orgasm rocketed through her body like a shockwave.

He pressed his fingers in as deep as they would go, stretching her as he massaged the inside of her pussy with the tips. Xia's legs shook with the force, thighs closing around his throat as wave after wave of pleasure sent her spiraling.

Stars danced along her vision when she came up for air, her head dizzy and body quivering. Their ragged breaths mingled and were the only sound against the flow of water still surrounding them.

Tendrils of shadow wrapped around her shoulders and held her steady as she swung a leg over Brooks and lay beside him.

"Holy fuck, Siren," he panted, and she huffed a laugh.

Xia lay in the aftermath, her muscles still trembling from the most intense orgasm she'd ever had. It wasn't long, though, before a sliver of doubt crept in. Would he be satisfied? How long until he lost patience and demanded to fuck her with his cock?

The Siren slithered back into the recesses of her mind, but the exhilaration and freedom of domination still pumped through Xia's veins. In that moment, as she basked in the afterglow of absolute control, Xia decided she wasn't ready for anyone to have that sort of power over her. She'd been given a taste of domination and had no intention of letting it go.

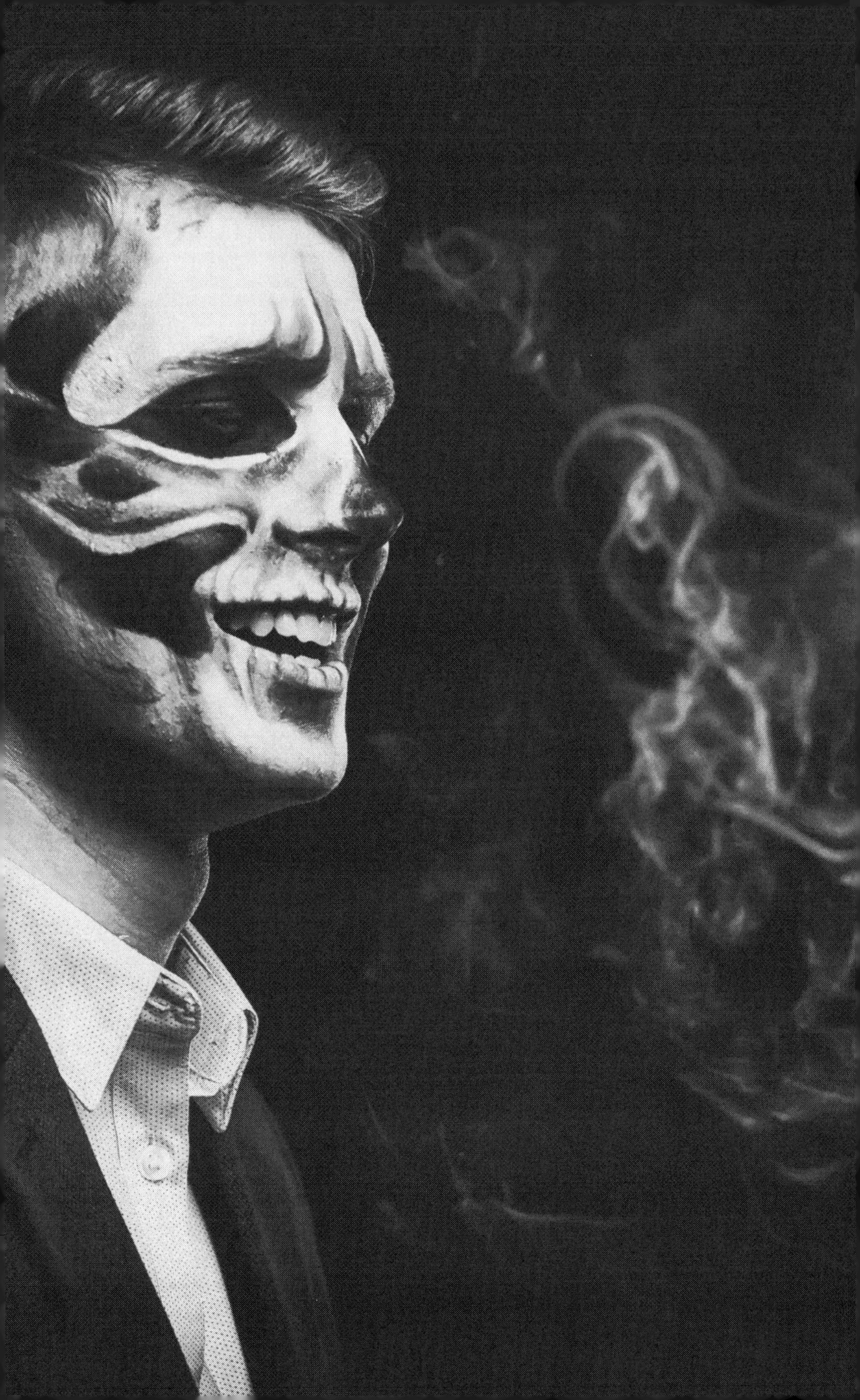

Nyx
16

Fury rolled off her shoulders in waves, steam lifting from her heated cheek as it met the chill in the air. Chaos was in Avyssos. What was she supposed to do? Shout to the sky and tell everyone their savior had come? That he was ready to take down Mount Olympus and set them all free?

No.

She couldn't. *Wouldn't.*

If her people knew their sovereign walked amongst them, Nyx would never be able to pull them back from the ledge. There was a fine line between faith and fanaticism, and the people of Avyssos had been through too much to lean toward faith. Nyx worked too hard to keep them alive, and all would be lost if they thought salvation was at their door. Besides, Nyx knew how it would end. Chaos didn't care about any of them. He would leave soon and her people would be left to starve and rot.

If that bastard would put in even half of the effort to save them as he used for that useless woman lying in Nyx's bed, the world would be completely different. That she knew for a fact, because she could feel it in her bones and her bones never lied.

It's what kept her alive

Nyx stormed through the night as their conversation played on a loop in her mind. *"I love this village, and I love these people. I would die for them. But I will not die for you."* And still, he didn't care. The broken damsel woke and he rushed to her side without a backward glance. For a single moment, Nyx drew on that shriveled piece of her heart that still hoped the god her people worshiped would save them. The god *she* hoped would save them

He might as well have placed a knife in her hand when he walked away, because Nyx cut that rotting piece of herself on the river bank..

Nyx walked until the sun crested over the hills and illuminated her home in a hazy light. She spent time searching for anything edible. She'd fed that bastard the last of their rations and was begging the desolate wood for an answer. Nyx was supposed to come back from Club Hel with enough valuables to take to the nearest Olympian outpost to trade. Sure, the daemon had their own tall buildings and shining cities just like the human world, but those were closer to Olympus. Her town was nestled far away from those godsforsaken cities. The pitfall to that was living like animals with no access to running water save for the river.

As it were, Nyx hadn't come back with shit.

Well, that was a lie wasn't it? She'd come back with more than she could handle. Rage and anxiety burned in her chest when she thought about her deal with the Devil. Less a deal and more of a race against the clock.

"Fuck!" she yelled, her voice bouncing off the trees and reverberating through the forest. "Gods, Nyx, think!"

But there was no room for reason. She couldn't see past the emotions boiling over. Nyx pulled her arm back and with one swift movement punched the tree next to her. She swung her fists over and over again, screaming her pain and fury into the world as her helpless soul raged. Bones cracked as splinters of bark flew, but the adrenaline kept her numb. Nyx swung until her arms were too heavy to continue, sobs wracking her starving frame as her knees hit the ground.

Her hands throbbed, knuckles no doubt shattered. Pain vibrated up her forearms and into heaving shoulders. But she didn't care. Nyx couldn't help herself, and now she couldn't help the people counting on her.

Nyx laid on the forest floor until there were no more tears left to cry. She stared at the copse of tree branches, moisture from the morning dew soaking into the tattered dress from the evening before.

Nyx was exhausted but knew sleep would not come. She rose, whimpering as her fingers pressed to the ground, and walked back to the village anyway. Back to her uncomfortable pallet made of straw and rags.

Birds sang overhead as she dragged her way back. Warm, sticky blood coated her palms but she didn't bother to wash them in a stream. Future Nyx could deal with that.

Right Now Nyx wanted to feel the throb of shattered bones. It felt better that way.

It was a small mercy that the village wasn't bustling with the rising sun. She didn't want anyone to see her broken in both body and soul.

Smoke drifted from embers that still burned between piles of stone. Makeshift hearths where people told their stories and warmed their hands, counting on blessings from a god who wasn't coming. She huffed a laugh. If only they knew. Just another reason to keep silent.

Their god had come, but he was more worried about a single woman than the whole of his creation.

When her crumbling home came into view, a small bud of relief bloomed. It wasn't fancy. It wasn't even really cozy. But, for now, it was hers. She made a silent resolution to die in that house. If they were all going to starve, she would do it in the one thing that belonged to her.

Nyx opened the wooden door and begged it not to creak. She wanted them to sleep in for as long as possible because, when they woke, reality would come all too swiftly. She stepped inside and turned to close the door as quietly as she'd opened it when a familiar presence made her stiffen.

Her heart pounded as that angry despair flooded back to the surface. If she listened hard enough, *felt* hard enough, she could have sworn that his heartbeat at the same tempo alongside hers.

"Did you miss me, Kitten?"

Nyx placed her head against the door in an attempt to gather herself before turning. Hatred filled her blackened heart as she turned to face the cause of her strife.

The Lord of Nightmares sat perched in one of her only chairs, his boots heating by the fire. His messy blonde curls were pushed back from his face and those wild white eyes stared back at her.

"What are you doing here?" she spat, her voice an angry whisper.

"Careful, Kitten. You know I like it when you're mean to me." His smirk sent shivers down her spine. If she had a knife she would cut it from his pretty face.

"Get out." Nyx pointed to the door, but his narrowed eyes said the gesture was futile. He didn't answer to anyone.

"I'm glad to see you made it off Anthemoessa alive. I knew a clever little thief like you would make it work."

"Yeah, no thanks to you, asshole. What did you do? Ride off in your golden chariot and drink ambrosia while you watched us all drown?"

"As a matter of fact, I did. The fear was absolutely engaging. I can't wait for the survivors to finally sleep. Their nightmares will taste like honey on my tongue. Much like you will, I imagine."

"You're fucking sick."

"What of our friend, Nyx?" He looked around and sneered before wiping at his pant leg, almost as if being in their presence made him feel dirty.

"You better stand up. You might get 'poor' on you from that chair."

Mischief flared in his eyes as The Lord of Nightmares stood, and she watched those expensive black boots stalk toward her.

To her shock, he stopped before reaching her. She'd anticipated him touching her. Grabbing her. Maybe even hitting her.

What she hadn't expected was him stopping in front of a petite brown-haired woman nestled around a sleeping blue-eyed girl.

Evangeline.

The Lord of Nightmares stooped low and twirled one of Evangeline's curls around his finger. Bile clogged her throat as she watched him with that curl. "Such a pretty thing, don't you think?"

"Please," she whispered as her fight drained.

"Children are my favorites." His smile shot ice through her veins. "Their nightmares are never worse than a grown daemon, but they are more vivid. Their fears are more imaginative. Unlike the rest of you." He stroked Evengeline's cheek with the back of his finger as he talked. "Useless tears as you're fucked against your will. Despair as your children's throats are cut. It's positively boring," he tisked.

What a sorry, dreadful piece of shit. She wanted to tell him that and how much she longed to see him die. But Nyx couldn't take her eyes off the blonde strand held delicately between his fingers.

Evangeline twitched. Her eyebrows furrowed as she frowned and turned into her mother's chest. Soft whimpers slipped past her lips and carried through the room.

"What are you doing?" Nyx said, her voice still low.

"I'm giving you a taste of what it looks like when you don't follow the rules, little thief."

Evangeline's little body jerked like she was fighting, and her whimpers turned into soft screams.

"The nightmares of a child taste like the finest of wines."

"What do you want? Make it stop and I'll give you anything you want." Tears spilled as her fists clenched.

He looked up to her with a fire in his eyes. "Boring. It's always 'what do you want' and 'please, I'll do anything if you stop.' Be original, Nyx. That's why I like you."

Original? She would show him fucking original.

Nyx didn't have a plan as she turned and flung the door open and walked back out into the chilly morning breeze. She was counting on him to follow. *Needed* him to. He was too close to Evangeline. Nyx wouldn't be able to reach her time if he decided to strike. Nyx ran like a mouse and hoped the cat followed.

Nyx didn't stop until she was behind the treeline and well into its shadows before she spun to face the Devil himself. That roguish smile she hated more than anything stretched so wide twin dimples appeared on his cheeks.

They stood and stared at each other, both tense and ready to spring. He'd stopped not even a breath behind her and she was glad for it. That icy stare made her feel things she couldn't begin to identify, and that fueled her hate fire until it seared her skin. She'd decided long before they reached the forest that she would be the first to act.

Nyx pulled her arm back as swift as a viper and swung her fist at his pretty face. Her broken knuckles made contact, a searing pain lancing through her entire side, but the satisfying crunch that filled her ears was worth the pain.

His head came back around slowly and he wiped the single drop of blood from his lips with a thumb. Nyx stood with her shoulders back and chest out, standing as tall as she could against this man made of nightmares. She would not back down.

"Again." His voice was so low that she wasn't sure she'd heard him correctly, but the unhinged gleam in his eye told her she had.

Nyx pulled back and swung again, landing a blow to his nose. His head flew back and a maniacal laugh bellowed from his chest. Nyx screamed as she raged and let her fists fly, punching him until her arms were too weak to swing and her hands too broken to hurt him, but she didn't stop there.

Nyx pulled her leg back and swung as she yelled. Over and over, aiming her kicks high and low. First the kidneys, then the thighs and shins.Nyx squared her body, aimed her foot right for his balls, and kicked with as much fury as she could throw behind it.

He grabbed himself and fell to his knees, laughing around coughs and moans as he placed his hands to the ground and held himself up with all four appendages.

"What is wrong with you?" she asked, tears stinging her eyes.

"Gods I love it when you tease me, Kitten." His voice was breathless, a smile lacing it. The Devil stood, his face bloody with bruises blooming in an explosion of color before he lunged. The Devil grabbed her by the throat and shoved. Her back slammed into a tree, the bark cutting like knives against her skin as he pushed. She screamed until his hand clamped around her mouth. The hand was replaced with a forearm as he rested his forehead against hers, their ragged breaths mingling in the silence of the forest.

"I underestimated you," he said between panting breaths. "So resilient for such a little thief." The Devil pressed his hips against her stomach and bit his arm to quiet his moan.

Nyx lashed out. Her hands were useless but she bucked against him, legs kicking and head swinging before he nearly crushed her windpipe with his arm.

"Settle down, kitten. No need to be so feisty." His lips were pressed against the hand covering her mouth, and she was thankful for the barrier.

"Now be a good girl and use one of those hands to reach into my pocket."

Nyx didn't move as she stared defiantly into the swirling whites of his eyes.

"Reach into my fucking pocket, Nyx. Or don't," he smiled. "I'll enjoy making you do it. We will take a detour, and I bet your pretty little hand would look delicious wrapped around my cock."

If hatred could kill a man through a stare, she would have mutilated him ten times over.

Her breath hastened as she glared and reached down into his left pocket. It brushed against his dick and the way he pushed against her made her stomach curl.

A piece of paper met her fingers and she struggled to make them close enough to pull it free.

"That's my good girl," he praised, and the way her body reacted to it made her want to die. "That's for our little problem."

Nyx furrowed her brows, a silent question as her fingers finally clutched the parchment. The Lord of Nightmares dropped her as he stepped back abruptly and Nyx nearly fell to her knees.

"The fuck is this?" she spat in between coughs.

"That is an invitation to Dionysus' club. That little piece of paper is worth more than a thousand of your shitty villages so don't lose it."

"What am I supposed to do with this?"

"Come now, kitten. You're such a clever thing. Don't let me down now."

Nyx fought to gather her thoughts, but she couldn't fathom why he would invite her to the club everyone had heard about, but hardly anyone had seen.

"Let me spell it out for you, Nyx. I need him there. Bring the Father of Chaos to this club, and your little Evangeline is safe."

Her heart skipped a beat.

"I'll even throw in something to sweeten the deal. Say, a steady supply of food and protection from the soldiers Ares sends to your door."

"Ha!" she laughed. "That's hardly a deal. At least Ares doesn't hold anything over our heads. He wants his money and he leaves." It would never be that simple with him. There would always be something more she would have to do to keep his protection. "I'm not signing my name on that line, asshole."

"That's my deal. You get it all, or you get none of it."

"Wait," she exclaimed, her hand flying up to placate him. "You said if I brought them then you'd leave Evangeline–"

"And then I changed my mind. You bring Chaos, I give you the girl, food, and safety."

Nyx threw her hands up as she paced. "Fine!"

"I knew you'd see it my way." His smile felt like acid on her skin.

"I fucking hate you!" she screamed.

"And I fucking like it." He grabbed his cock as the words passed his lips. It was pressed so tightly against his black leather pants she was afraid it would rip through.

They stared each other down for what felt like eternity before he turned and walked away.

"Wait!" she called as she glanced at the letter in her shaky hands. "I don't even know where this is."

The Devil looked back over his shoulder, but didn't turn. "The invitation is a portal. It will open when it's ready." He started to walk again, but then stopped. His posture was that suave relaxation that made her want to kill him, but the predatory gleam in his eye made her breath catch. "I like this game we're playing, Nyx, but I'd like it even better if you screamed my name when you cursed me. From now on, it's Tor, and you'd better start getting used to it because it will be the only name on your lips."

"I'm going to kill you," she seethed.

"I'm counting on it, kitten."

Unleash your Chaos

Brooks

17

He and his Siren lay in the quiet, watery confines of her making as their chests rose and fell in synchrony. As the sun rose over the horizon, its rays were caught in the water and reflected a brilliant rainbow of color against their skin. The colors were as liquid as the flowing stream above and Brooks let it wash over him, basking in the exuberance of the moment.

"What are you thinking about?" Xia whispered.

He sighed and said, "The meaning of life, how I'll get by without dried prunes, whether or not my abs will stay like this or if I have to work out... What about you?" He turned his head to smile at her and loved the way she lit up for him.

"I'm wondering whether or not your ego is going to fit back into those tight pants of yours."

"Don't hate on the pants, Siren. Everyone was wearing them at Club Hel. I fit in."

She scoffed, her laughter filling the small bubble containing their peace.

"I was actually thinking about how wondrous it is in here, and then dreading what happens when we leave it."

Xia rolled to face him and propped her head on her hand. "What does happen when we leave it?" Brooks pondered her question. His goal when leaving the illusion of the asylum was to find Xia. Find her, save her, protect her. He hadn't any other plans after that. Brooks was content to steal away with Xia and never look back. The planet could destroy itself and he would create a whole new one in her honor for them to live in solidarity.

It is more complicated than that. We cannot run from this problem. We owe death to her captor, and torture to those who plotted our downfall. Our power is dwindling, and this universe will fall with us.

Brooks rubbed at a gaping hole in his chest where his chaos used to flow as freely as running water, replenishing as quickly as it spilled. But now? It was moving like molten lava and drying on the surface rather than making its way back into the well. His power was lost to him and he needed to figure out why. He doubted his ability to create even a plant, much less building Xia a new home worthy of her.

And then there was the problem of the scrappy girl who brought him here. She was snappy and intolerant at best, but her revelation on the river bank stirred something inside that he couldn't quite shake. These people that felt so insignificant before felt longing, pain, and loss just as he did. They fought to survive and found peace in the moments in between.

Brooks reflected on his time in the asylum and recalled the bitterness and anger he'd felt at these self-proclaimed gods as they used the weak for their own agendas and made empty promises of peace to keep them placated. Lytta was the pinnacle of his revelation, and she chose to die to make sure he saw it.

Words in that raspy alto he missed so much flooded his memory. *"I gave myself to you so that you may wake and fix what he has broken."*

Lytta. She'd known suffering and devastation, and yet was able to find so much peace within the stars. She wasn't insignificant. Perhaps it was unfair to think the rest of them were

"I made a friend a promise and I need to make good on it." Her sacrifice resonated to his very core and, though he would never be the savior she deserved, Brooks would make this world right in her honor. No matter the cost. He turned to his side and mimicked her stance, except where she traced her fingers through the dirt, he coiled a lock of her hair around his. "But before I can do that, I need to figure out what's happening to me."

Xia's brows furrowed as she asked, "What do you mean something's happening to you?"

"I mean I was once all powerful. I could produce anything within the span of a thought and hold it in my hand the next. But now? I'm empty, Xia. Empty in a way I've never imagined possible. Something is wrong with the well of chaos, and I've got to figure it out before..." His words faded as a pit formed in his stomach.

"Before what, Brooks?"

"That's the scary part, Siren. I don't know."

Unleash your Chaos

XIA

18

The walk back to the village was quiet, but it was a steady sense of peace she'd never known. Brooks laced his fingers in between hers and didn't let go until they'd arrived back at the ramshackle town.

Xia didn't know what most of the world looked like. In fact, her feet had never left the black sandy beaches of her island. But she knew that this desiccated village was not a good representation of what lay in the great unknown.

Though she'd lived in captivity, her downy bedding and gilded furniture had been an absolute luxury compared to the living conditions here. It made her heart hurt.

As she and Brooks approached the steps, a small-framed daemon stood leaning against a fragile post holding up the roof of the porch. Her face was puffy and her hands were wrapped in linen that didn't hide the blooming blood underneath.

"We need to talk." Her voice was scratchy and the fury written across her brow looked like a permanently etched line. Brooks stepped forward and pulled Xia with him, but the girl stood straight and turned that hate-filled stare to Xia. "Alone," she ground out.

A prickle of cold danced along her skin as the navy of Brooks' eyes brightened to a defiant topaz.

"I'm not fucking around. You leave her outside or I keep my information to myself." The girl had no sooner finished spitting venom before she winced and a trickle of blood dribbled down her lip and dripped to the rotting wood.

It took Xia a moment to catch on, but she was horrified when she realized it was his doing. "Brooks!" she shouted and shoved at his shoulder. "Stop!"

He turned that piercing gaze to her and her breath caught.

"You're hurting her."

A door slammed to their right and Brooks scowled as black crept up the column of his throat.

"She's lucky I let her live."

Brooks cleared his throat and shook his head, eyes narrowing as he battled his other half. "I'm sorry," he said as navy bled back in to darken his irises.

"Well you don't have to apologize to me you dickhead. But you really need to go say it to her." She gave his shoulder a shove toward the door and he had the nerve to fake a stumble.

"Is this our first fight?" His smile made her want to punch him and kiss him all at the same time.

Xia crossed her arms and huffed. "You're unbelievable."

He looked at her for another moment before the smile fell, his eyes dipping down as he swallowed. Brooks exhaled a heavy sigh before finding her gaze again, and the fear and longing in them was a weight on her heart. She knew exactly what thoughts plagued his mind because they were running through hers too.

Xia stepped toward Brooks and cradled his jaw. "I'll be okay," she said gently. "This is real. We are here, together, and we don't have to pretend anymore."

The muscle in his temple jumped as his teeth clenched, but he gave a small nod and covered her hand with his own. "Okay. Just... Just don't go too far, okay?"

"I promise to only go as far as your secret shadow spies will reach." She touched the tip of her nose to his playfully and he leaned into her with the most beautiful smile plastered to his lips.

"Don't let them get handsy," he teased. "They don't think with their brains."

She joined him in a laugh before stepping away. Xia was saddened to drop his fingers, but she did it for his sake. He would be leaning on her strength for even the smallest of separations.

What hell it must have been to live in an illusion where you couldn't trust anything around you– including yourself.

"Go plan your battle tactics. I'm going to walk around the village, get to know this new world. Who knows, maybe I can be more than just a pretty face."

His gaze dipped down her body and blood rushed to her cheeks. "I can think of at least ten more pretty things on your body, Sunshine. But go dazzle them with your smile."

He winked and took the last few steps to the entrance of the house. With one more backward glance, he smiled in her direction and shut the door behind him.

Xia was left standing without a purpose and unsure what to do about it. She looked left and right, but the area was empty. A few empty fireplaces still smoked from the night before, and the makeshift shutters were closed on the two other houses at the end of the dirt road. They were on top of a small hill that overlooked a larger cluster of wooden buildings. The cover of darkness had hidden the bustling town below the night before, but with the early morning sun came a rustle of activity. Xia started down the path, eager to be among the crowd.

As she drew nearer, the smell of wood-smoke filtered through on the breeze as birds sang through the canopy.

Xia was enthralled.

Anthemoessa had been utterly silent until the Oneiroi moved in, then it was so chaotic with buzzing that not a moment of peace could ever be found. This place, however, was both of those.

When she stepped into the border along the first row of houses, a silence fell over those closest to her as they all watched her every move. Xia was all of a sudden too aware of the strappy nightgown she wore. Gods, how see-through and torn it must have looked. Her last altercation with the Devil had caught her unaware, and the last thing on her mind as she was lying on the floor was her clothes. She certainly hadn't been thinking about it when she was raging on the beach.

Xia kept walking as she held her head high and fought the urge to cover herself. The fact that she thought she could stroll into this place unseen was stupid, and she chided herself for it.

Xia stepped to the woman closest to her and asked, "Do you know where I could find some clothes?"

The daemon scoffed, her stringy brown hair falling from the mass atop her head. Several layers of old hide covered her shoulders and her shoes looked as if they'd been passed down through generations. "What makes you think we've got any for you? You should run along back to where you came from. Maybe they'll have more silk for you to play dress up in."

"I beg your pardon?" Xia shrunk back and twisted her hands in the hem of the gown.

The daemon only shook her head and turned back to building a fire in the pit before her. An empty rusted pot and a large charred stick sat beside it.

She guessed it was for cooking or purifying water, so she took another shot at conversation. "Do you need water?" The woman looked back, and Xia couldn't tell if it was incredulity on her face or anger. "I can wield water. It may make it easier to fill the pot rather than carrying it to the river and back."

"Fuck. Off," the woman spat. "We don't need help from the likes of you."

Tears stung her eyes, and just as Xia turned to run someone grabbed her hand. Relief flooded her system as she turned and expected to see Brooks, but froze when she saw an unfamiliar face.

"Thank you, Ariadne. I'll take it from here," the stranger soothed the hag. She turned to Xia. "Come with me and we will get you all fixed up."

"We don't have the resources to waste on her!" Ariadne called from behind, contempt lacing her scratchy voice.

"If I recall correctly, Ariadne, we didn't have enough to waste on you either, but we made do," she said as they walked away.

"It's okay." She offered Xia a placating smile.

The stranger was quite a bit shorter than Xia and more petite in build. Her nose came to a point and a small dusting of freckles dotted her pale cheeks beneath fuchsia irises. She wore a hood over her head but a single pink curl fell to the side.

What an odd color, Xia thought.

"We don't have a lot, but I think I know someone about your size who may be convinced to give up at least a shirt to cover you."

"Oh," Xia said, still a bit dazed. "That would be lovely, thank you." She tugged gently from the woman's grip again and this time she let go.

"I'm sorry about Ariadne back there. She's been through a pretty shit life and I think it wears on her."

"It's alright. I shouldn't have scared her like that."

The pink-haired daemon snorted a laugh. "You didn't scare her. Though I'm surprised she didn't scare you. That mess of hair is starting to look like a hydra's nest." She laughed again and Xia smiled tentatively.

"If you don't mind my asking, what is this place?" Xia waved a hand around toward the houses.

"You can think of it as a refugee camp. Daemon come and go. Some stay forever while others only stay for a night. This is one of the few places where the tainted chaos can't touch. They call it hallowed ground because, supposedly, this is a place of worship to some dead, long forgotten god. Unforgotten because he never deigned to care."

Xia pondered the answer before asking, "Tainted chaos?"

The woman quirked a brow as she asked, "Have you been living under a rock?"

If she only knew.

"Something like that."

"Well, after Zeus and the Olympians won Titanomachy there were a solid few years of peace. We rebuilt, and even started to flourish. Little did we know that a sleeping disease was waiting to take us out. And when it woke up?" She turned to look at Xia. "It woke up and *raged*."

"How do you mean?"

"Crops wilted, plague spread, water sources were soured with poison... It all just, I don't know. Fell apart. And it wasn't like this giant explosion happened as we were left dealing with the fallout. It crept in over years and we never saw it coming, until it was all we could see."

Xia's stomach dropped. Just how secluded had she been on her cursed island?

"Does everywhere look like this?"

"Ha!" the woman threw her head back with one loud laugh. "No. It's sweet you would think that."

Xia shook her head, totally missing the joke.

The woman sighed at her silence and said, "Think about it. What do those with more power than others do at the first sight of trouble?"

"I don't know."

"They step on those beneath them, climb to the top where all of the comfort is, and live like they don't have a care in the world while the rest are down here to suffer."

They continued at a slow pace down the dirt road. She avoided small rocks and lumps along the way, careful not to step on anything that may break the skin on her naked feet. Evidently she hadn't the rationality to wear shoes before raising the sea and destroying Club Hel.

"Wait here," the stranger said as she stopped in front of a single roomed home. "I'll go see if she has anything you can wear until we can figure something else out."

Xia nodded and stood with her arms crossed over her chest. She studied her surroundings and found that this part of the village looked just as the beginning had. Everything was made of graying, uneven wood and looked like it could collapse at any moment. Most of them were too small to house a hearth, so rings of rock and charred grass sat near many of them. She imagined it had many uses. Warming their hands, drying their clothes, boiling water...

Nothing like the luxury she was used to.

She found that she liked it.

Xia would trade material things for peace any day.

"Here you go." The woman came bouncing down the two steps with what looked like a brown knit sack in her hand. A few more pink curls the color of ripened berries fell across her forehead and she tucked them away hastily before handing over the cloth. "It's not much, but it'll cover all of your business and keep you a little warmer."

"Thank you." Xia slipped it over her head and put her arms through the uneven holes. The edges at the bottom frayed and had several lines of old stitching that tore the fabric in places. She realized that it really was a sack. One that had been mended too many times to hold anything properly. Evidently that meant it was to be repurposed to a shirt.

She found the extremes fascinating. Club Hel reveled in sin and luxury. Everything was expendable– even the daemon. But this village used every resource until it couldn't be repurposed any longer. She was sure that even at its last stop before death, the sack she wore would serve a final purpose.

"Did I hear you tell Ariadne that you wielded water?" Pink eyes to Xia. They moseyed through the village, away from Nyx's home and toward an open field.

"I do."

"That's great! I don't know where you came from, but it seems the taint hasn't reached out so far."

"Is it affecting chaos too?"

"Oh, yes." She nodded and scrunched her nose. "Those who only had small amounts are completely powerless. Even daemon with pure-blooded ancestors are feeling drained."

"I can't say I've felt any loss."

"Do you have pure-blooded chaos in your line?"

Xia dropped her features into what she hoped was neutral and answered, "No. I don't. My father was a water nymph and my mother a healer."

Lies.

Xia kept her heritage close to her heart and for good reason. The Lord of Nightmares coveted her because of what she was. *Who* she was, and Xia would not be chained again because of the blood running through her veins.

"That would explain the affinity for water then," the woman nodded. "Do you think you could help me wash the hides and linens today? There's usually a big group of us who do it, but some have gotten too weak to carry the water pots back from the river."

"Of course. It'll be no problem." Xia plastered a reassuring smile and the woman nodded in return.

"Great! It's just over here."

After a short distance, a clearing came into view. It was settled along the river bank but not so close that it would be washed away in a flood. Several large buckets were positioned side by side with wooden washboards in each.

"There are three stations with three buckets on each. One is to soak, the other to wash, and the last to rinse. From left to right and in that order."

"Got it."

"We need water in all nine…" she trailed off, a hesitant question unspoken.

"I can fill all nine." Xia smiled softly and turned to walk toward the river bank.

She stepped down the muddy side and put her toes in the frigid water. As cold as it was, the chill never seeped into her bones. Perks of being the daughter of Poseidon, she assumed.

Xia inhaled and put her mind, body, and soul into the current of water, letting its rush consume her until there was no beginning or end between the two. She pulled small rivulets from the river and sent them in bigger streams toward the buckets. She filled all nine in a matter of moments. When she exhaled to release the water, a small sense of longing remained. It always did when she lost the aquatic connection.

Xia turned back to the waiting woman and saw what she could have sworn was excitement or anticipation in her eyes, but it was wiped quickly and replaced with a generic smile.

"You just saved us over two hours worth of work."

"I'm glad I could be of use," Xia returned.

"I don't guess you can work some chaos to make it wash and rinse too, huh?"

"I'm afraid not," Xia laughed. "We will have to get them cleaned the old-fashioned way."

"It was worth a shot," she teased. "I'll wash, and you rinse. Maybe you can pull the extra water out of the clean linen so it will dry faster?"

"I can probably manage that."

They sat in front of the first set of wash bins and got to work in silence. Xia listened as her companion huffed, the short bursts of strength making her heart rate increase. It seemed a taxing job, and Xia hadn't seen many young or capable women on their walk through the town.

Xia let the monotony of the task soothe her mind as she put in the effort to rinse and pull water from the linen she hung to dry. The stranger beside her didn't speak, both content to work in the ambient sound of nature.

After everything was soaked, washed, rinsed, and dried, they stood and slung the water from their hands. Somewhere along the way, Xia's makeshift shirt had been soaked through and strands of her pale hair fell in strings. Xia looked up and found her companion in much the same shape.

"Here," she said. "Let me help. Wet and cold aren't a good mix." Xia connected her mind to the droplets of water and pulled it from their hair and clothes, letting it fall to soak into the dirt.

"That is *so* cool."

Xia nodded and brushed debris from her clothes. Just as she was going to ask what chore was up next, an all too familiar tingle shivered up her spine.

"Woah," the daemon said as she jumped back.

"Don't worry," Xia watched one curl around her arm like a cat. "They don't bite unless you ask them to." She repeated Brooks' words from earlier without meaning to, and her cheeks flushed at the implication she'd just spoken aloud.

Is that you asking, Siren? Chaos' voice whispered through the shadows and Xia swore she could feel the caress of a hand. A tendril of shadow stroked her hair while another gently tugged the skirt of her nightgown back toward the ramshackle house on the hill.

"I've got to leave now."

"Why?"

The question stumped Xia and she wasn't sure the reason. "I– I'm sorry?"

"Why do you have to go?"

Xia gestured to the shadows. "I came here with someone. He can manipulate shadows and these belong to him."

"So... he's calling for you?"

Xia's brows bunched as those words struck a chord she couldn't identify. "No, he's not calling for me. He had to discuss our plans with someone we're working with in private. He's just letting me know they're finished."

"I see," she said. "So he's debating *your* plans with someone else. In private. Without *you*. Don't you think that's a little, you know, controlling?" The emphasis on those words made Xia stop, confusion and doubt winding their way through her confidence.

No. She knew Brooks. Trusted him. Who was this stranger to question matters she knew nothing about?

"Thank you for helping me today, and allowing me to help you in return." Xia backed her words with steel. "I'm not sure how long I'll be here, but I would love to help in any manner possible while I am."

The strange girl watched Xia for a moment with pursed lips and a wrinkled brow. "That's very kind of you. I'm here if you need anything. Anything at all." She spoke slowly, emphasizing each word as her expression deepened.

Xia made it a few steps before turning again to say, "I'm sorry. I've been so lost in my own thoughts that I forgot to ask you for your name."

The woman tucked a strand of berry-pink hair back into her cap before she smiled and answered. "Ruby."

Unleash your Chaos

Persephone
19

Cold.

That was the first thought pressing into her waking mind.

Pain.

Icy rivulets streamed through every ounce of marrow in her bones as her back pressed against an unforgiving surface.

Misery.

Everything ached. Persephone willed her eyes to open, but even the simple act of inhaling was excruciating. Her throat was raw as if she'd eaten glass, and a pounding pressure resided in her lungs.

Persephone focused on her fingers and toes, urging them to move, but stopped when jolts of searing pain lashed down her body. Tears pricked her closed eyes and trailed down her cheeks, tickling her ear as they dropped to the floor.

Where was she?

A scratchy whimper left her lips as she tried to cry for help, but even that was too much to bear. She was going to die.

Or... had she already?

Flashes of terrifying memories filled her mind as she watched Narcissus assault and murder her all over again. The way his lips curved into a blissful smile, his hand pumping his cock until he'd come over top of her drowning body.

The tears came in earnest as the memories flooded, threatening to *drown her all over again. Pain rippled down her spine, but she couldn't stop the sobs wracking her broken body.*

What had he done to her?

She couldn't be in the warm, grassy knolls of her meadow. Her teeth chattered in the desolate cold and the sharp points beneath her had to be ice.

Couldn't think.

Couldn't breathe.

She should have never strayed. She should have listened like the good girl her mother begged her to be. Regret was a stone in her belly but didn't feel nearly as heavy as the sorrow. Persephone knew she deserved every second in the freezing hell she'd been condemned to.

She fell in and out of consciousness with no sense of time or its passing. Heavy drops of water fell somewhere in the distance, and she let its sound lull her back to oblivion. She imagined the sound to be the leaky spigot in her mother's greenhouse. There was always a small puddle beneath it, the ground never dry enough to soak it all in. Green bits of moss grew around the edges and Persephone loved to watch the water ripple as the drops fell.

The drips grew louder but kept their steady tempo, almost as if they were getting closer. Persephone attempted to rouse herself, pulling her mind from the edge of darkness and back to her torture chamber. She still couldn't open her eyes, but her hearing wasn't faulty. The sound was not water dripping. It was footsteps, and they grew nearer with each passing moment.

Persephone thought to force her body to stand, but she knew it would be futile. She couldn't so much as open her eyes, much less bring life to her shattered body. She would have to accept this new fate just as she had her punishment. A part of her was terrified it was Narcissus coming back to break her all over again. If she could cower into the darkness, she would. Maybe she could hide from him so he could never hurt her again.

Another voice spoke up in her mind. It was the same one whose defiance got her into this situation. Do not be weak, *it said.* Fight him. Do not be a coward.

"I can't," Persephone whispered to the surrounding darkness. "I'm not strong enough. I need my mother." The last word came out as a broken sob, her throat still raw from her fight to the grave.

"Shhh," a hushed whisper filled the space around her. "There, there, darling."

Only then did she realize she'd lost track of the footsteps as she wallowed in her misery.

A warm hand brushed the hair from her temple as a deep, melodic voice murmured words of comfort. He stayed until her tears stopped flowing, his hand never ceasing its soothing touch.

"I'm going to pick you up now," he said. "And it's going to hurt. But we're going to make you all better."

She said nothing. What could be worse than what had already happened?

One hand cradled her neck while the other slipped beneath her knees. He scooped her gently, but it didn't stop the hellfire of pain blazing through every corner of her being. Persephone sobbed while they walked, and he soothed her the whole way. The man held her close to his chest and the warmth of his body did its best to seep into hers.

She didn't know how long they traveled, but it felt like eternity. She begged for the ache in her body to pull her from consciousness. Blacking out would be a mercy. But, as she already knew, she would get none now.

A creak sounded as the thud of a boot on wood filled the quiet space. Light flared behind her eyelids and she moved to cover them, but found her heavy limbs still tucked at her sides. She whimpered at the burn, however it was nothing compared to the pain when he shifted her around in his arms, jostling every fragile cell of her being.

A scrap of fabric fell across her eyes and eased the ache. Persephone fell silent. Strong arms nestled her back into place and the rhythmic bounce of his steps continued.

"We're almost there. I know it hurts, flower."

Ice coated her spine. "Don't call me that," she croaked as she spoke around the shards of glass in her throat.

"What?" His heated breath brushed over her cheek, and she wondered for a moment what the man staring down at her looked like.

"Flower. Don't call me flower."

"Alright. What shall I call you then?"

Persephone thought for a moment. She didn't want to give him her *name. She was known across Olympia as Demeter's beautiful bud of obedience. Her mother would be ashamed when she found her daughter and learned of Persephone's downfall.*

"I see." The stranger huffed a small laugh through his nose, and she could imagine the beginnings of a smile touching the corner of his lips. "You need time to open up. I understand."

They'd stopped walking and the man placed his knee beneath her bottom to create a perch to free his arm. Fabric rustled beside her as he bent, careful not to jostle her. Whenever he was satisfied with his work, he slipped the arm back underneath and laid her down gently on what had to be the softest of clouds.

Something brushed against her feet and then fell heavily against her body, starting at her legs and ending beneath her chin. It felt like heaven against her frozen skin, and the weight brought a comfort like she'd never known.

"I'm going to help you lift your head. You need to drink something."

"Okay." She sounded so small, even to her own ears.

His hand cradled her head as the smooth lip of a cup pressed against her lips. She started with small sips, testing the limits of her tattered throat. The fragrant liquid stung on the way down, but left a coating that soothed the sores with every swallow.

"It's an herbal blend that will help heal you from the inside out. It will take time, and you'll need to have it everyday or the effects will reverse over time. Do you understand?"

Persephone didn't respond, just drank greedily from the proffered cup. Fragrant herbs danced across her tongue and brought her taste buds to life. Of all the beautiful plants her mother could grow, even Demeter had never made something so wonderful as the tea Persephone gulped.

As the last drop hit her tongue, she found herself already wanting for more. Persephone could feel the liquid lighting up her body, leaving a trail of warmth and healing in its wake. The effects were nearly instant and she sighed, the first drops of relief she'd felt in gods knew how long.

"What was that?"

Her voice was no longer cracked with abuse, but instead sounded as if she'd had a mild cough.

"Nothing too special. Just a few petals from healing plants, some herbs to soothe the tender parts, and some dried fruit to sweeten the bitterness. After you steep it together, it's really quite pleasant."

Persephone squeezed her eyes shut and this time, when she went to open them, it worked. Her vision was hazy, but the outline of her savior was clear as grass in the sunlight before her. She couldn't make out details, but knowing he was there was enough.

"What kind of fruit did you use? It tasted quite citrusy."

"Pomegranate. I grow them myself."

"Pomegranate." She repeated the word and rolled it around her tongue.

"Well, I'll leave you here to rest. The tea should help you sleep, and hopefully when you wake you'll be able to sit up."

He tucked the blankets back around her shoulders and stood to leave, but before he could walk through the door she called, "Wait!"

His form was still blurry, but Persephone could make out enough of the edges to see his head turn back.

"What's your name?"

He was quiet for a moment, and the anticipation made her heart thud a little harder.

"Hades."

Unleash your Chaos

Brooks

20

As he closed the door behind him, he caught sight of Nyx wiping her nose with a dirty, tattered rag. He may have caught a tear too, but would never ask her about it.

"What's so important that you need me alone?" His voice held more steel than he'd intended, but he'd come to the conclusion that it was better to be firm with her. "And where did everyone go?"

"Back to their houses. They sleep here when damages are being repaired." Nyx pulled something from the pocket of her worn pants but didn't meet his gaze as she passed it over.

He hadn't noticed until then that the same ratty cloth she'd used to wipe her nose had been torn to a few shreds to wrap her bruised knuckles. Patches of blood stained the fabric, fresh enough to still be oozing from the wounds. Brooks reached out and, rather than taking the letter, grasped her wrist to inspect her hand.

Nyx jerked her arm back and dropped the letter to the floor as she seethed, "Don't touch me." She stepped back and crossed her arms as she leaned on the counter. "That came in today for you."

Surprise stopped his movements and it took a moment to form the question. "Who would be delivering something to me?" When she didn't answer, suspicion coiled around the sinking feeling in his gut. "Nyx," he tried again. "No one knows who I am or that I'm here. Who would have known, and who would have sent a missive?"

He couldn't decipher the look in her eye. It was apprehensive, but something darker laid beneath the surface. Brooks pushed his chaos toward her mind to filter her thoughts, but he was drained and couldn't break through even the first barrier.

This is infuriating, Chaos seethed.

"I don't know." Her voice was low as she inspected her nails, boredom plastered to her face. "It was stabbed into your shrine in the center of town. Someone knows you're here, and evidently they want to invite you to their Freakshow."

"What the hell is a Freakshow?" He questioned as his fingers worked the trifold paper. Once he opened, he scanned the foiled lettering.

Dionysus Presents

A Menagerie of
GODS AND MONSTERS

For one night only,
come enjoy an exquisite collection of
FREAKS AND ODDITIES

When Selene bleeds, enter the
GARDEN OF EDEN

Explore your most luxurious desires
while indulging in depravity
WELCOME TO THE FREAKSHOW

"It's the most notorious party in Olympia and nearly impossible to get into." Nyx answered. She kept her arms crossed and a deep shadow formed in a permanent wrinkle on her brow.

She must not know who we are.

"She knows exactly who we are. You just make it impossible to be likable."

"Who is Dionysus?" Brooks' eyes read the paper over and over, but no matter how many times he read the lines clarity failed to follow. "And how do you know it's impossible?"

It just didn't make sense.

"He's the self proclaimed God of Pleasure and I've made a living stealing from the rich. Daemon talk."

That gave Brooks a pause, and he raised his brows incredulously at the insinuation. "As in..?"

"As in pleasure of all forms. Sex, intoxication, degradation, mutilation, you name it. If it brings someone pleasure, he becomes the master of it."

"So this Freakshow–"

"Is a house of illusion and his famous monsters."

Illusions...

"You don't think– It can't be linked to the Asylum."

How odd that an invitation to a mysterious gathering is pinned on a shrine built in our honor in a town as run down as this.

Brooks swallowed, the beginnings of dread unfurling. "Elaborate on monsters."

"I wish I could. I know as far as rumors go, he's a collector of different... tastes. I heard once that he keeps someone there who has the torso of a woman and the body of a snake, and that her hair isn't hair at all. But–"

"Snakes?"

"You guessed it." She pointed a finger at him in time with her words. Why did he feel like it was meant to be sarcastic?

"So what does this mean?"

"If you ask any more dumb questions I'm going to assume that either A, you're not who you say you are, or B, we're all fucked because our creator is in idiot."

Kill her, Chaos growled. Brooks tamped down the darker side of his mind and forced reasonable thought to flow.

"Your eyes flashed blue again." Caution rang through her voice as she tensed.

"It's none of your concern." Chaos mingled at the surface.

"Asshole," Nyx muttered under her breath.

He took a moment to collect himself before gathering the next sequence of questions he would need to ask. "I asked you to tell me about this world. I have more questions."

"Shoot."

"Portals."

"Is there a question in there?"

"I need every detail. I told you to assume I know absolutely nothing about your world."

"Alright." Nyx sighed deeply as she pushed away from the counter and sat in one of the unmatching chairs at the lone table. "Sit."

Brooks pulled out the one across from her, sat, and leaned forward to place his clasped hands on the table.

"Before we get started, can you at least manifest some food? Or a drink? Ambrosia or alcohol preferably."

He didn't have time for her games, and doubted there was enough chaos in his well for her demand. He wanted information quickly so he could regain the power taken from him. But, if he'd learned anything, it was that Nyx was obstinate. It suited his needs to give a little before he took a lot.

The presence of chaos is heavy here, and it trickles into us. We can manage.

He pulled a few strands of swirling darkness and willed it to become two glasses of the amber liquid he'd seen all over Club Hel and a loaf of warm bread with fresh cheese and dried meat. The same thing she'd fed him, but in better condition. He didn't need to be a part of their society to know that what she'd given him was past due expiration by a long shot.

Her eyes widened and he could practically see the saliva pooling in her mouth, but she hesitated. Did she think it was a test?

Brooks tore a small piece of bread from the loaf and popped it in his mouth. The sugar fueled yeast hit his tongue and he had to stop the appreciation manifesting as a groan.

"It's not poison."

Nyx closed her mouth and swallowed, her mask of indifference slipping back into place. "I didn't think it was. I'm just not impressed by your fanfare." She took the glass of ambrosia and sat back in her chair, sipping it slowly as she watched him contemplatively.

"Portals," he reminded her.

Nyx took another drink before placing the glass back on the table and kicking her feet up on the surface. "Portals are places where Olympians have pooled some of their chaos to create rips in space for quick travel. Unlike you, we can't turn into shadows to go wherever we please."

"I don't have to turn to shadows. I can just go." He didn't need to tell her that shadows were his only option for now.

"Semantics. Anyway, portals aren't open to daemon of lesser magic. Only those with pure lines of chaos can make or identify them. They're everywhere, but most can't use them. Think of them like a golden chariot for the rich. The rest of us have to find our own way."

"What indicates that there is a portal nearby?"

Her eyes narrowed as she quirked a brow, her mouth falling open in the smallest form of a gape. "Did you not just hear me dumbass?"

I want to feel her bones shatter beneath my hands.

"Stop being so dramatic. Likable, remember?"

I hate 'likable.'

Brooks cleared his throat before answering. "I did. But you've already told me that you're a daemon of lesser magic, and I'm not as dumb as you think I am, Nyx. Anthemoessa was an island hidden at the edge of the water circling the world, River Oceanus. It's not like you happened upon it, and I'm assuming it wasn't your first time there. How did you get there if not through a portal?"

Her eyes narrowed, but not incredulously this time. She was calculative, and their game of chess had only just begun. "Fine. I do what I can to make sure the people here have enough to survive." Her back straightened as she held her head high. "I will not be ashamed of keeping them alive. Being seen as small and weak sucks, but it usually works in my favor. Daemon underestimated me. It wasn't hard to follow the whispers and find someone going through a portal."

"And how many do you know of?"

"I think I'll keep that one to myself." Nyx took another sip of ambrosia. Her cheeks were turning rosy as the effects took hold.

Brooks' jaw clenched. He wanted to force the matter, and by the way Chaos roused Brooks knew he did too. "Tell me how many, Nyx."

"Why does it matter?"

Because he didn't have enough chaos to travel by himself, let alone with Xia.

He slipped a bit of his control to Chaos and caught the reflection of the neon blue eyes in her glass as it frosted.

"Two," she relented, although not happily. She looked as if she were ready to break a few more knuckles.

"And where do they go?"

Her teeth ground together, the subtle scrape filling the space between them.

"Where. Do. They. Go." Each word was backed by power that would make any lesser being cower. Nyx only glowered.

For some reason, it endeared her to him more.

That makes one of us, Chaos growled.

"Club Hel, which you've met, and the city of Dion at the base of Mount Olympus."

"Okay." Brooks glanced down at the invitation and reread it for the hundredth time. "How will I know where to find this one?"

"Beats me. You're the all powerful one. Should be pretty fucking easy for you."

"Your petulance is tiresome. Creating an entire universe was easier than getting information from you," Chaos spoke from his lips.

Glass slammed against wood, and he looked back up to see her ambrosia drained and her stare boring holes into his head.

"There are a lot of tiresome things about you. Where would you like me to start?"

Irritation was a rising tide and he needed something to help him settle it. Brooks reached through his shadows to find Xia, letting the darkness float her essence down to fill his senses. With every inhale of her, a little frustration released with the exhale.

Ignoring her question, Brooks continued. "What does 'when Selene bleeds' mean?"

"I'm assuming it's the blood moon. It happens sparsely, but we are due for one. I'd say three days time."

Three days.

Three days of simmering in his need for vengeance.

"Well, if that's all for now, I'm taking this." She pulled the platter of food into her arms. "And going to bed."

"It's daytime, Nyx."

"Yeah, and I spent my night dealing with you."

Nyx grabbed the food and swayed as she stood, her eyes blinking furiously as if to shake the exhaustion. The plate slammed to the table as she caught herself and closed her eyes, one fist rubbing furiously against them.

"Nyx?"

Her knees buckled and sent her crashing to the floor. Brooks stood and the force sent the chair flying backward. He rounded the table and knelt to her prone form, placing his hands on her shoulders to give them a gentle shake.

"Nyx!"

She panted, heart pounding as her fingers and toes twitched like she was in a dream. Her eyes were wide open and glazed a milky white as she paled, and Brooks was powerless to help her.

Unleash your Chaos

Nyx

21

Nyx dropped to the floor in a pile of flailing limbs and curses. When her visions had gotten so aggressive, she'd never know. She missed the small flashes here and there compared to the assaults of late.

"Okay," she sighed as she pushed to her feet and dusted the dirt from her knees.

Nyx stopped short when she realized how fucking ridiculous it was to wiping pretend dirt from her pants. This was a vision, not real life. But as she rubbed her fingers together the fine pebbles of packed dirt crumbled between them.

"Breathe, Nyx. Everything is fine. Maybe your chaos is growing, and your visions are more like hallucinations. More power equals more real. Please Zeus let that be the cause." Muttering to herself in the darkness was just the icing on the cake.

Nyx gathered her wits and inspected her surroundings just as she did every other time she was thrown into a vision. This one though...

It was unlike any other.

The cavernous space she stood in felt endless in the dark. There was nothing she could see to the side or above, only darkness.

However, a yard or so in front of her, a lone spotlight created a circle on the ground. Nyx stood just outside where the light reached and didn't dare step a single foot forward.

She'd never had a vision like this before and was terrified the thrum of her pounding heart would fill the room. Normally, falling into a vision was like opening her eyes, not crash landing onto dirt. She was like a specter standing in the middle of a busy sidewalk without the ability to see, taste, or smell. In this one, though?

She felt everything.

Electricity raised the hair on the back of her neck like the build of a storm, and Nyx was ready to get the fuck out of there. She'd never had much luck forcing the vision away, though, until it had shown her everything it wanted to.

The last time a vision felt this real, The Devil of Club Hel had looked her straight in the eyes. If he could see her... could he have touched her?

Hushed whispers filtered into the space around her. Nyx turned to check the darkness, but the void was impossible to see through. She checked both sides but couldn't tell where the voices were coming from.

"What the shiiiiit," she murmured, dragging the last word to give voice to the anxiety gripping her chest.

The voices sounded again, but this time a little louder. She turned to follow the sound and nearly choked on her surprise.

In the center of the light sat the biggest contrast of a woman she'd ever seen. Her soft, feminine form was lush with bountiful curves and skin that shone like silk. Long hair flowed in waves down her back and was the most unique mixture of vermillion and carmine. What was most stunning though was the harsh lines and bold features standing stark against the femininity of her body. There was nothing delicate about the menace shaping her brow or the sharp calculation brewing in her crimson eyes. There was a small beauty mark just above her lip that looked so dainty and out of place compared to the surrounding features.

Nyx was so entranced by the beauty sitting in front of a vanity that she almost didn't see the head of blonde hair settled between her thighs. His hands roved over her legs, the pressure from his fingers leaving blanched trails of red behind on her creamy skin through the dangerous slit of her skirt. The woman stared in the mirror with an unmoving, severe expression as if she'd no idea a man was trying to pleasure her.

"That's enough," the woman spoke, her voice just as harsh as her painted red lips.

The man pulled away and Nyx slapped a hand over her mouth to keep the gasp from drawing attention to her sliver of darkness. The Devil looked straight at her as he wiped the woman in red from his mouth. He stayed kneeled at her feet as if he were awaiting instruction.

"You're distracted." Her words were clipped, and she didn't deign to look at him.

Even from the darkness Nyx could see the fury written in every line of his face as his teeth ground, the muscles jumping along his temple. His stiff posture told Nyx everything she needed to know.

The Devil loathed the woman in front of him.

But why?

"I'm sorry, Mel. I can adjust if you–"

"Shut up. I'm so fucking tired of your mediocrity. Everything you touch falls to shit and I'm done cleaning up after you like a mindless hellhound."

He stayed silent, but Nyx could have sworn the shadows beneath him deepened.

"It was simple, Phobetor. All you had to do was drain the Siren of her chaos and this could have been done with. The club would have run itself. But you were so busy lording over it you forgot the point of it being there."

"What do you think I was do–"

His words were cut short by the red, daggered fingernails piercing his temples as she held him in a terrifying death grip under the chin. "Don't. You. Ever. Speak to me like that. Do not forget your place, you piece of shit. I do not need you. You're a convenient fuck and an errand boy at best and I've done you a service by letting you live. But make no mistake Lord of Nightmares," she taunted, his name rolling off her tongue in a spiteful mock. "I will not hesitate to rip the heart from your chest and eat it over top of your cooling body."

She pulled her nails free as she shoved him backward. He fell into the vanity and the force knocked bottles of perfume and various forms of makeup from the top.

"Clean this up."

Mel went back to assessing her reflection and didn't speak again until every item was arranged just as it had been down to the smallest details. Phobetor faced every label outward to be read and each tube of lipstick down so that the color swatch was visible.

Nyx had seen a lot of terrible things in her life. Lived it every day, to be honest. But nothing compared to the ice rolling off the woman in the spotlight. She was an evil unlike anything Nyx had ever felt.

"Here's what we need to do now, and you'd better listen. If there is one detail out of place I will slice off your dick and make you choke on it. Do you understand?"

Tor was back to kneeling in between her and the vanity, his head bowed subserviently. "Yes, mistress."

The ghost of a smirk lifted the corner of Mel's lip, but it was gone before Nyx could decide whether it had truly been there or not.

"Good boy," she purred and gave a gentle pat to his hair. Anger simmered in Nyx's veins, the mock in Mel's tone making her eye twitch.

"You've delivered the invitation to him, right?"

"Yes, mistress."

"And no one knows you were there?"

"No, mistress."

Nyx's breath caught as Phobetor's words settled. He hand delivered the invitation to her. She knew he was there.

He... lied.

"Perfect. At least you did that right. We're in a precarious position. He needs to be kept busy until I have what I want. Then we wipe the board. Did Dionysus tell you where the Freakshow tent will be set up?"

He didn't answer immediately and, if Nyx hadn't been watching closely, she may have missed the flash of his eyes toward her. "No, mistress."

"Hmm," she hummed. "Pity."

He swallowed hard, the Adam's apple in his throat bobbing as his fists clenched at his side. Gods, he had to be drawing blood with the force of it.

Mel opened a piece of folded parchment identical to the one Tor had given Nyx, and studied it for a moment before she looked back to Tor. "Retrieve my dagger from its sheath, pet."

Tor closed his eyes for a second before grazing his hand against her calf and slipping it under the hem of her dress.

"Slowly," she crooned in a voice that made Nyx's stomach curl.

The ring of steel filled the cavernous space as it pulled free from its holster. Tor handed it to Mel pommel first and the defiance written in every rigid muscle of his body filled her with dread.

If Mel killed him then... "Oh , Gods," she whispered.

"See how easy it is when you listen like a good boy?"

"I am not a godsdamned powerless underling for you to degrade, Mel." His face flickered between man and nightmare in a wicked display of power straining beneath its confines.

He tensed, his body preparing to launch itself toward Mel in a furious attack. Instinct flared and Nyx's body lurched forward without her permission, her heart acting before her mind. She needed to help him. If he died, then she would follow.

It didn't matter, though.

As soon as the toes of her boot stepped into the dimmest ring of light, Mel sprung forward, the epitome of a nightmare as she fisted his hair and swept the blade across his throat, the cut deep and precise.

Nyx slapped a hand to her mouth to muffle her scream as a line of fire ignited across her own throat. She dropped to her knees, tears blurring her vision and heart fluttering in erratic beats as if she were the one in the hands of a monster.

Arterial spray covered the malevolent beauty matching the glow of her crimson irises. She bathed in his blood, her head tilting back as she savored its warmth. Mel threw Tor to the side as if he were nothing but an inconvenience, and the thud his body made as it hit the ground made Nyx flinch. She looked down to the invitation once more before tossing it to the floor. Mel used the Devil's back to clean her blade before tucking it into the sheath strapped to her thigh.

She straightened her dress and fluffed her hair, putting herself back together as she spoke aloud. "You're lucky I wasn't carrying my obsidian blade. I've some business to attend to and I want this mess cleaned up before I come back. Do try to be quick about it."

One last glance in the mirror and she stepped from the light and into the waiting darkness. Nyx waited what felt like a lifetime before leaving her safe spot and running to Tor. She didn't know why she felt the urge to go to him after all he'd done to her– would probably continue doing to her. It wasn't something she wanted to look at too closely at the moment.

Act now, think later.

Nyx slid to her knees in front of Tor and rolled him to his side. Blood pulled beneath him, staining his clothes and skin. "Oh my gods, Tor." Nyx placed her hands frantically around his body as if she could find some way to help, but she didn't know where to start. "Are you okay? Of course you're not okay. Get it to-fucking-gether Nyx."

He coughed, blood spattering his chin as he whispered something unintelligibly.

"What? I can't– Tor I can't hear you." Tears stung her eyes and made everything blurry as a wave of dizziness hit. She wiped a hand across to clear them but fell to her ass when she realized her palms were covered in his blood. Blood she shouldn't be able to touch in a vision.

He coughed again and she brought her attention back to the words he was trying to mouth.

Focus, she reminded herself. *You have to focus. You can't help if you're freaking out.*

Nyx put her hands on the floor and leaned in to press her ear against his mouth. "Say it again, Tor. What do you need?"

"Invitation," he wheezed. Every breath was an effort, and it drew a cry from her lips. If he died, the people of Avyssos would be left to rot.

"I already have a stupid fucking invitation, Tor, just tell me how to help you. I refuse to die because you're too stupid to live." Nyx leaned down again, but he only repeated the same word. "Ugh!" Nyx yelled, frustration mixing with panic and clouding her judgment.

She scrambled to her knees and searched the floor around them until she found the blood-spattered invitation. It was identical to the one she gave Brooks, but Mel knew a secret they hadn't.

It was the blood.

In between the inked lines was the real invitation, written in a substance that could only be seen when soaked in blood.

Nyx laughed, the sound incredulous even to her own ears. "You genius, I could kiss you!" She turned to look back at Tor and remembered he was dying on the floor.

"Shit, shit, shit!" Nyx dropped and cradled his head in her hands. She tucked a leg under as gently as she could and laid his head in her lap. "I don't know how to help us." Her voice was low and raspy as tears fell to his cheek and she did a shit job of wiping them off before they ran down and dripped from his nose.

"Are you crying over me, kitten?"

"I would never cry over an asshole like you. I'm upset because your blood is staining my favorite pair of pants and, in case you forgot, I'll die right alongside you." He smiled even as his breaths were coming in short pants. He was fading.

A familiar heaviness hit her like Ares war hammer and godsdammit if it didn't always happen at the worst time. Her vision was fading. She would return to her home while he lay wherever he was, alone and dying. Would she go the same way? Dropped on her kitchen floor as the God of Chaos wiped his hands clean of her?

Nyx placed a hand over her eyes and pushed, willing her chaos to let her stay even a moment longer.

"Please," she begged. "Don't take me now. Just a few more minutes!"

She looked back down to Tor and a softness she'd never seen before eased the ever-present frown lines. That complicated look was the last thing she saw before her chaos jerked her back to reality.

Unleash your Chaos

Xia

22

"*Ruby*."

Xia let herself get lost in thought as she walked beside swirling shadows back to him. Back to *home*. She had mixed emotions about the woman she'd spent her day with. She'd been stunned when Ruby jumped to conclusions about Brooks when she'd never even met him.

Other than Ruby's curious behavior toward the end, Xia enjoyed spending the day with her. To not have to worry about what the night would bring and take on tasks as mundane as laundry while feeling so at ease was exceptional.

Knowing that Brooks was just up the hill from the main cluster of homes made it even easier to slip into a part of herself that had yet to be discovered. She'd spent so much of her life wearing armor made of tempered glass. It was too dangerous to take it off to figure out who she was without it.

Who was the girl underneath the glass? What if, just maybe, she was made of titanium?

Xia was determined to find out.

Maybe she'd done herself a disservice by not pushing to be a part of the discussion. Discovering the girl beneath the glass would mean speaking up for her needs and fighting for her wants.

Fighting... for herself.

She wanted this new life, and she knew down to her soul that she wanted Brooks to be a part of it. To build it with him by her side, but it wasn't possible until she did the work to love and trust herself. To be selfless was to be selfish, for one cannot know what parts of themselves to give if all they ever did was let people take the ones they wanted.

It was quiet this far away from the town, and she took her last few moments outside to marvel at the birdsong and splash of the river in the distance. It sounded like peace, and she could get used to it. Xia mounted the steps, pushed the heavy wooden door open and was standing in the entry room within a few strides. She stopped short when a loud crash echoed.

"Nyx?" Brooks' voice sounded behind the wooden table, deep and full of concern. Xia caught a glimpse of booted feet peeking out from behind and her heart fluttered.

Something was wrong.

"Nyx!" The urgency pulled Xia from her stupor, and she raced to his side. The pixie-like girl was lying on the floor, her mouth slightly agape as small tremors wracked her body. What caught Xia's gaze, however, was the absence of the violet irises she had been so taken by.

White, milky eyes stared at the ceiling as Brooks shook her fragile frame. Xia knelt beside them and placed her hands on Nyx's cheeks. She didn't feel warm to the touch, and the tremors weren't big enough that she would hurt herself. It was more a series of consistent twitches than anything, like she was lost in a dream.

Xia closed her eyes and focused on where their skin met.

"Can you heal her?"

Xia flicked her eyes up to catch the last moments of hope cross his beautiful face until it fell to concern. "No, I can't. Sometimes I can speak to the blood, but I'm not getting anything."

"What the hell does that mean, Siren?" he squeaked.

She looked back to him and would have laughed if the circumstances were different. Sitting in front of her was not the ageless God of Chaos. It was Brooks with his dramatic expressions and unique spark that she was so drawn to. Compassionate but at the same time unyielding.

For god's sake, focus.

"It's hard to explain." Xia removed her hands from Nyx and sat back on her heels, unsure what to do next to help the girl. There was no blood, no foam seeping from the mouth, and no indication as to the cause of the attack.

"I'm going to need you to try." Brooks still had his hands on the girl but was no longer shaking her senseless.

"I have–" she stopped, trying to pull a coherent explanation from her muddled thoughts. "I have an atypical affinity for water. I am a direct descendent of Poseidon, which means that my chaos is strong. Undiluted."

"And tell me how that relates to blood?"

"I can call to water in every way imaginable, in all of its forms. From the largest body of water to particles so small you can't see them with your eyes."

"I guess this is where the blood comes in."

"Zeus almighty, Brooks!"

He held up his hands apologetically but didn't speak.

"Our bodies are made up of *so much* water. Specifically our blood. I can't tell a whole lot from it, but sometimes if there was any sort of poison or substance ingested, I can sense it in the blood because it changes the water inside."

"What do we do?"

The fact that this all-knowing being was relying on her for knowledge and strength was endearing. Like they were a team.

"I guess we just... wait."

"Wait?"

"She will either come out of it or die." Xia shrugged.

"I don't know what I expected, but it wasn't that."

"Can't you do something for her?"

A battle waged inside him, so intense that every emotion filtered through to his expression. Fear melted into concentration before disappointment took over.

"I don't have anything left. It comes back slowly, but I can't–" Brooks ran a hand through his hair, leaving the wayward curls mussed in such a boyish manner it caught Xia off-guard. "I can't help her." The muscle in his jaw flexed as his troubled eyes watched the convulsions wrack Nyx's body.

"It's okay, Brooks." Xia forced as much compassion into her voice as she could. The world would be more than happy to place the weight of itself on his shoulders. Chaos may not have cared to carry that burden, but Brooks? Brooks would hold it until it crushed him. "Death cannot be helped here. We've lived and died for thousands of years. It's just the way it works."

They sat in silence and leaned against the furniture behind them as they watched. Waited. Nyx whimpered, her white eyes searching back and forth but never seeing. And then, something dawned on her.

Oh my gods.

Xia sat forward abruptly, breath lodged in her throat. Brooks startled, his body tense and ready to react to whatever threat had forced her into motion.

"What the fu–" he started, but she wasn't listening.

"*Seeing,*" she breathed.

"What?" His reply was cautious and lacking the surprise from moments before.

"She's a seer, Brooks! Phobetor kept a seer in Club Hel. I was roaming the belly of the island one night before– well, it doesn't matter, but I heard voices and was curious. I watched through the crack as Tor waited for the seer to come back from a vision. He didn't look like her though." Xia gestured to Nyx. "He stood the whole time and had this distant, far away look. They're so rare, Brooks, and as far as I know, the few remaining have little to no chaos. Some don't even have control over their visions."

"Why?"

"Zeus. When Tor brought the seer in, I heard him talking through the vent in my bathroom. Zeus had all of the seers imprisoned or killed so that none could be used to usurp him."

"She just dropped," he answered, his brows furrowed as he concentrated on Nyx. "She turned from the table to go to bed."

"She must not be able to control them. To have such a reaction..."

Neither of them knew what it meant. If she were locked in a vision, then they just had to wait it out.

No sooner than the thought crossed Xia's mind, Nyx sat up in a storm of flailing limbs and panic as she cried in earnest.

Brooks took Nyx in a firm hold, his hands braced on both arms, as he searched her face for recognition. Each time she turned her head or looked away, he followed with murmuring reassurances as her cries echoed through the room.

"Nyx, what happened?" he asked, his grip tightening further.

With no warning, Nyx froze, her body so still Xia feared she'd turn to stone. Her mouth was hanging open with tears drying on her cheeks, but Xia knew that look painted on her frozen face. Nyx was coming down and shuffling through memories. The body always reacted before the mind. Xia had been there more times than she cared to count after waking up from the nightmares Phobetor induced.

"The invitation," she whispered.

"Invitation?" Brooks asked.

"The invitation," Nyx repeated. "I need it. I need the invi–"

"Why do you need–"

"*I need the fucking invitation!*" Nyx roared.

Brooks sprang back, shock and confusion written in the set of his mouth and dip of his brow. He pulled a thick piece of parchment from his pocket and offered it with a tentative hand. Nyx ripped it from his grasp and stood, her movements rushed and clumsy.

She rummaged through a leather sack on the small kitchen counter throwing its contents until she found what she searched for. Nyx turned and Xia was concerned about the determined gleam in her eye, for in her hand was a dagger.

"Nyx," Brooks warned, Chaos rising to the surface to meet the threat head on.

Nyx rushed back and dropped to her knees between them, slamming the unfolded parchment on the floor.

She raised the dagger, her movements sure and efficient, and sliced it across her palm. The cut was deep enough to flash tendons before blood pooled in her palm. She smeared her injured hand over the elegant script, wiping once before Brooks grabbed her wrist and yanked it away.

"What the hell are you doing? This is the only lead we have and you're ruining it!" Chaos harsh tones mingled in his voice.

"Look!" Xia pointed to the smear as her pulse quickened.

Brooks dropped his gaze from Nyx long enough to follow Xia's finger. His first look was quick, but he did a double take. Xia knew he was seeing what she did when he released Nyx's arm and squinted at the paper.

Nyx saturated the paper and pulled back. Text that wasn't visible before appeared in the red stain, and Xia picked the paper up to read it aloud.

Dionysus Presents

A Menagerie of
GODS AND MONSTERS

For one night only,
come enjoy an exquisite collection of
FREAKS AND ODDITIES

When Selene bleeds, enter the
GARDEN OF EDEN

Explore your most luxurious desires
while indulging in depravity

WELCOME TO THE FREAKSHOW

A fucking psycho I may be, but I've yet to do my worst. I'll see you on Erebos.
With Love,
Dr. Kore

A FUCKING psycho I may be, but I've yet to do my worst.

I'll see you on, Erebos.

With love,

Dr. Kore

"I don't understand." Xia shook her head slowly before rereading the text to herself. "Brooks, what is this?"

Xia searched his face. What she didn't expect to see was Brooks leached of color and fighting back vomit.

"She's real," he whispered, his voice nearly a whimper. "I thought maybe she was just a bad dream. A nightmare pulled to keep me locked in my own dread, but she's real Chaos. All of the electroshock, and the torture... Gods, it was all real."

"Who's real, Brooks? Who hurt you?"

Their eyes met and his expression made her stomach drop.

"Dr. Kore."

Unleash your Chaos

Brooks

23

"I'm going to place your head gear now. Do try not to move."

"Do your worst, you fucking psycho."

That saccharine smile would be scarred into his mind for the span of his eternal life. Every muscle tensed and relaxed with each breath, his lungs holding less air with each squeeze. The heat of his palms plummeted to freezing and a film of sweat clung to every inch.

"Brooks? Are you okay?"

Why did she sound like she stood at the other end of a tunnel? He could hardly hear the voice he needed most over the pounding of his heart. He fought for every unbearable breath and the gasps echoed through his soul.

Hands pressed against his chest and his body lurched backward, the chairs crashing to the floor as the table overturned. Brooks clawed at the floor for traction and didn't stop until his back hit something immovable.

Trapped.

We are not trapped, and we are not helpless. Hold onto me, Brooks. I can take this away if you will only share the burden.

Gods he couldn't breathe. Couldn't fucking think.

Hold onto me!

His vision blurred and he pressed the heel of his hands to his eyes to clear the fog, but he only slipped further into the darkness. He laced trembling fingers through his coarse locks and clenched his hands until every follicle stabbed as sharply as a needlepoint. He needed the pain to ground him but all it did was pull him further under the rising tide.

I can ground you. Do not slip.

A malicious laugh reverberated through his skull and rattled what little security he'd found in this new world.

Brooks closed his eyes and begged silently for someone, anyone, to make it stop but to whom should he pray? He was the ultimate power. He held the key to creation.

No one.

No one could help him.

Godsdammit, Brooks!

The final ounce of dread from that thought grabbed his ankle like a vice and dragged his head under water. All of a sudden, he was back in the asylum, his body pressed against a splintered wooden table with worn leather holding him prisoner in the darkness. The omnipresent smell of antiseptic burned his nostrils and made his stomach churn as the sense of foreboding sat like a weight on his chest. That same laugh, cruel with intention, echoed through the room and he nearly sobbed.

The click of heels announced her presence beside him, and he forced his eyes to swivel as far as they could. He fought the strap holding his head in place but it was immovable. A white jacket with gold buttons stopped close and a cloying floral fragrance choked every particle of oxygen he inhaled.

He needed his head to turn, to see her. The anticipation of not seeing pain coming was enough to drag him deeper into the panic that had already swallowed him whole. A hand brushed the hair matted with sweat around his temple as she leaned forward and brushed painted lips against his ear before sinking her teeth into the lobe.

"I've been counting the days until I could see you again, Brooks. Oh how I've missed you."

He whimpered, the sound muffled by the leather strapped across his open mouth. Wood splintered beneath the force of his grip and stabbed into the soft flesh beneath his nails, but no bodily pain could ever compare to the wound tearing back open in his soul.

"We're going to have so much fun together, you and I."

She raised overtop of him, her red eyes shining bright with madness, and smiled.

"Brooks, please. Please come back to me." A soft, far away voice whispered in his ear. Desperation flooded his system in a staggering wave.

A phantom hand brushed his and he strained to look, but the strap holding him down was unforgiving.

"Let's play a game, shall we?"

Brooks' attention flicked back to the flame of red and fuschia hair tucked neatly away in a chignon on Dr. Mel. Kore. When she turned, a gleam of silver caught the eerie white light shining somewhere behind him. A subtle twist of her hand revealed a scalpel, sharpened and ready to mangle.

"Can you feel this, Brooks?" That voice... It was his beacon. "Can you feel it beating for you? This is real. *I* am real."

"Xia?" His voice broke, the panic clogging his throat making words nearly impossible.

Pressure against his hand made his heart stutter. Could that be his Siren? Was she holding his hand? That's why he'd loved her, even if she was a voice of his own creation. She was the embrace that held all of his broken pieces together and the sunlight that broke through the horizon every morning to chase away the dark.

"I always knew there was something wrong with your mind, Brooks. Don't worry. We will get rid of those voices even if it kills you. Now hold still."

Brooks closed his eyes to focus on the lifeline holding his hand. If he tried hard enough, he could feel the faint beat of a heart pressed against his palm. It matched the pounding of his own erratic beat.

A sliver of doubt made his hold on the tether slip. Was his blood pumping so heavily that he was feeling it down to his fingers?

"Hold on to me, Brooks!"

Dr. Kore lifted the surgical blade and pressed it to his forehead, her movements steady and sure. A smile lifted her lip before she pressed in earnest and a sharp, slicing pain erupted. Blood fell in rivulets over his face and neck, stinging his eyes and flooding his ears as she dragged the blade across his skin. Brooks' screams reverberated through the room.

"I'm going to open you up and see what's inside that deranged little head of yours."

"Let's just pretend." A brush of sunshine and sea salt filled his nose. "Just like we used to. Pretend you believe in me, Brooks, and that what I'm showing you is real. Pretend you can feel the rise and fall of my chest under your hand. That you're sitting beside me on a wooden floor, the smell of evergreen trees and woodsmoke clinging to our skin."

He clenched his hands against the assault but found his right one wouldn't close all the way. Warmth lay underneath it and his fingers expanded and contracted of their own volition.

"There you go. Feel my breaths. Stay with me."

Her voice was getting closer and with every inch she gained, the pain in his head stopped. Gods, he wanted to see her, smell her, touch her. He wanted to be fucking enveloped in her.

"Remember when we were on that beach, Brooks, just you and me? We were together and desperate to have each other."

He did remember.

He remembered the weight of her on top of his chest as her legs trembled around him. Could still feel how tightly her thighs squeezed around his neck as she lost herself to the rhythm of his tongue. The delicate way she ran her fingers through his hair as she guided him exactly where she wanted and the breathy sound she made when he got it right.

"That's it. You're safe, Brooks. I won't let her hurt you any more."

When he opened his eyes, no medical grade light scorched his pupils. Infinite darkness and cruel smiles didn't stare back. Instead, wood popping in the fireplace and the heat rolling from the stone wrapped around his senses, along with the sweet smell of sunshine.

Xia sat in front of him, holding his trembling hand to her naked chest, the fabric torn aside to give him direct contact to her warm skin. She felt so alive underneath him. Her cheeks were flushed the most beautiful shade of dusty rose and it reminded him of the skyline at sunset. Her eyelashes were clumped together by tears in her stormy green eyes and it shattered his heart.

Brooks reached out with his free hand and brushed the drops away. His fingers fell to graze against her neck before finding the silken strands of moonlit hair. They were always so soft between his fingers and he swore he could brush it for the rest of his life.

"Are you okay?" Her whisper was hoarse, fear and concern weighing heavily on her brow. She squeezed the hand he had pressed against her chest, one holding him to her while the other gripped his wrist.

Brooks swallowed against the dryness in his throat. "I am now."

Xia nodded as a new wave of tears sprang to her eyes. "What happened?"

He didn't know. And he didn't know what to tell her.

He panicked? That seemed too weak of a word to explain the absolute terror he'd been submerged in.

What happened was you lost your anchor and wouldn't accept help from the one person who could keep you grounded.

Brooks shook his head and closed his eyes, using every ounce of focus to the beat of what bound him to reality.

I *bind you to reality.*

She was here.

She was real.

She was his.

Brooks reached out and took one of her hands in his own and placed it against his heart, pressing just as firmly as did.

"Do you feel it?" she whispered.

"Yes," he breathed as he closed his eyes and swallowed. The rhythm beating under his hand was the same one thrumming in his chest. Their hearts beat as one. He opened his eyes then and stared at the woman that he... loved.

"This." She patted her hand over top of his. "It beats only for you. My heart is yours."

Unleash your Chaos

Persephone

24

It took Persephone the better part of a month to heal completely. Hades stayed by her side the entire time. She was most grateful for his presence after recovering enough to sort through her muddled memories.

Every bone in her body shattered upon impact to the icy floor. The back of her skull caved in and fragmented pieces stuck through vital organs. She bled on the inside, her own body killing her slowly.

Hades was her unlikely savior.

Demeter and the rest of Olympians spoke so lowly of him. She remembered countless dinners seated around the grand dining table in Zeus's palace where Hades was a hot topic of many harsh conversations. They talked of erratic behavior and secrecy, the illusive point of the trifecta of power.

The twelve Olympians had a fragile peace between them, each settling to rule their domain as the more powerful of them sat atop Mount Olympus. Zeus was, after all, the creator of humans and the piece of Earth they inhabited. A true dictator, he sat at the highest point watching, waiting, for any sign of rebellion.

The humans were his excuse. Everyone knew that he was really watching the other gods below him. Zeus was conniving and grew more hungry for power each passing year. Demeter spoke of the gleam of madness in his eye and the deterioration of his body.

Poseidon, Zeus's second brother, was more somber and didn't speak much. Persephone caught him on several occasions glaring at Zeus as he sipped ambrosia, his features set in restrained malice.

However, where Poseidon sat dutifully and tolerated his seat at the table for the sake of the game, Hades had abandoned them all. His seat at the other end of the table was always empty, and Persephone had found herself more than once daydreaming about the mysterious, missing king of the Underworld.

"I've no time for such things," he'd told her when she'd inquired about his absence. "Souls need tending, the gates need protecting, and I have no intentions to overthrow my brother. He leaves me alone and I stay out of his affairs."

His words said one thing, but his tone painted a different story. Demeter told Persephone once that Hades had been cast to the Underworld, that the prince of hell was the biggest threat to Zeus's platinum throne. "His power is the only that can contend with Zeus, so he was cast down to the darkness to ferry souls where he would wither alone."

What must it have been like to be cast down by a brother and locked away from the sunlight for eternity?

Persephone walked the halls of his home, making it further each day as she healed. It was a castle built of crumbling stone that stood in the middle of an eerie lake with water so black it rivaled the depth of space.

Hades warned her not to cross the water without him. He spoke of hellish beasts that not even her nightmares could conjure a face to.

"Mortal beasts like the chase," he'd told her. "Some will hunt you down until you're nothing but shards of bone in their teeth. But the monsters in Black Mirror Lake? They stalk you even through the windows, Persephone. They yearn for the blood pumping through your veins and the fire of light in your eyes. The moment you step close to shore, they will drain you dry."

Persephone had night terrors for days after and couldn't make herself draw the thick black curtains in her room. The lake surrounding the home was inescapable, but she didn't want to give lurking demons any more opportunity to stalk her throughout the house. She lay in bed as these thoughts rushed through her mind. The Underworld was disorienting since the sun never rose. The darkness made it hard to determine when she should wake and when she should rest.

Hades said that she would get used to it eventually, but she had her doubts. She was, afterall, a goddess of spring. She reveled in sunshine and notes of flora riding on the warm breeze.

That night after they'd retired to their chambers, Persephone tossed and turned in fitful sleep, reliving the nightmare of Narcissus all over again. She was at the worst part when something warm tucked behind her body. The heat pushed away the frigid water she was drowning in and she dreamt of laying in a field of her favorite blooms, tanning her skin in the sunlight. The heat was a steady presence throughout the night and brought her endless comfort.

When Persephone woke the next morning, she was alone in the bed. The pillows were untouched and the sheets unwrinkled on the other side. She was convinced she'd imagined everything but was grateful for the solace. When she'd sat up to stretch the stiffness from her body, a cup of fragrant tea steamed on her bedside table. There was no note, no gift of spring petals sprinkled around or a demand for her presence. Just a simple white tea cup filled to the brim with sweetened red tea.

The memory filled her chest with warmth, and she smiled as she turned to glance at her nightstand. Perched on the top was the same white cup filled with the same red tea. They never spoke of it, but Persephone knew it was his way of comforting her. An offer of kindness along with the indication that it was daytime in the Underworld.

The thoughtfulness of the gesture made her think that staying in the pit of darkness with the ruling prince may not...

It may not be so bad.

Persephone sat up and pulled a flowing insulated gown from her wardrobe and a fur shoulder jacket to ward away the cold. She was not made to live without the sunlight, but he did his best to keep her warm with furs and leathers of all sorts. Just another gesture of kindness that the other Olympians said he was incapable of.

Persephone sat at the mirrored vanity to brush out the deep pink locks tangled from sleep. Her brows drew together when she studied her reflection. The fuschia tones highlighted by the sun faded to pastel and the deep rosy red dulled, its once brilliant shine now lackluster. Her frame grew more gaunt by the day though she ate her fill and drank the healing tea with each meal. Bruised circles were a permanent decoration under her eyes and her tan skin paled to white.

Without the sun to nourish her, she was fading. She worried no amount of magic tea would help to replace the rays that once fed her soul. Anxiety clenched her chest. She would have to talk to Hades today about returning to the surface to regain bits of herself. She was worried he would think she wanted to leave him.

She didn't want to leave Hades, but... she did want to leave the Underworld. She missed the sun and the press of dirt between her fingers.

Persephone sighed and rubbed her hands over her face, wiping at her eyes and pressing at the throb in her temple. No matter how much she slept, exhaustion was a constant force pressing against her bones.

She lifted her head to face her reflection. She wasn't sure what she expected to see, but she didn't love the woman looking back, and her appearance had nothing to do with it.

Persephone pulled her hair back into a quick chignon and draped some wayward curls around her face and ears to hide some of the signs of deterioration. Would he feel guilty that she was withering? It wasn't his fault, she would say. Gods, he had been so good to her and asking to leave felt like such a betrayal.

She took a deep breath before standing and steeled her shoulders, telling herself that he would understand. His kindness said that he cared about her, and surely if he looked at her, truly looked at her, he would see that she needed to go.

Persephone retrieved the tea cup and left her rooms to walk the distance to the informal dining area where she met Hades every morning for breakfast. She sipped as she went and the warmness filling her belly eased the turmoil.

When she stepped through the door frame, she paused to appreciate the man sitting in the oversized leather chair he occupied every meal. It was worn from constant use and that felt like a novelty to her. Nothing in Demeter's perfectly arranged home was worn from signs of comfort. It was just ornate decoration to stay a key player in the game of clout and power.

"Good morning, Beauty." His eyes didn't lift from the game of chess he hunched over, but it made her smile, nonetheless.

"Good morning, Hades."

"Come sit. You know I don't bite."

Her belly tingled at his words, and she found herself wishing he would bite. Persephone scolded herself and shook the thought from her mind.

She strode to the chair on the opposite side of the checkerboard and observed his beautiful face as he concentrated. His chin rested in his hand with one finger placed over his top lip. She was fascinated by the small movements of his brow and the narrowing of his eyes when he'd put himself in a tough position and couldn't parry from the other side. If there was one thing she'd learned about him, it was that he loved puzzles and working through strategic maneuvers.

Maybe that's what got him cast to the Underworld. Hades, the one god smart enough to overthrow the ruthless power sitting atop Mount Olympus.

Persephone cleared her throat before she spoke. "Have you eaten yet?"

"Of course not. I was waiting for you."

A small huff left her nose as she tried to hide her smile. "Ever the gentleman, prince."

"A man does not eat until his lady does."

Her heart stuttered and she had to turn her head to tuck a strand of hair behind her ear to hide the shock. His *lady*?

"That's very kind of you." She recovered, but just barely.

"After we eat, I'd love to show you something." He looked from his game and stared into her eyes. The faintest shade of blue dotted his irises and mused white hair draped across his forehead. Hades was classically handsome with a sharp jawline, a perfect round nose, and broad shoulders. There was a hint of excitement that made her perk up. She was entranced and more eager than ever to please him.

"Of course," she answered with a smile.

Hades waved a hand over the small table between them. The chess game disappeared and in its place was an array of meats, cheeses, bread and fruits with two chalices full of wine fermented from a fruit beautifully balanced between bitter and sweet.

"Hades?" she said around a mouthful. "You never told me what fruit you ferment for wine. It's so fragrant and rich on the tongue."

"Pomegranate. It can only grow from soil fertilized by one of the five rivers of the Underworld. I have a grove of them."

"They're magnificent." Persephone gluttoned herself just as she did every meal. She ate more than her fair share and it was never enough. Her hunger grew by the day, but he seemed content to watch her eat what he provided. If he was happy, Persephone decided that she was too.

They ate in silence, and she tried not to feel self-conscious as he watched her devour every bite. He picked at the tray, nibbling here and there, but never took his eyes from her.

"We will travel over the Black Mirror today."

Persephone stopped, a combination of meat and cheese placed atop a bite sized piece of bread. Was he serious?

"Do not worry, beauty. There is nothing in this realm that I cannot protect you from. The beasts answer to me, but only to me. That's why it's important you do not travel alone. But, with me, you will be more than safe. They will kneel to you as if you were their queen."

She dropped the food back to the tray as she gathered her composure. The last time she trusted a man with her life, it ended in a scene so horrific she kept it from her mind at all costs. However, she hated to disappoint Hades by turning down his offer. He seemed so excited about whatever it was that she couldn't stand to see his face fall at her decline, especially by bringing up the fact that she was considering leaving.

"Okay," she agreed with a hesitant smile.

STEPPING from Hades palace was both terrifying and awe inspiring. Mist from the five falling rivers of hell coated her face and raised the fine hairs on her body. Though her instincts warned her to turn back, she was too awestruck by the morbid beauty of the Underworld.

Crossing Black Mirror Lake was effortless with Hades by her side. The water simply parted to let him walk on the lake bed. She avoided the milky white eyes that glowed in the wall of water despite the darkness, keeping her eyes focused on his back. They tracked every step she made, and Persephone had the distinct feeling that they were only watching her.

Hades explained the complicated tangle of webs that was the Underworld. There were five rivers flowing through the domain. Their purpose was to test the new souls and determine their place among the dead, along with two separate planes where they were sent for the final rest.

"There is Elysium which is very misunderstood," he explained. "Some believe it to be a paradise, but it's not. It just... is."

"What do you mean?"

"When a body dies, Beauty, its soul and chaos are ferried across the river Styx together. The soul endures several tests through the other rivers. After judgment, they fall to the special place I'm taking you. The chaos is siphoned and then the soul falls to Tartarus or Elysium."

"I've heard of Tartarus," Persephone quipped bitterly. "My mother used to tell me that if I disobeyed or didn't preserve myself that I would be dragged under to Tartarus and given as a sacrifice to the old gods."

He hummed, brows set before commenting. "She only got half of the story right. It was cruel of her to scare you into submission. Disobedience does not get you sacrificed to Tartarus, beauty. It's... more complicated than that."

Persephone turned his words over in her mind. Hades could be strategic with his words, but she was getting good at picking out the truths from his attempts at redirection.

"But some souls are sacrificed to Tartarus."

"Yes," he answered simply.

"What does it take to get sacrificed?"

They continued their trek through the bottom of the lake where the rivers converged and were approaching a cliff face in between falls. A set of stairs angled up the rock and a small door hole resided at the top.

"It's not up to the soul. Whether they were moral or not during life, it doesn't matter. The judgments are passed by the rivers and the rivers alone."

Another non answer.

"And what criteria do the rivers use to make this judgment?"

Hades remained silent until they'd climbed the steps and he released his hold on the lake. Water rushed in an unforgiving current, crashing against walls and spraying mist that clung like desperate hands ready to drag her under. Hades looped an arm around her waist and tugged her through the door.

She panted from the rush, but it deepened as she found herself pressed against him. Hades stared down at her, his heart thrumming against the palm she had pressed to his chest. The corner of his lips lifted before he let her go and kept walking.

The cave tunnel he'd pulled her through was eerily dim. Black metal sconces with years of wear were placed every ten steps or so and housed flickering blue flames. Their pace was slow and steady, but the silence between them was buzzing with tension. Or, maybe she was imagining things. A few glances at Hades and his neutral expression had yet to change.

"You didn't answer my question, Hades."

"I'm sorry, Beauty. You'll have to remind me what you've asked."

"What system do the rivers use to determine where to put a soul?"

"I'm afraid that even I am not privy to that information. The rivers have been in this domain even longer than I. I'm simply the power who guards the great cycle."

She nodded, accepting the answer, but something still seemed just the slightest bit off. Persephone chalked it up to the nerves she'd felt about walking through the Underworld after weeks of staying inside his palace.

The further they walked, the closer they got to an ethereal light emanating at the end of the cavern. It wasn't bright. Nothing in the Underworld was. The light shone like the bioluminescent foxfire that grew in damp areas surrounding Demeters estate. Her chaos was not capable of causing decay, but fungi was somewhere in between the living and dying. Persephone recalled her fascination with the fungus and how she'd worked countless hours nurturing it with her gift.

When they were mere steps from the entrance, the glow illuminated a vast field within the walls of a cavern.

"I've never shown anyone the wonder lying beyond this hall. But you, my beauty… You will thrive there. I want it to be all yours. My gift to you."

Curiosity filled her chest as she looked from the black eyes staring softly down at her to the opening of the mystery that was all hers.

"Go to it." He urged.

A smile spread across her face as she turned to run the last bit of distance between her and what little piece of himself he'd given willingly.

A secret place all her own.

When she reached the opening, she nearly fell to her knees. Persephone hiccupped a cry, the sound a mixture of joy and disbelief. She vaguely felt Hades stop at her side.

"This is the Asphodel Meadow. When the body dies, the soul and chaos fall here. The soul will soak into the dirt and rise to the River Styx where it begins its journey. The chaos, though, is a wonder all its own. No one knows how it works except Mother Gaia who placed it herself. Of course, some say that the great god of Chaos planted the first seed to bless us with this power. Either way, this is the reason chaos flows through us all."

There had to be thousands of blooms growing from stalks covering every inch of space on the floor and walls. The white pointed petals grew in clusters, the orange center standing stark against the glow of the cave. The most wonderous part of the room, though, was the giant tree that reached from the floor and grew endlessly through a non-existent ceiling as if it disappeared from time and space. Petals dotted the room like stars in the night sky.

"How is this possible?" *Persephone asked.*

"The meadow?"

"Well, yes. That and the tree. We are underground are we not?"

"What kind of lies do they spread on Olympus?" *Beneath the sarcasm was a fine line of incredulity.* "We are not underground, Beauty. We are in a plane outside both Earth and Olympus. Zeus likes to think it's below him because he cannot stand the idea of being under someone else. We exist out of time and space. Chaos embodies this place, and it shapes itself to fit the needs of the cycle. Just because you cannot see the tree from the palace does not mean it isn't here in the Underworld."

The concept threw her for a loop. Everything had an explanation. A reason for its mechanics. "So you're telling me that because of the chaos, nothing makes sense down here. It does what it wants."

"Something like that. This field is sacred and cannot be kept near the souls. It is the very center of the Underworld, yet it never touches it."

"What about the tree?" Hades wrapped an arm around her from behind and pointed up toward the never ending ceiling. Persephone's breath caught before she leaned into his embrace.

"It is the source of chaos. I imagine that the true form is incomprehensible."

"How tall does the tree grow?"

"Interestingly enough, it grows to the home of the three Fates. Clotho gave herself to the great cycle and made the ultimate sacrifice to the tree. At the very top, her body is preserved in the trunk as she spins the thread of life. She is a servant to the chaos and weaves only what it whispers to her."

Persephone knew of the Fates. One to spin the thread, one to measure the thread, and one to cut it. Birth, life, death. "Clotho uses chaos from the tree to create life. Lachesis measures the span of its life. Atropos cuts the thread."

"Put simply, yes. The Fates have a field just like mine, but they serve two different purposes. The Fates nurture the asphodel until they bloom and, when it's time, they cut the flower from the stalk. This is the birth, life, and death cycle. It then falls to my field and begins separating the soul from the chaos. Once the soul is taken, the bloom falls to the dirt and feeds the great tree its chaos. And so the great cycle continues."

She had no words. To be in the presence of something so magnificent and meaningful was an honor beyond comparison. She hardly felt worthy to be in the same room as the great tree of life.

"What happens if you pluck a stalk before its time?" Persephone looked to him just in time to catch the last flashes of warning in his eyes.

"Never cut a stalk. We prune wilting blooms. We never touch the stalks." His voice was assertive, maybe even a little angry, and she flinched. He seemed to realize his mistake and took a few breaths before continuing. "The stalks never change. They have been in the same place since the beginning. It is only the blooms that change. If you were to cut a stalk, the flow of chaos that ran through it would be lost to the cycle."

"Where would it go?"

His jaw flexed. "It would latch on to the closest source of chaos in order to get back to the well."

"Which would be..." she trailed off as the puzzle pieces put themselves together one by one. "It would be the daemon holding the stalk."

"Yes."

"Why haven't you used them to overthrow your brother? You could be ten times more powerful than him. I mean, just look at all of the power sources growing around you!" She gestured around the cavern, her eyes bright with discovery.

She was jerked from her revelation when a pair of hands took her shoulders in a bruising grip. She gasped and was face-to-face with Hades in an instant.

"Never," he said as he shook her, a frightening mask of fury slipping over his features. Shock froze her body, and Persephone was left staring. "Do not ever speak those words again, do you understand me?" Hades shook her in earnest now, her head dizzying from the force. "Do not betray me by sharing the one thing I trusted you to keep!"

"I understand!" she cried. "Please, Hades, let me go!"

The demon he'd slipped into faded away as Persephone sobbed. It was a physical thing as it left, neutrality settling into his features as he put on another mask. He released her shoulders, but it was a slow movement as if he were readying himself to catch her when she fell. Persephone trembled from top to bottom.

Hades dusted the front of his shirt and straightened the bottom as he collected himself. "I want you to tend to it."

"I'm sorry?" She couldn't believe it. Not the swift change in demeanor and subject or the fact that she'd just spoken of defiling such a sacred place and he still trusted her to be in it.

"The field needs to be maintained. The flowers must be pruned and cared for until they're ready to fall and fertilize the dirt to nurture the tree. I want you to tend Asphodel Meadows, Beauty."

"I couldn't," she breathed. "I'm no one, I can't just—"

"You are the great goddess of spring. You grow the most delicate petals and nurture them with a passion like no other. I want to give you this part of me. I want to share the most important part of life itself with you. I trust you, and I want you to share this life with me."

The poetic words he'd spoken wiped away the feelings from moments before, and she was overtaken by a sense of pride and longing. He only scared her because it was important to him. To the cycle.

He trusted her.

He wanted *her.*

To share in his life and secrets would be an honor Persephone would hold closely to her heart.

Their eyes bore into each other with a heat and intensity that had her palms itching to reach out and touch him. That ever-present electricity between them sparked, and she could see the moment he decided to catch fire with her. Hades stepped forward, his lips ghosting across hers.

"Can I kiss you?" His breath brushed against her and Persephone wanted nothing more than to feel his lips against her own.

"Yes."

Their kiss started gentle, testing the feel of their skin together and the tilt of their heads. As it picked up rhythm, hands roamed over whatever they could find, desperate to feel every inch as quickly as possible. Those roaming hands turned into needy pulls and scraping nails, two bodies eager to collide and become one.

Persephone whimpered as he dropped his mouth to her neck, his teeth nipping along the side until he licked along her collar bone. She tangled a hand in his hair to keep him there, every touch of his tongue sizzling in her blood.

"Hades," she cried, desperate for a touch she didn't know how to ask for. "More. I need more."

He was quick to respond as he grabbed her ass and pulled her up to straddle his waist. He was hard for her and the way he pressed himself against her was maddening.

"Please!"

"Tell me what you want, Beauty."

"The ache," she moaned. "I need you to make it stop."

That was all he needed.

Hades pushed her back against the wall and pinned her arms above her *head while his other hand worked to free his cock. There was no preparation, only desperation. He slammed inside her with a force that shook them both to the core.*

They were a tangle of limbs and the way he drove into her over and over was ruthless. His grunts were muffled by her hair, but she had no such compunction for her screams. His moans intensified as the ache in her belly grew. Slickness coated them both, his rhythm becoming more erratic with each thrust.

"Fuck," he moaned, over and over until he tensed and bit her shoulder, the pain sharp and intense. Hades pressed her relentlessly into the wall with the force of his orgasm, his moans ringing in her ear.

Gods she was so close, if he stayed right there, pushed a little harder against her–

He slumped, his hand dropping hers as he stepped away. Persephone's legs fell from his waist and she stood breathlessly on unsteady legs as he tucked himself away.

"You were even more beautiful than I imagined," he said as he stepped toward her and pressed a kiss to her cheek. "Come on, Beauty. Let's go back and have some lunch. I'm going to need to rest after that one."

He patted her ass and made his way back toward the entrance. Their panting breaths echoed off the wall of the great cavern, and she was left wondering what the fuck had just happened.

Unleash your Chaos

Brooks
25

"Who is Dr. Kore?" Nyx picked the blood-stained invitation from the ground and placed it on the middle of the table.

"It's a long story that I don't have the time to tell, Nyx." Brooks stared at the invitation. "She's no good. She's a malevolent soul that needs to be dealt with, and I will be the one to do it."

"Judge, jury, and executioner huh?" Nyx sat nonchalantly with her chin resting in her palm, and the easiness of her posture made him bristle.

Chaos bristled and the temperature dropped, black tinging his fingertips as he stared a hole through the smile on her face.

"So what's your plan then? Bust into the most underground, prestigious party in Olympia to murder someone? That's just another day on the mountain. No one is going to blink an eye. What's with the fanfare?"

He gritted his teeth as he fought for patience. "I don't have to explain myself to you Nyx."

"I'm not asking you to. I wonder why the great Father of Chaos has to travel across Olympia like a peasant to murder someone with his own hands when he could simply snap a finger to right all of his wrongs?"

"Some people deserve to stare into the eyes of those they hurt as the life drains from their soul, and those they hurt deserve to watch every last flame flicker to smoke as it happens."

"Shit, man. That's deep." Nyx's eyes bulged and a soft touch brushed his arm.

"I don't want to snap my fingers and end her. I want to hear her beg. I want to drown her in her own screams, and I want my face to be the last she sees."

"Noted."

Xia cleared her throat before interjecting. "So we're going to this party to find Dr. Kore. How will you even know what she looks like? If she could spin an illusion as detailed as the asylum, what makes you think you'll be able to find her there?"

"I'm counting on the fact that she doesn't have your Song this time. If she is without your chaos, I should be able to pull aside whatever vail she places over our eyes."

"You're seriously underestimating what happens at these parties," Nyx scoffed. "Party is an understatement. This isn't a fucking coming-of-age get-together. This is a place where the most powerful Olympians shed their skins and celebrate the darkest of their demons. Unabashedly, I would add."

"You told me they do that anyway. You spoke so highly of their cruelty," Brooks interjected.

"Yes. Cruelty. But you're forgetting the part where I told you the twelve Olympians have a truce. They aren't cruel to each other. So what do you get when you take the twelve most powerful beings in the universe and send them to a Freakshow?"

"I've no idea, Nyx, but I'm sure you're going to tell me."

"Depravity in the most extravagant forms. They decorate the walls with human sacrifices, take part in deviant sexual encounters, torture, and revelry. And in the center of it all? Dionysus shows off his infamous monster collection." Nyx held up a finger to shoosh him as he opened his mouth. "Dionysus is a collector of freaks and oddities. Anything he can put on a stage to wow an audience."

"Anything?" Xia asked, her face stricken.

"And anyone," Nyx finished. "I think I know where it's going to be, too." She looked down and picked at her nails as she chewed the inside of her lip.

"How could you possibly know that? Unless you're hiding something." Xia said with a raised brow.

"As I was thinking about it, it just kind of clicked and made sense. The Twelve would want a place no one else could reach. They will be vulnerable. Letting go for the sake of pleasure."

"And what kind of place would that be?" Brooks questions incredulously.

"A plane between Olympia and the Underworld where the living can mingle with the dead. No one except The Twelve are powerful enough to stay without starting the process of death."

"I don't understand." Brooks' eyes closed as he massaged his temples.

"Erebos," Xia breathed.

Brooks' eyes flicked up, his heart picking up speed as hers did.

"Erebos," Nyx confirmed. "How did you know?"

"Because," Xia swallowed as she clasped trembling fingers. "That's where the Onerioi are from. Where *he* is from."

"Who, Xia?" Brooks asked, though he had a feeling he knew. Chaos seethed under his skin.

"The Lord of Nightmares."

"Oh, he will for sure be there," Nyx added. "What better way to add onto the fun than to have a master weaver of nightmares?"

I do not trust her.

"And what about Zeus?" Brooks asked as he turned his icy stare to Nyx. Will he be there?"

Nyx's brows dropped as she threw her hands up. "Of course he will be there, you idiot! That's why I'm telling you you can't just waltz in there and start killing gods. Do you listen to anything I say?"

His thoughts drifted to the constellation in the night sky where he'd laid his best friend to rest. His heart ached in the empty space Lytta once filled. She was owed retribution and Brooks would be the one to see it done. He let Chaos curl into that missing hole and fill it with an anger so intense it froze rather than burned. His path to finding his power was going to have to take a detour for vengeance.

We will see.

"Don't you dare. You know how important she was to me. To us."

You forget yourself, Brooks. I do not meddle in the affairs of immortals playing gods. This is bigger than your feelings.

"And if you'd deigned to have any, you wouldn't be in this situation."

Brooks turned to Xia to see her pretty face painted with deep lines of fear and concern. "I made you a promise," he spoke low and sure.

Xia's brows dipped as her mouth opened to speak.

"I promised you," he interrupted. "That I would find who hurt you and make him pay tenfold for his crimes."

"You don't have to be a white knight riding in my honor, Brooks. If I wanted him dead I would do it myself."

"I told you once not to mistake my kindness for goodness, Siren, and I meant it. I am not a white knight Xia." Brooks pushed his darkness to the surface as he stepped one foot into Chaos' shoes. "I am yours. *Brooks* is yours. But Chaos is yours, too, and we will not stand for the crimes committed against you."

When Chaos brushed against the barrier between monster and man, Brooks welcomed the darkness with open arms. Ice coated the table where his palms met and wood split under the pressure of the cold. His eyes glowed an electric blue as his chaos bled like ink through his veins. His heart raced alongside hers, and when Xia leaned back with fear stricken eyes, he knew what she was seeing.

The eight-pointed star that bore him bloomed across his forehead, the bottom gleam settling in between his eyes as the other seven points stretched across his skin and spread like disease.

When he spoke, his voice was low and guttural, the weight of eternity lacing every emphasized word. "We will not stop until his blood paints the sky and his body lays dead at your feet. His soul is *mine*."

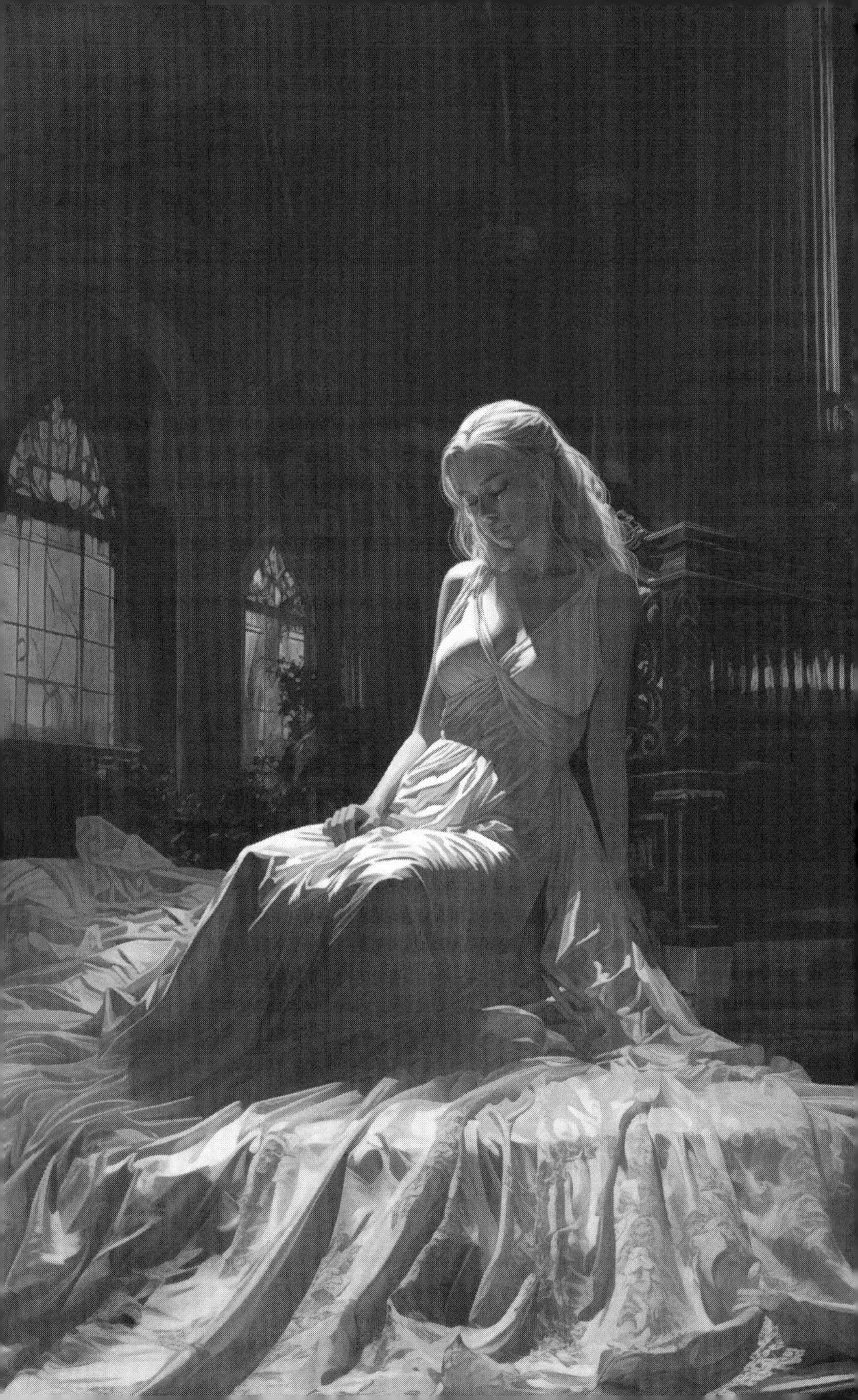

XIA
26

Xia's emotions warred as Brooks' words settled into her mind, her Siren slithering to the surface. She vaguely heard Brooks and Nyx arguing, but the buzz in her head drowned them out.

The kill is not his to take, she hissed.

"The kill is not for any of us. If we stoop to his level then we are no better."

We will finish what we started on that beach. He only got a taste of what was to come.

"You're going to get us all killed, and for what? A girl? Petty revenge?" Nyx spat.

"It is not petty and don't lecture me on affairs you will never understand." Brooks threw back.

"You don't think I understand wanting revenge? I would have killed you the first time I got the chance! I was almost killed as a plea for your mercy!"

The Lord's soul belongs to us, and we will swallow it whole.

"I don't want that. I don't want to be a monster."

The Siren hissed as she recoiled, anger bubbling over into Xia's emotions. It was suffocating.

Brooks was going to kill the Lord of Nightmares and there didn't seem to be anything she could do to stop it.

"Will you excuse me?" she said to the two daemon fighting a silent battle of wills beside her.

"Xia?' Brooks glanced up. "Are you okay?"

"Fine." She stood and shoved her chair away. "This dick measuring contest between the two of you seems like it's going to last a while, so I'm going to freshen up by the stream."

She ignored the small dip of concern on his brow. "You know I'd win right? My dick is way bigger than hers."

"You wish your dick was even half as big as mine, you ignorant ass hat," Nyx retorted.

Xia stepped through the door that'd seen better days.

An anxious flutter filled her chest like fleeing birds as she put as much distance as possible between herself and Brooks. His words startled her more than she would ever let him know. Not because she was afraid she would upset him.

But because... Xia wasn't sure she wanted the Lord of Nightmares dead.

She knew that's what she should want. Tor had done unspeakable things to her and, on that last night on her home island of Anthemoessa, he'd nearly killed her. The darkness she kept so firmly in check raged that night, and she'd been intent on killing him.

Until... Brooks saved her. A maelstrom to rival the power of Calypso whirled inside, sucking the woman she knew into an unforgiving darkness that prowled like a caged beast in her soul. The Siren wanted Tor's death.

I want to see him cut from neck to navel with his insides strung about the floor as he begs her my mercy.

"Stop," Xia cried out loud as she held her ears.

Death would be too kind of an end for him.

"That isn't me. I am not cruel."

Xia slipped down the riverbank and sat on its edge to dip her toes into the stream. The cool rush of water soothed her frazzled nerves, and she closed her eyes to connect wholeheartedly with the element of her heart. With her eyes closed and heart open, Xia dug into the tattered remnants of her soul to search for the answers to her questions.

Who is the girl beneath the glass?

For so long she'd been a victim living in a constant survival state. Her head stayed down, and she put valiant effort into staying invisible. If he couldn't see her, he couldn't get angry. If he wasn't angry, then he wouldn't hurt her. She had moments of defiance, but Xia learned quickly that it got her nowhere but half dead. In the aftermath of his violent destruction... it was different.

In those moments, she didn't want to survive. Her heart cleaved in two as Xia recalled the desperation to die but being too scared to do it herself. She was too weak to end her own suffering.

You are not weak. It is not weak to survive.

How many times had he shattered glass with her bloody face and left her with a broken shard in hand?

How many times had she stared at the mirrored fragment and sobbed as she held it to her wrist and pressed until blood welled in her palm?

And how many times did you listen and throw the instrument of death across the room because you were not ready to die.

"I was too scared to die."

No! I feed you my rage because we will not surrender to death. If death comes it will be forced upon us and nothing less. We will fight back, Xia, always, because we deserve more than this. We deserve to live and to do it because we choose to.

Xia rubbed her watery eyes with the heel of her palm to push the memory away, but her mind was too deep in the gaping crevasse to resurface.

She was weak.

Too weak to live, and too weak to die.

Who is the girl beneath the glass? Dig deeper.

"I can't," she cried, her voice a desperate plea upon the river breeze.

You must.

After I forced the glass from your hands, what did you feel?

She'd felt nausea squeezing her throat as the weight of the world pressed against her chest, making it nearly impossible to draw breath. Her bones would ache as the muscles forced them to move and support the weight of her body. Tears would well and fall from her bloodshot eyes, but the scream building in her chest was not from the pain or sorrow.

"Rage," she whispered.

Rage at a world that condoned the torture of others for pleasure. A man who hid his weakness by hurting those smaller than him. And a woman who was too scared to fight for herself.

When her island was taken, the smallest of fissures formed at the base of her soul. When her sisters died, those fissures broke under the pain and pressure. With each bloody brawl and mental war fought against Tor, the cracks fractured and webbed further into the growing void.

All of the times she'd taken that rage and shoved it down so deep inside, Xia thought she was making it disappear. But wrath was malevolent and it festered like mortal wounds, seeping into those fissures and eating away at her soul until they were gaping valleys of hatred and torment. Each swallow was a driving force into the wedge determined to shatter her.

It was then Xia realized that the monster standing on the black beach that night was one of her making. She let anger and hatred rot inside like a plague until it birthed the beast sleeping in her belly. Xia manifested her fury into a sentient being, and it was too hungry to let her go.

Who is the girl beneath the glass?

She let the discovery resonate and breathed until she was ready to take full responsibility for the evil she'd brought upon herself. She couldn't control her circumstance, and she didn't deserve the tribulations placed upon her shoulders. But Xia was the one in control of her actions and responsible for their fallout.

A responsibility I am eager to carry for the both of us.

The girl beneath the glass armor wore skin strong enough to live without it, and she would no longer hide behind a brittle illusion of strength. She would be fierce, and even the stars would quiver upon her reckoning.

Unleash your Chaos

Brooks

27

He stared into the violet eyes of the only person he'd ever met more obstinate than Chaos and sighed.

"I'm going with you. You're the walking cliche of ignorance and you won't last a minute without me."

"Be careful, Nyx. If you keep it up I might start to think you care about me."

The intensity of her gaze faltered as her eyes turned down to the table. She recovered quickly, but Brooks caught the squeeze of her throat as she swallowed.

"What aren't you telling me Nyx?"

Her eyes darted to his as the composure slipped back over her features. She watched him for what felt like hours, the silence heavy between them. When the tension was at its thickest, she broke the silence.

"I'm invested."

"Invested?" He couldn't stop his brows from disappearing underneath his hairline.

"Yes."

Brooks stared at his opponent as he determined his next move in their battle of wills. Though he'd only known her a few days, Brooks had seen enough to know something was off. She'd never shut up this long.

Chaos probed the walls of her mind. The sour tang of guilt laid heavily on his tongue as tingles of anxiety ran down the tenuous connection.

She's hiding something. Let me speak to her.

"I don't think that's a good idea–"

"When I met you, you were on an island far from home and playing games you had no business buying into," Chaos spoke aloud. "What are you really up to Nyx? And don't lie to me. I'll know if you do."

"Why does everyone keep saying that?" She murmured to herself. Her face hollowed as she sucked her cheeks, the wrinkles in her forehead deepening as she considered her next move.

"Someone threatened my family. Someone that I *know* will be at the Freakshow. Powerless daemon like me don't just get invitations to Olympian parties. This could be my one shot at making that threat go away and I will not let you stand in the way. Eternal being or not, I will escort you to the Freakshow or die by your hand fighting."

Brooks' jaw ticked, pain shooting up his temple as he clamped his mouth shut. She knew all the right buttons to push just to piss him off. Chaos probed her mind again, breathing in her emotions and fears.

The taste of deceit is still there, but no lie. It will have to be good enough until we unravel her truth as slowly as fraying thread.

"Fine. You show us the way and help us blend in, I'll get you into the Freakshow."

Nyx nodded but didn't say anything in return. She didn't have to. The embers in her eyes sparked to raging violet flames and admiration bloomed in his chest. The girl fought like she had nothing left to lose, but Brooks knew better. The fragile world she carried on her shoulders would shatter if she faltered. She crumbled as she carried it, sacrificing pieces of herself to foster the pressure, but she did not break.

He knew how that felt now and would do anything to keep his world safe. He couldn't begrudge Nyx for the strength she wielded. Brooks nodded in return to seal the silent agreement before moving onto what really mattered.

"How do we get there?"

Nyx's lips thinned as she tapped her fingers on the wooden table. Begrudgingly, she answered, "There's a portal to Dion here at your altar. The Olympians don't know we have it, and I want it to stay that way." She looked pointedly in his direction.

"Don't look at me like that," he scoffed. "Who am I going to tell, Nyx?"

"I don't know, but you have a tendency to leave people to die because you're bored so I'm making sure you know to shut the fuck up about it and not blab it to the first person who asks."

"I don't have any interest meddling in matters of your kind," Chaos' voice lingered with Brooks'.

"As you've made that brazenly clear for centuries now." Her eyes rolled and the ever-present annoyance scrunched her nose.

I still want to hang her by her toes over an abyss.

"I kind of like her," Brooks chuckled inwardly.

"Where is the altar, Nyx," Chaos demanded.

This is my last attempt at civility before I tear through her mind to find what I want and remind her what we are capable of.

"Just calm down, We're not going to get her to answer questions if you threaten her. If we are patient, she will soften."

I don't need her to be soft. I need her to be obedient.

"It's hidden," she shrugged and looked at her nails.

Chaos grasped control from Brooks and slammed his hands on the table as he stood, a resounding crack booming through the room as his chair shattered on the wall behind him. He called forth his chaos, sending his shadows flying like daggers to pierce her skin. They had Nyx out of her chair and pinned against the wall before she could scream. He sent curls of shadow through her nose and ears, each prodding her mind and bending it to his will. She screamed but was powerless to stop his assault.

He closed his eyes and inhaled deeply as he breathed in her memories and filtered through in search of thoughts around a portal. Images flicked across his vision one second after another, the scene like flipping the pages of an endless book until he found what he was looking for.

Nyx threw on a black cloak as she tucked daggers into various sheaths hidden along her lithe form. Shaky fingers tied the cloak tight and pulled the hood over midnight hair. She threw one last glance over shoulder to a messy head strung with different shades of golden curls. Both love and sadness filled her heart and the two warred inside. If Nyx couldn't find something to steal tonight, that little girl would starve.

She was just a babe, her innocence as pure as the brightest of blooms in spring. Evangeline didn't deserve to live in this desolate place any more than she deserved to be subjected to horrors outside of the altar's protection.

Bitterness was a sour stone in her gut as Nyx slipped out the door and into the night. She hated living in the shadow of a fake idol. Was it any better than living under the eyes of false gods? She'd never know. She hated all of them.

Across from the rundown building she called home was a tree line of evergreens that stayed thick and lively through every season. It was perfect to hide the sacred cave entrance to the altar of Chaos. Many holy men in the village maintained the sanctuary in His honor. Some had even taken vows of silence in hopes that their dedication would bring the god back to save them.

Nyx knew better.

Religious commitment only robbed men of the one life they were granted, and for what? Daemon-kind were all dust in the end, dying in the same shitty place and forgotten. The only difference between them and the holy men was that the committed died at the feet of a malevolent god who cared naught for their sacrifice.

Nyx broke through the tree line and stepped onto the worn trail that rose steadily just as the land did. It crossed and disappeared in places to give it the guise of animal trails, but the townspeople knew which direction to take by heart. Their religion resembled a cult, a fanaticism running so deep in the blood that they didn't know anything else. Even if it meant sacrificing children for the hope of a good harvest. She wished she could pull Evangeline from that, too.

Sticks crunched under her feet, joining the chorus of nightlife coming alive in the forest. Crickets and frogs chirped as wings rustled in the canopy. Helios, the golden god driving his steeds across the horizon to bring the sun, finished his ride across the sky and night had finally fallen in earnest.

Good. Nyx fucking hated the sunlight and could live the rest of her life hiding from it. She thrived in the dark. Where others stumbled blindly she navigated without error. It may even be possible that she saw better at night than she did during the day.

And the peace...

Nothing brought peace like the night sky.

The cave mouth was quite the trek from the town, but she could sense its nearness. Electricity buzzed against her skin and lifted the hairs off the back of her neck. The need to fight or run was an urge creeping through her blood, but she focused to push it back with deep breaths. Chaos was heavy in the air, and she hadn't even stepped through the entrance yet.

When the cavernous opening came into view she stepped eagerly into the dark and quickened her steps. She wanted to get through the creepy worship site as fast as possible. Something about grown men worshiping another grown man made her skin crawl.

No canals or side tunnels branched off from the main entrance and it sent beetles crawling through her stomach every time. Walking into a place where the only exit was the entrance was a death sentence.

The patter of her boots and heavy breaths bounced off the walls and echoed back, filling the empty space like tiny explosions. She wondered in passing if that was some sort of safety mechanism the holy men had in place to alert them to trespassers.

It was about a ten-minute walk through the winding hallway before she got to the great open room housing the statue and altar. She stopped as she did every time to survey the room of worship. Delicate flourishes were carved into every inch of wall space and up to the round ceiling. Splashes of color from crushed flowers and fermented fruits painted along the swirls in intricate patterns had long since faded, and the pews that used to hold hundreds of worshippers had crumbled to dust.

She let her eyes follow the single walkway between the rows of pews up to the main feature. Several steps covered in dripping wax candles led up to a well fashioned from fine metals and jewels, a silent sacrifice to the god who would never answer. If Nyx had her way it would be dismantled and sold to feed their town, but as long as there was a holy man occupying the altar she was shit out of luck.

The gilded monstrosity stood at the base of a great monolith where Chaos himself was carved into a single piece of marble. He stood strong, his naked body lean and carved with fine-tuned definition. He wore a crown of stars upon his head, the eight pointed symbol of his power accentuated in the middle.

Nyx stared into the eyes of the forgotten god and pushed back the anger. She would never, as long as she lived, understand.

"Protect me or else, motherfucker. These people believe in you and die upon your altar hoping themselves worthy enough of a resting place at your side. The least you can do is make sure I don't die as I risk my ass to feed and care for them." She used her hand to cross her chest in eight directions to honor Him, and then threw up both middle fingers as she walked down the deserted path to the well without giving Him a second glance.

Nyx made quick work of navigating the maze of ruined candles and side stepped the gaudy well to stop at the statue's feet. Illuminated in a soft blue glow was a free-flowing shape that rippled around the edges like a pool of water. The portal was faint and could be missed if you weren't looking, but the power radiating from it was unmistakable. Pure chaos charged the slice of marble between the great legs of Chaos, and it would bend to her will.

Tonight, Nyx had her mind set on the biggest target yet— Club Hel. Situated on the island of Anthemoessa was the epitome of sin where daemon of all types converged to revel in their darkest of desires. From the moment she heard whispers of its existence, she knew it would be a prize.

Nyx had spent weeks scoping the place out and it was now or never. She was out of options and people she cared for were starving. Tonight, she would break into Club Hel and steal enough from Level Pride to keep her town full for the coming months, even if she had to damn her soul to do it.

Brooks fell from the memory as Chaos receded back into the dark corners of his mind. His well was utterly drained. Chaos couldn't hold on long enough to see Nyx go through the portal, but Brooks was confident that the unforgiving part of himself found what he needed. Nyx slumped to the floor as the onslaught ceased and was a mess of curses and tears. Guilt was a heavy weight in his stomach.

"How could you have done that? You just shredded through her mind like she was nothing, Chaos! You can't do that to people!"

Next time, she will do as she's asked. She chose her actions knowing what consequences would follow.

"What the fuck did you do to me?" She coughed and sputtered, her words coming out choked as her brain fought to function.

"We will use the portal in your place of worship to travel to Dion," Chaos spoke. "The blood moon is in two days' time by your calculation, so we'll spend tomorrow preparing. By sunrise we'll be through the portal."

"And then what?" Nyx spat as she stood on shaky legs.

"Then we wait until the portal makes itself known as the invitation said," Brooks sighed.

"I know you don't know anything because you've been frolicking in delusion for the entirety of your life. Sit still and play house with your little girlfriend while I figure this shit out like I always do. You'll just get in the way."

"I will not sit idle just as I will not place Xia's fate in your hands."

She vented a frustrated growl as she pulled her hair. "You are so impossible."

Nyx paced the length of the open room and he stayed silent as he watched her wear the wood down step by anxious step. The click of a door closing sounded, but he was too focused on the girl in front of him to turn.

"Xia and I will be leaving by the second sunrise whether you like my plans or not. You will say your goodbyes and put your affairs in order if you want to come."

Nyx stopped and stared, her contemplative gaze boring a hole through his forehead.

She's probably trying to set you on fire with the chaos she does not possess.

"What did you do to me?" Her voice was low, but each word was said with deadly precision.

"I tasted your memories," he answered plainly.

"Meaning?"

"I scoured your mind until I found the answer to the question I gave you several chances to answer."

"You held me down against my will, entered my mind without permission, and then used it as a weapon against me?"

How could he explain that it wasn't him that'd done it? How even though he and Chaos shared a mind and body, they were completely different beings.

"Yes." His jaw clenched at the admission.

"Yeah," Nyx scoffed. "That's what I thought. Aren't you going to the Freakshow to hunt down and kill some doctor who did the same thing to you?"

Was that what he was doing?

"Yes."

"Maybe you should just join her since you're not any fucking better." Tears glazed her glowing violet eyes and the indignation in her voice hurt.

We are doing what we must.

Nyx turned her back on him and walked with silent, deliberate steps down the hall and to her room. He would never tell her that he could hear the soft sobs filtering through the thin walls, or taste the salt of sadness and despair radiating from her soul as she poured it out in private.

"Brooks?"

Xia's voice eased a layer of calm back over his body like a blanket, but he couldn't help but stare after Nyx. Her words were unsettling, and he wanted to crawl out of his skin.

"What was all of that about?" She spoke from the door without walking toward him.

"There was information I needed to keep you safe. She wouldn't give it, so Chaos took it."

"What do you mean, took it?"

"I…" He turned to face Xia and watched with sorrow as unease settled across her beautiful features. "I seized her mind to find the location of the portal. I did it so we could leave this place and get one step closer to our forever."

"Brooks." Xia shook her head as she stepped back. Fear turned to fury as the blues churned with the greens in her eyes. "You can't just hurt people to get what you want."

Brooks swallowed as the weight of what he was going to say rested on his chest. He knew she wouldn't like it, but he would not lie to her. Though Chaos was the one who hurt the girl, Brooks wasn't sure he would take it back. He met her stare and didn't falter as he said, "I am not a person, Xia. I am the Father of Chaos, and I will not hesitate to hurt or kill anyone who stands in my path. You are my priority, and if the world has to burn for it, then so be it."

Unleash
your
Chaos

Xia
28

Xia stood with her back pressed against the door and couldn't move, or breathe, or think. Her heart rate picked up speed as her mind tried to understand what she'd just seen and heard.

That was not the man she'd met in the asylum.

"I think we need to talk."

His brows knit as he swallowed and nodded, his hand gesturing down the hall to their shared room. Xia led the way and her body was all too aware of his presence at her back. They stepped through the threshold, and didn't turn as the door clicked shut. She'd wanted nothing other than to be in his arms for so long, but the man who walked out of that asylum was not the same one who was held prisoner.

He told us that. You simply refused to listen.

"I need to understand what's happening," she whispered. "Who this person is." Xia turned to face him then but kept her distance. She didn't want the needs of her body to muddle those of her heart. "I need to know that you're a safe haven to stand by me as I heal. I don't need another captor, Brooks."

"Xia, I would never–"

"Not intentionally, I know." She cut him off. "But this innate need to protect isn't going to allow me to grow. It's going to suffocate me. Do you understand that?"

He looked to the floor as a single tear caught the moonlight and fell to his feet. "I just want to give you everything," he whispered.

And you will take everything.

Xia closed the distance between them in two long strides and held his face between her palms. "You *are* everything, Brooks. I don't need you to be more than that. You kept me tethered to this world when I wanted nothing more than to see it end. You deserve a partner who makes you better by complimenting you in every way, and I want to be that for you," she swallowed as her Siren rose and lended her strength. "I don't need anyone to give me what I want. If it's important, I will take it. If I need it, I will ask. If it involves me or my life, I will make the decisions. I want to stand by your side. Not in your shadow."

Xia dipped her head to catch his gaze and urged his chin upward. He needed to know what she felt for him, and how much he meant to her.

He needs to know that we are not weak, and we do not bow. We are survivors.

"I've never second-guessed us, Brooks. From the moment I saw you on that beach, it was us. I will walk by your side wherever you want to take me, but I will not follow behind."

Brooks nodded, the different shades of blue in his navy eyes highlighted by the white light pouring through the window. "I'll learn how to be better for you, Sunshine."

Xia leaned in to press her forehead against his as she held the man who owned her heart. "You're perfect for me." The rawness of her confession thickened the space between them. "The balance to my darkness."

Brooks brushed his nose against hers, the ghost of a kiss whispering across her lips. She leaned in and pulled his mouth to hers, the stubble on his chin leaving tingles across her skin. His kisses were tentative and his hands stayed pinned behind his back.

"You can touch me," she said as she nipped his lip.

"I don't want to make you–"

Her Siren burst through the surface as she gripped his neck and forced him to the wall, the structure groaning under the pressure. Iridescent scales dotted her hands as a shimmer cast down her arm. *"I did not ask,"* she hissed. "You will touch me, God of Chaos, or I will bring you to your knees."

Chaos rose to her Siren's call, his ice coating the floor meeting her fire head on. "And if I prefer to be on my knees, Siren? What then?"

Xia gripped tighter and smiled as black veins bulged from his neck and forehead. His eyes closed, the muscle of his jaw flexing under clenched teeth. She leaned in, brushed her lips against his ear and whispered, "Then I will relish watching the almighty Chaos as he falls to worship his queen."

Xia reached behind and grasped a hand to place around her waist. His palm covered the expanse of her lower back and radiated warmth against her skin. She shivered as she placed kiss after kiss along his jawline, pleased as his grip tightened around her gown.

Emboldened, Xia reached for his other hand and placed it on her breast as she arched into him. His breath stuttered as a fine tremor shook his hands.

"How do you do that to me with just a touch?"

His grip tightened around her waist as the other hand slipped from her chest to the curve of her face. His fingers laced into the hair behind her ear and he used the grip to hold her mouth to his.

"You taste like fucking sunshine," he moaned against her, the desperate pull of his words stoking the fire in her belly. "It drives me crazy, Siren."

Xia pressed her body into his and giggled when the door rattled under the impact. He smiled against her lips and she used the opening to slip her tongue in to lick against his. The action churned the desperation between them and he responded in force.

Unleash your Chaos

Nyx

29

Nyx stepped into the inky night with quick steps. She didn't know where she was going, but she needed to get away from the noises in the room next to hers. If she'd done the people staying in her house any favors, it was finding them somewhere else to sleep while her new *guests* were in residence. She already couldn't fucking wait until they were gone.

The cold nipped at her heels as she chased the puff of steam clouding with each breath. Winter had come in full force and they'd never been less prepared. She knew she needed to check in on everyone before she left with Chaos and Xia, but a leaden ball of dread soured in her gut. She loved the people she protected and would never leave them behind. Sometimes though...

Sometimes the weight was *so* heavy.

"Pull yourself together, Nyx. Weak people don't leave their mark, and they don't die with honor." She steeled her spine and turned to walk toward the quiet village nestled in the valley between two hills. Nyx had called Avyssos home for as long as she could remember, and assumed she would die just as she'd been born– alone. A pawn.

At least her mark would be left. There would be people to remember her and what she did for them when they couldn't do it for themselves.

No candlelight burned in the windows and the plumes of smoke floating from the makeshift chimneys spoke of dying fires. She made a note to check their stores of firewood to make sure everyone stayed warm while she was gone. They were already starving. She wouldn't let them go cold, too.

The first rays of sunlight crested the horizon as she met the bottom of the town. One main road ran straight through the middle with housing on either side. There were no stores or markets, no shops for people to buy and sell. Everything was shared, because that's what happens when you scrounge for every resource.

Some smaller paths branched off the main road with clusters of smaller homes. Back when the town was closer to thriving, children were born and raised and then settled in houses behind their parents. Some of them moved on to bigger cities or went on grand adventures, but the heavy religious practices in Avyssos taught that this was the only safe place, and most of its citizens took that to heart. The majority of the children born there would never leave, and now they paid for the sins of their parents.

Homes disintegrated over time and fell to ruin. Parents grew old and sick, and when they died the oldest of their children took over the main house. That was the natural order of events. As the Olympians grew greedier, however, there was less travel to and from trade posts. Money stopped flowing, and the land was too desolate to be farmed. Soon, women lost their fertility to starvation. Children stopped filling those smaller houses, and the town didn't have the resources to maintain something that would never be of use again.

Nyx swallowed past the lump in her throat. She'd failed the people of Avyssos in more ways than one when she refused to die. She took their hope, and as it died so did their will to thrive. All was lost. They were alive, but was this any kind of life to live? There was an insecurity inside that wondered if she'd done them a disservice by living. Would they have been happier with her death?

Just as she hit the bottom of desolation, a laugh as precious as chiming bells rang through her memories. Beautiful blonde curls born of honey and sunlight bounced around her mother's legs as she played hide and seek. Nyx smiled through her tears as she relived the memories of chasing Evangeline down the river bank and jumping out from behind hanging linens to scare her.

Evangeline... The only child born to Avyssos since Nyx was old enough to retain memories. The pregnancy was a miracle. Everyone showered her with food and blankets woven from the softest furs.

The holy men claimed that the babe growing in her womb was a sign from Chaos himself. Evangeline was the morning star and would guide them into salvation. Nyx didn't have the heart to tell them that it was just a one in a million chance.

Evangeline's mom, Adriana, had been sent to a trade post in search of autumn seeds to sow in hopes they would be blessed with ripe fruits and grains. Since the loss of her daughter Persephone, Demeter no longer blessed the fields of Olympia. They were left sullen and empty just as her heart was. The goddess of harvest and fertile lands left the world to die, just as it had left her only daughter.

It was a pity everyone else had to suffer the consequences. Such was the petty, immature nature of The Twelve. Demeter couldn't see that she was making an entire population suffer her fate. Women lost children every day to hunger or sickness, but it mattered not. If Demeter was suffering, so too was the world.

Adriana had been gone for weeks and they'd all assumed she abandoned them or had been killed. It was a shock when she came back. No seeds or dried meats filled her bag, but she carried something even more precious.

Nyx would give the holy men some credit. The town's spirits were raised and, for a time, everything seemed like it would be okay. As time passed, however, with no signs of Chaos, gloom settled back into their hearts.

Nyx studied that despair as she walked through the quiet street. Straw rotted on top of woven branch roofs and wooden planks split and crumbled from the walls. It made her heart sick, but she was only one person. Nyx worked day in and day out to keep her house as shapely as she could to provide shelter in times of need, but she couldn't thatch every roof or replace every rotted structure.

The sleeping town stretched as it woke, murmurs floating

through windows and kettles being placed in the fire. The smell of cooking oats wafted through the air and Nyx's stomach rumbled. She'd given that ungrateful asshole of a god her last ration of bread, cheese, and meat. Privileges like fruit and honey had long since run out, so every meal consisted of boiled oats. It wasn't nutritious, but it kept the stomach full.

Another wave of guilt hit when she thought about the platter of food he'd provided for their talk. Nyx hid it away in hopes that Brooks would forget he ever summoned it. She wouldn't be sharing it with the town, but she also wouldn't be saving it for herself.

Evangeline needed it most.

The moan of wooden hinges broke the easy quiet and a man stepped through the door. He was tall with muddy hair and a beard that needed trimming for the last few years. Nyx could imagine that in another life he would have been handsome and well built. His frame was thick and corded muscle shaped his arms, but starvation hollowed his cheeks and hugged his ribs.

"Andreas," she nodded in greeting. He was the man in charge of logging and splitting firewood in the town. He'd produced less and less over the years, but she was grateful for whatever help he was willing to lend.

"Hey, Nyx. It's a bit early for you to be out. What brings you down from the hill?"

"I..." She stopped short. "I'm going away for a while."

Concerned deepened the lines in his forehead and widened his forest green eyes.

"Not like that," she hurried. "My last trip was a bust. I couldn't get anything worthwhile, so I need to start looking somewhere else."

The concern was still etched, but it softened just a touch. "That's no good," he admitted. "I know you'll find something for us to use, though. You always do, Nyx. That's why we depend on you."

In that moment, her responsibility felt more dire than a weighted backpack on her shoulders. Instead, it felt like a ball and chain locked around her ankle, and Andreas had just pushed her overboard into the sea.

Could she swim?

"I won't let you down, Andreas."

"I know you won't." He studied his shoes coming apart at the seams, but the purse of his lips told her he wasn't done speaking. "My wife had a dream last night that you found us a miracle." He looked back up with pleading eyes and Nyx nearly faltered under the burden of it. "You found it and everything changed. We had more food than we knew what to do with. Her cycles returned and her belly swelled with the promise of a new start."

A tear fell down his sun-worn cheek and the fractures of her soul cracked a little further.

"Keep that hope, Andreas. We will need it to get through this winter."

He nodded and Nyx gave him a silent moment to gather composure. "So," he sniffled and wiped at his nose. "How long will you be gone this time?"

Nyx looked at the river and the straw lined banks. "I'm not sure. I have a big lead and it may take me a while to make it work. I won't be coming home in between. This is a one and done."

Andreas nodded and Nyx turned back to catch his gaze, holding it stern and steady. "I need your help while I'm gone. Someone is going to have to make sure Evangeline is taken care of and that my great room stays open for anyone who needs it." Nyx considered telling him about the food stores, but she'd seen the desperation in his eyes. There was no need to put that burden on his conscience.

"I can do that."

"Good. I promise I'll be back before spring, and I'll have the money Ares requires." Nyx clapped him on the shoulder in dismissal before walking away. She didn't do goodbyes.

Nyx filled her morning with chores alongside the people she loved. Together, they gathered water to boil for drinking and dumped in large wooden buckets to clean tattered linens. Firewood was carried to the main stock shed to keep it safe from falling snow and straw collected from the river bank to reinforce their roofs for winter. Mud would need to be gathered to fill in holes and bind planks to insulate for the coming cold. So much to do, and so few able bodies to do it.

Usually she was the one to delegate tasks, but Nyx didn't have the fortitude to lead like that today. She busied herself by carrying bucket after bucket of water from the slippery banks back to the waiting wooden barrels. The monotony blurred her surroundings and soon she lost track of them altogether.

On her seventh trip back to dump the water, a hand brushed her shoulder. Adrenaline flared as she spun the bucket, intent to throw her attacker off with the water before maneuvering them to the ground, but when the water stopped mid-air, Nyx stumbled backward.

The hovering liquid gathered into a stream and poured itself into the waiting barrel. Standing in front of her was the pale woman she'd been so desperate to avoid.

"You scared the shit out of me!"

"I'm sorry." Xia smiled placatingly, and Nyx wanted to wipe it from her pretty face. "I didn't mean to. I called your name a few times, but I guess you didn't hear me."

"Huh," Nyx huffed.

"You seemed lost in your work. I thought I could come to help."

"Help with what? What do you know about what this place needs?" Nyx answered defensively.

"Not much." Xia's response was neither sarcastic nor passive aggressive. Her brows dipped, lips thinning as she looked away.

"Well." Nyx brushed nonexistent dirt from her shirt as she grasped for words. "What can you do?"

"Anything you need. I don't have a wide range of skills, but I'm a quick study and don't mind getting my hands dirty. I helped Ruby with the laundry yesterday. Maybe I could start there."

"Who the fuck is Ruby?" She knew every single person in the village, and not a single one went by the name Ruby.

"She saved me from Ariadne and was kind enough to find me this shirt." Xia gestured to the worn flax."

"What did she look like?"

"I... I'm not really sure. She was just a woman. Petite. She wore a gown with her hair tucked under a hood. She had the most stunning pink eyes though. I've never seen anything like them."

Nyx tucked that information away for later. She would find this Ruby and figure out why the fuck she was living in Nyx's town unannounced. It could be that she blew in on the wind while Nyx was away, but someone would have told her about the newcomer by now.

Right?

"Okay. Well, Right now I'm just gathering water. We need to fill all ten of these barrels. Most will be divided into the homes and boiled for safe drinking. About four of them will stay for washing. We need to prep water to store for winter and give the linen a final scrub. Winter brings sickness, and the last thing these people need is dirty linen to lie on while trying to heal."

Xia nodded and accepted the bucket Nyx handed her. Nyx didn't look back as she walked toward the river. If she had to explain how to fill up a fucking bucket she would just send the damsel back to her prince charming.

"Nyx?" That sing-song voice called from behind and grated on her nerves. How could someone's life be so perfect? Nyx bet Evangeline's dinner that Xia had never known a day of strife. Even Aphrodite would weep in her presence.

Bitch.

"What, princess?" Annoyance oozed from her voice as she kept walking. When no answer came, Nyx scoffed and knelt by the waiting pool of water. She pressed her bucket to the top, careful not to collect too much debris, when the water shivered. Ripples went against the current as tendrils rose and drifted seamlessly behind her.

Nyx turned and watched in awe as Xia used her chaos with ease. Xia's feet were planted and her body moved as delicate as the water she wielded. Her arms ebbed and flowed like the tide. The crystalline streams thickened as they traveled and filled the buckets. A fine mist sprinkled Nyx's upturned chin as fine as the morning fog. When the streams stopped, Nyx stood and damn near ran back to where ten full barrels sat.

Incredible.

"How did you do that?"

"I'm a Siren, Nyx. I live and breathe the water. I understand it better than anyone or anything in the world."

Nyx fell back to reality and crossed her arms. She wasn't supposed to be impressed. She risked her ass and her town to save the dainty female and haul her brute of a boyfriend back.

"Good. Now you can save me time and take the barrels where they need to go. Four to the laundry, six to the town. You'll need to gather pails from every home, fill them up, and return for boiling. It'll take you the better part of the day, princess, so you better get moving."

Nyx turned to stomp away, but Xia called her name again.

"It's already clean."

"Excuse me?" Nyx spat.

"The water. It's clean and ready to drink."

"That river is full of shit and bacteria. It needs to be boiled."

"It's clean, Nyx." Xia said each word slowly and with care as if she were speaking to a child, and fuck if it didn't ruffle Nyx's feathers even more. "I've also been thinking of a way other than this to provide water for the people. If we could dig a hole deep in the ground, we could tap into water from the river. The minerals in the ground would filter anything harmful from it and the heat from the ground would stop it from freezing.

"I'm not risking people's lives on your word. Do the godsdamned work or go back to your castle." Nyx turned and didn't look back.

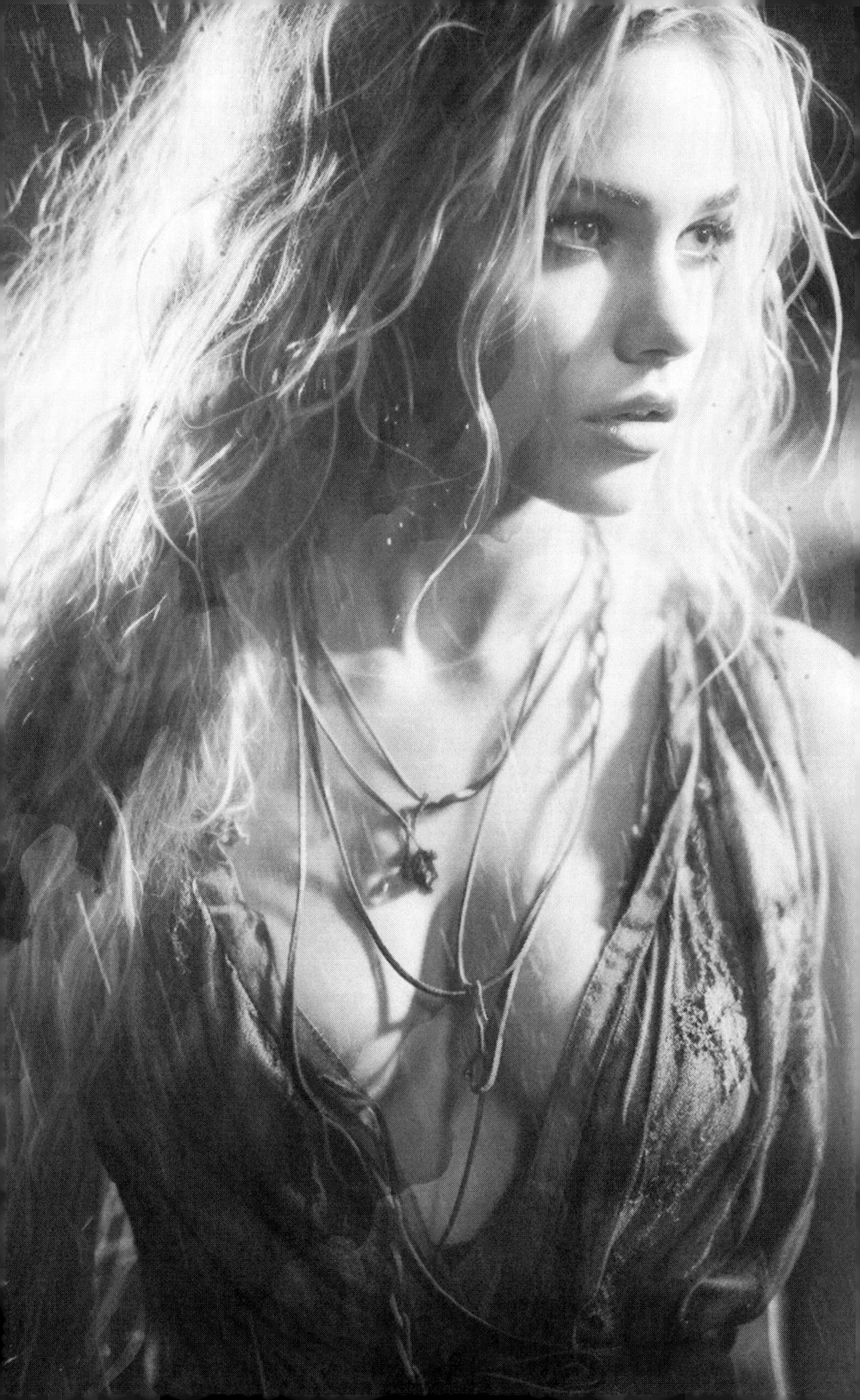

Xia
30

She watched in silent apprehension as Nyx stomped toward the waking town. The girl was high-strung and lived in a constant state of sassy retorts and defensive curses, but Xia recognized it for what it was— her shield.

Everyone's armor is made of something different.

In many ways, Xia had been a princess locked in a gilded tower. She was surrounded by luxury with every basic need met. A princess, just like Nyx said. From the outside looking in, Xia had no reason to be miserable.

She will never know what it was like for us there. She may struggle for resources, but there are people who love and support her. We had nothing.

Maybe Xia had hoped she could find a kindred spirit in Nyx. Someone who could understand what it was like to have to live within a coat of armor to survive. To don something every day that protected the softness within.

"Perhaps that's why her words hurt."

We do not need her.

"No," Xia sighed. "We don't need her, but it would be nice to have her. We've never been allowed the luxury of daemon connection. Do you not think it would be good to have a friend?"

Putting your trust in another is simply handing them a blade to stab you with.

Xia shut her Siren out as frustration roiled inside. They may share a mind, but that didn't mean they had to agree. Xia wanted Nyx's friendship, and so she would keep trying.

"I just have to give her time and change her mind." She talked aloud as she worked to fill the water pails. She wasn't sure what the townspeople did after boiling, and Nyx didn't seem to trust that it was clean, so she did what she was told. Xia could have had it done in minutes, but instead she worked with her hands to pass the time and soothe her mind.

Collecting and filling the buckets had been the easy part. Carrying them back to their homes, however, was a different chore. The weight pulled at her shoulders, and she had to take more than one in each hand to finish before sundown.

By the fifth trip she was sweating. By the tenth she feared her heart would jump out of her chest.

When the fifteenth came around, a brush of shadow curled against her chaos and whispered, *"Is everything okay?"*

Xia leaned against a barrel and wiped the sweat beading along her brow. *"I'm fine,"* she huffed. *"Just doing some manual labor."*

"Good. I've only known one thing to make our hearts race like this, and I thought I was going to have to come–"

"Do nothing," Xia scolded.

"You're right. I could at least stand behind in case you needed me."

"No need. Unless you want to come help carry these buckets of water."

"Sorry. I have to clean between my toes, and that takes ages. Rain check?"

"Have I ever told you that you're insufferable?"

"A few different ways, actually, and a lot of different times, but it's a good reminder, Siren. After last night, I'd say 'insatiable' fits better, don't you?"

"Go away or I'll drown you."

"Talk dirty to me!"

"Goodbye, Brooks."

His chuckle faded as the presence of his chaos drifted from hers. She'd left him fast asleep in their shared bed. Her cheeks heated as she recalled the thin sheet draped over his thighs as the rest stayed on display. Finely corded muscle flexed as he dreamed, and the smile she caught as she rolled out of bed chased away the cold.

"Do you need some help with that?"

Startled, Xia turned toward the intruding voice to see Ruby leaning against the barrel beside her. It would seem Nyx wasn't the only person losing track of their surroundings.

"Hey, Ruby," Xia smiled. "I'd love a hand if you're free. All of the barrels are full. I've just been filling the buckets and taking them back to their houses."

Ruby frowned as she looked between Xia and the barrels. "Why are you taking them back?"

"Uh, well, that's what Nyx wanted me to do?" Xia was caught off guard by the question and sounded a bit more dumbfounded than she would have preferred.

"You can filter the water, can you not?"

"Well, yes."

"So why are we not taking the barrels to the winter storage building?"

"I... I'm not sure. Nyx seemed to think we should boil it just in case, to lower the risk of illness."

"Interesting." Her tone combined with the purse of lips led Xia to believe there was something she wasn't saying.

"What's interesting?"

"Oh, nothing." Ruby swatted the air in dismissal and bent to pick up four full pails of water.

"You can speak freely, Ruby."

One pink strand fell from the white linen cap as she nodded contemplatively. After a moment, she put the buckets back down and crossed her arms. "It just seems a bit disrespectful. Like she doesn't think you're good enough to do what you so clearly can."

"She doesn't really know me though, Ruby. She just wants to keep her people safe."

"Maybe. I've seen her do that to a lot of people here, though. She makes some really bold assumptions and is quick to condemn."

"I'm sure it's hard to trust outsiders. I haven't done much to prove I'm not a hindrance. She will come around."

"I hope so for your sake. I remember when I first settled here and she was away, but no one would tell me where she went or why, which was super weird. Anyway, not the point. The point is, I came from a modern place. Electricity, running water, food you could glutton yourself on for days."

Xia nodded, all too familiar with the benefits of the more lavish side of life. She was curious as to how Ruby ended up in a primitive town, but didn't want to ask. Ruby could flip the question and Xia wasn't prepared to trust someone with that information.

"When Nyx came back," Ruby continued. "I asked to speak to her about some ways we could improve, but she refused to see me."

"Why would she do that?"

"I'm not sure. Everyone says she's secretive. Comes and goes as she pleases but they don't question it because she brings back money or supplies. Keeps them fed, you know? And you don't bite the hand that feeds."

"Is she from here?"

"I've never asked. I would hope so since she takes the most accommodating and well-kept house in the town. It could very well house several families, but instead she lives there alone."

"Several people sleep in the great room by the fire," Xia countered. There had to have been ten or more people tucked away in the great room when she woke that first night to find Brooks.

"Yeah," Ruby scoffed. "Only if you offer her something in return."

The statement stunned Xia, her stomach lurching. Nyx hadn't seemed the type of daemon to require a trade for a warm place to sleep, but what did she actually know about the girl?

Xia offered a valid solution to make village life easier. A central well accessible to everyone with a consistent source of freshwater, but Nyx wasn't even willing to let her finish explaining. Had she judged Nyx the wrong way? Instead of a strong daemon willing to fight and claw to save her town, could she be looking at a bitter woman holding helpless people under her thumb?

"What did you want to talk to her about? What improvements?"

"Running water. We live in a valley between two big hills. With a little bit of planning and hard work, we could easily create a sort of watershed pond that we control with a dam. I was foraging for the few fruits and herbs that grow here this past summer and came across a familiar patch of red soil that was cracked along the top. It was a bit brittle, but so dense. I took a closer look and realized it was the same soil my mother used to wet and mold. I was so excited that I dropped my pail and ran straight back to town to find her."

"What's so special about the red soil?"

"It's clay!" Ruby exclaimed. "You can mine it and use it to line the bottom of a hole. It's nearly impossible for the water to soak away into the ground."

Xia's face lit up as she realized the intention behind her suggestion. She grabbed her companion by the arms and shook her gently. "Yes! Ruby, you're brilliant! We could structure a small drain off the river that tunnels down to a large hole lined with clay. We build two dams– one at the very start of the drain entrance so the water doesn't erode a large path through the town, and another one that crosses the length of the pond. We use the dam to control the water flow. Over time we could build off of it and get running water to each house!"

"I know! No more wasted time or energy breaking backs to carry water from the river just to sort and carry somewhere else. A day's work could turn into a matter of minutes. It would take a while to find enough clay to mine, but we could make it work."

"You said it holds water right?"

"Well, yeah. More so in the winter and spring I would think, since the ground stays saturated with rain and snow."

"If you took me to the place you found, I could determine how much water it holds, look for the similar spots, and mark it. Then we wouldn't have to search. We could focus time and energy gathering it rather than finding it."

"You can do that?" Ruby came alive like a mad scientist, and Xia was her partner in crime.

"Yes! It would be easy. As far as I can tell, my connection to water is infinite. I love it and, well, it loves me back. It's a bit wild, actually. It's like we're drawn to each other."

"You must have a crazy amount of chaos running through your veins."

Xia pulled back, cleared her throat and attempted to cover the awkwardness with a laugh. "I wouldn't say that. My father was a gifted nymph. Just following in his footsteps, I suppose."

"Either way, you're a real prize, Xia. We will be lucky to have you."

Xia climbed the hill leading to Nyx's house. Blisters lined her palms from carrying pails and her feet ached, but the pride and satisfaction were worth it. She would prove to Nyx that she wasn't a useless princess.

She questioned for the millionth time why she cared what the bitter girl thought of her, but every time she asked she knew the answer never changed.

When she and her sisters were younger and happy on Anthemoessa, life was bliss. The love between them ran soul-deep. Like every relationship, it wasn't always sunshine and rainbows. They bickered often and sometimes bickering turned into fights. When it was really bad, the fights morphed into endless days of silence.

Since there were three of them, it typically meant someone was always caught in the middle. Xia learned early not to take sides when her sisters fought. Two against one was never fair, and women had the ability to hold grudges for millennia. Xia watched her sisters fight a hundred times, and each argument consisted of smart remarks and surface level insults. When Brooks and Nyx bickered, it was like diving into a piece of her past. They acted just as her grappling sisters had, petty anger and taunting jabs.

Xia realized then why she was drawn to Nyx. It was more than a shared bond through trauma. Nyx reminded Xia of oldest sister, Molpe.

Molpe was dangerous. She had a spirit composed of fire and acid but was the coldest of them all. Molpe was hard on Xia. If Xia stumbled and scraped her knee, her sister would punch her in the shoulder and tell her to stop feeling sorry and stand up.

"Don't let anyone see you cry. If you show them weakness, they will break you. You're either a fighter or you're dead, Xia. Do you understand?"

Nyx was Molpe reincarnated. It both warmed and shattered Xia's heart. She couldn't save her sisters, but maybe she could help Nyx save herself.

Xia shook her head and looked to the sky hoping to dry the tears before they fell. She didn't want to think about those years. Moving on meant remembering the good and the bad, but it didn't do any good to dwell on the nightmare.

Xia walked up the steps and chewed her nails as she used her last seconds forming a plan to mend what Brooks may have broken. He had breached a major line of trust, but Xia hoped the line was bent and not broken.

Nyx would have to understand that he was new to this world. As all knowing as he was, he was ignorant to the complexity of relationships and feelings. Brooks may have been soft-hearted, but Chaos was an unforgiving force with no such compunctions.

Xia pushed through the door and found Brooks sitting at the table staring at the bloody piece of parchment from the night before. Her heart squeezed as her thoughts flickered back to the panic that held him tight as a vice.

"Hey, you," she said gently so as not to startle him.

Brooks looked up and she caught the remnants of haze clearing. "Hey, Sunshine. Did you enjoy your morning?"

"I did. I helped Nyx prepare the water for winter and then..." she trailed off, unsure as to whether or not she should mention Nyx's behavior. That was what couples did, right? Confided in one another? "Nyx got kind of upset and left, so Ruby came to help me."

"I'm going to have to meet this Ruby you're spending so much time with to make sure she's safe to be around."

A small flame of agitation sparked in her chest as her Siren hissed, but she tried to brush it off. Days ago he couldn't trust anyone or anything. Why would she expect him to just let that go?

"He was joking," she thought. *"He's just having a hard time adjusting from the asylum."*

He is testing our patience.

Xia shook her off before saying, "No need, you big bully. I am completely capable of judging someone's character all on my own."

"Obviously not. Look at the company you keep." Brooks gestured toward himself and the most obnoxious snort laugh burst past her lips.

"Now that I think about it, you're right. Please vet her for friendship starting with a thousand-page questionnaire about her intentions. And while you're at it, fill one out alongside her."

"You're brutal, Siren." He shook his head and waved her over. "Don't just stand there. Come sit."

"I'd love to. My feet are killing me."

Xia sat in the chair beside him and moved to pull the worn shoes from her feet, but before she could reach them, her chair was sliding around abruptly. Brooks turned her to face him and pulled her legs up to rest in his lap. He unlaced both shoes and dropped them to the side before settling her feet in an accessible position.

"Is this comfortable?"

"This is perfect," she whispered. Xia closed her eyes as she rested her head against the back of the wooden chair.

Brooks applied gentle pressure to massage the pads of her feet as he stroked his thumb along the bottom, rubbing smooth circles with his other fingers. When he was pleased with the amount of attention given, Brooks moved up and started working her calves. The tenderness pointed to how sore she would be the next day.

"Nyx was in a really foul mood this morning. More so than normal, I mean. I scared the shit out of her when I asked to help. She seemed pretty lost in thought."

Brooks was silent for a beat too long, the space between them growing thick with tension. "I haven't seen her since our... you know."

"Oh. Okay. I guess that makes sense."

Brooks had been overly protective since arriving in the town, and it seemed to get worse every day. That included reading too hard into everything, and Xia had never been good about hiding her feelings.

"Makes sense for what?"

"Just that she was... upset."

"What aren't you telling me, Xia?"

Xia sighed, resigned. If they were going to be partners, then there shouldn't be lies and half truths between them, right? "She said some things to me this morning that I don't think she meant. I wanted to talk to her again, but wasn't sure when the right time would be. I was hoping she'd come back here to calm down, but it doesn't seem that was what happened."

A chill nipped the air as neon flames sparked in his eyes.

Careful, God of Chaos.

"What did she say to you?"

"The words don't matter, Brooks. Just the resolution."

"I want to know what she said. She's already on thin ice as far as I'm concerned."

"She has every right to be upset. If you did to me what you did to her I would be furious. You crossed a serious boundary, and most people aren't so forgiving."

"I would never do that to you unless I had to."

The Siren sprang to the forefront of Xia's mind as she spit and hissed.

Xia pulled her feet from his lap and raised her voice an octave. "*Had* to? What the hell does that even mean Brooks?"

"If it was a matter of your safety, I wouldn't hesitate to search for the answer in your memories, Xia."

"You are so fucking unbelievable. Did last night mean nothing to you?"

He looked down as he answered, "It meant everything to me."

"My words, Brooks. Did my words not make it through that thick skull of yours? I asked you to stay by my side as I grew, to be my safe space as I figured out who I am. You said you would learn to do better. And then I gave you my body because I trusted you to keep that word."

"I am trying, Xia." His eyes were pleading, but she wouldn't let that deter her from driving the point home.

"Boundaries are important." Her voice rose as the Siren laced herself within it. "I don't want to be some damsel who can't save herself. I've lived that life and I never want to go back. I cannot survive going back." Xia pressed her hands to her forehead and paced as the silence grew to a chasm between them "Do you understand that? This isn't doing better, Brooks," she gestured between them. "This is tightening the noose."

Scales rose along her arms as her Siren slipped free, their combined fury begging to be unleashed. "I don't want to be the spoiled princess living off the broken backs of others. I want to stand on my own and make an impact I can be proud of, and that starts by proving to Nyx that she didn't risk her home by helping us."

"Is that what she said to you?" His head jerked up, his gaze intense and accusing.

Xia stopped and stared at him, her gaze narrowing in as if to pierce his soul. Her spine trembled as the Siren clawed to lash out. "Unbelievable. You are un-fucking-believable. Out of everything, that's what you heard."

"I heard you, Xia. I am listening. I value everything you're saying."

He lies!

"You sure don't act like it," she whispered. Xia shook her head and walked out the door she'd stepped through not even twenty minutes before. Xia rushed to the river where she knew the solace of water waited but stopped short when a messy head of black hair showed over the bank.

Was she supposed to turn around? Maybe go to the river access where they did laundry?

No, she thought. *I can't let others stand in the way of relationships I want to forge. This is for me.*

Xia approached slowly but stepped purposely on dry leaves and twigs so as not to scare her. Nyx was fast and scrappy, and Xia had no doubt the girl kept a blade or two ready.

"You don't have to be weird about it," Nyx said without turning. Her legs were tucked up to her chest, arms wrapped around her knees as she looked out over the horizon.

"I'm sorry," Xia answered. "I wasn't trying to be weird. I just didn't want to get stabbed." She huffed an easy laugh, but her smile fell when it wasn't reciprocated. Nyx was going to be a challenge, but she was one Xia was willing to take on. Something about this girl told Xia that any trouble would be worth the reward of her friendship.

"Trouble in paradise?"

"No," she lied. "Well, maybe a little."

"Let me guess. He ripped your mind apart to see if the legs over the shoulder position or from the back was your favorite." Nyx's tone was so matter-of-fact that Xia wasn't sure how to respond for a moment. Her cheeks flamed at the forwardness.

"Not exactly. Although I expect we will draw up a complete set of analytics on performance later."

Nyx huffed a laugh and, though Xia didn't want to ask the question, she had to. "You, um, you heard us? Last night?"

Nyx turned, eyebrows lost in her hairline as her eyes bulged. "The whole fucking underworld heard you. Are you serious?"

Xia laughed as she tucked a strand of hair behind her ear, her eyes dipping to look anywhere other than at Nyx. "Sorry about that. It wasn't intentional. That was very rude of us. You've been such a great host and I'm thankful for your hospitality. I'm sorry if we crossed a boundary."

Nyx nodded, one corner of her lip upturned in what could have been a half smile. "You're such a pretty liar. It makes me a little jealous."

"What?" Xia's head whipped to Nyx, confusion clouding her thoughts.

"I've not been a good host, and I've said a countless amount of shitty things to both of you, so we will call it even. If you suck him off again so close to my room, though, you're both sleeping in the water shed."

Xia choked on saliva, and she worked to regain her composure.

"Don't worry, princess. You'll get used to it. This world is too deplorable to stay innocent for long."

"I'm not innocent, I just... I'm not used to someone being so forward. Especially about private matters."

"Are you kidding?" That expressive look of incredulity painted her face again, and Xia found she was warming to it. "Princess, those walls are literally made of sticks. What you did was no more private than me taking a shit in a hole in the ground. Everyone does it. You shouldn't be ashamed. Just like, put an olive branch on the door next time or something."

"An olive branch?"

"Yeah. It's like a peace offering. It says 'we're trynna fuck so go somewhere else.'"

"Peace usually means both sides get something out of it. What do you get out of being kicked out of your home because there's a branch on the door?"

"I get out of you screaming at him while I'm trying to sleep."

The two smiled at each other and laughed, an honest and genuine sound. Maybe even companionable.

"I'm sorry," Xia blurted. "For what he did to you. That was crossing a major line, and I would understand if you can't forgive him for it."

"You don't have to play peacemaker, princess. I'm a big girl and he's a grown man. I can work it out all on my own."

"I know you can." She nodded and looked down at the hands laying in her lap as she fought the urge to pick at her nails. "I'm not asking you to forgive him. I'm just asking that you don't give up on him. I know that you understand tribulation, Nyx. Like you, he's been through a lot of it. More than anyone deserves to go through."

"How do you know what I've been through?" The question wasn't angry or spit with venom, just bitter curiosity. Both of them made the silent decision not to look at each other as they spoke. Instead, they watched the sun fall from the sky knowing that everything changed when it rose again.

"I don't, but I can take a few general guesses."

"Like what?"

"I know you must feel an incredible amount of responsibility for people in this village if you were willing to risk yourself at Club Hel. The Devil is not a nice man, and I can't imagine what he would have done to you if he knew why you were there."

A flicker of movement caught Xia's eye and she couldn't help but glance discreetly. Nyx picked at her nails, the skin around them blistered and scabbed. Something else they had in common.

"He knew. I only made it two floors before I got caught," she scoffed. "Some clever thief I am."

"Well, don't be too hard on yourself. There wasn't a fleck of dust in his club that he didn't know about. To say he has control issues would be an understatement."

"I got that."

"I hope he didn't hurt you." Xia's voice was small as it worked around the rising lump.

"Well he sure didn't please me."

"What floor did he take you to after that?"

Nyx huffed another bitter laugh. "He had me tied up, gagged, and thrown into his office."

Xia's stomach squeezed. The Playground was something she wouldn't wish upon her worst enemy.

"He talked about selling me," Nyx continued. "But that was about the time your lover boy started tearing shit apart, so he forgot about me. What floor were you patroning when it all went to shit?"

"What makes you think I was patroning any floor?"

"Look at you." Nyx gestured between them. "Girls like you don't work at Club Hel. They get lost in it. You can't fool me, princess. There's no need to be ashamed of your tastes. I mean, I'm totally going to judge you for it, but that doesn't mean you have to hold back."

Was she serious? "I'm honestly a bit offended."

"Oh, don't play coy. Spit it out."

"I was not there for pleasure. I was... I was his captive."

"Pffft, yeah. And I was his dominatrix."

We will show her what he did to us and then give it to her tenfold, the Siren hissed. *She will never understand us.*

Furious tears built in Xia's eyes. She did everything she could to contain them but, as most storms do, she broke. "You know, for someone who claims to hold the world on their shoulders, you sure aren't sympathetic to others buckling under the weight."

Xia stood, her legs trembling as she took the few short steps to the water. When she was knee deep, she tilted her head back to bask in moonlight, surrendering to the two parts that came together to make her whole. The sound of feet slugging through water sounded to her right, but Xia was too furious to acknowledge Nyx.

A light touch brushed her arm. "Are you being serious?"

"Why would I lie about something like that? I don't need your pity, Nyx."

"I just thought–"

"Thought what?" Xia faced Nyx and didn't hold back the venom. "That someone who looks like me can't feel pain? Couldn't possibly suffer like you do?" Xia towered over her, the Siren rising in every lapping wave of the river. "Let me tell you something, Nyx. I didn't make assumptions about you when I walked through your decaying town. I never judged your strength or struggle based on your appearance, and I never once perceived you as naive because you were a child way in over her head." Storm clouds gathered in the sky as Xia's canines elongated. "Instead, I valued the parts you were willing to share and respected the ones you wouldn't, and you've not once given me the same courtesy."

"Xia, I–"

"No! I'm not finished and you will listen because I will *never* explain myself again." Lightning flashed overhead as the wind picked up speed. "I am a Siren. In fact, I am the *only* Siren since the Devil and his brothers slaughtered my sisters. I am born of the moon and tide. I am the epitome of alluring, Nyx. Do you know why? I'm assuming not, since you don't care to look any further than the surface," Xia spat. Her hair whipped in the breeze, stinging her cheeks like the lash of a whip. "My beauty is a mask to hide the serpent inside of me. Do you get that? I look like this so I can pull blood from the skies to satiate her hunger. Men and women alike fall at my feet and die because of it. The only reason the Devil didn't kill me is because I was a lucrative asset."

Nyx struggled to stay upright in the maelstrom as the thrashing water fought to pull her under. "I'm sorry!" she screamed over the roaring wind. "Xia, I didn't know!"

"I lured people to his club and I'm the reason that someone I love and care for was stuck in the most horrifying place imaginable. The Devil stole my chaos, my song, and used it to feed Brooks' illusion while he kept me locked in my mind, reliving nightmare after nightmare!" The sky opened up and wept with its mistress. "I watched my sisters die a thousand times just to rise from the mutilation and tell me it was my fault. And when he got tired of that, do you know what he did, Nyx?"

"Xia please!"

"Let me tell you so that you don't have to assume," Xia spat as she seethed, all of the rage and despair pouring out of her shattered heart along with the Siren raging in her chest. "He got creative with the nightmares he projected into my head. He raped me. Beat me. Killed me. Ripped me apart one layer at a time as I screamed through the agony. All to be left on the floor picking up the pieces of myself alone. Do you know what that's like?"

Before Xia could finish, Nyx wrapped her arms around Xia's shaking frame and held her in an embrace so tight she thought she may break. Xia tucked her head into the crook of Nyx's neck and squeezed back. Nyx didn't say a single word, just held her through the storm.

Unleash your Chaos

Nyx
31

Rain pounded down from the sky and sliced like knives against her skin, but Nyx's hold on Xia never faltered. Gods she'd been so fucking wrong.

Being quick to judge was one of her less attractive personality traits. She'd never hated that side of herself more.

A sliver of warmth hugged her back and curled around her shoulder. Nyx pulled back just enough to see a tendril of shadow wrapping itself around them. The pressure in her chest increased as the shadow pulled them into its embrace and moved to nuzzle Xia's cheek.

She nearly shit her pants when that hazy tendril formed a hand, and from that hand grew an arm. In a matter of moments a man made of shadows stood before them. His shape was familiar to Brooks, but his eyes were a piercing shade of neon blue and he wore a permanent scowl that softened just a touch as he watched Xia cry.

Energy emanated around the figure and it was nearly impossible to stand in his presence, but Nyx wouldn't leave Xia alone with it. He closed the distance and wrapped his arms around them both.

"What is this?" Nyx whispered. The figure turned those menacing eyes and Nyx nearly crumbled under the intensity.

"Brooks?" Xia pulled her face from Nyx's shoulder, her voice thick and trembling.

"Not quite. He wanted to give you space. I didn't want you to be alone."

"Chaos." Xia's eyes lit and a small smile graced her lips.

"I'm here for you, Siren. Always."

Xia pulled back from the group hug. The rain and wind stopped blowing as the clouds cleared and the moon hung bright in the sky once more.

She turned to Nyx and squeezed her hand. "I'm sorry. I didn't mean for any of this to happen, but I do appreciate you getting me through it."

"That's what friends are for." Nyx's words were tentative as her hands trembled.

"Do you mean that? That we're friends?"

"Oh, for sure princess. Before you know it we'll be braiding each other's hair and sleeping in the same bed."

The temperature dipped as Chaos' eyes narrowed.

"Okay." Each syllable was elongated as Nyx considered her next steps. Should she run? Or maybe back away slowly and look to the ground? Fuck. She needed to touch up on her 'escaping dimwitted predators' knowledge.

She went with the backing up slow option and held her hands out submissively. Nyx thought she heard Xia giggle under her breath, but refused to take her eyes off of the shadow god. "You made your point," she said.

Xia slammed into Nyx once more in a gripping hug tucking her face into the crook of Nyx's neck. "I'm so grateful for you, Nyx. Really."

Nyx chanced a look at the beauty and gave her an awkward pat on the shoulder. "I appreciate you too, princess, but if you don't let me go your guard dog is going to bite my head off."

Xia's eyes narrowed, the pupils splitting vertically before she said, "Fine. I'll let you go for now. I guess I'll see you when we come to bed?"

"No need. The house is all yours tonight. I assume that the man and the monster need to have a chat with you, and the last time that happened I had to sleep somewhere else anyway."

Xia's cheeks flamed with the most beautiful shade of summer peony, and the innocence there made Nyx want to protect her at all costs. She turned without another word and trudged back toward the house. With any luck, Brooks was out of sight and she could slip in unnoticed.

She huddled against the cold within the folds of her ragged jacket. She may not have been affected by the night, but she was damn sure a victim of the cold. Nyx's teeth chattered the whole way to the house. When she stepped through the door she found the great room blissfully empty. She was annoyed, however, to see the fireplace missing a fire.

"Worthless. Creator of the godsdamned universe but doesn't know how to stoke a fire." She stopped herself from throwing in another. "Nope. If they're going to let it go out, then they can be cold."

Thoughts of Xia sent dread curling in her stomach. She needed to leave and get out of there before the pair came back. Nyx rushed to her room, changed into some dry clothes, and grabbed the bag she'd packed with the food to give to Evangeline.

When the sun rose, they would leave for the city settled at the bottom of Mount Olympus– Dion. Nyx didn't know what they were going to do once there, but she couldn't think about that now. Her hands trembled as she opened the bag to check that everything was there and swallowed against the anxiety tightening her throat.

"One step at a time, Nyx." She blew out a shaky breath. "You only stumble when you try to take more than one."

Rather than risking running into the pair at the front door, Nyx removed the makeshift board of planks that covered the window in her room. She slipped through and landed on the dirt flawlessly. There were perks to being a thief. You got stealthy or you got dead. Poetic, really.

She tucked her head and started a slow jog down the hill leading into the village. Evangeline and her mom Adriana lived in one of the furthest houses from Nyx's. As she ran, her mind raced. The devastation Xia threw out in the river, a pain so deep it ripped the sky apart, was all because of a man–

"Stop!" she rasped as she fisted her hair and blinked back tears.

Nyx stuck to the deeper shadows. She wasn't fit to run into anyone tonight. She needed to take Evangeline the food and then go somewhere to panic in peace. The way Xia clung to her in the river, and the look in her eye when Nyx called her a friend...

Nope. Not going there. First food, then panic. Get a fucking grip.

Windows were shuttered and doors locked for the night as thick plumes of smoke drifted from each makeshift chimney stack. Families would be huddled against the chill in their front rooms. Soon, they would move their beds there for the winter. Supplies ran too short in the town to provide each room in a house with a fireplace.

When Evangeline's home came into view, Nyx pulled the bag from her shoulder as she stepped up to the door and knocked. Adriana was the first to answer.

Nyx pulled back her hood. "Is Evie still awake?"

"Yeah. She's pulling our blankets out now." Adriana stepped to the side as she opened the door. The woman's eyes drooped heavily into dark circles. Her pale face spoke of a bone deep weariness.

Another drop of anxiety fell into the pool filling too quickly in Nyx's chest. If she didn't find somewhere to be alone soon, she was afraid it would burst at the most inconvenient time. Small footsteps pattered down the hall soon followed by bouncing blonde curls and a gappy smile.

"Nini!" Evangeline smiled and dropped her blankets to the floor as she ran toward Nyx with open arms. Nyx couldn't stop the smile taking up the entirety of her face.

"Evie!" The girl slammed into Nyx and held her in as tight of an embrace as her little arms would allow. "Are you getting ready to tuck in for the night?"

"Mhmm! Mommy says we get to have a sleepover by the fire tonight! I was getting all of my blankets so we could snuggle tight." Evangeline pulled back, but before Nyx could speak the girl's eyes widened and sparked. "Mommy! Can Nyx stay for our sleepover too? Please, please, please!"

Adriana's weary smile was weak as she nodded. "Sure, baby. If Nyx wants to stay, she can."

Evangeline jumped up and down, her squeals both breaking and warming Nyx's tattered soul. It hit her then that she may not come back from the mission. This could be the last time she heard those sweet giggles that chimed like a symphony of bells.

"I would love to, Evie, but I don't think tonight–"

"Please, Nini," the girl whined. "I miss you so much."

"I know you do, sweet girl." Nyx swallowed back the tears threatening to fall.

The joy fell from Evangeline's face as a somber frown took its place. "You're going away again, aren't you?"

Nyx looked down to her feet as she nodded. Evie didn't need to see the despair she knew was so plainly written there. "Yeah. Yeah, Evie, I am." Nyx put on her bravest face as she looked into Evie's crystalline eyes, the blue so pure and innocent. Those eyes were always Nyx's reminder that she could not stop fighting. She could never back down and dying was not an option, now or ever.

"I don't want you to go." Her lips trembled as those sweet cherub cheeks dampened with streaks.

Nyx pressed her forehead against Evie's and grasped her shoulders. "Remember what I always tell you? You've nothing to worry about Evie. Have I ever not come home?"

"No." The girl plucked at the strings fraying from her nightgown as her little body twisted back and forth.

"And have I ever left you behind?"

"No."

"So this time won't be any different, right?"

"I guess not." Evie ran her small hands through the hanging strands of Nyx's hair.

"Whose job is it to keep everyone in line when I'm gone?"

Evie fought the beginnings of a smile. "Me."

"That's right. And who has to keep Mommy safe?"

"Me!"

"That's my girl." Nyx smiled and placed a quick kiss to the girl's nose. Evie giggled and pulled back, wiping invisible saliva from the tip. "Now come on. I've got some things to give you before I go."

"Yay! Presents!"

Nyx stood to grab the discarded blankets and settle them into neat pallets on the floor before going back for the bag she brought.

"Sit on your blanket, love-bug." Evangeline settled on the floor and clasped her hands as she waited for Nyx to join her. Nyx placed the bag in her lap and patted it as she said, "Alright. Are you ready?"

"Yes!" Her voice was pure, unadulterated joy.

"Okay. I've got…" Nyx rummaged through the bag dramatically which drew even more giggles from the girl as she pulled the contents one by one. "Two loaves of bread. Two blocks of cheese. And a few days' worth of meat."

"I can share with mommy."

"I know you can love-bug, but it's mine and mommy's job to protect you until you're so big and strong that not even Zeus could win a fight against you."

"I am almost six," she said matter-of-factly.

"You are. Just another year and a half and I guess you have to move into your own house."

"I will! I'll build a house all by myself right next to yours, Nini."

"That sounds like the best of plans, Evie." Nyx brushed a wayward curl from Evie's forehead and tucked it behind her ear.

Evie's mouth stretched wide as she yawned. Nyx cherished the last few moments she would get with the girl, memorizing every delicate feature of her face. Lying to Evie sucked, but Nyx would never voice the truth. She wouldn't make it home from the Freakshow. She just had to hope that Tor stayed true to his word and would feed and protect the town once she brought him what he wanted.

Once she betrayed Xia.

Nyx swallowed against the aching lump and looked to the ceiling as she blinked to clear the pooling tears. Her voice was ragged as she said, "I've one more thing before you go to sleep."

"Is it more bread?"

"No, sweet girl." Nyx pulled the roughly sewn stuffed toy from her bag. "I made you something so that when you're scared or missing me, you have something to snuggle."

What was supposed to be a chimera ended up being some sort of fur and linen conglomeration, but Evie's eyes lit as she snatched it from Nyx's hands.

The little girl looked the animal over and rubbed her fingers along the stitches. Nyx put it together with hide from her last hunt and pieces of her favorite blanket. She and Evie spent many a cold night under that blanket together and Nyx hoped Evie would take it when she...

Well, when she didn't come back.

The forest-green blanket was hand knit and colored with a mix of dyer's weed and indigo. The color faded with time, but Nyx couldn't make herself throw it away. It was the only thing she had from a childhood she'd never known.

"I love her!"

"I'm glad! She's a chimera. She has the head of a lion and the tail of a snake. She's one of the strongest and most cunning creatures out there, just like you love-bug. She will help you be strong when you're scared."

"Thank you, Nini!" Evangeline embraced the stuffed toy, her little body swaying back and forth as she hugged it tight.

"Of course. Anything for you." Nyx smiled and placed a kiss on the top of Evie's head as she took one last sniff of her hair. There were no words to describe the smell of a child. Even if there were, they wouldn't do it justice.

Evie poked the two black button eyes and the strip of leather Nyx had cut for the nose. "She's so cute."

"Good, now lay down. I'll tuck you in tight."

"Do you have to go?"

"I do. You'll never sleep if I stay. You like games too much."

"I would too sleep. I've done it before."

"That you have, kiddo. I promise we will snuggle tight under my blanket when I get home."

Evangeline laid on the makeshift bed as Nyx tucked her into a fur blanket.

"How long will you be gone?" The girl asked around another yawn.

"I'm not sure, baby, but it won't be long."

"Promise?"

The lie caught in her throat as traitorous tears tumbled down her cheeks. Nyx looked down in hopes that Evie wouldn't see. She nodded as a response, not trusting her voice to answer.

"Okay," the girl said as she scratched the surface of a button. "I'm going to miss you, Nini." Her blue eyes looked up to Nyx, and Nyx felt the world crumbling around her.

"I love you so much, kiddo. Now get some sleep, and I'll be home before you know it."

Nyx barely hit the treeline before the wracking sobs hit. Her feet pounded against the ground as she tore through the night. Maybe, she thought, if she ran fast enough she could get away. Get away from what tomorrow would bring, or the cost of what she was leaving behind.

When she was so deep into the woods she was sure no one would find her, Nyx dropped to the ground and let the tears fall in earnest. The burden of her situation was one she couldn't bear any longer. The pressure of her responsibilities had thrown her into the mortar years ago, but tonight the pestle made its final turn. Nyx had nothing left but the dust of her bones to give.

She thought of Xia on the riverbank as she ripped at her hair and screamed. Though they knew nothing of each other, a bond tethered by shared trauma weaved itself into them both, and it would be there forever.

Forever, until the weight of her betrayal cut the threads.

Nyx was working side by side with the man who brought her friend to life just to kill her again. She was lying to Brooks and leading them both to their deaths. She was the driving force of their demise, but the worst part was that she couldn't stop.

Wouldn't stop.

Nyx promised herself a long time ago that Evie came before anything.

"Fuck!" She screamed into the canopy, the sound ripping from her chest in the rawest form of despair.

Xia's words flooded her mind one heartbreaking line at a time. Nyx clamped her hands around her ears, but nothing stopped the guilt from pouring in.

He raped me.

"Stop," she begged, saliva stringing from her mouth as she cried out.

Beat me.

"Please!" She curled into herself, hoping to get so small the words couldn't find her.

Killed me.

"I'm so sorry." An endless void of darkness descended until it consumed her. Nyx was left staring back at the emptiness of her soul.

Ripped me apart one layer at a time as I screamed through the agony.

"I have to protect her." Her chest seized as her ragged breaths grew shorter and faster.

All to be left on the floor to pick up the pieces of myself alone.

"Please understand." Black spots danced in her vision as she gasped, the panic overtaking every cell of her body.

Do you know what that's like?

She didn't.

Evie's voice was the last Nyx heard as she surrendered to the darkness with the smallest hope that she wouldn't wake back up.

I'm going to miss you, Nini.

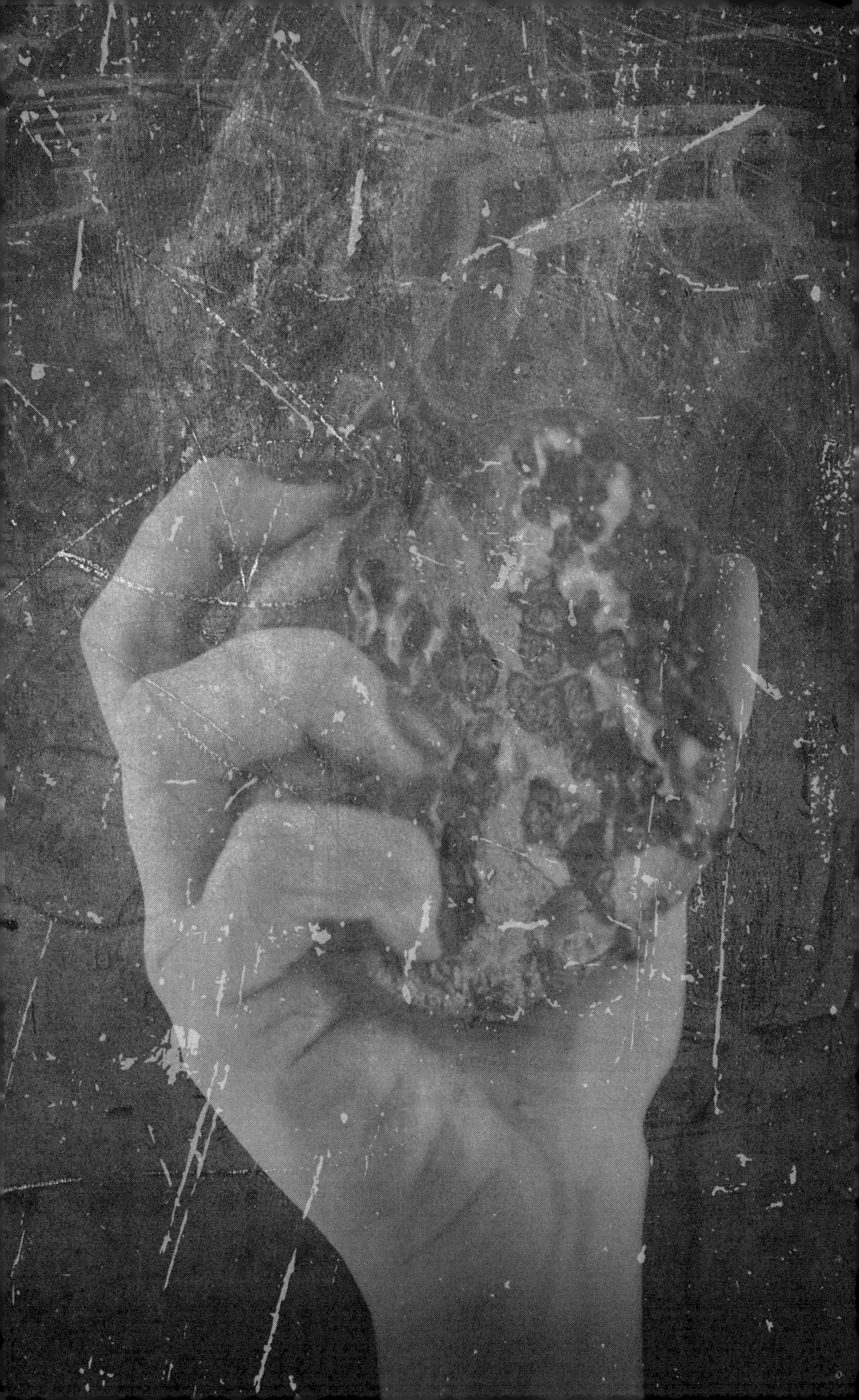

ASHES
ASHES
IT ALL BURNS DOWN

Unleash your Chaos

Persephone

32

Persephone spent her days in Asphodel Meadow, sweat beading on her upper lip as she worked the soil and pruned the wilting petals by hand. Her chaos was useless in the Underworld. Persephone was the budding life of spring, but Hades domain was death.

She was left alone with her thoughts nearly all hours of the day. Hades escorted her to the fields every morning after breakfast and retrieved her every night before dinner, only appearing once more to bring her lunch.

Each time she saw him it was like the sun blooming in her chest. No one, not even her mother who'd held her close, had ever been so thoughtful.

Hades never missed a meal with her and filled their time with conversation and mind-bending puzzles. He was more cunning than she, but Persephone was a quick study. With two wins under her belt, Persephone proposed a gamble. She wagered that she would win five matches against him before the one-year mark of her arrival.

She sat back on her feet, twisting side to side to ease the tension in her back and shoulders. Her fingertips tingled and the ache in her knees worsened, the pain growing worse every day like her body was breaking down from the labor.

Persephone's hand closed around the thermos of healing tea she kept close and popped the lid, swallowing the last of its contents as she wondered for the hundredth time who pruned the stalks before. It truly was an all day job and it never ended. When she asked Hades about it, he simply said, "I did, of course. Imagine my joy when the goddess of spring landed on my doorstep as if the Fates put you there with their own hands." He'd laughed, but her stomach churned. How cruel the Fates were if they thought she deserved her path to hell.

Sometimes her mind wandered a little too far and her thoughts turned spiteful. On her darkest days, she resented Hades for the task. However, It never failed that guilt followed each thought as swift as a swinging blade. He trusted her as he had no one with the sacred meadow. The cycle of life was in her hands and it could mean the damnation of them all. Hades knew that, and still he believed in her with such conviction.

"Persephone, darling, are you ready?"

His voice brought a smile to her face and she rushed to stand. A wave of dizziness caused her to stumble, but Hades was there to catch her, just as he always was.

"Careful, Beauty. We can't have you damning the world with your clumsiness."

She laughed, the sound half-hearted even to her own ears.

I'm not clumsy, she thought. I'm just dizzy from spending all day breaking my back while you lounge about playing chess.

He tucked her under his arm and they walked back to the palace side by side. He even carried her thermos. It was one of many traits she loved most about him.

Love.

That's what she felt for Hades, and she planned to tell him when they were wrapped up in each other's arms, sheets tangled around their ankles after passion.

She'd spent the first few months of her life in the Underworld sleeping in separate quarters, but things changed as they grew closer. He'd invited her to his bed and she accepted the offer with a shy kind of joy. They made love that first night and she'd been so embarrassed to tell him of her inexperience, but he took it with grace. Hades was patient as she learned what he liked, guiding her each step of the way with gentle corrections and words of encouragement.

Falling for the king of the Underworld had never been the plan, but her love for him was as impossible to stop as the breaking of dawn.

Nerves crept up her stomach at the thought of laying another piece of herself at his feet, but she had to take the leap. He'd trusted her with the world, so she would trust him with her heart. After all, they did beat as one.

Persephone noticed it after their first night together. She was bathing in the afterglow, head resting on his chest as she listened to the rhythmic sound of his snores. At first she thought it was just the beat of her own heart rushing through her ears from the fallout of their passion. As her body settled, though, she realized the truth.

She marveled at the revelation for days after, and it still made her stomach flutter when she thought about it. Every night, she lay on his chest and listened. Persephone wanted to ask if he'd noticed it too, but every time she began, the question died on her lips. She was too afraid of his rejection.

"You're quiet tonight, Beauty."

She startled as his voice interrupted her thoughts. He'd led her all the way to the palace doors and she hadn't even noticed. "Just lost in thoughts, I suppose. My body aches worsen each day and it jumbles my thoughts here of late."

"Surely you don't complain over a single chore? I'm running an entire realm while you pick flowers."

While she knew he was jesting, Persephone was not amused by the quip, but she stayed silent as they walked to his private study. He lowered her into the chair across from his and poured wine from a decanter into both chalices. Hades sipped from the more ornate of the two cups. Intricate scrolls and flourishes spiraled from lip to base, the body studded with jewels and with no signs of wear. Hers, on the other hand, wasn't decorated at all. Just a tarnished silver cup. On her worst days, she wondered why he would conjure such a monstrosity for her as he sipped from luxury. On others, Persephone reminded herself that they were both cups that served the same purpose no matter the aesthetic.

Hades sat and motioned for her to drink. Food appeared with a wave of his hand, but her stomach soured at the thought. Months ago, Persephone couldn't eat enough, finishing every meal with a greedy glance around for more. The past couple, however, she was never hungry.

"Tell me about your day, Persephone. How were the asphodels?"

"Flourishing as always. How about yours?"

"Busy. Many matters required my attention today."

She used to ask him about those matters, to take an interest in her newfound home. Hades made clear long ago that he was not willing to share, so she stopped asking about his daily affairs along with those of his court. The Twelve had a staff of servants and a few even held advisors. They let more elite daemon who worshiped them live on their estate and hosted parties for entertainment. However, Persephone had never seen another living soul in the Underworld. He truly was a master of deflection.

"I'm glad you were able to attend to them."

They ate for a few moments in silence with nothing but the clink of silverware to fill the space. "What is it you'd like to do this evening, Beauty?"

It was a trick question. There was nothing to do. It was the same routine every night– drink the wine, eat the food, play a game of chess, go to bed. Sometimes sex after chess, but not too often.

"Just spend a quiet evening by your side." She smiled and he returned it as she pushed her found around the porcelain platter.

"Have some food, Persephone, and finish your wine. I'll get you another glass."

"I'm okay with just the one tonight."

"No, I insist. Tonight is our anniversary after all."

"I'm sorry?" Persephone pursed her brows as she looked up from the table.

"You've been in the Underworld for a year now."

"I thought that wasn't for another week? I've been marking the calendar you gave me and I'm sure I haven't messed it up."

"No worries, Beauty. It's easy to get confused here, but that's why you've got me." He lifted his chalice toward her with a nod and then drank to his praise.

"I'm just sure I haven't messed up my days." Persephone used her calendar religiously to track the time. It'd been hard enough to adjust in a world with no sunlight. Marking the days brought a sense of comfort she couldn't explain. It kept her grounded.

"No matter, Beauty. You were very close to death when I found you and slept through many of the first days. I'm sure your miscalculation came *from there. Trust me, Persephone. It is tonight. This big reaction to such a small problem is unnecessary."*

It ate at her for the rest of the night like a toxin. She was so sure of herself, but alongside that confidence was doubt. Hades knew this world better than anyone. Could she perhaps have missed a few in the beginning? A shiver raised the fine hairs along her arms as she narrowed her gaze toward him, her neck prickling with caution before she shook it away. Narcissus birthed that distrust and she wouldn't let him get in the way of her relationship with Hades.

Persephone decided with a deep breath to drop it and trust Hades. He'd had nothing but her best interest at heart, and what did the misjudgment of a few days matter anyway? She loosened her shoulders and focused on their evening.

Her head spun after the second glass of fruit wine, and by the end of the third she was loose with her tongue and laughing at every one of his jokes. By the fifth, she couldn't keep her hands off of him. Persephone sauntered over and straddled Hades in the oversized chair. She placed kisses down the column of his throat, her hips grinding in time with each roll of his hips. His hands roved over her body, cock straining in his pants as he palmed her breasts.

She moved her kisses to his lips and he opened to her, a man too hungry to wait. He kissed her greedily and sat up straighter with every moan he coaxed from her. "Beauty," *he groaned.* "I'm going to fuck you on this chair if we don't make it to bed soon."

Her belly clenched and she found she wanted that more than anything. They'd never had sex anywhere but his bed, and even then there was little exploration involved.

"Do it," *she breathed.* "Fuck me on the chair."

"You know I prefer the bed."

"Please, Hades."

A low rumble vibrated through his chest against her nipples. She was so desperate for more, she would barter anything to have it.

"Please what, Persephone?"

An impatient whimper escaped her swollen lips as she begged. "Please fuck me on the chair."

He stood in a rush and ripped the gown from her body as he bent her over the arm. "Do you trust me, Persephone?"

"Yes!" she cried out. Her body's reaction to his dominance left her desperate.

"Do you love me, Persephone?"

"Gods, I do. I love you with every part of my being, Hades."

"Good," he growled. "Relax, Beauty."

He slipped two fingers into her pussy and dragged them up the back.

"What are you—"

"Do you trust me, Persephone?"

"Always," she breathed after a moment of hesitation.

He repeated the motion and she closed her eyes to revel in his touch.

Hades pressed the tip of his cock to her entrance and pushed into her, his moan guttural as she clenched around him.

"Don't stop, Hades."

He pulled out and thrust in again, this time even slower than the first. She was desperate for him to pick up the pace and drive her to the brink of madness.

When he pulled back this time, he slipped free of her completely and the anticipation turned her throb into an ache. Hades grabbed her hips and she braced for the slam of his body against hers. That was what she wanted, but it wasn't what she got.

Instead, he used his cock to spread her slickness around the entrance of her ass and thrust himself all the way in. Her back curled as she cried out, the pressure of his intrusion the worst sort of fire that only burned hotter as he kept going.

"Do you love me, Persephone?" he grunted.

"Hades, it burns—"

"I asked if you loved me, Persephone!"

"Yes," she cried, tears falling to the worn leather of his chair where her nails scarred the surface.

Hades never lasted long in bed and what was usually a curse became a blessing. In only a few pumps, an orgasm rocketed through his body. He slammed into her with each pulse, oblivious to her cries. When he was done, Hades slipped free and reached for the decanter of wine.

Persephone couldn't move. The ache in her behind throbbed with her racing heart and she wanted nothing more than to curl into her own bed and hide.

"Get up, Beauty. Let's have another glass of wine to take the edge off. I nearly fell to my knees that time. How unfortunate it would have been to slip free during the best part."

Hades sauntered over to the chair and placed her cup on the table, standing over her for a moment before taking hold of her shoulders and forcing her up. Persephone cried out, but he took no notice.

"It will go away faster if you move. Great, isn't it? A whole new kind of pleasure." He poured wine into his own chalice as he spoke with his back turned to her. "Before you came, and when I was most lonely, I experimented with all sorts of pleasure. That one was one of my favorites and I thought you'd like it. I love pleasing you, Beauty." Hades turned, a flicker of disgust flashing through those eyes before he softened them again. "Persephone, stop your sniveling. Don't you remember the first time someone had you? It hurt for a while, but you love it now, don't you?"

Her body trembled and each movement made the pain worse, but she didn't want to anger him. Persephone forced a smile and nodded as she sniffled. "Yes. Yes I love it."

His smile returned and he gestured toward her cup. "Drink. The wine will help."

She didn't want to drink. She wanted to run, to be alone until she could heal and process, but under the pressure of his watchful eye, she was caged. Persephone put the cup to her lips and gulped until the last drops dribbled down her chin.

Who was this man standing in front of her? He must have known he hurt her. She stood vulnerable before him, handed over her heart and he turned it to dust with a smile. He didn't ask permission, he just took it. Just like Narcissus. Just like the men who lined up on her family estate to ask for her mother for the grand prize.

They stole and they desecrated and they **ruined**.

Her stomach gave a mighty squeeze as it cramped. Persephone dropped the chalice and bent at the waist, wrapping her arms around her middle.

Pain flared as her muscles spasmed and fire spread through every fiber. Her throat swelled to twice its size and made it impossible to breathe.

Hades walked a slow circle around her as she struggled. His gaze was calculative and a single eyebrow lifted a fraction, his lips pursed and jaw clenched. It was the same face he made across the chess board when he placed his pieces to make the winning move.

Persephone fell to her hands and knees and coughed as her lungs seized, red spattering the rug below. Her arms buckled from the tremors and her face hit the stone floor, nose breaking on impact. Persephone's throat was closed, her body bleeding from the inside out and, for the second time in her miserable life, she was dying at the feet of a man who betrayed her.

Hades' feet blurred in her line of vision as he stopped, the world fading to gray as her body failed. "One day, Beauty, you'll learn to stop trusting and start playing."

Unleash your Chaos

Brooks
33

When Chaos had come back with Xia tucked safely beneath his arm, Brooks didn't speak. He'd known he needed to apologize, but hadn't worked out exactly what for. After she stormed out, he and Chaos argued for eternity before his dark passenger left to be with her.

He still didn't know whether or not he should have been the one to go to her. Maybe that's what he owed an apology for?

They didn't say a word as she crawled into bed beside him. Chaos laid tucked in behind her until he was too weak to stay. Xia had fallen asleep on his chest and that's how they'd stayed until morning. The space between them remained tense as they rose and prepared for what lay ahead. His stomach fluttered when he thought about what the day may bring, but knew he couldn't dwell on it. Keeping Xia safe meant staying aware. He still wished he could tuck her away in the village as he carried out revenge, but he knew she would refuse.

They sat in silence around the table, both fiddling with wooden cups filled with water Xia filtered from the river. A door creaked open down the hall and they turned to watch Nyx trudge into the room. Her eyes were a swollen red, her upper lip puffy and skin pallid.

"What happened to you?" he gawked. Xia kicked Brooks under the table. "What?"

"Mind your own fucking business." Nyx slapped the back of his head as she walked by. She was lucky Chaos was recovering.

"Message received," he murmured as he rubbed the spot she'd hit.

Nyx turned to lean against the counter, facing the two of them with a dead look in her eyes. She looked like a girl with nothing to lose, and those were the most dangerous of them all.

"Are we ready?"

Xia looked to Brooks, her brow drawn in silent question.

"Uh, we were waiting on you. You're the one with the grand plan, remember?"

"Huh," Nyx scoffed. "Why the hell did you tear my brain apart looking for a portal if you intended for me to lead you there anyway?"

"I said I was sorry, Nyx."

"Yeah well, sorry doesn't always cut it, now does it?"

"I suppose not."

"Oh, you suppose? Perfect."

"Nyx?" Xia's voice was gentle as if she were approaching a rabid animal.

"Let's just get this over with already." Nyx pushed herself from the counter and stomped toward the door.

Xia and Brooks shared a final glance before gathering the parchment invitation and chasing her down. The two stayed well away from the leader and watched every step she took as if they could analyze the problem based solely on her stomps.

"We need to be careful with her," Xia whispered. "She's obviously upset and looking for a fight."

"Well Chaos will be the one to give it to her."

"No!" Xia scolded. "Both of you will keep your shit together and take every punch she throws, because that's what she needs."

"Will you two shut up? If I have to hear your high-pitched voice one more time, princess, I'm going to tie a gag to your mouth."

Chaos stirred, but Brooks pushed him back.

"I'm sorry, Nyx." The hurt in her voice made him want to slam that scrawny ass girl into a tree and rip her face to shreds with the bark.

Nyx stopped dead in her tracks and whipped to face them. "Don't be sorry. Sorry is weak, Xia, and I don't do weak. I refuse to be killed because you can't keep up. So beef the fuck up or stay back and fill water barrels while I clean up your mess."

Nyx turned back and stepped into the treeline. The path was familiar– the same he'd watched her walk when he stole her memory. They walked in silence, not even daring to look at each other. Brooks' palms stung from the force of his nails digging in, but if Xia didn't want him to intervene, he would do his best.

For now.

Nyx had about three more crude remarks before he took care of the problem.

Try one. Her soul would be satisfying going down. Normally he disagreed with his darker half, but on this topic? They were on the same page.

They traveled in tense silence for a while before the winter cold dropped to numbing temperatures. The atmosphere rippled and a giddy flutter filled his stomach.

Chaos once flowed here in great force.

"Tell me about it, bud."

"Did you say something?" Xia glanced over, but kept her voice low so as not to enrage the small beast stomping ahead.

"Just talking to the demons, Sunshine."

Her smile was genuine and it felt like a bandaid on the wound their fight left behind. Maybe it was the beginning of a tenuous apology. He was ready to go back to normal.

Stop whining. It's hard to live in here when all you do is pine after someone you've already got.

Rather than answering out loud, Brooks took the conversation inward. *"Oh, it's hard to live in my head? You can exit at any time."*

And leave her with you? Not a chance. You'll be hand feeding her grapes in an iron prison.

"Oh, really? You're the one who gets possessive at the most inconvenient of times. It's hard for me to give her space when every step back I take, you take two forward. This is just as much your fault as mine."

I will tear you apart from the inside.

"Good luck, buddy. Your shadow ass won't have anywhere to live then. How are you going to restore order to the cycle of chaos if you don't have any hands to choke someone with?"

Silence. Grumpy, brooding silence.

"You can just tell me I'm right, you know. It wouldn't kill you. I, too, have a brain capable of problem solving."

You're not right. I just don't have a good comeback.

"Exactly."

Brooks let a moment pass between them before he went inward a second time. The relationship between him and his darker half was something he had no clue how to navigate. Before, it was as if Brooks were the one living inside Chaos. He was the part that longed for connection and beauty, while Chaos was the great Father of Darkness. It was clear that Brooks didn't know how to drive just as much as Chaos didn't know how to be a passenger.

"Look," he thought to Chaos, "I know this is hard. It's been you and me for eternity, but maybe this is a good thing. We went to sleep because there was a piece missing, and that piece crumbled until it was a gaping chasm. I can do this, Chaos."

I don't like you being in control. The little beast was right. *Weakness makes you hesitate, and hesitation gets you killed. Us killed.*

"You know we can't die."

I don't. We've never been this separated from the energy that makes us what we are. Of all the worlds we've created and watched destroyed, the chaos stays balanced. This is an unknown, and I do not like it.

"That may be the first ounce of vulnerability you've shown in the history of ever."

I will slit your throat and wear the inside as a necklace.

Brooks huffed a laugh as he focused on the forward movement of his feet. Dried leaves crunched and made the birds scatter from trees. The breeze carried the musky smell of decaying flora and pine off of the evergreen trees. Brooks inhaled deeply. How long had he been stuck in that asylum and deprived of the simplicity life had to offer?

Too long.

"We're here," Nyx called from ahead.

Brooks pulled his thoughts from the woods and focused on the task at hand. The cave entrance was overgrown with thorny vines and foliage that was woven in deep layers. From their vantage point, it seemed almost impenetrable.

"How are we supposed to get through that?" Xia voiced from beside him.

"Afraid to get your hair tangled, princess?"

Xia set her brow and pushed forward until she stood before the tangled mess blocking the entrance. She only needed a moment to study before she smiled, looked at Nyx, and stuck her hand straight into the thorns.

Brooks lurched forward. "Xia, what the hell are you–"

"It's an illusion," she said to Brooks before turning back to Ny who continued her stomp up the hill, muttering under her breath the whole way. Brooks just stared, a combination of awe and pride welling in his heart, along with...

Insecurity.

Are you afraid she may use her brain to leave you behind?

"Shut up," he told Chaos. "She's been through a lot and needs someone to watch her back while she's vulnerable. You're supposed to be with me, not against me."

We want different things. I want to rush to her side to catch her should she stumble. You want to throw her over your shoulder and weather through the obstacle for her. She is not helpless.

"No. She's not," he submitted. "I... I can't lose her."

Then stop hovering.

He had no words. 'Fuck off' didn't feel powerful enough. Instead he decided on silence as he stepped up to the illusion of thorns. Instinct roared to turn back, but the electricity of chaos fueling the illusion begged him to stay. Chaos sighed, a satisfied sound rumbling through his psyche.

This place feels like home.

Brooks stepped into a dark cave mouth that narrowed into a single tunnel. Footsteps reverberated off the walls and he followed the sound through the dark. He inspected the walls and was intrigued by the drawings marking nearly every inch. When he'd walked this path in Nyx's memory, she'd been so forward focused that he hadn't seen them.

They resembled ancient scrawlings of a mad man. Hundreds of different languages were layered on top of one another in every direction. They didn't care if they were marking through someone else's words, as long as they had space to write. Every line, though, had one thing in common. Each sentence ended in the eight-pointed star. The star of Chaos.

"How do they know about the star?" Brooks whispered out loud.

Of the many sentient beings I've molded, this planet houses the most observant of all. There was a time when I showed myself freely. Never walking among them, per say, but not hiding either. I would create from the ground rather than the sky. The mark is forever carved into my skin. Evidently, it had an effect on the first of them.

Brooks chewed that over before a realization hit. "I suppose we're lucky for it. Had they not passed it down, these sacred places may never have been built. If every point of access to chaos had been found by the taint..."

We would have never woken.

The weight of the statement sat heavily in his stomach, nausea making his mouth water.

"Can you read this junk?"

Brooks jumped, incoherent curses echoing off the tunnel walls. "Fucks sake, Nyx."

"Oh, I'm sorry. Did I scare you?" Her smile mocked him.

"You know, sometimes I wish I could hug you so hard that I accidently kill you. Assume that I mean 'accidently' in the loosest sense of its definition."

"Well you can assume that the feeling is mutual." Nyx rolled her eyes so hard she nearly lost them.

Perhaps we could just snap her neck and call it an accident.

"So can you?" Nyx motioned to the scribbles on the wall. "Read it, I mean?"

"At one time, maybe."

"Not even a single one? Dude, there are like a million languages here. Do you know how old this place is?"

"I've not the faintest clue, Nyx, but I'm sure you're going to annoy me until I drag the answer from you."

"Oh yeah. One letter at a time, too. Better get your stick out and write it down on the floor. Unless you can't spell, of course. It wouldn't surprise me."

Chaos reached for the reins, but Brooks was quick to shut him down. He wasn't fast enough to stop the temperature drop.

"Geez you're so easy to rile."

"It's not me you have to worry about."

"Who then? Are you just a projection of the god you're supposed to be? Are you a messenger of God? A shepherd, perhaps?"

Fuck it. Brooks took one hand off the leash and let his passenger slip to the surface and surrounded her with his shadows. *"We are one, you petulant child, but he's kind enough to spare your life. I am not so merciful. The next time we meet under these circumstances may very well be the last."*

Nyx jumped back, hands shielding her body as fear sparked in those violet eyes.

Chaos pulled back of his own volition with a satisfied hum and Brooks asked, "Does that answer your question?"

Nyx dusted imaginary dirt from her clothes and cleared her throat. "It does, along with a few others."

"Good. Shall we keep walking?"

"After you." She gestured, her voice trembling from the dying adrenaline.

Brooks continued down the funneling walkway and examined the etchings in the stone. The further they walked, the older the languages became. So old, in fact, that he could read them.

His brows drew together. *"Are you seeing what I am?"* He asked Chaos.

I'm always seeing what you do.

"Goddammit, I know that, but are you really seeing?"

Dozens of eight pointed stars were scored into the wall and, when the artist grew tired of etching, they drew in blood. This section was different from the others, though. Encompassing the star was a circle, and on either side was a crescent shape with the points facing outward.

"What does it mean—"

"Why is your star surrounded by moons?" Nyx pulled him from his silent conversation.

"Moons?"

"Yeah," she nodded and traced the shapes with her finger. "This is the waxing crescent, then the new moon, and the waning crescent."

"Moons. They're moons." His passenger was silent, but apprehension rolled in waves through the both of them. *"What do you know? What aren't you telling me?"*

"Are you guys coming?" Xia's voice rang from the end of the darkened path.

Nyx shrugged her shoulders and kept walking, leaving Brooks to stare at the symbol alone.

"Brooks?"

"Almost there," he called, before turning to go. He jogged the last few paces until he hit the wide opening to the cavern. It looked exactly as it had in Nyx's memory, and the crumbling details were even more stunning in person.

"I know it's grand, but we really need to get moving." Nyx said as she pushed past him. "The portal is up here." She jumped through the mess of candles in the same path as the memory. Upon the altar, she ran her hand over the well and stepped up to the foot of the statue.

Brooks looked at the figure and exhaled. It was nearly an exact likeness. The only detail out of place was the star. Rather than being carved into his forehead, it was extended across his naked chest.

"They did more than see you."

Us. They saw us.

"Whoever they saw, apparently it was a face they'd never forget."

Brooks couldn't blame them. Chiseled into the marble was a

scowling god standing to judge them all. His narrowed eyes were a solid piece with no details and added to the portrait of malice.

"Are you coming or not?" Nyx shouted from his feet.

Xia stepped up beside him and brushed her fingers against his knuckles. "Are you okay?"

Brooks shook the haze from his mind and nodded. "Yeah, I'm fine."

"Must be weird to see proof of how dedicated an entire race was to you. It would make anyone with a conscience feel guilty for leaving them to die. Good thing you don't have one." Nyx patted him on the shoulder before walking away.

"Good thing," Brooks whispered around the tightness in his throat.

They walked in silence past the candles as Brooks contemplated the meaning of the cavern. People gathered to worship a god who had no intention of stepping in to help them.

You know why we cannot.

"No," he thought. *"I really don't. We're doing it for Xia because losing her is not an option. We are not the only beings who experience such longing and loss. Why do we deserve it more?"*

Chaos sighed, but did not respond.

As he and Xia approached the well, the ever-present current of electricity surrounding the cavern intensified. Brooks ran his hand around the lip and peered into the darkness. Raw chaos thickened the air inside, but it was hardly a large source of power. The flow was ebbing, and the world was not being supplied with the chaos it needed to be sustainable.

"They used to sacrifice people you know," Nyx whispered beside him.

"How?"

"It was a huge ceremony. Servants of the temple would bathe the servant and dress them in all the finery imaginable. The ceremony was celebrated by a seven day fast to show you their dedication as they watched the servant feast. For seven days that person was provided with the best life had to offer, including–" she swallowed and looked anywhere but at him as she picked her nails. "Including a grand house placed on a hill above everyone else so that the daemon could look upon their chosen."

A stone dropped in his belly as an uncomfortable wave of guilt crawled over his skin.

"Some argue that the week begins with the holy day because that's when the fast started. Others say the week ends with it because that's when the sacrifice was made. However you look at it, a daemon was promised luxury while being prepped for slaughter."

"Was the servant aware of their fate?"

"No," Nyx shook her head as silver tears rimmed her eyes. "The sacrifice was never a resident of the town. They came from outside. That's why it's seven days of prep. Seven days to wash the taint from their system and refill it with whatever religious bullshit they thought would please you."

"And they just did that? With zero proof that help or paradise would ever come?"

"Yup. Holy men were quick to excuse any crime for members of their ministry as long as it's in the name of religion. The scariest part wasn't the act done in the name of God. It's the devotion they can manipulate from people by playing on their most carnal fear."

"Which is?"

"Final death. They can't bear to think that death is their end. Can't comprehend that when their loved ones die, they are just gone. Enter holy men. They swoop in and make promises of eternal peace. As long as you live by what they preach, your future is guaranteed. Even if what they preach is murder with a purpose."

"You sound like you've had a while to think about these things."

"I have. I've never been to the human world, but I've heard a few things from my travels and it's just as bad there as it is here, if not worse."

"Oh yeah?"

"Yeah. They run countries and fight wars in the name of a god they've never met. They think that we are gods. That the strongest of daemon are who created their world and will grant them an afterlife.

So the way I see it is if they're wrong, then we're probably wrong, too. I know that Zeus is a piece of shit who engages in cruelty for pleasure, and he is their god."

"But he is real."

"What?"

"Cruel and manipulative he may be, but he is real."

Nyx turned her contemplative gaze back toward the well, her eyes glazing over to some far away place. "I'd rather live in a world where I didn't know he was real. At least then I could die knowing that I'd never met such cruelty."

"For what it's worth, I'm sorry."

"Sorry for what?"

"You've a lot of passion about this. I can only imagine it's born of scorn and bitterness. And, in this cavern, it's because of people who believed in me."

"I used to believe that people who did good deeds would be rewarded, you know? So I tried for so long to live in that mold, doing what they said was good even when it felt wrong. Eventually, I grew up and realized that it *was* wrong. I shouldn't be doing bad things in the name of a god because I'm scared to die. Killing an innocent daemon to guarantee my happiness is evil incarnate. I want to do good because it's the moral thing to do. Not because I'm afraid of a malevolent spirit looking over my shoulder."

A sense of deja vu sent his head spinning. It wasn't long ago that he decayed in that fucking asylum thinking the exact same thing.

"Powerful people don't have the right to make decisions for the innocent," she continued. "Powerful people don't deserve the title of a god. In the end, we're all dust scattered about the stars."

"So what, then, defines a god, Nyx?"

She huffed a cynical laugh. "There is no god, Brooks. Only evil men fighting for the title."

Brooks took a moment in silence to turn her words over. Nyx didn't believe in a god, but lived among powerful daemon. She didn't believe in a god, but there he was. The creator of her species and the ground she stood on. "Is the true god not the creator of all?"

"No. He's just the most powerful man in the room." Nyx stopped and shook her head, her brows knit as she determined her next words. "Here you stand before me, just another man with power enough to destroy them all, but no god. No, I don't think the true god is a person. I think he's an idea. He's the power of the universe. He is what we cannot comprehend, and yet strive to put a label on."

"Brooks? Nyx?" Xia interjected. "We really need to go."

"We're coming, princess." Nyx patted the well twice before turning without another word. Brooks didn't quite understand her words, but he grasped the heartfelt intention. To Nyx, the ideal of one god put too much power in the hands of the one who claimed the title.

"This way, assholes." In the span of a blink, Nyx was through the portal in between the feet of his statue.

"Uh, did she tell you how this thing works?"

Brooks shook his head and answered, "No. She didn't."

"Okay then. I guess we just countdown and go, huh?"

"It's as good a solution as any."

Xia swallowed as she nodded. "Alright. Do you want to go first?"

"No. Let's go together. We're a team, Sunshine."

She smiled and laced her fingers through his. "Together."

They stepped through the portal, a wave of electricity tingling over their skin as their stomachs lurched. Vertigo hit fast and hard but disappeared almost as quickly as it had come. When Brooks and Xia opened their eyes, they staggered.

Nyx stood to the side rubbing the goosebumps prickling her arms. "Welcome to Dion."

Unleash your Chaos

XIA

34

Blinding red light flashed in stark contrast to the night sky. Xia covered her eyes and rubbed at the spots dancing in her vision as she pressed into Brooks for stability. When she opened them again, the surprise remained.

The trio stood in a darkened alley with the haze of neon lights filtering in. Spotlights atop buildings shone different hues of red, pink, and purple and moved about the city. Of course the moment she opened her eyes, one would be pointing right at her.

The twin buildings they stood between were several stories high with no windows. Voices bounced off of the masonry but Xia couldn't see anyone else through the darkness.

"We need to go," Nyx's voice whispered through the dark.

"To where?" Brooks whispered back.

"Anywhere. Just away from the portal. And stick together. It's easy to get lost here and, once you're lost, you're likely to never be found. Follow me, keep your head down, and act natural."

"How do we act natural if we're not looking up?" Brooks squeezed Xia's hand, their fingers still wound together from stepping through the portal. It was a silent question. Are you with me? Are you okay? She squeezed back in response.

"You can look up if you want, but I wouldn't recommend it unless you've got money lining those tight ass pants of yours."

"Let's just go," Xia urged.

Nyx's silhouette nodded against the hazy light and turned. Brooks was hesitant, but walked when Xia pulled his hand forward. When they stepped from the alley, Xia found it hard to follow Nyx's rules.

Two parallel streets were split by a canal and lined with extravagant brick buildings that were five stories tall or higher. Each of them had their own unique flares like gilded window frames or intricate designs carved into the corbels supporting the awnings. No barrier protected the walkway from the water except for a few bridges that connected one street to the other. Cast iron street lamps spaced every couple of feet with grape vines winding down the posts, and the sweet smell of evergreen drifted off the canal breeze with the scent of ambrosia lingering underneath. Though they were all various shapes and sizes, at least six windows lined the front of every building and Xia nearly stumbled when her brain caught up with her eyes.

Xia looked up at the city around her and was mesmerized by every detail. Subtle flourishes decorated the lampposts and reflected the sultry glow of the neons. Bodies swayed in every glass frame as males and females alike tempted bystanders with a night of carnality. Signs flashed over every door boasting the unique pleasures that could be found if only you were brave enough to follow the temptation.

Xia was mesmerized by the vast beauty. It was not the same as the tranquility Nyx's town and the surrounding river brought her, but they both struck that dizzying cord in her heart that released a slow leak of adrenaline. A knock to the right caught her attention and Xia stumbled backward. Brooks caught her before she hit the brick walkway, but she couldn't turn away from the man in the window.

His tanned skin was slick with oil that reflected the purples and reds in a tantalizing display. He wore nothing but a studded loin cloth and matching bands around his biceps. Where Brooks was lean and athletic, the man in the window bulged with muscle over every bone. He ran a thick hand down his chest and drew her hooded eyes to his waist band. He slipped it under and grasped–

Xia shook her head as her Song flooded her veins, fighting back the lesser chaos permeating her senses. Sitting atop the muscled shoulders was the head of a bull, his black eyes beady in the droning light. A gold studded ring pierced through his septum with a hanging chain that attached to his collar. His ivy thorns curved and pointed above his head but, where she expected deadly points, were golden caps. Xia studied the caps and was horrified to find the head of four small screws holding the caps firm to the horns, tiny fissures webbing down from each entry point. Gods, how that must have hurt. Had he done it to himself? Or was he just as much a slave as she'd been? She held his gaze, working to decipher the emotion there until a sharp pull of the hand landed her back in reality.

"Xia?" Brooks's eyes roamed anxiously over her face. "Are you okay?"

"Yeah, I, um–" Xia looked back to the window, but the man was gone.

This is what happens when daemon are afraid. The strong are chained so that the weak may hide behind a false sense of security.

She shook her head and tried again. "I'm fine. Stupid me, broke the first rule. I'll do better." Xia laughed, the sound dull and weak.

"Shocker," Nyx mumbled.

Brooks shot her a sharp look before tugging Xia's hand again. "Come on. We need to keep moving."

Xia tucked her head and followed, her eyes never leaving the back of Brooks' heels. Water pooled in small puddles where the walkway dipped, small ripples forming from the vibration of bass-heavy music and traffic. She focused on the sound of splattering under her feet from the wet cobble.

Dion was the epitome of everything Level Lust stood for. Silhouettes danced on the walkway from each window, their shapes elongated in the reflecting light enticing daemon to veer from their path and indulge.

Gods, she was so tempted to look up again. Curiosity rang like a cacophony of piercing bells and they grew louder with each passing moment. Nothing intrigued her more than the bull-headed man's ability to influence her mind. Raw chaos flowed through her veins and she'd yet to meet anyone else who could seduce the mind as well as she could.

They passed a building with lambent purple light and the sickly-sweet smell of opium drifted from the open door. Another detail woven into the Club Hel ambiance to seduce its customers.

"We're almost there." Nyx murmured to Brooks.

"Where is 'there'?"

"Just trust me."

A few paces later, they stepped back into another alleyway hazed with red lights and missing lampposts. Xia kept her head down, not willing to risk being caught in another situation, until a finger crooked under her chin and urged it upward.

Brooks' soft smile filled her vision. "It's safe to look up now."

"Thanks," she sighed, relief releasing the tightness in her shoulders. "Did it affect you, too?"

"A little bit. Maybe even more than you. Nyx had to shake me out of it too, and I don't even like taking dick."

Xia had to slap a hand over her mouth to cover the laugh.

"Are you crazy?" Nyx hissed. "Shut the hell up before you get us killed!"

"I don't understand how laughing is going to get us killed, Nyx." Brooks's eye-roll was evident in his voice. "They're all laughing out there. If anything we will look suspicious because we're walking head down and not talking at all."

"That's because you don't know this place like I do."

"And how do you know this place?"

"Seriously? Did you not see the people out there? This is a huge city full of horny, dumbass men who are easier to pickpocket than a newborn."

"So you steal money from the daemon in Dion?" Xia inserted herself into the conversation.

"Of course, I do. How the hell do you think I keep Avyssos floating?"

Brooks huffed a laugh. "Seems like you could just pick a window and earn plenty."

"Zeus all-fucking-mighty," Nyx sighed and rubbed her face. "Let me explain it to you in the simplest terms I can. This city was built for two reasons– filling the pockets of The Twelve and controlling daemonkind. Everyone here thinks that their ruling gods are so gracious as to provide them with a playground."

"Makes sense."

"The Twelve do not share. The people working here do not get paid because that's sharing. Which means..?" Nyx made encouraging yet sarcastic motions with her hands as if she expected Brooks to answer the question.

"They're slaves," he answered, the temperature dropping a fraction in the alley.

"Bingo. Wow buddy," she patted him on the shoulder. "You get smarter every day. I am seriously so proud of you."

Chaos flashed through those neon blue eyes. "Do not mock me, girl."

Nyx stepped backward and saluted, but her teasing smirk remained.

"Why are we here, Nyx?" Xia asked, her arms crossed and voice flat.

As the last syllable left her tongue, the air thickened and the fine hairs on her neck stood on end. Brooks and Nyx both went rigid, his eyes darting about while Nyx swallowed, her eyes crinkling as panic settled over her face. Black inked Brooks' arms as Chaos inched toward the surface.

The fine tingle along her skin morphed into an awareness that shivered down her spine. There was a power in the air that called to her chaos, and it unfurled in response. Iridescent scales dotted her arms as she searched the night. The Siren raised her head and pushed against Xia's mind.

Let me in, she hissed. *I know this power, and the God of Chaos is too weak to fight it. It will take what is ours.*

"So," Nyx said suddenly, a slight tremble in her voice. "Do we have a deal?" The girl shuddered and flinched as if something raked its claws against her mind.

A whisper of power brushed against Xia's skin. It was familiar and yet so... dissonant.

Xia's lip curled, hackles rising as she peered around and placed herself against Brooks. One look at Nyx and the point was clear– play along, or die.

"Uh... Can you lay out the terms one more time?" Brooks asked.

"Sure thing, big boy. My friend and I are willing to pay you to patronize one club of your choosing here." Nyx cleared the tremble from her voice. "As long as you end the night with us."

"Both of you?"

"Both of us. Isn't that right?" Nyx looked to Xia, a small nod of encouragement.

We must mark him. She needs to know that he is ours.

"Ours?"

"Both of us," Xia repeated. "And we get to join you."

"Your terms are fair." A cool mask had slipped over Brooks' face, no emotion showing except that of a businessman deep in negotiation. "How do we seal it?"

"Like every deal in Dion is sealed. In blood."

Take him, the Siren urged.

The slightest line formed between his brows, but Xia was quick on her feet as the possessive hunger of her Siren flared and took hold. Her canines extended as she lunged, their points sharp as blades to pierce the skin.

Xia pushed Brooks against the wall and grabbed his throat with brute force as the thrill of possession and bloodlust rang through her essence. She tilted his head back and ran her nose up the column of his neck, dragging in his scent like she was starved for it. Xia pressed her body against his, heart pounding as she pressed a kiss against the pulsing vein in his neck.

Shadows unfurled as Chaos rose to meet her Siren. Brooks' hands gripped her waist as Chaos pressed into her from behind, his shadows enveloping as they tickled her skin. Xia sank her teeth into his neck and moaned as the blood hit her tongue, each greedy drag pushing her further into euphoria.

"He tastes like mine."

He tastes like ours.

Xia was too lost in the frenzy to feel the tug at her arm. She missed the shadows melting away as they became too weak to stay. The air thinned as whatever presence stalked the night disappeared, and yet Xia still couldn't stop.

She clawed at Brooks' shoulder, clinging to him like a feral cat refusing to let go. Her greed turned to desperation, her teeth sinking in deeper to tear the artery open so it flowed more freely.

Before she could act on it, a powerful blast of chaos rocked her senses and challenged her own. The Siren spit and hissed as Xia lurched backward and fell into Nyx, her small frame nearly buckling under the weight. Brooks stood against the wall, his eyes glowing as Chaos flowed black through his veins and an eight-pointed star bloomed on his forehead. Their breaths mingled in the air as puffs of steam in the icy temperature.

Xia's darker nature was made of raw chaos and near insatiable, but Chaos was a reckoning and even her Siren would bow to him.

The weight of Xia's actions slammed into her tenfold as she watched Chaos recede. Brooks was pale and leaned heavily on the wall behind him, blood drenching his charcoal shirt in pools of black. His life force was still warm on her chin, her tears mixing in as they dripped to the ground.

Xia moved away from Nyx, her hands covering her mouth as horror turned her stomach. "Brooks, I–" she started, but her words caught underneath the lump of despair forming in her throat.

He is not lesser, Xia. He can handle us. Do not apologize, and do not balk.

"It's okay, Xia. I'm okay." He pushed away from the wall and swayed, his hand reaching back to steady him.

"It's not okay! I could have killed you!"

"Not likely, Sunshine. You've nearly killed me twice now, but I'm not counting tonight as one of those times." He winked.

"This isn't funny, Brooks." Her cheeks warmed and anger soured her stomach. Why was he not taking her seriously? Did he not understand just how close she'd come to losing herself?

"I know. I'm sorry. I shouldn't have joked." He dropped his hand from the wall and stepped toward her, but Xia couldn't let him get too close. Her Siren was still straining to be free, and Xia feared she couldn't control her a second time.

"Just stay back. I don't want to hurt you. Let's just go and get this over with."

"Xia–"

"I don't want to talk. I just want to leave. Please, Nyx, just get us to where we're going."

Nyx nodded, her body still rigid and soaking everything in with those clever eyes. "We're almost there."

Rather than turn back toward the neon lit streets, she walked deeper into the alley. Brooks and Xia followed silently. Every sidelong glance made her skin crawl, the unspoken words hanging in the air between them like a suffocating fog. Xia quickened her steps until she was in stride with Nyx.

"You didn't come up here for a snack did you?"

"Just don't. Please. I'm not going to hurt you."

"If you say so."

Xia sidestepped the comment. They reached a fork at the end of the alley, each darkened path leading to a series of other trails. Dion was a lot bigger than Xia imagined if the network of alleyways was any indication, and Nyx navigated as if she could see through the darkness with a crystalline lens.

"What was that thing back there?" Xia asked.

"Lamia. Do you know what that is?"

"I've no idea, Nyx, and I feel like you knew that."

"I did, but I'm not going to pass up a chance to make either of you feel like idiots."

Xia's Siren hissed as she coiled in Xia's chest.

"Lamia, Nyx."

"Oh, right. No one really knows anything about her."

"That's it?" Xia said incredulously.

"What do you mean 'that's it?'"

"You call me an idiot for knowing nothing, but the only thing you know is her name?"

"Well it's more than you knew wasn't it?"

Petulant child. The God of Chaos should have eaten her soul when he had the chance.

"Where are we going?" Xia sighed as she massaged her temples, irritation simmering underneath her skin.

"An inn of sorts."

Xia waited for her to continue, but Nyx seemed satisfied with the answer she gave. "That's a suspicious lack of information."

"You and papi soul-eater back there are strictly on a need-to-know basis."

"You've such a winning personality. I can't imagine why you work alone."

"I already told you why I work alone. Weakness gets you killed out here, and I refuse to risk my ass for someone who can't do what needs to be done. The only person you can trust is yourself, princess, and you'd do well to start learning it."

"Gods you're fucking impossible," Xia growled as her fists clenched, patience thinning with each poorly timed quip.

"Whatever keeps me alive, princess."

"What if I threaten to kill you? Would that make your information flow a little faster?"

Nyx gave Xia a sidelong glance as if she were assessing the comment in earnest. Xia didn't want to threaten Nyx. She even dared to think they'd formed a tenuous friendship.

She does not care for us. Was never sincere or willing to accept us. We do not need her, Xia. She's a deceiver.

"That is not true. Relationships ebb and flow. What we shared was real."

"I'm not going to stop asking, but I may start taking your advice, Nyx. If you don't talk I will consider making you."

"You wouldn't hurt me." The tension in the firm line of Nyx's lips was all Xia needed to know that Nyx was testing her.

She'd just consumed chaos in the rawest form, straight from the source and called on the fresh well of it simmering in her blood. The power was stronger than any she'd had before and she wielded it with caution. Xia didn't know what she was capable of, but she didn't want to really hurt the girl.

You may not be willing to, but I am.

Xia's Siren lunged for control and Xia was too slow to stop her. The Siren clawed her way through Xia's mind, shoving her down into the darkness until she was no longer in control.

"*Nyx!*" Xia shouted, but no one could hear her. She was just a passenger now.

Nyx stopped walking, eyes bulging as a small stream of blood flowed from her nose. "What are you doing to me?" Each word was an effort, her voice thin and cracked.

"Do you want to know a secret about me, Nyx?" The Siren stepped toward the girl, her back turned to the God of Chaos, as she donned her true form. Scales tore through the surface along her arms and cheeks, pupils narrowing to serpentine slits as her canines elongated. Her opalescent skin glinted in the stray beams of light and her nails sharpened to claws.

Nyx didn't answer the question. The Siren doubted she could.

"I'll give you a leg up on me and just tell you," she hissed. "I lied to you that day on the riverbank. I can manipulate water in *all* of its forms. Did you know that your body is mostly water, Nyx?"

No answer.

"I can pull the blood through every pore and leave nothing but a husk behind. A dried up strip of hide that crumbles in the wind." Malice laced her words as red blurred her vision.

"Do you want to know the Siren secret, though? Something I've never told anyone." She lifted a hand between them and opened her fingers. "I am the master of blood. I sing my Song and it *pours* for me. The blood in your body will do my bidding and I can control you in every sense." Xia's fingers began to close, the movement near imperceptible, as Nyx grabbed at her chest with panicked wheezes. "When I'm done with you, Nyx, I'll pull the heart from your chest and I will be the last you see before it bursts."

Xia squeezed the struggling organ for emphasis before letting Nyx go entirely. Nyx fell to the ground and scrambled backward as she held her chest. Tears fell freely, but she wore hatred as a shield as she coughed. "You're a fucking psycho, just like he is!"

"No, Nyx. I am a goddess, and you will do well to remember it. The next time you call me weak, perhaps you should consider that I'm just being kind enough to let you lead."

"Xia, what did you do?" Brooks knelt beside Nyx but she swatted him away.

"I did what was necessary to make her understand that she is starting games she doesn't have the power to play, let alone finish."

With those words and a final cold stare, the Siren receded back into the dark as Xia rushed forward. Xia stumbled as she regained control, her heart racing and tears building behind her eyes. She looked to Brooks trying to find the words to explain, or apologize, but stopped short. He was still weak. Xia could see it in every trembling limb as it fought to hold him up.

"You didn't have to do that to her. She would have come around– she would have talked. All you had to do was show an ounce of kindness and patience."

We are done being nice, and will no longer be their pawn. You would do well to remember that.

Concern etched itself in the fine lines of Brooks' forehead as he looked at her. He helped Nyx stand even though he was struggling to do so himself. They both stumbled, each leaning on the other's strength to get upright. Xia wanted to go to them, to help them up and make sure they were alright.

They will learn faster if we let them struggle.

Nyx wiped the blood from her nose with the back of her hand as she glared at Xia. She turned without a word and strided down the alley with Brooks only a few steps behind. Xia kept her eyes forward as she followed and fought to temper the well of emotions still threatening to overflow.

They made three more turns before Nyx stopped and faced one of the building walls. Xia couldn't draw much detail from the dark since her Siren withdrew, but it seemed that some of the bricks were a few shades lighter than the others. In the dark, they almost glowed.

Without a word, Nyx stepped through the wall. Brooks looked at Xia, the space between his brows wrinkling as his lips thinned, and followed the girl through.

Was he... mad?

How fucking dare *he be mad!*

"What?"

We protected him and his precious side-kick from the Lamia, and they're angry at us?

"You nearly killed them both tonight!"

Xia was met with a thunderous storm and returned it to her Siren tenfold. A hurricane raged inside as they clashed and gray clouds swirled furiously in the night sky.

If you would trust me, trust yourself, more than you trusted others tonight could have been different. I am starving, *Xia. I am bitter, enraged, and just as much a prisoner as you were in that godsforsaken club. I am a part of you and yet you cage me like an animal.*

"Because you destroy everything you touch!" Xia squatted in the alley as she fisted her hair and panted. Thunder clapped and vibrated the ground.

It's better than destroying myself as you seem so determined to do.

Xia yelled through clenched teeth as she tried to shut her eyes to the world, but as lightning flashed through the sky, Xia saw the ghost of her Siren standing before her.

I was patient, Xia. When you wanted to tear me from your soul, I went willingly. When you wanted to hide, I slept in the dark.

"Please," Xia cried as the Siren knelt in front of her.

I stayed silent as you were degraded and bloodied because you were too afraid to let me in. I ate all of your fear and anger, consumed your despair, and absorbed every ounce of bitterness so that you didn't have to bear it all on your own. I have always *been with you, Xia. Even when you did not want me, I was there.*

Xia hugged her legs tight as she fell back to sit and cry into her knees. A taloned finger brushed her hair back as a warm palm cupped her face.

The longer you deny who you are, who we are, the more you will suffer. You wish to find yourself, Xia, but you're only searching one half of the map.

Xia sniffled and looked up at her Siren. "I don't want to be like this anymore," Xia whispered out loud.

Those serpentine eyes softened and blood red tears fell down her cheeks. *I want you to love me the way I do you. I need you, Xia.*

Xia let those words resonate as all of the pieces came together. Her Siren was not a monster. She was all of the emotions Xia refused to feel, the mirror she couldn't make herself look into, and the darkness she feared.

Brooks' voice drifted through her mind as the last piece of her puzzle locked into place.

"No creature can be made only of light. There is always a flaw, or a taint. Everything is capable of being corrupt. Only those who learn to let their darkness find solace within the light can control their outcome. It's part of us all, Xia. Embracing your chaos means finding peace in your heart and living with all parts of who you are. Even the ones you hide from."

The Siren stroked Xia's cheek with her thumb as she held it in her palm. Xia let out a shaky breath and nuzzled close. For the first time in her life, she wasn't afraid of the chaos within.

Xia cradled the Siren's hand with her own as she said, "You are the shadow to tame my light when it's blinding, and I am the beacon to guide you through the dark when you're lost. Apart, we are devastation, but together... we are salvation."

Unleash your Chaos

Brooks
35

Brooks stepped through the wall and fell into a sleazy tavern, but he couldn't focus on the scene. The memory of his Siren's face in that alley would live on for millennia in his memory.

Gone was the feminine blush of her cheeks and in its place were patches of scales shimmering off of cheekbones angled so sharply they could slice. Her eyes were a hundred shades of malevolent green with pupils slit like a serpent and her talons were sharp enough to carve the heart from Nyx's chest.

The biggest change, though, had been her scent. Her sea salt essence bittered to something more metallic.

Like… blood.

Nyx shoved through the room until she reached the bar and dropped a few stolen coins on the top. A small glass of amber liquid slid in front of her and she gripped it with trembling hands as she threw it back. A quick wave to the daemon behind the bar made another appear in her waiting hands.

Brooks left her to it and faced the wall he'd come through, but Xia wasn't standing there. Where was she? Had something happened after he stepped through? Gods, if whatever that thing was in the alley returned…

"Should we go check on her?" He threw the silent thought to Chaos.

I would love to say no, but I'm getting cagey.

"You're always fucking cagey."

Not the point. Go back through. I need to see her.

Before Brooks could raise his foot, Xia stepped through the wall with a scowl. She stopped as if she weren't expecting him to be there and then sidestepped.

"Xia, wait." He followed her through the crowd. "Xia, where are you going?"

"Anywhere to be away from the two of you," she called over her shoulder.

Xia wound through the mess of mismatched tables until she reached an empty table placed on the opposite side of the tavern.

"She wasn't kidding. She is as far away from us as she can get."

Speak for yourself. She said 'the two of you' which means you and that infant of a girl. She said nothing about me.

"Don't you fucking dare go over there. We are a team."

We are no such thing. You're the one who can't handle her Siren. This speaks nothing toward my ability.

"I didn't say I couldn't handle it."

It's nothing to be ashamed of. She is powerful and has been left untamed for too long. She needs a darkness deep enough to match her own. You and Xia are a perfect match. It is her Siren I want to dance with.

"Are they not the same?"

They are as we are, and that is why they are perfect for us.

Brooks chewed that over as he watched his Siren from afar. Her table was seated by the large fireplace off in the corner next to a single stairwell. The firelight chased the shadows from the table, but her expressions were heavy enough to carry their own.

Everything in his gut longed to join her at the table, but would she want him there?.

Brooks looked back to Nyx and the sour expression plastered on her face and decided he didn't want to be there with her either. What had she done to make Xia so angry?

She is a moody child and you'll gain nothing by asking her.

"I don't think Xia wants to talk to us right now. I'll start with Nyx. If she lies, you can eat her soul."

That's the best news I've heard all damn day.

He sat on a rickety barstool beside her. Brittle and torn vinyl pricked his thighs. This place had definitely seen better days.

"Cheers, asshole." Nyx put her drink into the air before tossing back just as she did the first.

"How many of those have you had?"

"Lost track at five."

"Don't you think you're too small and underfed to drink that much ambrosia?"

"Don't you think you're too stupid to make that assessment? And it's not ambrosia. We can't afford that here. It's whatever fruit doesn't get used in the kitchen and is stuck in a bucket until it goes so bad it melts and then fucks with your brain. So piss off and let me drink in peace."

Brooks nodded as he tapped a finger against the scuffed bar. Names and profanity were etched into every surface, some worn down over years of sliding glasses and resting elbows while others were so fresh that the color of new wood hadn't been taken over by grime.

"What did you say to her, Nyx?"

Another full glass was placed in her hand, but she paused before downing it like the rest. Her hand came away before she circled the rim with a finger.

"What makes you think I said anything to her?"

"I've never seen her look like that before."

"Well if I'm hearing things correctly and, trust me, I am, you've only known her just as long as I have."

"I've known her longer than you have," Brooks argued.

"That's not what it looked like on that beach."

"We've known each other for a while. We just... We hadn't ever met in person."

"That's disgusting. You two are way too attached to not have met less than a week ago."

"That's not the fucking point Nyx. I want to know what you said to her in the alley." Brooks grabbed her shoulder, spinning her chair to face him.

Nyx slapped his hand and leaned back, her reddened eyes struggling to focus. "Don't you touch me. I am done being touched by the two of you for a lifetime."

"What. Did. You. Say?" he ground out.

"I just told her that she couldn't trust anyone but herself, okay? And I meant it. Relying on others gets you killed. Their weakness becomes your weakness, and I've got too much on the line to take on someone else's baggage."

Chaos growled, That doesn't make any sense. She's hiding something.

"No way that would make her lose her shit like that," Brooks threw back at Nyx.

"Well, I don't know what to tell you, buddy. That's all we talked about. Now, if you don't mind." Nyx stood and waved the daemon serving drinks over again. "I need two rooms. One for me, one for my friend."

"Joining?" the man asked.

"Fuck no," Nyx hiccuped. "Far 'way as you can get us." Another hiccup followed as he slipped two keys from under the bar and into her hands. Nyx slammed one of them down in front of him and patted his shoulder. "You and that one are sharing a room 'cuz I need some time alone." Her words slurred as she stumbled, but it didn't stop her from navigating through the tables full of daemon and up the steps.

"Room number's on the key," the barkeep said as he wiped down a clean glass. "Clean sheets and towels are free, food and drink's not." He nodded and walked to serve a daemon hanging over the bartop reaching for a bottle of gods knew what.

Brooks looked back to Xia's table and found her staring at him. Her expression was flat and the fire in her eyes banked to embers, but there was still something brewing under the surface. He was hoping she'd calmed enough to at least go to their room and rest.

He held the key up and tilted his head toward the stairs. She didn't come to him, just walked toward the steps and up without a backward glance. Brooks took the steps two at a time and found her leaning against the wall, waiting to follow him to their room.

Brooks wiggled the old key into the hole and twisted. The lock was old and caught at nearly every turn, but eventually gave way. He held the door open for Xia as she stepped through.

"Wow, I'm surprised I get to go in first. Don't you need to check the room for rabid bunnies or sharp corners? I may fall and hit my head on one, you know."

Brooks sighed as exhaustion crept in. "No, I don't need to check the room, Xia."

She nodded and Brooks could see the reply sitting on her tongue, but rather than spitting it at him she turned around. The room was basic– yellowing walls accompanied by a single bed with a green comforter that was probably black at one time. The sour smell of old food and fermented fruit drifted from the tavern and clogged his nose. He didn't even want to know what the bathroom looked like.

"I'm sorry, Xia. This is terrible. I can go ask for something cleaner."

"It's fine, Brooks. I don't need luxury. I'm not fragile."

You're really fucking this up.

He swallowed the building frustration. "I know you're not fragile." Brooks walked in and shut the door behind him, locking the single rusted mechanism in the doorknob. Only one lock was not ideal, but it would have to do. He would use his shadows to stand guard–

She drained us when she fed.

Xia opened the bathroom door and stared for a few seconds before shutting it again. "Neither of us will be bathing tonight. Do yourself a favor and *do not* open that door."

"Fucks sake." He rubbed a hand over his eyes as he flipped through their options. Surely there was another place in Dion they could stay for the night. "Maybe we could go somewhere else. I assume we need money, which I don't have, but you could use your Song to influence–"

"No."

"No?"

"No. I'm not calling on my chaos again."

"Sunshine," he whispered. "You didn't do anything wrong."

"I don't want to have this conversation again."

"We hardly had it the first time, and I really think we should talk about it."

"I'm done talking tonight, Brooks. I just want to sleep, and I think you should too."

"You shouldn't hide from it, Xia. If you keep pushing it down it's going to take control of you. You'll lose who you are, and I know you don't want that. Gods, and you look so much more alive now that you've fed."

"Stop!"

"You don't have to kill another daemon to feed your chaos anymore, Sunshine. I can be that balance for you–"

"I said *stop*!" she screamed, her voice an inhuman roar that rattled through the building. Xia pulled at her hair as she bent at the waist as if whatever was lurking couldn't find her if she got small enough. "Just get out."

"Xia, please, I–"

"Just get out, Brooks! Get out, get out, get out!"

Tears pooled in his eyes as the pain bottled in her voice shot through the air like shrapnel. She screamed over and over, her words echoing through the room until he stepped into the hall and closed the door behind him. His chest squeezed as he leaned against the door, the sound of her sobs the ultimate torture.

"Take it away," he said out loud. "Take it away, Chaos."

His passenger didn't say anything, only laced his shadowed fingers through Brooks' and flipped their hands. When Brooks opened his eyes again, he was seeing his body move from someone else's eyes. The pain in his heart still remained, but the anxiety released the vice in his chest and the exhaustion fell away, all handed to a god who felt nothing but ruthless logic.

Go rest, Brooks. I've got us.

With those three words, Brooks lost himself to the darkness wondering if he'd ever resurface.

Unleash your Chaos

Persephone
36

Persephone thought death would be weightless, her soul like the feather of a bird drifting with a summer breeze. She thought that her mind and body would finally be at peace, that the wrongs of the world would be a physical thing as it lifted from her. Persephone knew she wasn't dead, though, because everything hurt and dying would be a blessing. Just like when Narcissus left her at the bottom of a pond. Somehow, Persephone was alive and she dreaded opening her eyes to find out why.

"Are you awake, Beauty?"

Persephone squeezed her lids tight before prying them open. Through blurry lashes, all she could see was the cracked ceiling of his office stained from wood-burning smoke. "What did you do to me?" she croaked.

"I've secured myself a life partner in this dreadful place."

She couldn't see him, but his voice filled her ears from every direction.

"What did you do, Hades?" Persephone tested her limbs and flinched. It was painful, but they did move.

"It's complicated. I'm not sure you have the mind space to keep up."

Anger fueled her movements as she rolled to her side and tried to sit. "Try me," she ground out through the pain.

"Do you know why I live in the Underworld, Persephone?"

"You know I don't."

"I do, and that's why explaining it to you is going to be a waste of my breath."

"I think I deserve it after what you've done." She sat up and faced the man she thought she loved. He was laid back in his chair with one leg crossed over the other like he was waiting for an artist to paint him.

"I'm here because my brother cursed me."

That caught her attention. "What?"

"Zeus. We were losing the war against the Titans, you see. Overpowered and outnumbered. Desperate to find something that would tip the scales. That was when those three cunts of fate showed their faces. They made us an offer we couldn't refuse– chaos enough for two. Zeus and I would hold the power of a Titan and win the war, but with great power comes grave consequences, they warned. The Titans were tyrants because the chaos drove them mad, and that was to be our fate." Hades sipped from his chalice and followed her with watchful eyes as she pushed from the floor and moved to occupy the chair in front of him. He waited until she was settled to continue.

"We accepted the offer, of course. How could we not? We defeated our elders less than a year after that. Ten long years of war, and all it took was a bargain with fate." He scoffed as he shook his head, taking another sip from his chalice. "By the end, the overflow of chaos was already taking its toll. Zeus became paranoid and exiled anyone he thought could challenge him. Including the brother who fought by his side. We swore an oath upon Styx when we accepted that deal. Even daemon as strong as The Twelve have to keep promises bound by the river. I won't go into details, but he outmaneuvered me. Tricked me into breaking my oath and the river Styx claimed me. I've been exiled here ever since."

"Are you dead?"

Hades rolled his eyes. "No, I'm not dead, you dense girl."

"You said the Underworld was no place for the living."

"I did, but I hold the power of a Titan, Persephone. I can do everything," he ground out, "except leave this godsforsaken place. Trapped within the inner circles of hell and going mad."

"So you trapped me here because... because you're **bored**?"

"Well, when you put it that way it sounds rather daft."

Her head was spinning, unable to comprehend the words laid out in front of her. "I want to leave, Hades. I want to go back home. Demeter will pay a heavy price for my return."

"I'm afraid I can't do that, Beauty."

"I'm serious, Hades. She has the hand of Zeus. We can bargain for your freedom—"

"Persephone," he tisked. "I want that for the two of us more than you know. Unfortunately, it will never happen. I'm bound to the Underworld just as steadfast as you are."

"I'm still alive, Hades!" Persephone gestured to herself frantically, hands waving up and down as she pressed her point. "I can—" she stopped as something odd caught her eye, body frozen and chin trembling. Persephone looked at her shaking hands and choked on a sob as she turned them over. The outline was hazy and her skin was faintly transparent.

"The dead cannot walk among the living, just as the living cannot walk among the dead. If you're in the Underworld, Persephone, you are either dead or dying." Hades sipped his wine as the mad gleam in his eye dipped to her feet and back up.

A tear fell from the pool in her eyes as his pompous smile sent a wave of ice cold horror washing over her body. Persephone shuttered, her breaths coming in shallow pants as she closed her eyes and turned to follow his stare. When she opened her eyes, she stopped breathing all together.

"Oh, gods," she whispered, her head shaking as denial crept in.

Pale pink irises clouded by death stared into the void. Light danced over her pallid features, highlighting sunken eyes and concave cheeks that lay in vomit. It must have been her body's last feeble attempt to dispel the poison and save the girl who'd trusted too much.

"What have you done to me?" she whispered.

"I cannot walk the surface with you, so I brought you to me." His head dipped as he aimed to catch her eyes. His brow was soft, encouraging even, but the madness in his eyes was a spark she hated herself for not seeing before. It was there, bright as Polaris in the night sky. "You're my soulmate, Persephone. The other half of my beating heart. We belong together."

"Your soulmate?" Her voice rose with each word as her vision tunneled. "What beating heart? I've no heart left to beat, Hades!"

"You don't need one, Beauty. As long as mine beats, we live. That's the wondrous part. I am sorry it had to be this way. If I could have joined you on Mount Olympus, I would have. Alas, that's not our fate."

"Fate? How dare you speak of fate to me! You are the cause of this. Not fate. You!"

"Our hearts and souls are bound, Persephone. It would have ended this way no matter the course. I simply sped it up."

"What do you mean sped it up?" She exclaimed, brows knitting as she tried to piece together her downfall. "How did I die, Hades?"

"Slowly and with as much grace as the Underworld allows."

"So you didn't even have the nerve to do it yourself. You just let your prison do it for you like a coward?"

His nostrils flared the moment before he crossed the space between them and struck her face with the palm of his hand. Persephone's head whipped from the impact as the smack reverberated through the office. "Do not forget who you speak to, girl. Cursed I may be, but I still hold the power of a Titan. I can call forth flames and summon the beasts in Black Mirror Lake with little more than a thought. You died by my hand because I showed you mercy. I could have let the rivers take you, cursed you to endure their wrath as I had to. Instead, I fed you the fruit of the dead and let you die peacefully."

Something coiled in her belly then, an unfamiliar presence brewing from the rage simmering in her blood. "The fruit of the dead?"

His lips curled, venom dripping from his smile. "The pomegranate is a beautiful fruit. Did you know that it can only grow if watered by the rivers of the Underworld?"

Persephone wracked her mind for memories of the fruit. Hades' voice filled her mind from the day he'd carried her broken body to his bed. "It's an herbal blend that will help heal you from the inside out," he'd said. "Pomegranate. I grow them myself."

Another memory tugged at her of Narcissus plucking fruit from the hanging trees around his pond and cracking it open to expose the seeds. "This is a pomegranate. All of these red sacks are filled with tiny seeds and juices. They're truly delightful. Here. Give it a try."

Demeter had been right all along. Stupid. Weak. Head in the clouds. And now she had her death to show for it. "Narcissus. Was he part of this, too?"

"Ah. Disgusting isn't he? Black Mirror Lake is the parallel to his beloved lagoon. A small pool of water from the Underworld that bubbled to the surface. The rivers have a mind of their own, Persephone, and wouldn't pass up an opportunity to steal a soul. Narcissus made it too easy, really. There's nothing he wouldn't do in exchange for the freedom to leave the waters gaze upon himself in their reflection. I must admit, my interest was piqued when he requested your innocence, but it was worth it to get you here."

Persephone's fingers flexed, fists clenching as hatred reddened her vision. "Requested?" she spat, low and menacing. "As if it were yours to bargain?"

His features fell as his head cocked to the side. "Of course it was mine to barter, and I'd do it again to get you here. Hasn't it all been worth it in the end, Beauty?"

His words rang through her skull like the clamoring of bells, each chime driving her closer to madness.

Never wander too far, Persephone. Don't talk to anyone without my permission, Persephone. Be a good girl and listen to your mother, Persephone.

Gong...

Bloom the brightest petals, Persephone, because men like their wives to be the epitome of beauty. Don't eat that Persephone, men don't like plump women. Sit down and be quiet. Men don't like opinionated women, Persephone.

Gong...

Defiance is not obedience, Persephone. Never be loose with your words, Persephone.

Gong...

Narcissus took the only choice she'd ever made for herself and twisted it into a malignant evil. Hades picked up the pieces just to shatter her all over again.

Gong...

A rage, as ancient as the bones Olympia was built upon, iced her dead veins and something vital cracked inside of her, the fissure in her soul an irreparable scar. Her innocence and stupidity died with the girl on the floor, and a phoenix rose from the pyre ashes as a goddess of malice and wrath was birthed by the flames.

Her corporeal form flickered between life and death as the blooms of spring wilted and left behind a forest of thorns that mutilated and twisted the chaos inside until it was as dead as she was. Ruby red talons extended from each finger as Persephone became the piece on the board Hades never considered.

"Come now, Beauty." Hades extended a waiting hand. "If you're done having your tantrum, I'll take you to see the rest of our kingdom."

Persephone closed the distance between them and grasped his hand. A smile was his only warning before she struck with lethal speed and grace. Her clawed hand plunged through Hades' chest and Persephone breathed a deep, gratifying sigh as she ripped aside bone and muscle to pull the beating heart from his chest. Hades gasped, the fleeting moments of shock lingering in the rattle of his breath.

"Your pompous attitude was always your greatest weakness, Hades," she whispered. His head rested on her shoulder, body slack and leaning against her. He wasn't dead yet. He was a daemon with the power of an Olympian and Titan combined, but a soul could not inhabit a dead body.

A pearlescent light drifted from his open mouth and Persephone hummed as she consumed it. "As weak and gullible as I was, Hades, I was observant while you were quick to dismiss it. I want you to know it's your arrogance that got you killed."

She bit his earlobe, the sharp point of her canine coaxing forth a bead of blood. His eyes moved back and forth, pleading silently for a mercy he wouldn't receive.

Persephone pushed his lifeless form to the floor and sneered as she watched it fall before kneeling by the shell of who she was. She allowed herself one moment of remorse to mourn the ingenuous girl at her feet and everything she could have been.

Persephone stared into those unseeing eyes before she closed them for the last time with a brush of her hand. She leaned forward, placed a gentle kiss on each eyelid, and rested her forehead against the girl she used to be.

Persephone lifted and wiped away the tears as she let her newfound darkness fill the gaping hole in her chest. She opened the rib cage of her corpse and replaced her withered organ with Hades' still-beating heart. It was faint, and fading fast, but it wasn;t gone yet.

She didn't know what to expect since Hades words were her only guidance. Soulmates only needed a single heart to survive. Whatever cruel trick of fate or chaos that was, it was disgusting and she would see it crushed.

The heart melded seamlessly and began the work of regeneration and reanimation. Before long, the remnants of Persephone's past was sitting in the chair across from Hades'. The body was near lifeless, staring into the flames, mouth slackened, but it would do.

She sat in Hades' chair and pulled his chess board close. To her shock, the game had changed. Gone were the generic pawns and crowned queens. In their place were pieces of obsidian carved in the likeness of all of the most powerful daemon in Olympia, and standing beside Hades was Persephone. Her name soured on her tongue as she stared at the pieces.

She was not that girl anymore. She was a goddess torn in two, split between maid and monster.

As she stared at the ongoing game of gods, a name bubbled to the surface worthy of her new prowess. "Melinoe," she whispered.

Melinoe circled a taloned finger around the remaining piece of Persephone on the chess board before crushing it in her palm and looking at the pink-haired girl staring into the flames. "We're going to do great things, you and I. You will walk among the living and be my eyes where I cannot see, my ears where I cannot hear. You and I are going to make them all pay, Rue."

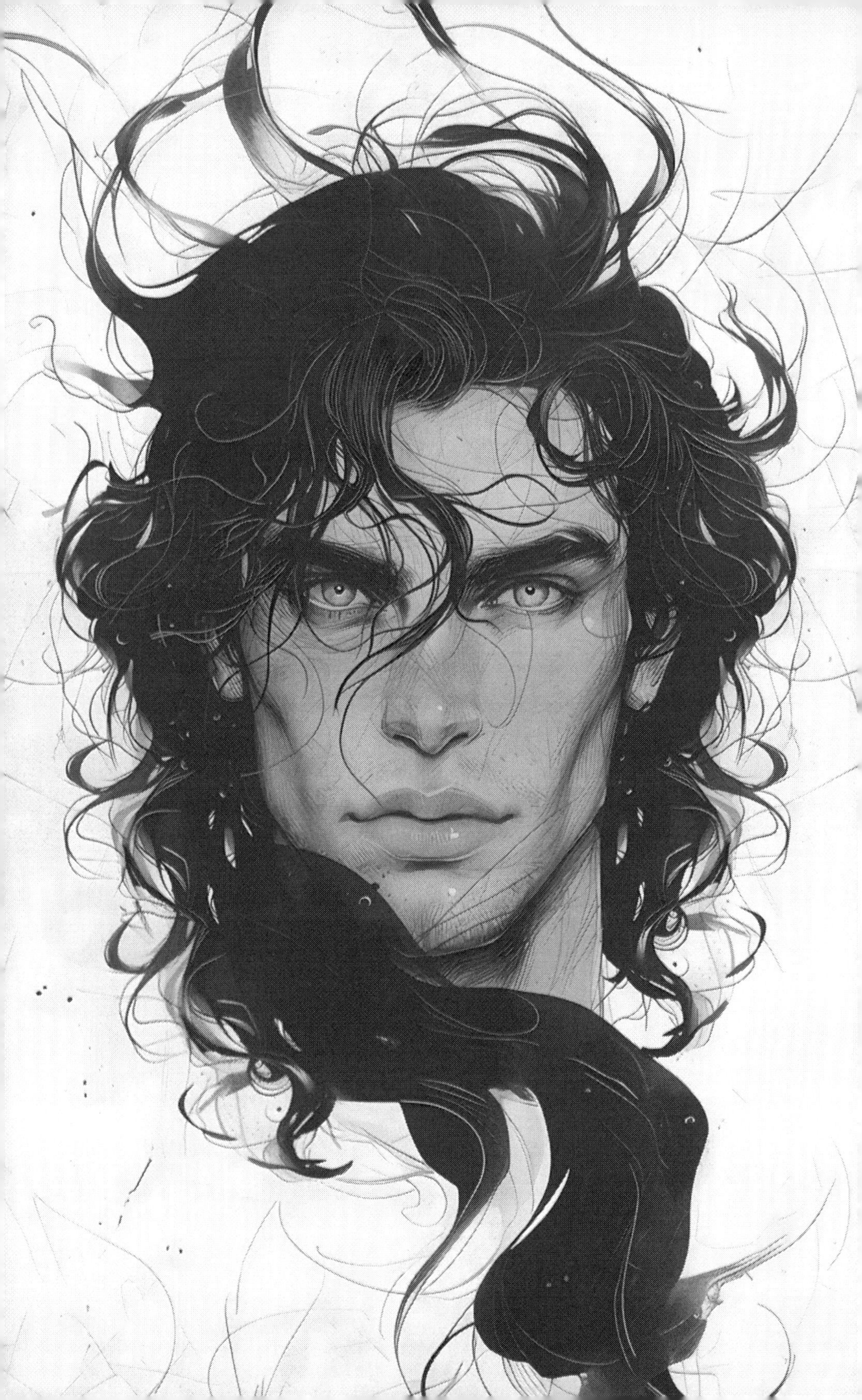

Chaos

37

Xia's shouts from the other side of the door sent a wave of emotion rolling through his system that he didn't quite understand. Brooks was his better half, the part of him capable of analyzing emotion and empathizing alongside it. Chaos could identify it in others, but sympathy was as far as he could get.

The girl raging just inside the room, though? He loved her. Loved her more than he loved himself with no comprehension as to the hows and whys. Even the darkness growing inside of her called to the very core of his being and he longed for the both of them.

No matter. Comprehension wasn't important. His role in the universe was not gray– it was black and white, something Brooks would never understand.

He took a deep breath and assessed the situation. His purpose was different from either of his companions. Their emotions were too involved– revenge on the captor, confronting the doctor from the Asylum, and setting the scorecard even. None of it, though, was as important as the cycle of chaos.

The blood moon was in twenty-four hours and Xia's demon drained him dry. They didn't know where the entrance to the Freakshow was or how to make it appear. He didn't have enough chaos to summon a shadow, much less be of any aid in the face of danger.

A flutter of unease passed through his stomach, but Chaos was quick to squash it. All logic pointed to a true death if anything happened while his stores of power were so low. It wasn't an option. If he ceased to exist, then so did Brooks. If they were dead, there would be no one to protect Xia. The short-term answer was to get a quick fix of chaos and there was only one way to do it.

Chaos swept a furtive glance around the hall and stopped toward the room furthest from his. He knew his Siren well enough to know that his actions would impact her, but they were necessary to protect both her and himself. The least he could do was start as far away as possible in hopes she would fall asleep before he reached the adjoining rooms.

Chaos planted his feet in front of room number one, closed his eyes, and pushed his awareness out in all directions. The bar below was in full swing with the late hour. Countless bodies were crammed in the small space below, scraping tables and clinking glasses adding to the cacophony drifting up the staircase.

It would work in his favor. No one would hear the screams.

He examined the bodies below, each appearing as a thin, glowing outline in his mind as his baser instincts detected their body heat. In the center of each mass was a black void that indicated the amount of chaos the daemon carried. Not a single patron below had enough to satiate his needs.

Pity. They would all be taken for the cause.

Chaos pulled his awareness from the lower half of the building and sent it out to the level he would start with. Every room apart from his and Nyx's had at least two daemon, all of which were asleep except for Xia and four down the hall in room ten.

He took a moment to focus on Xia. The well of chaos in her center was massive, covering the entirety of her chest and belly. The last he'd checked, it was large but was still a calm, round mass in the center. Since she'd fed from him, though...

The difference was drastic. What once rippled like a clear pool of water now crashed like the blackest seas.

Chaos cleared his throat and refocused on the task at hand. He had an obligation to the universe to identify the cycle disruption and fix it. Two daemon slept in room one, and they would be the first to fall. He twisted the knob, its rusted lock no match for his strength, and swung the door open as the broken pieces of brass fell to the carpet.

Sleeping peacefully in the bed was a man and woman. Their bodies were intertwined, his hugging her from the back with their fingers laced and held over her heart. The dark circle of chaos within their centers was as small as a pin prick, barely enough to conjure a shadow in the palm of his hand, but every drop was imperative to survival.

The first few rooms were going to be the most painful. He didn't have enough power to ease the transition from life to death. However, there was no room for remorse or regret.

Chaos approached the couple and stood over their prone forms. He placed a hand on the sleeping man's shoulder and used the connection to call forth the chaos residing in his soul. It was hesitant at first, fighting to stay latched onto the essence that kept it alive.

It was the only flaw to his power and one that he could never fix. The universe demanded balance, and even he was not capable of defying it. If the chaos was removed, so too was the soul. Whatever force brought him into existence decided long before his birth that one could not be the master of souls and chaos at once.

Chaos gripped the bead of power with more force and tugged. Although the power fought, it was no match for him. The man sat upright with a gasp, his pupils blown and eyes bulging. He grabbed at his chest as he fought for air, every vein in his body swelling near to bursting. He turned that panicked stare on Chaos, but his body already knew what his mind couldn't yet comprehend– he was going to die.

The woman rolled toward her thrashing partner, her eyes still foggy with sleep, until she opened them enough to see Chaos standing overtop her dying partner. She screamed and threw the sheet aside, her legs tangling in the flying fabric and forcing her to the floor. She kicked as she crawled away from the bed and huddled against the furthest wall and sobbed, her body too fear stricken to flee.

Desperation urged the man to fight. He threw his body to the side and kicked his legs, but he was no match for Chaos. Chaos rolled the man back over and placed a knee on his chest to keep him still as he forced the bead of power out in earnest. The man's body seized as his chaos drifted past his lips and into the air above. Different shades of red and purple bloomed along his torso as the organs burst, his muscles clenching and releasing in relentless spasms as the last shreds of his soul were torn free. Chaos closed his eyes and inhaled the floating orb of power. Though it had given a valiant fight to stay inside the man, it joined his well eagerly.

He turned his eyes to the woman huddled against the wall, her pleas unintelligible through the screams. Chaos rounded the bed and stopped to kneel in front of her. Their eyes met, hers bloodshot and brimmed with tears. She dug her heels into the wooden floor in a desperate attempt to run, but there was nowhere for her to go.

"I am sorry," Chaos murmured. "Your sacrifice is necessary."

She screamed as he placed his hands on her cheeks, inky shadows crawling through her veins in search of its likeness.

Chaos held her stare and watched every moment of her death through her eyes. She clawed at his wrists and she coughed blood, the spatter dotting his face and neck as it ran in rivulets down her chin. When he'd taken the last ounce of chaos from her soul, he stood and let her body slump to the side in a heap of useless flesh.

All through the night, Chaos went room to room gathering bits of power to store and, when he was done with the top level, he moved to the tavern. His shadows enveloped the room and pulled chaos from every patron before the thought to fight could cross their minds. He didn't stop until every last drop of chaos was torn from its soul.

Chaos stood and gazed upon the desecrated bodies strewn about, not a single bead of remorse dripping from his blackened soul. When the sun rose, whispers of his massacre would travel with the breeze to every shadowed corner of the universe and, under the grand menagerie tent of the Freakshow, every daemon would know his name.

Not the Father of Darkness. Not Chaos, the Deathless God or the Void Between the Stars. The Soul Eater was coming, and they would pay in blood for their crimes.

Unleash your Chaos

XIA
38

"Get up," a voice hissed. "Xia, you have to wake up!"

Xia pulled her mind from the depths as her body shook back and forth.

"Xia come on, please! We have to go!"

Her eyelids opened and blinked against the rays of sunlight, stomach lurching as adrenaline forced her into motion. Xia sprang up from the bed and away from the intruder, her arms up defensively as she called on her chaos.

"It's me," the blurry figure whispered. "We have to go."

Xia wiped her eyes to clear the fog and opened them to see a figure clad head to toe in cream robes. Her pink irises looked desperately between Xia and the door, a single strand of fuchsia hair falling over a freckled cheek.

"Ruby? What are you doing here?"

"Something's happened at Avyssos, Xia. Something bad, but I don't have time to explain it to you right now. We need to get out of here before he comes back."

Xia's heart pounded in her chest as her mind worked to both wake up and take action. She needed more information but couldn't focus on which questions to ask first.

"Please, Xia."

"Where's Brooks?"

Ruby set her jaw, but pity touched her eyes.

"Ruby! Where is Brooks?"

"We have to leave him."

"What? Why? What happened?"

Ruby looked away. "They're dead, Xia. The villagers. He–" she choked, "he killed them all."

Ice ripped through Xia's veins. Brooks wouldn't.

That mask of pity slipped through the tears, and Xia hated the way it made her feel. Like she was a stupid, blind girl with no knowledge of the world.

"I tried to tell you. He is so controlling, Xia. Watching your every move and quick to decide your next. I worried about you, but who was I to stop you from going with him?" Ruby stepped toward Xia with every word, her hands out placatingly as if she were a wild animal ready to flee. "I saw the signs, Xia, but I didn't know how to make you believe me."

The Siren squirmed as it worked to understand the information.

"He is the god of the gods, Xia. Zeus is cruel, but the Father of Darkness rules with an iron fist. He does not have the ability to love or empathize."

"Yes, he does." Xia stood tall, every bone in her body rigid and defiant. "I've felt his love. I have seen his love."

Ruby's mouth thinned again, and there it was. That fucking pity.

"No. You've seen the man's love. You haven't seen the monster. He ripped the chaos from every daemon in our town and shredded their souls to do it. Do you understand what that means? He took their power and they are just... gone. No chance at the cycle of life and death. Their souls are wiped clean from the universe. And now that the Chaos has been fed, he will be strong enough to destroy the man and take back his throne of darkness."

"No..." Xia stumbled. "It doesn't make sense."

"I know. Gods, Xia, I swear I know it. But you know their cruelness. You've lived it first hand, and that was just from some low level daemon. If the Lord of Nightmares was capable of that cruelty, what do you think the god of us all is capable of?"

Xia swallowed. When it stuck, she tried again but nothing made it past the lump in her throat.

"I... I can prove it. I don't want to have to, but we need to leave before he comes back. I'm afraid he's consuming power so that he is strong enough to take yours. You were so strong on that river bank, Xia. He's going to need your chaos in order to take on the rest of Olympia."

"How do you know that's what he wants?"

"What else would he want? You say he loves you. Do you think he doesn't want to avenge you?"

"I asked him not to, Ruby. He wouldn't go against my wishes–" Xia stopped.

He has gone against our wishes every step of the way, the Siren hissed. *He said he would kill them all, and then lock us in a pretty cage to keep us safe.*

"Come on." Ruby held her hand out. "I think seeing it is the only way to understand the danger you're in. That *we* are in."

Xia couldn't move. She stared at the proffered hand for what could have been the span of a heartbeat or years. Brooks couldn't have hurt anyone. Not after the asylum. Gods, he was tortured in that place, his mind ripped apart and sewn together only to be shredded again.

But...

Xia knew firsthand how that rage felt. How the beast inside simmers until the pressure releases with the force of a supernova. She'd lost herself on the black sands of her home, Anthemoessa, and she was only a daemon. The Twelve proclaimed themselves gods, but what would it be like if the true god of them all decided the world deserved his wrath?

Xia placed her trembling hand into Ruby's and let the woman lead her from the room. The moment Ruby opened the door, the stench of copper assaulted her nose.

Blood. A lot of it.

Dread hit her harder than the Lord of Nightmares ever did as Ruby walked her directly across to the hall to room nine. The door was cracked and fragments of rust and metal lay on the ground in front of it.

When Ruby's hand touched the door, she hesitated and looked back at Xia. With a squeeze of the hand, she whispered, "I'm so sorry, Xia."

Ruby pushed the door open and pressed her back against it, her head bowing and bottom lip trembling. Xia let go of Ruby's hand, closed her eyes, and lowered her chin. She allowed one last heavy breath before facing the reality of her situation. When she opened her eyes, though, she wished she hadn't.

A boot mark was imprinted with blood into the carpet beside her foot. It was twice the size of hers. There was no denying that it was a man's, but that didn't mean it was Brooks'.

Did it?

Her gaze followed each print down the short entry hall until they ended and the massacre began. The bed was soaked in pools of blood so thick it had yet to dry. Black spots stained the carpet and spattered against the wall furthest from the door.

Tears streamed down Xia's face, dripping from her chin and joining the boot prints on the floor. Apprehension set her stomach to roiling, the contents threatening to spill with each step she took.

Xia stepped around the largest parts of the mess, but there was too much gore to avoid it completely. Her eyes closed each time her bare foot made contact, a sob escaping with every sticky pull. When her vision crested the edge of the bed, Xia wished she'd turned around at the sight of blood. Wished she'd taken Ruby's word and gone no further.

Xia fell to her knees, the stiff ends of the carpet digging into her skin as she screamed. Nothing could have prepared her for the sight. She bent forward and retched, the need to both vomit and breathe warring with her soul shattering cries.

Piled together against the wall was a mess of flesh and ichor. Xia had seen a lot of terrible things in her existence, but nothing rivaled the daemon laying dead on the floor. Their mutilated bodies looked like they'd been torn apart from the inside out. The exposed flesh was riddled with gaping holes and patches of deep reds and purples as if every organ and vessel exploded outward.

Xia couldn't move, or think, or breathe. She couldn't believe that Brooks would do this. He wasn't capable of it, and she had to believe that he wouldn't allow Chaos to do it either.

"He couldn't have done this, Ruby. I know him and he wouldn't have. He wouldn't have done it," she sobbed as her body rocked back and forth. "I know he couldn't have." Tears mixed with her nose drippings, spit dotting her chin as she cried.

A hand rubbed smooth circles on her back as another cupped her cheek. Ruby appeared in her blurry vision, shushing and whispering with her forehead pressed against Xia's.

"How do you know? Ruby, how do you know it was him?"

Ruby focused those pink eyes on hers with an intensity Xia felt down to her bones. "This is every room, including the tavern downstairs. Every room, Xia... except yours."

Xia cried out as grief poured from her in waves at Ruby's implication. She wanted so badly to believe it wasn't Brooks, but who else would leave her untouched? To murder every single daemon in a building?

Every single daemon... but *one*.

Xia grabbed Ruby's arms in a crushing hold as desperation consumed her. "What about, Nyx? Is she okay? Please, Ruby, tell me she's okay."

Silver lined those eyes, and it was answer enough. Xia wanted to go back to sleep and pretend it had never happened. Curl up in a ball and never wake up again. Her heart couldn't take it.

"I know it's hard to understand right now, Xia, but we've got to go."

"Just leave me here. I can't, gods, I can't... It's too much."

You do not deserve to die here, her Siren hissed. *Do not let him do that to you. I will drag us out of here if it's the last thing I do.*

Ruby gripped Xia beneath the arms and pulled, forcing her onto trembling knees as Ruby led her from the room toward the stairs.

"When we get to the bottom, don't look, okay? Xia?"

Xia nodded but as they hit the landing, she couldn't help herself. The scene in room nine was but a preview to the real massacre. She turned her head into the crook of Ruby's neck as she gagged.

"Shhhh, I know it, sweet girl. It's okay. I'm going to get you out of this. We're going to go through the kitchen and out the back door so no one sees us, and then I'll take you somewhere safe."

Xia focused on putting one foot in front of the other as her friend led them out into the dawn. She didn't ask questions when Ruby took the back alleys instead of the streets. She didn't even ask when Ruby helped her into a black carriage with two crossed sickles on the door that shone like diamonds against the morning light.

Ruby settled Xia on lush black cushions while she talked to someone outside. Xia was too numb to keep track of what was happening. She felt nothing as Ruby got back into the carriage to help her lay down, covering her with a blanket. Colors blurred to gray as she sunk into the deepest recesses of her mind where she would hide until she felt strong enough to face the horrors of the day.

With her head settled in Ruby's lap, the carriage rocking rhythmically back and forth, and fingers combing through her hair, Xia submitted to the nightmare that would haunt her forever.

"They're all gone, Xia. The villagers. He killed them all."

Unleash your Chaos

Chaos

39

The city of Dion was a cesspool of the worst sort of daemon. Chaos spent the night lurking through the shadows listening for any whisperings of the Freakshow and stealing the chaos from anyone carrying enough of it to make a difference. The trail of bodies in his wake was adding up and would double before he left.

He'd gained enough chaos from the tavern to move through the night without issue, but was careful with how much he used. Even if he ripped the soul from every daemon in Dion, it wouldn't make up a fraction of what he once held. Chaos told himself for the millionth time that night that it would have to do. He was lucky that Brooks was silent throughout the night. He needed a clear head, figuratively and literally.

Though he didn't learn anything of the infamous Freakshow, he did get some background on the city. Dion was an empire soliciting every debauched deed imaginable. From intoxication to fetish and torture, it was a playground for the wicked named in honor of Dionysus and was the main settlement of his worshippers. Daemon who frequented the city to party were wary of the crazed followers, but the consensus was that if you didn't bother them, they wouldn't bother you.

He'd mapped out the entirety of the city during his exploration. A river ran from the top of Mount Olympus and branched into several streams at the base. Built around the centermost stream, the neon lit buildings sat on either side and funneled citizens to a large, marble temple.

Chaos visited the temple and scoffed at its grandeur. Villages like Nyx's starved while a power-hungry daemon had a monstrosity of granite erected for looks. At least fifty steps were carved into the mountain leading up to the shrine that stretched the entire length of the bluff. Columns stood at the entrance of a grand foyer. Grape vines sprouted from trunks and climbed the walls on either side, overflowing with ripe fruit even though there was no water or sunlight to support their growth. It was a disgusting display of a daemon abusing the chaos he'd gifted them.

Through the foyer were a few steps leading into the room where his cult held rituals. A gaudy statue of Dionysus was the focal point, standing proud in the middle with a wreath of evergreen placed on his head. Ivy leaves accented with needles and cones from pine trees draped his form. The man carved in marble was handsome, each limb and muscle pronounced in a masculine and elegant fashion. An altar encircled the stone under his feet, dripping with candle wax and fabrics of all colors. Bottles of wines littered the floor and flesh sacrifices lay amongst the offerings in different stages of rot.

Chaos nearly left the second he lay eyes upon the monstrosity, but the cold rage darkening his veins made him stay. He circled the altar multiple times before sweeping an observant glance around the rest of the room. Grape vines climbed the walls like a pest and covered nearly every inch, but nothing else was to be seen.

Or so he'd thought.

Just as he'd turned to leave, one of the neon spotlights roving over the city made a pass through the temple and glinted off something on the back wall. Chaos stepped to it and pulled back the mess of vine and ivy. Underneath was a gilded mirror that had seen better days. The surface was close to ruin with all of the scratches and cracks running through it, and the gold around the edge was coated with years of grime.

Chaos called the temple a loss and left for the bustling streets of Dion once more. With the arrival of dawn, however, he was ready to lay in bed beside his Siren and catch up on rest before the blood moon.

He navigated the back alleys until he arrived at the discolored bricks marking the front entrance. Chaos stepped through and the floating stench of decay struck his senses.

Fuck, he thought.

Perhaps he should have cleaned the mess before leaving. He'd even thought about it, but shrugged it away. He couldn't expend the chaos necessary to do it, and there was no way in hell he was doing it by hand. He ran a wary hand over his eyes and decided bed was more important. He would figure out the bloody situation after some rest.

Rest had never been necessary during the eternity he'd been alive. The exhaustion weighing his vulnerable form was a new feeling he'd grown to hate. Not only did it weaken his body, but it strained his mind, too. It was a dangerous game he didn't care much for playing.

When he reached the landing, Chaos dropped the hand rubbing his eyes and stopped, every muscle going rigid. A single light shown from a room on the left side of the hall toward the end. A room that he was positive had a brass sign labeled 'twelve' on the side.

Chaos stalked toward the door and pushed it open the rest of the way. "Xia?"

No answer.

He lunged forward in a panic, his fury rising at the sight of his empty bed. The sheets were tossed aside as if she'd been pulled from bed, and her shoes were still in the corner where she'd tossed them.

He turned and shoved open the bathroom door, but she wasn't there.

"Xia!" he bellowed. The chaos he'd collected from the night before rose to the surface like coiling snakes, ready to attack on his command. Shadows seeped from his hands as he struggled to leash the rage and fear overwhelming his thoughts.

The girl, his shadows whispered. *Where is the girl?*

"Nyx," he spat.

Chaos busted through her door within the span of a breath and jerked the blanket off. Alcohol and sweat permeated the air with the rush of the blanket as he threw it to the side.

"Get up!" he roared.

Nyx jumped, her eyes crazed as she rolled from the bed and hit the floor. She was a mess of flailing limbs as she fought to stand and fight, but he didn't have time for her bravado. Chaos lunged and pinned her against the wall with his arm across her chest.

"Where is she, Nyx?"

"I don't know what the fuck you're talking about. Put me down you brute!"

"Xia," he ground out. "She's not in the room. Where is she?"

"I've been here asleep the whole time and, last I checked, I wasn't your princess's bodyguard. So let. Me. Go!"

Chaos slung his arm as he turned to pace. The temperature in the room lowered to near freezing and her breath frosted in front of her eyes. Despite the cold, sweat rolled down her spine as nausea swirled in her gut and vertigo nearly swept her off her feet. Nyx bent at the waist and placed her hands on her knees to ride through the whirlwind. She begged whoever would listen that it was just the last few shots of alcohol in her system.

Of course, it couldn't be that easy.

Another wave of vertigo hit and she reached out for Chaos. "Protect my body," she slurred. "I'm gonna…"

He caught the girl as she fell, latched onto her chaos, and spiraled into the vision with her.

Nyx fell in a tangle of ivy as her back was thrown against a wall.

"I hate my fucking life," she murmured.

She opened her eyes to darkness and froze, using her other senses to glean information about what hell hole she'd been thrown into this time. Nyx kneaded her hands into the ground, using the tips of her fingers to test the surface. Packed dirt stuck under her nails as blades of grass tickled in between her fingers. No breeze rustled her hair just as no smell wafted through the air.

She hadn't expected it to. Up until recently, she was just a ghost in her visions. Since she met the Devil, though? Textures were apparent and she could be seen. Well, by him at least. She didn't want to test the theory on anyone else.

Nyx strained her ears for any noise, but couldn't pick up anything solid. She stood, careful not to ruffle the ivy or trip over the creeping vines. The last thing she needed was to announce herself.

Her hands reached out in search of anything to guide her steps. She was met with some sort of vinyl on one side and ran her fingertips along as she walked. After a few paces, a dim yellow lamp glowed to shed some light on her path.

She walked on a dirt road with trampled grass, her fingers gliding along a worn red and white striped fabric that ran from the ground and into the air. It was so tall that she couldn't make out the top, and wide enough that her fingers never met its end.

"What the fuck?" she whispered.

Her steps slowed, more tentative the closer she got to the light. Nyx didn't dare step into it, but she needed it to find what her chaos wanted her to see. There was always a point, and she would be stupid not to find it. Maybe it would help her find Xia. Or, better yet, the entrance to the Freakshow so she could hand Chaos over and go back home.

A pang of guilt struck a chord in her heart, but she shoved it down. Chaos was, after all, the creator of everything. He could handle himself, and he would have to understand why Nyx had to do it. She couldn't lose sight of her purpose.

Low mumbles pulled her from the frantic thoughts and she focused on the voices. She left the tent to her left and crossed the shadows to another she could see peeking through the light.

The closer she got to the new tent, the more her vision let her see. The same fabric draped over metal framework, but this one was smaller than the other and yellowing around the edges. A light glowed from within and two silhouettes appeared on the outside. The tent flap was closed and Nyx wouldn't risk opening it.

She crept around the shadows and kept the light to her front to make sure she didn't add her silhouette to the tent. Nyx settled close enough to hear the voices without touching the tent.

From the new angle, she made another body laying on a cot, one of the others reaching out to stroke their cheek.

"We're almost to the end now," they whispered.

The voice was meek and feminine that held an edge of... compassion? Fondness?

"I've done my part," she continued, still stroking the unconscious daemon. "I hope for your sake that you've done yours."

The second silhouette shifted from one foot to the other and took their time answering. If Nyx were a betting woman, she would say they were nervous.

"My pieces are in place," the second answered, the voice so low that Nyx nearly missed the words. She leaned in closer, straining to hear every word.

"Mistress will not be happy if you come up short," the feminine voice said.

"I will not come up empty. It is not your job to supervise me or the tasks I've been given. Your task was just a pawn on the board."

"A pawn it may have been, but without my move, your board would have fallen useless."

A chill ran down Nyx's spine as the man's silhouette expanded on the vinyl. Tattered wings rose from his shoulders as claws extended from his fingertips, twin spikes protruding from either side of his head. Nyx blinked as her mind fought to catch up with her eyes. The middle of the silhouette was black as ink and shaped like a man while the monster outlining his frame was lighter, but still very much a part of him.

"You don't scare me, Phobetor," the female crooned as she continued stroking the figure on the bed. "Put your nightmare back where it belongs and do your part. I won't be punished because you can't perform. Now leave my tent. Xia needs her beauty rest for the grand finale of the Freakshow."

The man huffed, the silhouette of his monster trembling. With fear or rage, Nyx wondered. "Whatever you say, Rue."

Chaos slammed back into his body as Nyx lurched forward and wheezed.

"She's not in the tavern," he said as frost spread across the floor.

"How do you know?" Nyx peered at him as her eyes widened. "Brooks, what did you do?"

His jaw clenched as black webbed his veins and shadows rolled off him in waves. "Brooks is no longer here. I am Chaos, and I've done what I must."

Unleash your Chaos

Epilogue

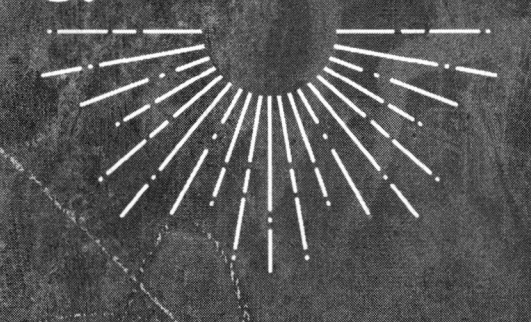

Melinoe rested on an ivory throne carved from the bones of men as she stared into Hel. A red talon grazed the fine hairs along her cheek, mind churning over the faults in her plan. Her temper flared, lip curling as she replayed the moment from days before in her mind.

"Phobetor lost the Siren, mistress. The Father of Chaos has taken her."

Melinoe tapped her fingers against the bleached armrest as she contemplated the words and tamed her fury. Crashing doors broke the silence as Phobeter sauntered into the room.

Mel quirked a brow as he approached. "To what do we the pleasure of your company—" She stopped, a touch of malice lacing her words as she mocked him. "What shall I call you today? The self-proclaimed Devil of Club Hel? Or perhaps the Lord of Nightmares?"

"Whatever pleases you, mistress."

She smirked as a small huff escaped her lips. "So docile today, Phobetor." Mel uncrossed her legs and leaned forward as she glared in his direction. "Have you come to talk me out of your death?"

"I've come to seek your mercy, mistress." His head bowed, though she caught the grimace he tried to hide with subservience.

Melinoe waited a moment to respond, pleased to let him simmer in anticipation. "I'm listening."

"What Rue says is true. Siren has gone with Chaos, but I've set a plan in motion to get her back."

"Oh? Do tell."

"I can get both of them to the Freakshow on Erebos. A seer stalks my club and I've made her an offer she can't refuse. I will deliver an invitation and make it clear they're to come. With some assistance from you, mistress, I can guide her way with strategic visions."

"Are you going to haunt her nightmares, little lordling?"

A muscle jumped in his temple as his fingers twitched. "No, mistress," he ground out. "Due to your generosity, I've consumed my brother's powers. Now that they belong to me I can bend her chaos and force a vision."

"I know." She smiled. "I just like to hear you say it." Phobetor straightened and defiance flamed in his eyes. His rage tasted like ambrosia on her tongue and she longed to glutton herself on it. "I doubt their intelligence, though, and want no room for mistakes, Phobetor. You and I will spell it out. After you fuck me, I want you on your knees in my dressing room and we will put on a show. Your little birdie needs to trust you if this is to work."

"Yes, mistress."

"Now get out of my sight."

He left with a stiff nod and Melinoe turned her stare back to Rue. "And you?"

Rue's brow dropped, her mouth slightly agape as if she'd been trapped in a spider's web. Smart girl.

"I'm at your will and mercy, mistress."

"You disgust me. Weak. Pathetic. The only good thing that bastard of a man ever did was rip me from you." Rue's head bowed, jaw trembling as she picked the skin around her nails. Melinoe sneered, incapable of being in the same room with who she used to be for even a moment longer. A surge of chaos flared in her chest as she reached out to the Underworld and called forth three souls. "Take two of them with you to the mortal world, Rue. I want to know where Phobetor's seer is taking my Siren. Once you find them, gain her trust. Separate her from the group. Bring her here alone. If we have the Siren, Chaos will follow."

"Yes, mistress."

"Cover your hair and for Hel's sake, do not call yourself Rue. We can't run the risk of Chaos recognizing you."

That confused expression returned as Rue asked, "What should I call myself?"

"I don't care!" Melinoe snapped, her voice bouncing off the stone and echoing through the room. "Make it simple and easy for you to remember. Call yourself Ruby and be done with it. Just get. The Siren. Here."

Melinoe hated being dead. With her soul bound to Rue and nothing but chaos to fuel her wrath, she was forced to put her game pieces in the hands of others as she sat on Erebos staring through the looking glass. Just another ghost unable to pierce the veil of the living. Fury and wrath were too shallow to describe the depth with which her hatred simmered.

Melinoe pushed away from the throne and called forth Hades' chess board. She paced around the ornate table observing each piece and calculating their next move. Chaos ripping free from her illusion made things complicated, but Melinoe liked a challenge. What was a game of warring gods without a good parry now and then?

Her eyes roved over the checkered pieces, past the Siren carved from obsidian and the god of Chaos. She looked past the caged demon she controlled and the weaker half of her soul. Dionysus' piece on the board was no matter, and neither was Zeus sitting atop his platinum throne.

Pawns, and all of them useless.

That ancient malice rumbled in her bones, and with a war cry Melinoe threw the chess board and kicked the table from the dais. Her bellows shook the in-between and rattled the Underworld where even the shadows seemed to shrink and hide. She turned to the artistry behind the throne, a sculpture of her own making hanging displayed for all to see. Faded skin torn down the seam of a spine and ribs broken outward spread like wings. Arms were outstretched to either side and nailed into stone, the insides forever draped on the outside. A trophy. A memory. Reminder.

"I'll be back, Beauty," she whispered to the man on the wall. "Do try not to miss me too much. Longing never suited you, Hades."

Melinoe summoned her chaos and vanished from her palace on Erebos, the kingdom she'd built in between life and death, and stepped from the shadows into the rubble that was once the home of Hades. She took a look around, disdain curling her lip, before stepping into Black Mirror Lake. Melinoe swirled her hands in the water and smiled as a whisper of scales brushed against her palm.

"It won't be long now, pet."

She waded through the water until she reached the door Hades had taken her through all those years ago. Melinoe walked through the tunnel lit by black flame and stepped into Asphodel Meadows. Wilted petals covered the ground, falling from stalks left unattended for centuries.

Melinoe had been so careful, only consuming one section of stalks at a time. Never enough to risk attention from the Fates or wake the Deathless God. However, she was tired of waiting, and sick of scheming. The Deathless God was free from her illusion, the daughter of Typhon clung to his side, and a soul-walker guided their way. Melinoe needed to strike while they were still unaware of the power in their pocket.

She mustered the rage and spite and indignation from every fiber of her being, squeezing every drop of accelerant from her psyche to *finally* watch them burn. Melinoe cried out and ripped stalk after stalk from the sacred ground. Petals fell in a flurry and a buzz rent the air as if the Earth was shattering. Orbs of chaos slammed into her chest from every direction, the power trying to overcome her as she swallowed more than her form could handle.

Melinoe didn't stop until every stalk lay dead on the ground and watched as they all turned to ash. She looked up to the never ending tree and set her brow as she approached. Melinoe placed her hand on the trunk and reached for her chaos, the black well overflowing with stolen power and hissing on her fingertips. Hades' voice whispered through her mind as she closed her eyes, the chaos spreading like a toxin through her veins.

"If you were to cut a stalk, the flow of chaos that ran through it would be lost to the cycle."

"Where does it go?"

"*It would latch on to the closest source of chaos in order to get back to the well.*"

The power inside tugged as it gravitated toward the sky and pulled her spectral form with it. The journey was as fast as a flash of lightning in the night sky, and when Melinoe opened her eyes again she could taste destiny like opium clinging to air.

Two sets of unseeing eyes shedding glistening blue tears turned to her, one with a crown of thorns and the other a crown of stars. Their mouths hung open as their bodies froze.

"Lachesis. Atropos. It's nice to finally meet you. I'm Melinoe." She plastered on her most saccharine smile as she looked at the Fates. "I'm sorry to have come unannounced, but I'm sure you were expecting me."

They didn't move. Couldn't speak or draw breath.

"Oh, I'm sorry." Melinoe feigned innocence and placed a hand on her chest. "I just assumed that for three daemon as powerful as yourselves, you would know when you had a guest coming. Forgive me. I've a small matter to attend to and then I'll be on my way."

The Fate with the crown of thorns stepped toward her, but as Atropos opened her mouth to speak, Melinoe seized the shears in her hand as swift as the five flowing rivers beneath them.

Melinoe delivered a brutal kick to the Fate's knee and, as she buckled, Melinoe grabbed her by the front of her gown and growled, "I'll show you the mercy you never cared to show me."

"Wait–"

Melinoe stabbed the shears up under Atropos' chin, pushing through sinew and cartilage until she hit bone. She didn't waste time watching the Fate fall after pulling the shears free, only inhaled her chaos and lunged for Lachesis. The goddess held her hands up as if it would stop her death, but Mel swiped outward and opened her neck from ear to ear.

Her well of chaos doubled in size, and she turned to stare at the last of the Fates. Clotho rested in the tree, suspended in a state of sleep that she would never wake from. Her body was frayed like ribbons and intertwined with the trunk of the tree, and though she must have known her sister's fates, she never woke.

Melinoe closed the distance between them and gazed upon the weeping goddess. An extra trail of red fell from her eyes as she wept for her sisters. Melinoe sliced through the tendrils of life holding Clotho to the tree, severing every connection before shoving her body from the hollow onto the ground.

"I was an innocent when you placed me into the hands of men and watched as they tore me apart. You are cruel, sister Fate, and your day of judgment has come, for I am damnation and will not stop until this world burns."

Author's Note

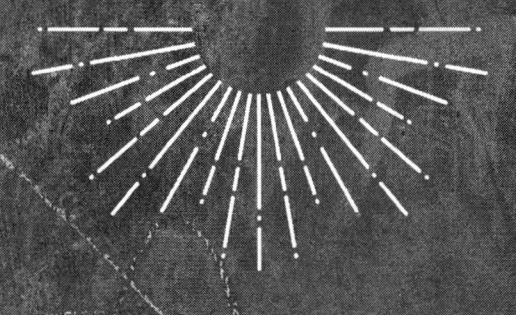

It feels like only four months ago I was releasing my debut novel.

Oh, fuck, wait, I was.

I dove head first into this author thing and you, Darling, made sure I had no regrets. One Little Nightmare was rough around the edges, but I appreciate everyone who stuck through and saw it as the diamond in the rough I thought it was. You've allowed me a safe space to take all of the chaos, all of the darkness inside, and produce something that helps me to embrace it all. If you take one thing away from this series, I'm hoping that can be one of the lessons. You are who you are, and repressing the parts you hate doesn't make them go away. It makes them build and build until they swallow you whole.

Learn to live with them, Darling. I promise you'll feel happier and healthier.

I hope One Saccharine Dream gave you something to cling to and at least one character hit close to home. They are all a part of me, and connecting with you through it all is one of the greatest honors of this crazy journey I'm taking.

Embrace your chaos, Darling, and get ready for the epic conclusion to the Of Gods and Monsters series. I'm not done breaking you.

Acknowledgements

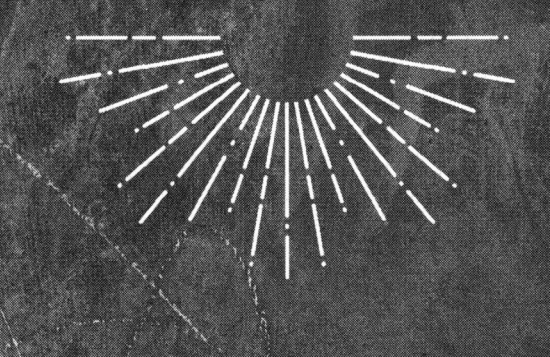

There were a lot more people who had to deal with my shit this time around, so buckle up buttercup.

Mr. Darling and all of his muscles. Someone had to carry me over the editing finish line and I am not petite. I like cheese and soft drinks. So.

Can we get a round of applause for the Spice Girls? Chaos bless my beta readers and allllllllll the whining they had to hear from me.

Ginger Spice and every ounce of positivity you bring to my ever present imposter syndrome.

Scary Spice because... You scare me, but also because your scary critiques make me good, but your loyalty and friendship make me even better.

Posh Spice for being the only one capable of bringing any sound reasoning to the table most times. Your logic keeps this author on the ground.

Sporty Spice and all of your shenanigans. I know life has been making you swim pretty hard, but you're doing GREAT! So stop apologizing in the group chat. Or else.

In case anyone was wondering, I'm baby spice. Evidently I'm soft.

I am endlessly grateful for your support and friendship. Without you, I would have never and the lady balls to publish One Little Nightmare. Without you to love my characters just as much as I do, they would have never come this far. Thank you, friends.

Props to my author besties Geneva Monroe and Cassandra Aston. You let me bitch, freak out, scream, cry, and everything in between. You the real MVPs because this bipolar girlie is a hot mess on a good day and yet you still answer my texts.

Jessica Jordan. Jessica Freaking Jordan. All the 4am editing sessions. Every repetitive word, plot hole, redundant statement, and flat out confusion you helped bring together.... this book would have been a lot less without your friendship and guidance. If anyone ever needs Alpha read edits, Jessica is your girl. Unless she has to pick your book to work on over mine. Then she's not your girl. She's busy, so go away.

I took a leap of faith this year and it was one of the best decisions of my life. To my Kickstarter Darlings, I have never felt so fucking supported in any career field than what you've made me feel. Mr. Darling's muscles had to hold me up a lot through the tears.

To my Darling Obsession backers... Godsdamn.

I don't even think my kids like me as much as you do. I hope every tiny detail I'll be putting into this can show just how much I appreciate you all. **María Tharp, Marron Edwards, Becca Penrod, Amanda Corbin, and Gini Eynstone**... thank you for taking this leap of faith on me. You will never know how much it means to this Hufflepuff.

To Traci Bookstagram who stepped into **A Darling Horror Story** unfazed and ready to face the dark. I'll hold your hand if you'll hold mine!

To my Darlings who stepped into **A Land of Gods and Monsters** to face their demons, I salute you. It can be scary in there, but I'm willing to take that ride if you are. **Chelsea Rothstein and Jensa Brenna**, thank you SO much for your support.

I'll end my Emmy acceptance speech with a nod to you, Darling reader. YOU are what makes this happen. Every page turned, every like and share, and every investment you make into me, I will never be able to say thank you enough. You are all godsdamned rockstars.

Are You Invested?

If I'm your own special brand of heroi— shit. Never mind. That's probably trademarked. Let me try again.

If you're loving what I'm doing and you want more, I've got big plans to keep you busy for 2024!

Dying to chat about the chaos you just read? Join my Darling Reader Group on Facebook. One of us! One of us!

Preorder leftover Kickstarter goodies on my website!

If you want all of the inside scoops, my Patreon is the place to be. My book boxes include exclusive engraved edges I won't sell anywhere else, ARCs WEEKS before the public, a never before seen book I'm introducing as a serial, and BTS looks at all art, formatting, news, and book teasers. Make sure you subscribe to get the first chapter of the serial, or sign-up to my newsletter for the free download. Be warned, though. You will get addicted, and you will want more. Kat and Black are intoxicating.

Make sure you're following my profile on Kickstarter. I'll be releasing the pre-launch link for the next one soon!

DARLING READER GROUP

PATREON

KICKSTARTER